Catherine Marsh

The Life of the Rev. William Marsh, D. D.

SALZWASSER
VERLAG

Catherine Marsh

The Life of the Rev. William Marsh, D. D.

1st Edition | ISBN: 978-3-75253-449-8

Place of Publication: Frankfurt am Main, Germany

Year of Publication: 2021

Salzwasser Verlag GmbH, Germany.

Reprint of the original, first published in 1867.

THE LIFE

OF THE

REV. WILLIAM MARSH, D.D.

THE LIFE

OF THE

REV. WILLIAM MARSH, D.D.

BY HIS DAUGHTER,

THE AUTHOR OF 'MEMÓRIALS OF CAPTAIN HEDLEY VICARS.'

'He had eyes lifted up to heaven, the best of books in his hand, the law of truth was written upon his lips, the world was behind his back. He stood as if he pleaded with men; and a crown of gold did hang over his head.'—PILGRIM'S PROGRESS.

FIFTH THOUSAND.

LONDON:

JAMES NISBET & CO., 21 BERNERS STREET.

HATCHARD & CO., 187 PICCADILLY.

1867.

PREFACE.

This biography is no record of stirring events, nor is it connected, excepting by passing allusion, with any public matters. But it may serve to show what were the doctrines, opinions, and practice of the Evangelical School of the last century; and to prove what a blessing an English clergyman, with his heart full of love to God and man, may be, in his quiet sphere.

To those who best knew the beloved Father of whom I have written, he seemed to have been moulded by Divine grace into the ideal of a Christian manhood: and his life to be such an one as

> '. . . dares send
> A challenge to the end,
> And when it comes, say "Welcome friend."'

Yet was his *only* hope of a happy eternity centred in the Person, the Work, the Atonement of Him 'who liveth, and was dead, and is alive for evermore.'

During the last few months of my father's life, no sentence was so frequently on his lips as those words of the dying Saviour, 'IT IS FINISHED.' It was 'the anchor of his soul, sure and steadfast.'

The publication of this book has been delayed beyond the time proposed, by the difficulty of attending to its preparation during the four months' prevalence of cholera, last year; when an opportunity of attending on some of the sufferers appeared to be my duty for the time being.

It has also consequently been completed in a less careful and finished manner than I could have wished. May I therefore hope that those who read it will do so with lenient judgment, as well as with generous consideration for one who could not have ventured to undertake so great a responsibility, with the strain of feeling it involved, had it not been laid upon her as a sacred duty.

My warmest thanks are due to all who have aided me by counsel, letters, documents, or personal recollections of my father's life and character, and for the great assistance rendered by my sisters; and by my two nieces who were constantly associated with him—without whose untiring help I could not have completed a task at once most painful and most precious.

No fact is mentioned in this book which is not attested by the witness of at least two memories; no conversation recorded which was not taken down at the time; and no statement of his views made which is not familiar to his family and friends, and thoroughly authenticated by his writings.

In conclusion, I venture to entreat that those who read would pray that the blessing of God the Holy Spirit may rest upon these memorial pages, so that, by them, in death—as in life—he may win wanderers to arise and go to their FATHER, and persuade those who have already been won, to seek for more entire consecration to God and His service, and for a more full and unbroken 'fellowship with the Father and with His Son Jesus Christ.'

CONTENTS.

CHAPTER I.

EARLY DAYS AND COLLEGE LIFE.

'He went in the strength of dependence
    To tread where his Master trod,
To gather and knit together
    The family of God:

As one whose home is in heaven,
    To pass through this world of sin,
With a heart diffusing the balm of peace
    From the place of peace within.

With a conscience freed from burdens,
    And a heart set free from care,
To minister to every one
    Always and everywhere.'

The Three Wakings.

EARLY DAYS AND COLLEGE LIFE.

William Marsh was born on the 20th of July 1775. He was the third son of Colonel Sir Charles Marsh, the descendant of an old Norman family who served under Lord Clive in the conquest of India, and distinguished himself by his cool courage and gallantry throughout each campaign, and especially at the siege of Pondicherry.

He returned to England with an ample fortune, which was subsequently lost by a speculation. His death took place before he could meet all the liabilities in which this misfortune had involved him; but they were afterwards discharged, out of a limited income, by his son William.

Sir Charles Marsh married Catherine, daughter of John Case, Esq., a gentleman of independent fortune, who resided chiefly at Bath. Though not sixteen years of age at the time of her marriage, Miss Case was already distinguished for her clear and cultivated intellect, and her sparkling wit. Her mother was one of the personal friends of Pope, and other leaders of the literary society of the day, of which Miss Case became a brilliant ornament.

The children of this marriage, five in number, were remarkable for their personal beauty, gifted minds, and attractive manners. But amongst them William seems to have been the object of his parents' peculiar delight, not merely on account of these outward attractions, but for his sweetness of disposition, which seemed to his mother so faultless that she used playfully to say of him, 'He was born before the Fall.'

Even in his early childhood, a tender sensitiveness, which lent an almost feminine grace to his maturer years, was balanced in its infantile measure by the same steadfastness and power of self-sacrifice, which formed the groundwork of his character, when, by the grace of God, it was moulded into an example of real manliness, as consisting of 'all that is pure, and noble, and true, and strong, and tender, and lasting.'[1]

An aged friend of the family remembers that his mother spoke of him as the peacemaker in the childish dissensions of the nursery. In any dispute about toys, William would run to her and say, 'Oh! give them my little horse, or my cart, or anything of mine, if only they won't quarrel.'

Another anecdote which has been handed down to us amongst the few reminiscences of his childhood, shows his honesty in circumstances of strong temptation for a

[1] Extracted from a Sermon preached by the present Archbishop of York, in Westminster Abbey, June 1863, to the Volunteers of London.

little boy not then four years old. For some small offence he had been shut up by his nurse in a store-room, and left there until long past his dinner-hour. The nurse had forgotten that dishes of oranges, apples, and cakes, were arranged there within his reach. On looking through a window, she saw the hungry little boy gazing at each by turns, with his small hands firmly clasped behind his back, and she heard him saying to himself over and over again, 'Billy must not touch them, Billy must *not* touch them. They are not Billy's own.'

During his early life, he had little religious instruction, excepting that which he received from an unmarried sister of his father. She loved little William, and during her visits to his father's house, she had the child often with her, and read him stories from the Bible. His great love for these lessons in Holy Scripture caused his brothers to call him 'Bible-Billy,' a name which proved truly significant of his devotion to the Word of God in after years. With all his gentleness and docility of character, there was mingled a constant overflow of boyish spirits and energy, which at times expended themselves in fun and mischief; but were never known to degenerate with him into coarseness or profanity.

When dangerously ill, in his eighty-eighth year, he mentioned, with an expression of anguish on his countenance, a single deviation from this rule. He had *once*, he said, at the sinful taunt of a butler, uttered an oath. This man had said, in the presence of several of the servants, 'Master William is not man enough to swear.' He fell into the snare laid for him, and with trembling lips, for the first time and the *last*, wilfully took the name of his God in vain. Scarcely was the sin committed, when, like Peter, 'he went out and wept bitterly;' and the recollection, after the lapse of eighty years, caused him keen distress.

Until he was eleven or twelve years old, he continued to attend the Grammar School at Reading, whose head master at that time was Dr. Valpy, well known for his classical learning, and as the author of several standard works for the use of schools. William was afterwards instructed by a private tutor under his father's roof.

A different career seemed now to be opening before him from that into which he was afterwards led by the good hand of his God upon him. In acknowledgment of Sir Charles Marsh's services in India, a commission in the army had been granted to each of his four sons. The two eldest had already begun to distinguish themselves in India, where shortly afterwards each found an early grave.

But before William had decided on joining his regiment, he received another and a higher commission, and surrendered himself to the service of the great Captain of his salvation, as at once the profession and the *reality* of his life. Thenceforward, by that Saviour's grace, he fought manfully under His banner, against sin, the world, and the devil, and continued His faithful soldier and servant unto his life's end, never laying down his arms until he was called to receive the victor's crown. Previous to this change, which took place when he was eighteen years old, he was entering with all the gaiety and ardour of youth into the amusements provided in his father's house, and amongst his large circle of acquaintance. His most frequent visits were made at Caversham Park, then the home of the Earl of Cadogan, who resided there for many months in the year with his charming and gifted family. From one of its members, at that time the rector of Chelsea, rich spiritual blessing was shortly to flow into William's soul; and another, then a little child, was in later life to bring gladness to his home, after it had been darkened by sorrow and death.

It was in the bright scene of a ball-room, and amidst the excitement of dancing, in which he delighted and excelled, that he was first to hear the voice of God, speaking with power to his soul, by the sudden death of a young man, who fell by his side without a moment's warning.

For the first time William realized the solemn nearness of eternity, and returned to his home in deep concern for his own salvation.

That night sleep forsook him, driven away by anxious thoughts of death and the unknown future. He arose ill and exhausted, and the anxiety of his mind brought on fever, which lasted for some days. After three or four wakeful nights of uneasy thought and uncertain prayer, his weary eyes at length closed in a troubled sleep, and he dreamt that the Judgment Day had already come. He stood before the Great White Throne, awaiting in trembling dread the sentence of condemnation. But before the words had been uttered he awoke, thanked God that it was a dream, and that time was still left him to seek for mercy. From this moment the question was continually recurring to his mind, 'How shall I stand in the Judgment, and find my place in the congregation of the righteous?' Under this solemn impression, with none to advise him, he inquired of a bookseller for some religious work, and was recommended by him to purchase a volume of Roman Catholic devotions.

At such a moment of anxious search after salvation, this book might have diverted the whole current of his history; but the Holy Spirit of God, who had already been speaking to his heart, kept him from error, and guided him, step by step, to a clear knowledge of that Saviour who is the Way, the Truth, and the Life.

The book failed to satisfy the deep yearning of his soul, or to relieve the anxiety of an awakened conscience; so he exchanged it for the Autobiography of the Reverend John Newton, whose friendship and Christian counsel he was afterwards to enjoy. The reading of this book led him to decide upon beginning a diligent study of the Holy Scriptures. His self-appointed task was to read four chapters daily, in order to enable him to finish the Bible in the course of the year. At first he found it a burden, but he persevered in it, until, at the end of three years, the Bible became the 'man of his counsel' and 'the joy and rejoicing of his heart.'

He was also in the habit of diligently searching the Scriptures, always noticing the bearing of the context, and making the Word of God its own interpreter, by the comparison of one passage with another. In quoting any passage, he was very particular to be exact in every word, and was in the habit, in after life, of recommending this practice to his children and friends. On one occasion, in a large clerical meeting to which he had been invited, a discussion arose with respect to a quotation which presented a difficulty to the minds of many assembled. He suggested that they should look at the passage, to see the precise words, and on referring to it, the difficulty at once disappeared, as no such passage was to be found.

To him the great object of the Bible seemed to be to unfold the character of God, especially as shown in the prophecies and history of the Lord Jesus Christ. More than once he has said that if he were asked to choose a motto for the Word of God, it should be, 'Acquaint now thyself with Him, and be at peace, thereby good shall come unto thee.'

From this time to the close of his life, the study of the Bible continued to be his unceasing delight. One evening, within two months of his death, whilst reading with his usual intentness, two friends entered the room, and stood by his chair for some time before he perceived them. On looking up, he greeted them with a bright smile, saying, as he held out the sacred volume, 'With this staff have I travelled through my pilgrimage, and with this staff I will pass over Jordan.'

About the year 1793, the Honourable and Reverend William Cadogan was appointed Vicar of St. Giles's Church, Reading, and thus the blessing of a wise Christian friend was provided for William Marsh at the time he so greatly needed it. Mr. Cadogan's earnest and scriptural ministry, clearly setting forth the full message of present pardon and peace through the finished work of

Christ and the sanctifying power of the Holy Spirit, brought numbers of thirsting souls with joy to 'draw water from the wells of salvation.' Amongst them was William Marsh; and probably no ground on which the good seed was sown by that faithful preaching brought forth richer or more abundant fruit than that which was seen in his life and ministry. The impression already made was greatly deepened by a sermon preached by Mr. Cadogan from the words, 'What shall it profit a man if he shall gain the whole world, and lose his own soul?'

It was a period in which many members of our Church, both amongst the clergy and the laity, were careless or prejudiced; and it involved some degree of reproach even to attend at a church where the preaching was of a distinctly evangelical character.

Like Nicodemus, who came to Jesus by night, William at first went to St. Giles's for the evening service only, and when there, stood behind a pillar to avoid being recognised.

This did not last many weeks. When once the message of the Gospel had been believed by him in his heart, then 'the fear of man which bringeth a snare' was broken and trampled under foot. There came a night when the fetters were struck off, and even as he entered by faith into 'the glorious liberty of the children of God,' he quietly stepped from behind the pillar which had hitherto concealed him, and thenceforward bore his share of the reproach, and took his place amongst the acknowledged hearers of the gospel—that gospel so truly described by a Brahmin, when conversing with one of the noblest missionaries of modern times, as 'PEACE TO-DAY.'

From the time of their first acquaintance, Mr. Cadogan's heart was drawn to William Marsh with no ordinary warmth of affection, which strengthened year by year, and was returned by his young friend with an equal depth of attachment. Brothers could not have loved each other more truly.

On Dr. Marsh's last birthday, in an address given to his parishioners, with that freshness of memory and feeling which was one of the peculiar charms of his green old age, he thus referred to this friend of his youth :—'Seventy-one years ago, a faithful and revered minister of Christ taught me to love my Bible, showed me that it was the Word of God, and the only book in the world which could teach us the way of salvation. That man was Mr. Cadogan.'

With William Marsh's change of heart began an entire change of life. Even whilst living in the world, and sharing with vivid enjoyment in its amusements and interests, his conduct had been singularly blameless. 'What a monument of grace is your son!' remarked a Christian friend to Lady Marsh, several years after his conversion. 'You never made a greater mistake in your life,' replied the mother, with almost pardonable indignation at the seeming aspersion on her son's lovely nature; 'grace never had so little to do for any character as for my William's!'

The family party at this time consisted of his father and mother, his only sister Matilda, his brother Henry, and William himself, who was now the eldest surviving son, and heir to a considerable fortune. They became great favourites in the society in which they moved, from their pleasant dispositions and the charm of their conversation and manner.

When Harry Marsh was only fourteen years of age, he was sent by his father to the hustings at the time of a county election. He was the bearer of a note to the Tory candidate, to explain the unavoidable absence of his father, from whom he had received at the same time a charge to stay for the 'show of hands,' and to hold up his own on the Tory side. The boy went off in high spirits with his commission, but after delivering the note, and listening to the speeches on both sides, his convictions were so strongly in favour of the opinions expressed by the Whig candidate, that he mounted to the hustings beside him, and made a speech so full of wit and talent, that it turned the whole current of feeling in the crowd into the Whig interest, and mainly assisted in the unexpected triumph of their candidate. This incident gave the colour to his after-life, and determined his political opinions, so that from henceforth his ruling passion became the furtherance of the Whig cause by every means in his power, especially by seeking to secure the return of Whig members, and in this his success was unrivalled, both in his own and the neighbouring counties.

But the promise which he thus early gave of distinguishing himself in a public career, was not fulfilled according to the expectations of his friends. In his eighteenth year he married a young and beautiful widow, who was the owner of a small estate in Hampshire, and his devoted attachment to her, which continued unaltered during the fifty-three years of their married life, induced him, in compliance with her wishes, to decline the repeated proposals which were made to him, either to stand for the county, or to represent his numerous friends in the borough of Reading.

According to the fashion of those days, when comparatively few families amongst the country gentry went up to London for the season, but passed the winter months instead in the nearest county town, Mr. and Mrs. Henry Marsh made Reading their metropolis, where their presence was always hailed as the centre and spring of good humour and merriment.

During Sir Charles Marsh's lifetime, this 'season' was always spent under his roof; and although the strong brotherly affection which ever existed between William and Harry remained undiminished till death, their interests and pleasures at this time presented a strange contrast. From the period of his conversion, William's chief object in life had become the glory of his Saviour in the salvation of sinners; whilst Harry, then unconvinced even of the truth of Revelation, lived for enjoyment, though preserving an unblemished morality.

The change in William subjected him at first to his father's severe displeasure; but it was impossible for his kind heart and genial nature long to retain feelings of anger against a son whose dutiful and affectionate conduct, guided by 'meekness of wisdom,' left him no fault to find with him except he should 'find it against him concerning the law of his God.'

Anxious now to make each son happy in his own way, Sir Charles would give his large drawing-room on one evening to Harry for a ball, and on the next, to William for a Bible-reading. These gatherings for reading the Word of God, and for prayer, were frequently presided over by Mr. Cadogan; at other times, they were conducted by William himself, with the help of two or three excellent laymen, amongst whom may be mentioned Mr. French and Dr. Ring, men 'full of the Holy Ghost and of faith.'

Now and then, to his great delight, he was able to obtain the honoured presence of those men of God, John Newton and Richard Cecil, and other leaders in the evangelical revival of the last century, whose ripened experience and fatherly wisdom were of deep spiritual blessing to many amongst this little band of Christians, and especially to him who was the means of drawing them together.

But whilst William Marsh was thus endeavouring to make known the good news of salvation, as he had opportunity, to his acquaintance and friends, and to draw closer the bonds of Christian fellowship, he was not unmindful of the Lord's words, 'Return to thine own house, and show how great things God hath done unto thee.' Constrained by the love of Christ, and by his deep home-affections, his first and most earnest care was to seek to win his own family to know and serve the blessed Saviour.

His faithful efforts were soon crowned with joy, in the conversion of his beloved mother and sister. Matilda was the first to receive Christ into her heart as 'the hope of glory.' Young, lovely, and possessed of all which makes life attractive, it is not surprising that she was almost wholly occupied with the gaieties and vanities of the worldly society in which she had been brought up. One Sunday morning she yielded to the persuasions of her brother to go with him to St. Giles's

Church. Mr. Cadogan had chosen for his text that day, the third verse of the fifty-third chapter of Isaiah, 'He is despised and rejected of men,' and the heaven-taught and solemn words of his sermon sank into Matilda's heart, and sent her home in deep distress of soul. The rest of the day was passed in sadness, and when the time came for evening service, she was thankful that William asked her to attend it with him. Mr. Cadogan's sermon was upon the seventh verse of the second chapter of the first Epistle of St. Peter, 'Unto you therefore which believe He is precious.' He spoke of the preciousness of Christ to the believer in His work, His character, and His offices. The Holy Spirit—who had, by the preaching of His Word in the morning, convinced her of sin, in having hitherto chosen the world instead of Christ—in the evening brought peace to her troubled heart by revealing the salvation purchased by the blood of the Lamb of God; and her right by faith to enter at once into all the privileges of grace here, and the joyful prospect of glory hereafter. As Matilda entered her home that night, she clasped her hands, saying, 'He shall be precious to me; He shall be precious to *me*.' From that hour, the testimony of her life was—

> 'My heart is fixed, eternal God,
> Fixed on Thee;
> And my immortal choice is made,
> Christ for me.'

She had been permitted to have a glimpse of Him who is 'the chiefest among ten thousand,' and 'altogether lovely;' and in the brightness of His glory the charms of earth seemed faded to her eyes. As she grasped the higher happiness she let go her hold of the lower. But the great change which now transformed her whole heart and life did not appear to her to render less binding a sacred engagement into which she had previously entered, although it was to make her the wife of a man of the world. She was on the eve of marriage to a distinguished naval officer, who had been attached to her from her childhood, but in whose heart religion had no sway. She concealed nothing from him as to the change in herself, but frankly said that to cherish the spiritual life given her, she must forsake those amusements in which she had hitherto delighted.[1] Her marriage took place shortly afterwards; at first all seemed bright before her, and she had hope that the crowning joy of seeing her husband sharing her highest happiness would be granted her. But clouds arose, and her after life was one of peculiar and continuous trial; yet throughout all, her faith in Christ remained unshaken, and whilst passing through tribulation her spirit was enabled to rejoice in God her Saviour. As the time of her death drew near, her joy rose into triumph and burst forth in the hymn,—

'I 'll praise my Maker while I 've breath,
And when my voice is lost in death,
Praise shall employ my nobler powers.
My days of praise shall ne'er be past,
While life, and thought, and being last,
Or immortality endures.'

[1] It was for his brother-in-law's sake that Mr. Marsh wrote his first tract, taking, at his sister's request, for its subject, 'Nonconformity to the World.' It was afterwards enlarged, and republished in the year 1857, under the title of *The Right Choice*.

She died a few minutes afterwards, saying, 'Happy, happy! Christ is all!'

It was about the time of his sister's marriage that the desire entered William's heart to devote himself exclusively to the service of God by entering upon the ministry of the Gospel. The position of an evangelical clergyman seventy years ago was not an enviable one in the eyes of the world. Promotion was a thing rarely known amongst them, and they bore the reproach of Christ in no slight measure. But these were considerations that had little weight with a character like that of William Marsh; and the earnest counsel of Mr. Cadogan, who saw his eminent qualifications for usefulness as a minister, decided him in his choice.

In the year 1798, he entered as gentleman-commoner at St. Edmund's Hall, Oxford, having chosen this college in preference to others on account of the Christian character and evangelical views of its Principal, Dr. Crouch, and several of its undergraduates, amongst whom was Daniel Wilson, afterwards Bishop of Calcutta, who formed a friendship with Mr. Marsh, which continued unabated to the end of life. On the last return of the Bishop of Calcutta to England, he visited his old friend, then incumbent of St. Mary's, Leamington, to enjoy the refreshment of personal intercourse with him after those many years of separation. One day, whilst conversing with Dr. Marsh's family, the Bishop spoke of the calm and holy beauty of their father's manner of life in Oxford, and of his earnestness in promoting, and perseverance in carrying on, meetings amongst the undergraduates, for prayer, and for the purpose of interesting each other in missionary work. The Bishop added, 'Would you like to have the key to the wonderful knowledge of Scripture that your father possesses, so that he has the Bible at his fingers' ends; and if you set him off at the 1st of Genesis he could almost go through it to the 22d of Revelation? Well, I can give it to you. He never wasted an opportunity of studying it at odd moments, besides his regular hours of reading. He had an open Bible always before him whilst he was dressing, and even when shaving he was learning chapters by heart, regardless of consequences in slips of the razor, although he was the handsomest man in Oxford.'

Another friend, who continued faithfully attached to him throughout life, was the late Rev. Thomas Tyndale, of Trinity College, Oxford. They had been school-fellows, and on their meeting again at the University, William at once made use of their early friendship to avail himself of every opportunity of striving to awaken in Mr. Tyndale a desire for salvation. He soon met with a rich reward in his friend's conversion, and entire dedication of himself to the service of the Lord. Mr. Tyndale was three years younger than any of the little band of earnest Christians at St. Edmund's Hall, and was known amongst them then, and as long as they lived, by the familiar name of 'Young Tom Tyndale.'

In the year 1820, Mr. Tyndale left Woburn, in Buckinghamshire, where his labours are still remembered with affection and respect, to become Rector of Holton, near Oxford, where for above forty years, he preached the pure Gospel of Christ. 'There was,' wrote a clerical friend after his death, 'a simplicity and power in Mr. Tyndale's public ministry which made it peculiarly acceptable to the poor, and among them there were numbers who have testified by their life and conduct that the Word was not preached in vain—numbers known in the church on earth, how many more to be manifested in that day when the secrets of all hearts shall be revealed! His original mind firmly grasped great truths, and with one great object always before him, the glory of God and the good of his fellow-creatures, he suffered no opposition to daunt him, no hindrances to impede his work. He stood boldly forward to resist every form of error, which, during his long life, rose up under different phases in our Protestant Church. He had ever one appeal, to the "law and to the testimony;" and in the early beginnings of that infusion of error which has in later days led so many of our clergy to leave the Church of their fathers, he saw and protested, both by writing and preaching, against the first deviation from the straight line of scriptural truth.'

Thus, 'following after righteousness, faith, charity, and peace, with them that call upon the Lord out of a pure heart,' William Marsh passed through the ordeal of his college life.

A few days previous to his ordination, he was invited, with several other candidates for the ministry, to meet at the house of the Rev. Richard Cecil, incumbent of St. John's, Bedford Row, in order to spend a day in the study of the Scriptures, conversation, and prayer. Sixty years afterwards, he referred to it with the same freshness of enjoyment and thankfulness as if it had been but the day before. 'Mr. Cecil,' he said, 'was most happy in the art of illustration. Wishing to impress upon our minds the importance of ever making prominent in our preaching Christ and His atonement, he told us an anecdote of his former life. He had been a great sufferer for years, and none of his medical friends had been able to ascertain the cause. At length Mrs. Cecil was told of a physician, who was extremely skilful in intricate cases, and whom she entreated him to consult. On entering the physician's room, he said, "Welcome, Mr. Cecil, I know you well by character, and as a preacher. We must have some conversation after I have given you my advice." Mr. Cecil then described his sufferings. The physician considered for a moment, and then said, "Dear sir, there is only one remedy in such a case as yours; do just try it; it is perfectly simple,"—and then he mentioned the medicine.

'Mr. Cecil, fearing to occupy too much of his time, rose to leave, but the physician said, "No, sir, we must not part so soon, for I have long wished for an opportunity of conversing with you;" so they spent half an hour more, mutually delighted with each other's society.

'"On returning home," added Mr. Cecil, "I said to my wife,—You sent me to a most agreeable man, such a fund of anecdote, such originality of thought, such a command of language." "Well, but what did he prescribe for you?"

Mrs. Cecil anxiously inquired. There was a pause, and then Mr. Cecil exclaimed, "I have entirely forgotten the remedy, his charms of manner and conversation put everything else out of my mind."

'"Now, young men!" said Mr. Cecil, "it will be very pleasant for you if your congregation go away saying, What eloquence! what original thought! and what an agreeable delivery! TAKE CARE THEY DO NOT FORGET THE REMEDY, the only remedy, Christ and His righteousness, Christ and His atonement, Christ and His advocacy."'

To *one* of Mr. Cecil's hearers, at all events, this advice was not given in vain. It became one of the marked characteristics of Mr. Marsh's ministry, that everything was subordinated to the setting forth of the love of God, as manifested in the free salvation provided by the life and death of His Son; and he frequently urged upon his brother clergy that no sermon, on whatever subject, should close without the way of life being plainly set forth. 'There might be one present,' he said, 'whose last or only opportunity it would be to hear the faithful saying, that Christ Jesus came into the world to save sinners.'

Speaking on the same subject, Mr. Cecil continued, 'My daughter plays beautifully on her pianoforte in the next room to my study; it does not divert me from my reading and writing in general, but now and then she touches a chord; down goes my pen, and I do not see a word in my book, all I can do is to listen. Now, my young friends,' he added, 'whilst you are preaching, one has wandered in thought to his farm, another to his merchandise, a third to converse with his friends, but touch the key-note, set forth a Saviour's love,—for "the love of Christ constraineth us,"—let your own heart be well in tune with it, and theirs will respond.'

CHAPTER II.

FIRST YEARS OF MINISTRY.

'He was a shepherd, and no mercenary,
And though he holy was and virtuous,
He was to sinful men full piteous;
His words were strong, but not with anger fraught;
A love benignant he discreetly taught,
To draw mankind to Heaven by gentleness
And good example, was his business.

. . . . .

But Jesus' love, which owns no pride or pelf,
He taught—but first he followed it himself.'

CHAUCER

ST. LAWRENCE'S CHURCH, READING.

THE ABBEY GATEWAY LEADING TO THE HOUSE WHERE

FIRST YEARS OF MINISTRY.

At Christmas, in the year 1800, Mr. Marsh was ordained to the curacy of St. Lawrence, Reading. Solemnly, yet joyfully, he entered upon that career of usefulness, which was to be pursued with unwearied patience and increasing delight for upwards of sixty-four years. His first sermon was preached at one of the week-day services, on the words, 'Behold, the Judge standeth before the door.'

As the church had to be closed for repairs before the following Sunday, his valued Christian friend, Dr. Ring, invited Mr. Marsh to spend that day with him at his mother's house in Basingstoke, promising him the opportunity of preaching, as the curate of the parish church had offered the pulpit.

The rector had been for some time non-resident, but returned unexpectedly that week. On hearing of the arrangement that had been made, he said to his curate, 'That evangelical young Marsh shall not preach in my church.'

When this news was announced to him on his arrival, he received it with his usual serenity of temper, merely replying, 'Then I am to be a listener instead of a preacher to-morrow. But I can *pray* as much as I wish —no man forbidding me!'

The cheerful and unruffled calmness with which he met this disappointment distinguished him throughout life, and arose from no want of keen sensitiveness, whether to kindness or unkindness, but had its source partly in a native sweetness of disposition, combined with a power of making prompt and large allowances for the peculiarities of others, and a happy knack of giving a playful turn to little annoyances; but, above all, from a habitual realization of an Almighty Father's hand arranging and overruling every circumstance of life: the language of his heart was—

> 'Ill that God blesses is our good,
> And unblest good is ill;
> And all is right that seems most wrong,
> If it be His sweet will.'

The Master in whom he implicitly trusted had otherwise planned that Sunday's work for him.

Early in the morning a messenger came from a clergyman, who had a small church in the suburbs of the town, to say that he had been seized with an attack of inflammation in the chest, and that he would be most grateful if Mr. Marsh would undertake his duty.

Gladly accepting this opportunity, he went forth to preach the gospel of Christ from the words, 'Behold the Lamb of God, which taketh away the sin of the world.'

At the conclusion of the sermon, he offered to give the congregation an afternoon service. Between the services the news spread about the town that the young clergyman who had been refused the pulpit of the large church, was to preach again in the small one. With the generous impulse of Englishmen to take the side of any one whom they fancy to be injured, the numbers who pressed to hear him were so great that the congregation overflowed until the churchyard was crowded. Even the choir deserted from the parish church, in order to testify their sympathy with the young clergyman who had fallen under the rector's ban.

Amongst the crowd in the centre aisle there stood a man so noted for his ungodliness and profane language as to be known in Basingstoke by the name of 'Swearing Tom.' He was a leader in sin and profanity; and for seventeen years he had never entered a church. It was only curiosity which brought him now. The text was taken from the prophecy of Ezekiel, 'I will put a new spirit within you.' Towards the close of the sermon, the preacher quoted the words, 'If ye then, being evil, know how to give good gifts unto your children; how much more shall your heavenly Father give the Holy Spirit to them that ask him?' (Luke xi. 13)—remarking that, contrary to the conclusion which might have been expected, 'the offer was not to children, but simply to those who asked. There was nothing therefore between the worst of men and this most blessed gift from heaven, but to ask for it.' He then added, 'If the most wicked man in this church would go home, and pray that God, for Christ's sake, would give him His Holy Spirit to change his heart, God would hear and answer that man's prayer.'

These words went straight to the heart of 'Swearing Tom.' 'I am the worst man here,' he said to himself; 'I will go home and pray.' As he went, he had to pass by the familiar public-house, but, unmoved by the calls of his companions, he refused to turn in. On reaching his home, he threw himself upon his knees, and tried to pray in the words which he had heard from the pulpit. The prayer was answered. From that time he became a changed man, and his name of 'Swearing Tom' was soon altered for that of 'Praying Tom,' by which he was known till the day of his death. He placed his leisure time at the disposal of his clergyman for visits to the sick and afflicted, and was made a great blessing, for upwards of half-a-century, in his native town. It was not until Mr. Marsh preached again in that church, after a lapse of thirty years, that he became aware of the blessed result of his first Sunday's sermon, when Tom himself asked leave to speak to him in the vestry, and told him the story of his conversion.

Many years later, as Dr. Marsh was going up the stairs of Exeter Hall for the last meeting there of the British and Foreign Bible Society at which he was able to be present, a stranger met him, and asked if he was not Dr. Marsh; on receiving the reply, he said, 'Ah! dear sir, "Praying Tom" of Basingstoke is now "Praising Tom" in heaven. His last hours were blessed indeed, for he died as he had lived, rejoicing in his Saviour.'

In the year 1801, Mr. Stonor, father of the present Lord Camoys, who, while himself a Roman Catholic, had a deep respect for Mr. Marsh's holy and devoted character, offered him the two small livings of Nettlebed, and its adjoining parish, the united incomes of which only amounted to £25 a year. These he afterwards accepted, still retaining his curacy at St. Lawrence's, which he served gratuitously during eleven years. Every third Sunday he exchanged duty with his curate, and officiated at the two little churches, sleeping at Mr. Stonor's house on Saturday night. On these occasions, and between the services on Sundays, he had much conversation with Mr. Stonor, who became warmly attached to him, and with the domestic chaplain, a Roman Catholic priest who had been brought up abroad, and was remarkably liberal in his views. Mr. Marsh frequently urged upon both the need of coming as sinners to the Saviour, and trusting only in His all-sufficient sacrifice, *once* offered for the sins of the whole world. After a time Mr. Stonor allowed his young friend to read the Bible and pray with him, and their affectionate intercourse remained unbroken until the death of Mr. Stonor.

Before Mr. Marsh's ordination, his chest had been considered delicate, and he had spent two successive winters at Clifton for the sake of milder air. He had been told by more than one physician, that, if he took orders, his work must be limited to one service on Sunday. But from the time he was ordained, three full services on every Sunday, besides diligent supervision of the schools, became his rule. Nor was the week less fully occupied in his Master's work. In addition to a Tuesday evening service, and a catechetical lecture to the children, he added a short extempore sermon of an expository character, to the regular morning prayers at the church on Wednesdays and Fridays; for he held strongly then, as he did to the day of his death, that the preaching of the gospel should always accompany the prayers of the Church. He was in the habit of quoting, with reference to this subject, these words of our Lord and Master, and of His inspired apostles, 'Preach the gospel to every creature;' 'It pleased God, by the foolishness of preaching, to save them that believe;' and also the example of the apostles, who went about 'preaching EVERYWHERE in the name of the Lord Jesus.' In the parish, his pastoral labours amongst both the healthy and the sick were unceasing, so that it might almost be said of him, in the words of Scripture, that 'daily in the temple, and in every house, he ceased not to teach and to preach Jesus Christ.'

Among the many young people to whom his preaching was blessed, was one whose remarkable energies became entirely consecrated to her Master's service. Miss Sarah Hooper became well known in Reading for her works of love. She first organized a distribution of tracts amongst the poor, and visited in the worst localities, seeking by kindness, charity, and faithful words to win souls to Christ. Her love for God's ancient people, learned also under Mr. Marsh's ministry, led her eventually to devote herself entirely to them. In later years she took a small house in London in a retired court in the city, in order to be in the immediate neighbourhood of many Jewish families. Twice a week she received a large number of poor Jewish women, to whom she gave tickets for articles of food and clothing, towards the expense of which they contributed a part, while the rest was supplied from her own resources and the liberality of Christian friends, amongst the foremost of whom was Dr. Marsh. After giving them refreshments, she usually read aloud a chapter from the Old Testament. Her great object was to convince them that they were loved by Christians, and to prove this she was ready to sacrifice ease, health, home, and property. She died not many years ago, resting upon her Saviour's atonement, rejoicing in her Saviour's love.

Whilst the pastor's heart was cheered from day to day by the fruit he saw ripening around him, in lives made holy and homes made happy, the good seed of the Word, as faithfully sown by him, fell also upon some hearts in which, though it lay apparently dead, it brought forth fruit 'after many days.' And the Lord of the harvest, from time to time, refreshed the soul of the earnest labourer in His field, by bringing to his knowledge some unexpected instance of blessing on his preaching and teaching.

During his ministry at St. Lawrence's, Mr. Marsh, at the week-day services, preached a course of sermons on the Commandments. It happened once that, owing to heavy rain, his congregation consisted only of the boys of the National School. The subject for that morning, 'Thou shalt do no murder,' the preacher felt to be most unsuited to his audience, but as it came in the natural order, he proceeded with it. One passage in the sermon had reference to the crime of suicide, and contained the following sentence: 'If any man, in the full possession of his senses, take away his own life, his last act is an act of sin.' Many years passed away, and Mr. Marsh was walking in one of the streets of Weymouth, when he was stopped by a respectable-looking man, who looked earnestly in his face for a moment, and then said, 'Thank you and bless you, sir, for saving my life.' 'I think there must be some mistake,' he replied, 'for I do not remember having ever seen you before.' 'But I have seen *you*,' said the stranger, 'and never can forget you. I was one of the boys in the National School at Reading, and heard you preach on the Sixth Commandment. A single sentence of the sermon was all that remained in my mind. I commenced business in this town, but after some years of prosperity I was brought, owing to unfortunate circumstances, to the brink of ruin. In my despair I resolved to drown myself, but as I stood on the breakwater about to throw myself into the sea, the words which I had heard fifteen years before, "If any man in the full possession of his senses takes away his own life, his last act is an act of sin," flashed upon my memory, and with all my heart, I said, By the help of God, *my* last act shall not be an act of sin! I returned to my home and found comfort in the Bible and in prayer, and that evening I heard a sermon preached in one of the churches, which led me to seek and find peace with God. The next day's post brought me a letter from an uncle, enclosing a cheque for my present relief, and from that time my circumstances gradually amended until they became prosperous, as they have continued to this time. This has been a great mercy—but the salvation of my soul, when I was on the brink of destroying it for ever, is infinitely greater, and I owe it under God to you.'

The chaplain of the jail in Reading was at that time in failing health, but he could not afford to resign his appointment, as he had a large family to support. Mr. Marsh offered to assist him, without salary, in the weekly services, and in visiting the prisoners, in which duties he forthwith engaged as earnestly as if that had been his only charge.

About the fourth year after his ordination, he resigned Nettlebed, having been presented by his father to the livings of Basildon and Ashampstead, the united value of which was £300 a year, exclusive of the vicarage house of Basildon. He felt it to be his duty to retain the curacy of St. Lawrence's, as the vicar was unable to take any part in the services of the church, owing to an accumulation of debt in which he was, unfortunately, involved, and from which Mr. Marsh (as we have learnt since his death), by diligent attention and exertion, was at length enabled completely to extricate him.

The retention of the curacy of St. Lawrence's not only involved Mr. Marsh in much fatigue and inconvenience, but also in considerable expense, as it made it necessary for him, after accepting Basildon and Ashampstead, to have two curates to share with him the duties of these parishes. But he felt then, as he expressed it in after-life, 'the more work we have to do for God, the more we are indebted to Him.'

An aged farmer, then residing near Reading, who was in the habit of spending his Sundays there, lately mentioned that when Mr. Marsh preached in St. Lawrence's, the church was crowded to such an excess that he believed nearly three thousand persons must have gained admittance; and that, when he preached at Basildon, people flocked from all the villages round to hear him.

The following letters were written about this time:—

ON THE STUDY OF THE BIBLE, ETC.

'I think it desirable that we should possess a kind of general knowledge of the Scriptures. This may be obtained by reading about four chapters every day, which will carry you through the Old and New Testaments within the year. But for the purpose of real devotion and growth in grace, I recommend the following plan:—

'Whatever chapter you may read, at the end of it ask some such questions as these—"What *doctrine* does it contain? Do I *believe* it, and see its practical tendency? What promise does it contain? Do I feel my need of it? Do I pray that it may be fulfilled in my experience? What precept does it contain? Do I humbly implore God's Holy Spirit to write it on my heart, and to enable me to reduce it to practice?" A plan of this nature, steadily and conscientiously pursued, must, I think, be attended with considerable advantage in the end. We may meet with much opposition to our progress in the knowledge, experience, and practice to which I have here alluded, both from the fiery darts of the wicked one, and from the unbelief of our own hearts; but if we humbly depend on God's mercy through Christ, and seek, in the use of means, the teaching and help of the Holy Spirit, we shall, without all doubt, find that our labour is not in vain; we shall, without all doubt, be brought off more than conquerors, and be conducted safe into those happy regions where sin has no existence, where Satan cannot pursue us. "Where the Lamb which is in the midst of the Throne shall feed us, and shall lead us unto living fountains of water, and God shall wipe away all tears from our eyes." . . .

'I need not advise you daily to commit yourself to the Lord, to trust also in Him, with this confidence, that He will bring that to pass which shall best promote His own glory and your eternal benefit. "Who art thou, O great mountain? before Zerubbabel thou shalt become a plain." . . . I have often read on the subject of Providence, and often spoken upon it, but was never so particularly called upon to exercise special faith in it before. May we be daily enabled to exercise this most useful grace! May every exercise strengthen it! There is no rest for the mind but in God. Happy is it for the soul when it can say of the riches of His grace, of the conduct of His providence, and of the presence of His Spirit, "With these things will I cultivate acquaintance; here will I rest, for I have a delight therein."

'Before the Most High I daily feel myself to be a condemned, guilty, helpless creature, but the Scriptures have taught me to expect eternal life, with everything that shall meeten me for it, as the "GIFT OF GOD THROUGH JESUS CHRIST OUR LORD." Here is my only hope, and I know your soul is supported by the same anchor. . . .

'What will not love lead us to attempt? This principle, when it predominates, readily undertakes the greatest hardships, and cheerfully submits to acts of the greatest self-denial, for the sake of the object upon which it is fixed. It thus developed itself in our blessed Lord towards us. May the Holy Ghost so lead us to muse over it that the same divine flame may be kindled in our breasts towards Him, and burn brighter and brighter.

'I thank the Author of all holy desires for your pious breathings relative to the blessed event we are about particularly to commemorate.[1] You lament your want of gratitude. I feel as you do; but let us remember that for this also *Jesus died*, as well as for every other sin, that the guilt of it may never keep us from approaching the mercy seat, since Divine grace can alone remove it. Do you not, for this among other reasons, desire a place amidst the spirits of "the just made perfect," that you may be unfeignedly thankful, without any mixture of ingratitude or distrust, and worthily magnify His holy name?'

AN ANSWER TO DOUBTS AND FEARS OF A SPIRITUAL NATURE.

'Of the truth and reality of the change in you, both from what I have seen, heard, and read, I have not the shadow of a doubt.

'Whence your acquaintance with your own heart? Whence your dissatisfaction with the mere form of religion? Whence your present uneasiness because you feel not that heavenly-mindedness and liberty in religious exercises which you deem essential to the Christian cha-

[1] Christmas Day.

racter? Whence, I say, do all these arise, but from your having been quickened from spiritual death and made alive unto God through Jesus Christ our Lord? I doubt not the experience you describe, however contrary to your present view of the matter, will eventually be made, by the power of the Holy Spirit, to produce the most desirable effects. It is the will of God that *self*, which cleaves to our fallen nature like ivy round an ancient wall, should be annihilated; and that Grace, as it is manifested in the atonement, works, and gifts of the Redeemer, and in the operations of the Holy Spirit, should be exalted *alone* in our salvation.

'Now, will not your present feelings force you, as it were, to depend entirely on the record which God has given of His Son? on the obedience unto death of the Lord Jesus, for pardon, justification, and eternal life; and on the Holy Spirit as the author, preserver, and perfecter of spiritual life in the soul? Recollect, we are called upon to walk by faith during our abode here, and not by sight. Hope, and not fruition, is the anchor of the soul, whilst tossing on the waves of this tempestuous ocean. Is not Christianity a *warfare*? and whence would be the painfulness which that term denotes, if we were always basking beneath the beams of the Sun of Righteousness? It is no proof of our want of grace, but rather of our possession of it, if—when we find we have a heart of unbelief, a subtle, powerful and invisible enemy, and a world which lieth in wickedness to encounter—we feel our inability to overcome those foes, and grieve that we so faintly pursue them, and are at times too successfully repulsed by them, and driven from our standard. Think not, therefore, that any strange thing has happened unto you. "The same difficulties are accomplished in your brethren that are in the world." It is the common lot and experience of at least the majority of the children of God. However, permit me to give you this advice. Though you may feel no present benefit or comfort from studying the Holy Scriptures, *yet still be occupied therein.* Though you may feel spiritually dead and lifeless at the throne of grace, yet *continue* to wait upon the Lord. "Though the vision tarry, wait for it." "They that wait upon the Lord shall renew their strength." "Call upon Me in the day of trouble, I will deliver thee; and thou shalt glorify Me." Though the Holy Spirit will be grieved by the indulgence of evil, even in thought, or the omission of known duties, and on these accounts may withdraw His comfort from us, yet if we are desiring His return we are still under His influence, and shall not be finally forsaken by him—(Ps. lxxxix. 30-33). Apostasy from God is never complete till we have lost all desire of going forward—of enjoying His favour—of obtaining His grace, and participating in His image. I know your present language is, "Oh that I were as in months past,—as in the days when God preserved me." May that blessed peace be restored, and in the meantime may you be enabled to rely on the faithful Word of God—an UNCHANGING GOD. May we believe that in all these things whatever is, is right. He hath done all things well! He doth not afflict willingly nor grieve the children of men. "God is love," and all His dispensations towards those who seek Him are the results of love. Love employs infinite wisdom to plan, and infinite power to execute His designs. How then can they fail? God has not spared His co-equal, co-eternal Son. He has promised His Holy Spirit to them that ask Him. He has sent His Word, preaching peace by Jesus Christ; and when we are "come of age"—when properly educated, and fit for the station we are to fill—He will put us in possession of the purchased possession, and give us fulness of joy and pleasures for evermore. Truly "GOD IS LOVE."

'Here may our faith be fixed, as on a rock. Here let us cast anchor. We may be tossed to and fro for a season, but cannot be entirely overwhelmed or eventually sunk in the deep waters. Such tempests alone shall arise as shall give the best opportunity for the glorious display of the great skill of our wonderful Pilot; and those winds only shall blow which shall keep us in the right channel, and waft us to the shore of eternal rest and peace. May the Spirit be poured upon us from on high. "Then the wilderness will become a fruitful field;"—"instead of the thorn shall come up the fir-tree."

'How beautiful is the whole of that chapter—(Isa. lv.) What a generous call in the first verse! "HO, EVERY ONE!" Is it not a call to the children of men in general, who are naturally thirsting after happiness, but seeking it in wrong directions; and is it not a particular call to such as thirst after the pardon of sin, the favour of God, the sanctification of the soul, and eternal life;—and are not they expressly invited who feel themselves destitute of all spiritual good, and every qualification necessary to meeten them for that world which is reserved for the righteous? May we find by happy experience the Father's love, the Son's merits, and the Spirit's grace, to be as water, wine, and milk to our souls, purifying, strengthening, and refreshing; and may we find prayer, hearing and reading the Word of God, the holy Sacraments, godly conferences, to be indeed streams which make glad the city of God!

'My dear friend, have you not an habitual thirst after spiritual mercies? Can you suppose that this proceeds from any source but "the fountain of all goodness!" and will he not finish this work of His, and fulfil the desire He has excited in the soul? Wherefore dost thou doubt?

' "Grace will complete what grace begins,
To save from sorrow and from sins;
The work which wisdom undertakes,
Eternal mercy ne'er forsakes."

'Lord, thou hast heard the desire of the humble. Thou wilt prepare their heart. Thou wilt cause Thine ear to hear. He who has made us sensible of our need of holy influences, and made us willing to be partakers of them, will not withhold them. Let us ever lament our unbelief, ingratitude, and want of spirituality; but let us never despair of obtaining from the God of all grace, eventually, a victory over sin, Satan, and the world, and a seat in the heavenly kingdom. "I will heal their backslidings"—read Hosea xiv. "Lord we believe, help Thou our unbelief." "Let thy mercies come also unto us, O Lord, even thy salvation, according unto thy word." "Be it unto us even as Thou hast said."

'I am just going to talk to my young friends of Balaam's words: "God is not a man, that He should lie." My dear friend, are you not looking to Him for free pardon, divine teaching, and holy influences, and has He not promised these things to them that ask Him? and is He not faithful that hath promised? May the sure word of an unchangeable God be our constant companion and delight, then shall we "have good success."'

It was about this time that Mr. Marsh was invited to spend a few days with his friends, Mr. and Mrs. Reade, of Ipsden House, Oxfordshire. A visit there always refreshed his mind and heart, for in them, and in those whom they were wont to gather around them, the charms of cultivated intellect were hallowed by the graces of Christianity.

Amongst the guests assembled at this time was the only daughter of Mr. Tilson of Watlington Park, in the same county. Her winning countenance and manners were the expression of a refined and cultivated mind, warm affections, and a sweet, self-sacrificing nature, which made her the centre of joy in her home.

Although this was their first meeting, they scarcely met as strangers; for they were already known to each other by report. At an early age Maria Tilson had given her heart to the Saviour, and, relinquishing the pleasures of the world, to which she had ready access in their most attractive form, she had consecrated herself entirely to His service. As in those days such decisions were rare, it had been much spoken of in the county, and from the same cause Mr. Marsh's 'manner of life from his youth' had also become well known to her.

With such a ground-work of the highest sympathies, the attachment which quickly sprang up between them was one which many waters could not quench, and which remained unchanged through years of separation, silence, and hopelessness.

After permitting an engagement for several months, Mrs. Tilson conceived it to be her duty, in consequence of Sir Charles Marsh's sudden loss of property, to require that it should be entirely broken off. This hard trial was borne with uncomplaining patience and obedience to a parent's command, with such high honour that, for upwards of three years, Miss Tilson denied herself even the comfort of hearing from mutual friends of the welfare of one so deeply beloved.

Some years after her death, a manuscript book was found by one of her children, containing quotations from Mr. Marsh's letters to her during the time of their engagement, on the title-page of which was written, 'Extracts from the letters of a beloved and valued friend. "The Lord gave, and the Lord hath taken away; blessed be the name of the Lord."' One letter, and that the last of this series, has been preserved entire, and manifests with what characteristic unselfishness, at this painful crisis, he kept his own feelings in the background, in order to support and comfort her.

(It was written a few days before Good Friday, 1802) :—

'May the infinite love we are about to commemorate be shed abroad in our hearts by the Holy Ghost, that we may look unto Him whom we have pierced and mourn,—

> "Henceforth may sin have all our grief,
> And Jesus all our hearts."

May we live unto Him who died for us!

'I trust you will pray before you read this letter that some thought in it may comfort you, and that your mind may be supported by the invisible hand of an ever-present and ever-gracious God, and be led to derive all the benefit designed by this and every trying event, and that we may both be enabled to manifest the power of Christianity in employing and supporting the mind under tribulation, and leading it from the creature to the Creator for happiness.

'In whatever state we are, GOD ONLY can *satisfy the mind*. Without His immediate blessing the apparently most happy state in the world would only be full of vanity and vexation of spirit. Who therefore has resisted His will without cause to repent? And who ever submitted without cause for joy and peace?

'I think, in Bishop Beveridge's sermons, there are some exceedingly excellent and useful thoughts on Providence, from this text,—"THE LORD REIGNETH." Remember "it is the Lord, let Him do what seemeth Him good." In every dispensation He saith, "It is I, be not afraid." We are, like children, without judgment; and left to ourselves, should choose what might please for the moment, though it might prove injurious. Should I hear that your mind is satisfied with the apparent determination of Providence, I shall, with much greater cheerfulness, proceed in the path which is clearly marked out for me. Take this hint from Flavel:—"Providence is like a curious piece of art made up of a thousand shreds, which singly we know not what to make of, but put together they present us with a beautiful history." Although "affliction cometh not out of the dust, neither doth trouble spring from the ground, yet man is born to trouble as the sparks fly upward."

'In this respect there is one lot to him that serveth God, and to him that serveth Him not, but with this essential difference,—to the former, the curse is turned into a blessing. "All things work together for good to them that love God," and all His dispensations towards His children proceed from fatherly affection,—are we afflicted, are we grievously afflicted, are we disappointed in our hope of that which we thought would have been the most happy event of our lives?—let us not forget that our heavenly Father's never-failing providence "ordereth all things." He performeth the thing that is appointed for us, and He sees the end from the beginning. And therefore He alone can judge what would be best. However severe our trials, we have cause to say, "Shall a living man complain?" How great a mercy to be in the land of the living, and not in the place where hope never comes! And how is the mercy heightened if we are in any measure alive to God and hastening towards the eternal enjoyment of His unclouded presence! These considerations should in some degree quiet the mind under the most painful trials in the present transitory life.

'May your faith, beloved friend, in the sayings and promises of Holy Writ on those subjects be much greater than mine is, or ever has been. God grant to you and to me grace to glorify God, and to manifest the power of Christianity in supporting the mind when creature-comforts fail, whether those we had possessed or anticipated. You may remember that, at the commencement of our correspondence, about eleven months since, I observed that I viewed our mutual attachment as designed either to be a peculiar trial, eventually for our spiritual benefit, or to lead to an union which would increase and intensify all temporal happiness.

'I have till lately indulged the latter hope, but the circumstances which have now arisen confirm me in the opinion that it has been permitted for a trial. "Shall we receive good at the hand of the Lord, and shall we not receive evil?" He is

> "Good when He gives, supremely good,
> Nor less when He denies;
> E'en crosses from His sovereign hand
> Are blessings in disguise."

'O Lord, grant us faith and patience under every trial. Save us from murmuring, and bring us into a humble submission to Thy will; help us to believe that good is Thy will concerning us, and with a degree of cheerfulness to acquiesce, even when it most opposes our wishes and most deeply tries our feelings.

'My dearest friend, you have already been an instrument of much good. Our gracious God has still work for you to perform, but not just where we intended. "Be steadfast, immoveable," and, according to your station and ability, "always abounding in the work of the Lord." You will then experience that peace which creatures cannot give; or at least be preserved from sinking under the waves of this tempestuous ocean, and at the last be conveyed safe into that haven "where the wicked cease from troubling, and where the weary are at rest."

'May the Holy Spirit engrave this truth deeply in our hearts,—"GOD IS LOVE."

'If we believe this, we shall, in proportion to our faith, be satisfied with this dispensation. Oh for faith to say, "All is well!" Glory be to God it is so, even when we cannot take the comfort derived from believing it. In Providence, as well as in Redemption and Grace, we may say, "Great and marvellous are Thy works, Lord God Almighty; just and true are Thy ways, THOU KING OF SAINTS." His ways are in the deep, and His paths in the great waters, and his footsteps are not known, yet for the comfort of those who call upon His name, He has said, "When thou passest through the waters, I will be with thee, and through the rivers, they shall not overflow thee; when thou walkest through fire, thou shalt not be burned, neither shall the flame kindle upon thee." The most highly favoured servants of the Lord have no promise of exemption from trials in the present life, but rather the contrary; but all have the promise of the sanctifying presence of the Lord Jesus in the furnace, so that they shall lose nothing but their dross. "He knoweth the way that I take. When He has tried me, I shall come forth as gold."

'I now know what self-denial means, and I trust I shall experience the efficacy of faith in things "unseen and eternal," to support the mind under the loss "of things seen and temporal." "We are journeying to the land of which the Lord hath said, I will give it thee." Let us keep the end of our pilgrimage in view; this will preserve us from fainting by reason of occasional rough roads, tempestuous weather, the attacks of robbers, and other inconveniences which most Christian travellers endure. Let me still ask for your prayers. You will ever have mine.

'With respect to Religion, this is my earnest, last advice. Be satisfied with the Remedy infinite wisdom has appointed for the disease under which Adam's fallen race labours. Believe the record that God hath given of His Son. "And this is the record, that God hath given to us eternal life, and this life is in His Son." Seek daily after the holiness which His religion enjoins and promises. Let your soul rest on that "covenant which is ordered in all things, and sure." Constantly approach the throne of grace, and read, mark, and learn the Word of God, and pray that by the power of the Holy Ghost "you may inwardly digest it."

'Regard it as sinful to disbelieve the inestimable truth "that Christ died for our sins according to the Scriptures;" therefore the law having been magnified, and justice having been satisfied, we may "come boldly to the Throne of Grace, assured that we shall obtain mercy and find grace to help in every time of need." You will ever find Christianity a warfare. Evil in some shape or other will ever be present with you in this life, but waiting on the Lord, your spiritual strength shall be renewed, and shortly you will see that every dispensation was perfectly consistent with St. John's heart-cheering revelation of the Divine name, nature, and character of the Most High—

"GOD IS LOVE." It is only in this short life we are called upon to submit to His *trying* dispensations. Trusting in Christ, and being brought to hunger and thirst after righteousness, here *only* we can suffer in the heart. Fulness of joy and pleasures for evermore await us.

'In every period and situation of life I shall feel myself honoured and happy in being permitted to subscribe myself your most sincere and affectionate friend,

WILLIAM MARSH.

' "Farewell! but not for ever," Hope replies—
"Trace but his steps, and meet him in the skies." '

'It added not a little to Miss Tilson's trial, that her mother, from time to time, urged upon her acceptance some offer of marriage more brilliant in point of rank and wealth. But here she felt it to be her duty to God, to the heart she had won, and to her own peace and purity of soul, to resist as firmly as she had hitherto implicitly yielded. Marriage was too holy in her eyes to be degraded into a matter of mere worldly advancement, or entered upon with anything less than her whole heart's affections. Mr. Marsh's attachment was not less steadfast and devoted. At the same time, he supported her in the fulfilment of her severe duty, by not attempting the slightest renewal of intercourse. One way alone was left open to them for reaching each other's hearts; this was the way round by Heaven. No earthly authority could claim the right of closing that door. In the sanctuary of the presence of their God, their spirits could still meet, yet break no law, divine or human. And He set the seal of His approval upon their constant affection. Miss Tilson's filial submission to the will of her Heavenly Father, under these trying circumstances, so deeply touched her mother's heart, that during a prolonged illness which ended in death, she gave her full and willing consent to her daughter's marriage with Mr. Marsh.

Nor was even this all the joy that God had reserved to bring forth for her. In the midst of her sorrowful watching, during the last days of her mother's illness, she had the sweet testimony from that mother's dying lips, that her child's conduct had so convinced her of the reality and power of religion, that she had sought and found 'like precious faith' in Christ Jesus.

It was in the month of November, in the year 1806, that William Marsh's marriage with Maria Tilson, took place. From that day forward until the 24th of July 1833, when the desire of his eyes was taken from him, the holy and blessed love which God had given to them only grew and gathered strength as years passed on, from their union of purpose that in all things Christ should have the pre-eminence.

My father's first curate and beloved friend, the Rev. James Haldane Stewart, thus wrote of my mother after her death,—'It was my privilege to know her in the morning of life, when, although surrounded by friends among the higher circles, she was led by Divine grace to enter willingly upon the duties of a clergyman's wife in a country parish. It was early in life that she preferred to sit at the feet of Jesus and to hear His word; and this ought especially to be noticed in order to remove an error into which some fall, that the sincere followers of our Lord, who enter upon His service, do this from disgust or disappointment. No, there was no disappointment here. It was in the bloom of her days, when all was cheerful and pleasant around her, that she took her station as the willing helpmeet of a pastor's duty in a country village. And here she made good her confession; for frequently in conversation she made known her principles, declaring that her dependence was altogether on her Saviour ("found in Christ"); and her aim to be conformed to His image—Jesus her Lord, Jesus her Saviour, Jesus her Advocate, Jesus her Righteousness, Jesus her example, Jesus her all in all. And this faith manifested itself by cheerful piety, by readiness for prayer, by constant self-denial, and by lively zeal and enlarged benevolence. That which used to strike me much, was the sound good sense and superior wisdom which enabled her, whilst so spiritually-minded, diligently to attend to the ordinary affairs of life, uniting in her measure those rare graces which shone so brightly in our blessed Lord. He, though so conversant with heavenly things as to speak of future glory as mansions in His Father's house, was yet so attentive to minute concerns, that He commanded His disciples to gather up the fragments that remained, that nothing be lost. There was in her also an enlarged spirit, a spirit ready to sacrifice the pleasure she derived from the society of her beloved husband, though none more delighted in such society, and willingly to permit him to pursue his duties unconstrained, upon this truly Christian principle, that "although," as she beautifully said, "his Master's service gives me less of his society now, I shall enjoy it more when we reach our home." For her religion was not of that character which blazes high and soon expires, which hears the word with joy, but in time of temptation falls away: it was the steady flame which Divine love kindles, partaking of that "charity which suffereth long and is kind, which seeketh not her own, which beareth all things, hopeth all things, endureth all things."

'This was her religion as I almost daily witnessed it for some years after her marriage; and, although the great Husbandman latterly placed us in different parts of His vineyard, I have since seen and heard quite sufficient to enable me to say that she continued in this same blessed course.

'But *I* need not bear testimony to her continuance in well-doing. Ask her dear family what were her daily employments. Ask the numerous friends who shared in her correspondence. Ask the many young persons who have since been instructed by her counsels, encouraged by her kindness, soothed by her consolations, and above all, blessed in answer to her fervent prayers. Ask *them* what her religion was, and they will say that her path was that of the just, which is as the shining light which shineth more and more unto the perfect day. Her faith became more simple, her hope more assured, her views of the Divine character more clear, her sense of the vanity of the world more strong, and her confidence in her Saviour more entire.'

At another time, Mr. Stewart remarked, 'Mrs. Marsh

was always planning how she might do good to others, and especially for the benefit of the poor, and that with so much excellent judgment, arranging everything for them to the best advantage. She had a peculiarly sweet manner in visiting them, helping them both temporally and spiritually.'

Amongst other acts of our parents' self-denial which Mr. Stewart named to us, he said that, not long after their marriage, they gave up their carriage and horses, and then turned the coach-house into a schoolroom for the children of the village.

Two or three times in a week the children came to her for private instruction; and another hour was occupied in the same manner with the children of a school established on a hill at some distance.

In the month of May 1807, Mr. Simeon, of Cambridge, paid his first visit to Basildon Vicarage. He bore a strong and ever-increasing affection to both my father and mother, and more than once, after taking long journeys with my father for missionary purposes, he wrote of him as 'that loveliest and most heavenly-minded of men.' At this time he came for rest, having lost his voice from continuous over-exertion. One day, when he was beginning to recover, he said to my mother, 'The Lord deals with me in the greatest mercy, He has been doing some little good by me; now He has laid me by, and this is the time to get good for myself. My curate, who took an under part while I was in health, is now exceedingly growing in grace, and is wonderfully acceptable to my dear people. I am not wanted at all; but, if it please God to place me again in a post of usefulness, I hope to serve Him with all my strength.'

During a short absence from home, Mr. Marsh thus writes:—

ON TRUSTING IN THE SAVIOUR.

'*July* 1807.

'YOUR soul resembles the needle, which may be agitated from its point, but will return to it again. What a proof is this that the invisible influence has attracted you! Rest on the work of Jesus when self appears all sin. This removes shyness. This brings the soul to the throne of grace without slavish fear. This draws peace and succour from above.

"If I ever loved at all,
Help to love Thee more, I pray;
If I have not loved before,
Help me to begin to-day."

'It is your prayer. It must be answered. Who created anxiety in our hearts for peace with God? Who taught us that to walk with Him is our honour and our happiness? Who gave us a taste for the beauties of holiness, and a view of the suitableness of the adorable Saviour to our case? "He that hath wrought us for the self-same thing is God." And I am confident He will perfect, and not forsake, the work of His hands. "Trust in the Lord and do good, and verily thou shalt be fed." This is true in more senses than one. Adieu, my most beloved wife. Peace be with you.—Ever yours, W. M.'

In the summer of the year 1810, the eldest son of one of the devoted evangelical clergy of that day, the Rev. Basil Woodd, came on a visit to Basildon Vicarage. To the deep grief of his parents he had been led astray into evil courses: but one hope always remained, he never disbelieved the truths of the Bible. A deep impression of the happiness of religion was left on his mind by that visit. In the autumn of the same year he gladly accepted an invitation from his sister, who lived in the neighbourhood of those friends whom he had begun to prize so highly. On the first Sunday after his arrival, he walked to Basildon Church in the morning, and finding that Mr. Marsh was to preach at Reading in the afternoon, followed him thither, but returned in the evening in time to be present at the exposition of Scripture, which my father gave at the vicarage to his family and the villagers. The subject that night was our Lord's meeting at the well with the woman of Samaria. Among other remarks, Mr. Marsh said there was nothing between her soul and salvation but prayer: 'If thou knewest the gift of God, and who it is that saith unto thee, Give me to drink, thou wouldest have asked, and He would have given thee living water.' This thought was made 'the power of God unto salvation' to young Basil Woodd. Thenceforward, he consecrated his rare attractions and talents to the service of his God. But it was for the eleventh hour only of his brief life that he was to be permitted to work in the vineyard. When soon afterwards a rapid consumption set in, deep was his regret and penitence for time lost and life wasted. Towards the close of his illness, he expressed an earnest desire to see his beloved father in Christ. As Mr. Marsh entered the room, the dying youth clasped him in his arms, saying, 'Oh, my dear friend, you were the instrument of bringing me to God.'

Every day his sense of sin deepened, and at the same time his trust was strengthened in his Saviour's atonement, mercy, and love. And every day more brightly shone the glory set before him, until the veil was removed, and he saw face to face—Him, 'whom having not seen he loved.'

Twenty-eight years after Mrs. Marsh's death the following letter was received by one of her children from a stranger:—

'*April* 6, 1861.

'THE thought of writing to you arose from reading a short account of your sainted mother in the *Family Treasury*. I shall have to bless God to all eternity that ever she lived.

'When Dr. Marsh was Vicar of Basildon, the parish of Ashampstead was under his care, and when there he used to sleep occasionally at my grandfather's, so that "our old house at home" obtained the appellation of "The Episcopal Cottage," and many a reminiscence of him, of your sainted mother, and the pious Mr. Stewart (curate), has been told round our hearth, till we have all blessed God that such saints ever visited our village. Much fruit remains to the present day, and some is gathered into the heavenly garner. One day a thoughtless lad was running about that house, and your blessed mother put her hand upon his head and offered up a prayer, not I believe the only one, for I think she prayed much for him, and then she put a book into his hand consisting of a number of tracts. He was first bound as an apprentice in Reading. One day, just before he went home to see his friends, he thought, "Mrs. Marsh will be asking me how I like the tracts; what shall I say? I have not read them; I had better just look into them? then I can say I have commenced." He looked, and the first thing that struck his eye, and heart too, was, "solemn thoughts about eternity;" and deep conviction seized his mind. He read and read on, and grew much troubled, until some short time after, while hearing the Rev. James Sherman preach, his load of sin was removed, and his spirit rejoiced in God his Saviour. That change has been permanent, lasting till now, some forty-six or forty-seven years. That lad is now my father. When I was born he was upon his knees in the room underneath; and when my first cry fell upon his ear, he gave me up to God; and He who is faithful heard his prayer. After I had lived twenty-one years in sin, his prayer was answered, and this heart was changed by Divine grace; and now, blessed be God, I am a missionary in Ireland. I covet no higher station. I see no higher one on earth, for I have the glorious opportunity of pointing poor sinners to the slain Lamb. Thanks be to God, I have had the happiness, during eleven years, of seeing hundreds of poor sinners crying for mercy, and finding peace through the blood of the Lamb.'

Mr. Marsh held the curacy of St. Lawrence's for about eleven years, and the living of Basildon for seven. At the recommendation of the bishop, and with the consent of the governors, he was then appointed to St. James's, Brighton. A veto, however, rested with the vicar, who was determined to exercise it; for, although he expressed the highest admiration of Mr. Marsh's character, he had been prejudiced against his religious views by certain anonymous letters. The chapel, nevertheless, was opened, and Mr. Marsh began his ministrations there with the bishop's consent, in the hope that the vicar might withdraw his objection; but as this was not the case, Mr. Marsh resigned after some months, and the chapel was closed until another appointment should be made. The vicar was afterwards raised to the bench, as Bishop of Worcester, and became one of Mr. Marsh's warmest friends, supporting him most heartily in a somewhat similar difficulty, which occurred many years afterwards at Leamington.

In referring, at his first visitation dinner, to the circumstances of his early acquaintance with Mr. Marsh, the bishop remarked: 'Had I known him then as I know him now, never would I have allowed him to leave the chapel at Brighton. Even then I could not but see that his conduct throughout was that of a perfect gentleman and blameless Christian.'

In the following letter, written from Brighton, to Mrs. Fuller Maitland of Park Place, Oxfordshire, after informing her of the birth of a daughter, and congratulating her on the birth of a son, he writes: 'May all that is contained in the promise, "I will be a God unto thee, and to thy seed after thee," be the portion of both parents and children. Great is the encouragement which may be derived from the nature of God, the declaration of Scripture, and the conduct of the Redeemer, to hope that our families may be nurseries for the skies.

'Our contest here is not yet decided. By misrepresentations and other weapons I have been attacked, but I am not yet dead of my wounds.

'These oppositions are trifling. We have to contend with much more formidable enemies; but the God of all grace will not suffer us to feel our weakness, and call on His name for strength, and then leave us a prey to their power. Yet a little while, and eternal victory will open to our view. May we daily catch those glimpses by faith, which will animate us in our course.

"For us is the Forerunner entered;
For us He contended and conquered."

'Through Him we shall conquer. The belief of this will lead us to praise Him, and make us desirous to declare His mercy and power to others.'

Whilst Mr. Marsh remained at Brighton, people of all ranks flocked to hear him, and numbers dated their first knowledge of a Saviour's love from that blessed period of his ministry. The uncertainty of his stay from week to week, and the possibility that each Sunday might be his last, gave additional solemnity and earnestness to his preaching. The late Rev. Henry Venn Elliott, incumbent of St. Mary's, Brighton, when preaching one of the funeral sermons for Dr. Marsh, alluded to that period as follows:—'I remember him in the early days of his ministry at Brighton, when I was an undergraduate at Cambridge, with what beauty of holiness he appeared amongst us—with what attraction of manner and countenance—for really, as some said, he looked the Gospel, as well as preached it. With what a copious variety of sound argument out of the Scriptures he handled his topic, and invited us to accept all the grace of Christ crucified. It was in the "fulness of the blessing of the Gospel of peace" that he came to us. His whole soul was in his work at St. James's chapel for the nine short months that he occupied that pulpit, and his ministry was as life from the dead; for those nine months were harvest months of immortal souls. Everywhere, in every society and conversation, in every letter, call, or interview, his Lord and Master's name, uppermost in his own heart, found an entrance—and not a forced or injudicious entrance, "out of season"—as it might have seemed with another man. He had the faculty to convert it into "in season." He was then in the prime of his strength and activity. I remember hearing him called the St. John of the Church of our time, the beloved disciple;—a remarkable appellation, which he owed, I think, partly to the sweetness of his natural disposition—a little, also, to the graces of his person—but much more to the refinement, the holiness, the love, that breathed in all his words, and looks, and actions—both in public and in private life."

CHAPTER III.

LIFE AT COLCHESTER.

'GIVE alms: the needy sink with pain;
The orphans mourn, the crushed complain.
Christ, through His poor, a claim doth make;
Give gladly for thy Saviour's sake.

Give words, kind words, to those who err;
Remorse much needs a comforter.
With the sweet charity of speech,
Give words that heal, and words that teach.

Give thoughts, give energy, to themes
That perish not like folly's dreams.
Hark! from the islands of the sea,
The Missionary cries to thee
To aid him on a heathen soil,—
Give thoughts, give energy, give toil.'

LIFE AT COLCHESTER.

From Brighton Mr. Marsh removed to Colchester, where the living of St. Peter's, in those days not exceeding in value £300 a year and a house, had been presented to him by his friend Mr. Simeon. During the fifteen years of his residence here, there was perhaps a greater outpouring of the Spirit on his work than at any other period of his ministry.

Twenty-two missionaries and clergymen were sent forth from his congregation. Associations were formed in connexion with the Bible, Church Missionary, and Jews' Societies, the three grand causes which he loved to forward; but others were not forgotten.

He supported the societies then in existence for missionary work in Ireland; the Prayer Book and Homily Society, the Religious Tract Society, and others; but his energies were chiefly concentrated upon his own parish and neighbourhood. In all his labours of love there, he was heartily aided by his wife, of whom it might truly be said that she 'diligently followed every good work.'

To a valued friend we find him thus writing of his duties and interests :—

'*August* 1, 1816.

'I HAVE been more than usually occupied of late in attending Bible Society meetings in the neighbourhood, etc., as well as by full work at home. And now I have to prepare for Thursday on a subject new as far as discussion goes. I am to prove to the Jews that Messiah was the Angel Jehovah that appeared to the fathers. The subject would make any man who believes the inspiration of Scripture, at least no mere Unitarian. It is evident there is a plurality revealed—a Being with the name, attributes, and worship of Jehovah, and yet distinct from the Father, and assuming an inferior nature and office for the deliverance and comfort of guilty, miserable man. I have no doubt of this, that no man hath seen the Divine Essence at any time, and yet that in the person of the Son He has in all ages manifested Himself to man. Our world is restored, and saved, and guided, and comforted by a Mediator, or what St. Paul would call, "God manifest in the flesh;" or St. John, "the Life who was manifested and became the light of men." Philo, the Chaldee Paraphrasts, Jonathan, and the Jerusalem Targum, prove the ancient Jews had very different views of the Messiah from the moderns. I am culling what flowers I can from bouquets which have been already formed. I find it a delightful subject for meditation. Infinite power, and other infinite attributes confound me; but when I see them actually exercised by a Mediator, the Friend of sinners, the Saviour of man, my heart can contemplate them with peace and hope. St.

Paul has the thought in 2 Cor. iv. 6, and shows the effect of it in 2 Cor. iii. 18. May this knowledge increase in us, and draw our hearts to their proper centre.'

Although my father's sermons were preached from notes only, and he had great fluency of speech, yet he set apart much time for study in their preparation, and for prayer for the Holy Spirit's guidance and teaching; so the result frequently bore witness to this truth, '*The Lord gave* the word.'

A lawyer who was the leader of an infidel club in the town was met one evening by an acquaintance at the turn of the street which led to St. Peter's Church. The lawyer was only walking for his amusement, but his friend rallied him with the words, 'What, are you turning Methodist? going to the evening lecture at St. Peter's?' The spirit of opposition was roused, 'Why not, if I choose?' he replied, and turned down the pathway. Seeing him enter the church, just before the service commenced, my father, who was sitting by my mother's side, called her attention to the unexpected arrival, and told her that the subject of his sermon was one against which the unbeliever had especially levelled his attacks. 'Shall I change it?' he whispered. After lifting up her heart in silent prayer, she answered, 'No, let it be the one you intended, I believe God has a message in it for him.' The next day the lawyer came to my father, to tell him that his sermon had such an effect in removing his difficulties as to the inspiration of Scripture, that he desired further instruction in the Word of God; and after this he frequently came for reading and prayer. This resulted under the blessing of God in his complete conversion. From this time he earnestly endeavoured to spread the knowledge of the truth as it is in Jesus. His younger children, whom he now trained in the Christian faith, early received Christ into their hearts, and surrendered themselves to His service. Two of them became devoted missionaries in connexion with the Church Missionary Society.

Some time before this, Mr. Marsh's interest had been greatly deepened in the Jewish cause, by an incident which he used to tell with great animation. He was staying in London for a few days, when his friend, Mr. Simeon, sent for him. 'I am advertised,' said Mr. Simeon, 'to preach at Stroud for the Jews' Society, and now I am too ill to leave my bed. Would you go for me?'

'Gladly, if I knew more of the subject. But although I have subscribed to that Society from the first and like its object, I know too little about it to undertake to preach for it the day after to-morrow.'

'Have you a grain of humility? if you have, you will preach my sermon!'

Mr. Marsh laughed, and said, 'If that be the criterion, I think I have.'

On his arrival at Stroud late on Saturday evening, the portmanteau in which the manuscript of Mr. Simeon's sermon had been packed, was discovered to be missing. Driven by this accident to give his own thoughts from the pulpit, he spent several hours that night in prayerfully searching the prophecies concerning the Jews, and ended by writing a running commentary on Romans xi.

Just before the service began on the following morning, a waiter from the hotel came to the vestry door to say that the portmanteau had arrived.

'Shall I fetch the sermon?' asked a lay secretary of the Society who was aware of the dilemma.

'No!' said Mr. Marsh, 'Mr. Simeon is not to preach to-day; and I am not to preach; St. Paul is to preach!'

The Society was the richer for that sermon; and incalculably the richer for the intense interest awakened in my father's mind by those hours of deep study of the Word of God touching the chosen nation, the present duties of Christians towards them, and the glorious hopes for their future. From that hour he devoted himself with the tranquil and enduring enthusiasm of his nature to the cause of that Society, and to the temporal and spiritual welfare of the Jews.

'*July* 17, 1817.

'LEWIS WAY is going at his own expense on the first mission to Russia respecting the Jews. He takes a converted Rabbi, now ordained a deacon in our church, to place him probably in the Crimea. Dear Way presses me also to be his companion. I should be three months absent; but, if my own flock can be well watered and fed, I am ready to go.'

'*August* 13, 1817.

'YOU will be glad of a line to hear that I am still in England. C. preferred the tour to taking my duty, therefore he accompanied Mr. Way. The Reverend N. H., K., and young Mr. M., the artist, are of the party. The ship little knew the value of its cargo. The object of the tour is simply to make inquiry as to the state of the Jews in Poland, Russia, the Crimea, and probably as far as Palestine, and to stir up the Gentiles in their favour.

'Our sermons and meetings were well attended, and above 300 guineas will go to the parent Society.

'The parting with Mr. Way was truly affecting; but I left him on board quite calm, and ready for a useful life, or a Christian death. This is a new thing. A man of great wealth and talents, resigning the comforts of an English home, and everything that earth can give, for the fatigues of land and water, and the frozen regions of the north. Some indeed have gone thither for pleasure, and some for gain; but he goes for the benefit of God's ancient people. May the God of Abraham, Isaac, and Jacob accompany him and his companions! I have never before witnessed such a scene as took place in my vestry that evening.

'A Polish Jew, a Tartarian Mahometan, and British Christians, on their knees together, in the name of Jesus, weeping and praying and imploring blessings on the Church and people of England, and embracing each other as brethren in Christ!'

In the year 1818, my father went with Mr. Simeon to Holland, to inquire into the religious condition of the Jews. To Miss Hooper, who has been previously mentioned as taking so deep an interest in the Jewish nation, my father thus writes:—

'AMSTERDAM, *June* 22, 1818.

'You know the object dear Mr. Simeon and myself had in view. I trust our tour has not been in vain. We have made some curious discoveries, and, perhaps, by the blessing of God, may prepare the way for our brother, who is coming as chaplain to this city. We have conversed with several Jews, and find there are three descriptions—the strict, the liberal, and the convinced.

'The *strict* object to every kind of innovation, though not altogether to overtures of friendship; the *liberal* are desirous of a good understanding between Jews and Christians, and to further the education of their children; the *convinced* are afraid to confess Christ, lest they should be put out of the synagogue.

'I do not wonder at this, when I consider that they would not only be excommunicated by their own people, but would also be suspected by ours. It requires almost the spirit of a martyr. I trust persecution on the part of many of the Jews will soon cease, from a remarkable circumstance. The president of all the Portuguese Jews, a very learned and respectable physician, informs us that the Spanish Jews never approved of the crucifixion of Christ. They venerate His character and moral instructions. The use we shall make of it is this: If you disapprove of the crucifixion of Jesus, ought you to persecute those who believe in Him? This circumstance, when known, may bring Jews and Christians a little nearer together, and shelter Jews who believe. Had

Nicodemus made much greater progress than some of these Jews when he first went to our Lord? Their civil privileges in this country are very great. One is at this time a member of the Government. The King of the Netherlands has issued an edict that all their children shall be instructed in Dutch and Hebrew.

'Our church here is small, but the station is very important in many points of view. Lift up your heart for us, that we may be useful to Christians and Jews, and especially that our brother who is coming as chaplain may be filled with wisdom, and patience, and love. It is like the work of raising this country out of water, it requires industry and perseverance. What a mercy it is to be delivered from that unbelief, which is not peculiar to the Jews! What a mercy to know our need of a Saviour, and to have been led to "the Lamb of God, which taketh away the sin of the world!" May we live a life of faith on Him, and a life of devotedness to Him. This is the only happy life. May His Spirit be with you all!'

The following letters, written at about this date to two of his old friends and parishioners in Reading, Dr. and Mrs. Hooper, will show that, amidst new duties and interests, he did not forget former pastoral ties:—

ON 'THAT BLESSED HOPE.'

'*March* 21, 1817.

'AND now, my dear friends, you have all to guard against a mistake so natural to us, looking down into the *grave* instead of looking up *to the* SKIES. It is not your dear Jane who lies in the tomb. She is before the throne of God and of the Lamb. It is not Jane who is among the dead. She is written among the Living in Jerusalem, and has joined the spirits of the just made perfect. Her human frame was but the tabernacle which lodged the immortal spirit during the abode on earth. That frame is laid aside, and thus she is indeed concealed from your sight, but even that shall be reanimated and appear like Christ's glorious body, in splendour, resembling that which Peter, James, and John witnessed when they saw their Master transfigured on Mount Tabor. Oh great salvation! The Lord Jesus will not rest satisfied till He has done all that He has spoken to us of. He will swallow up death in victory. Long before that, our spirits shall enter Paradise, and rest with infinite content till the Resurrection morn. Let us look steadfastly towards heaven, and live in joyful hope of soon meeting our departed friends in the Lord. While here may we have grace patiently to suffer, or actively to perform His will, and, having filled up our measure of suffering and duties, our only hope being in Christ, we also shall fall asleep in Him, and rise to be for ever with the Lord. "Wherefore comfort one another with these words."—Believe me always, yours most affectionately,

WM. MARSH.'

ON TRUE COMFORT.

'COLCHESTER, *December* 5, 1822.

'MY VERY DEAR FRIEND,—Not a word has reached me from any quarter respecting your visit to London. I thank God you have passed through the operation, and pray all the expected benefit may result. Exercised as you are with self-knowledge, you receive trials as Fatherly chastisements, and murmur not. You shall find they are real blessings. Believers in our blessed Lord and Saviour not only recover what they lost in Adam, but their trials in time will promote their great good in eternity (2 Cor. iv. 17, 18).

'While we take the most humiliating views of ourselves, we should indulge the most exalted hopes in Christ. Two texts of late have afforded me much pleasure: "Him that cometh unto *Me*, I will in *no wise* cast out;" and, "A cup of cold water only," etc., "shall in *no wise* lose its reward." What an encouragement to *sinners* to come to such a *Saviour*, and to *believers* to serve such a *Lord!*

'Time is indeed rolling on, and what is it, but as it has a happy influence on *eternity?* Its trials, vexations, and cares will be as "waters that have passed away!" But what will eternity be? Who can tell further than as it is revealed? (1 John iii. 2:) "And there shall be no more curse: but the Throne of God and of the Lamb shall be in it; and His servants shall serve Him: and they shall see His face: and His name shall be in their forehead" (Rev. xxii. 3, 4). This is quite sufficient for the present. It will consist of knowledge, holiness, and love. The works and Word of God will then be better understood by the lowest saint, than now by the wisest philosopher and best informed divine. The service of God will then be without interruption and without imperfection. May our hope of this happiness be steadfast.—Ever yours affectionately, W. MARSH.'

'*February* 8, 1825.

'There is a wonderful shaking among the Jewish dry bones. The King of Bavaria has just ordered all synagogues to be shut that will not prepare young men as preachers, and allow a sermon to be preached every Sabbath in the language of the country. He wishes them to be informed Jews, and not to remain in their present Rabbinical ignorance. He does not allow that this is persecution, because all that he requires is, that they should be taught their own religion as taught by Moses. Nevertheless it will be regarded, I suppose, as persecution, because it is not voluntary on their part.'

'*August* 1825.

'Thanks for the Traditions, though I almost wish there had never been such things in our world: for the most part they obscure the light of truth, and mislead the children of men. I trust the day is dawning, and the Day-star arising, which will disperse them all. How joyful will be the time when truth shall triumph, and Jew and Gentile become one fold! We should desire it and labour for it, though we may die "without the sight."

'Yet I believe we shall see it. Heaven is not a corner of the universe, where we can hear and see nothing connected with the honour of our Redeemer on the earth. I do not like these corner views,—they are dark.'

Whilst at Colchester he held two evening services every week in the church; and on alternate Tuesday afternoons the schools for the upper classes were invited to attend at the large infant-school room, which, with the assistance of friends, he had built. When each young person had been called upon to repeat a verse of Scripture from a portion selected at the previous meeting, my father would give a catechetical address, in a manner peculiarly adapted to sustain the interest and win the hearts of the young. After an interval of six-and-thirty years, one of his daughters met three ladies who told her that it was in those meetings they had first learned to seek, and then to know and love, that Saviour, who had led them all their life since.

Both my father and mother devoted much care to the sick and aged. As St. Peter's Church stood on the brow of a steep hill, such as were infirm amongst the poor who lived in the valley, were invited to dine between the services in the laundry of the vicarage, where meat pies, made the day before, but warmed for the 'Sunday dinner,' were provided for them. After they had dined, the old people spent their time in prayer and in singing hymns, until the hour for afternoon service. On summer days, when the door was open, the children, as they walked in the garden, have heard their dear old friends praying for a blessing on their beloved vicar and his family, and on the work in his parish. At the christenings of the son and youngest daughter, who were born at Colchester, the same sort of gatherings took place in larger numbers. From dinner until tea-time, and from tea-time till supper, the hours were spent with unflagging interest in reading the Bible and singing hymns—in Christian conversation and prayer. The day was concluded by family worship, conducted by my father, in the largest room in the vicarage; and then the happy old people returned to their homes.

There were some delightful characters amongst these old people, and their conversation was often racy, as well as profitable. One old man had read Scott's 'Commentary' three times through; another, wishing to see if he could puzzle him on Scripture subjects, asked him whether Peter was the worse or the better for his fall? He thought for a moment, and then replied, 'He was the better for his *recovery*.' Some of them were remarkable for their exercise of self-denial, in order to enable them to give out of their pittances to aid the Bible, Jews', and Church Missionary Societies. One old woman, on parish allowance, gave up drinking milk and sugar with her tea, which was her principal meal, that she might give the little sum thus saved to these good causes.

Amongst the curates who were successively with him at Colchester were the late Rev. John Harrington, vicar of Little Hinton; the Rev. Vicesimus Toriano, vicar of Donyland; the Rev. John Sandys, formerly incumbent of St. Paul's, Islington, now rector of Rockland; and the Rev. John Burt, vicar of Seething; men of God who have uplifted the standard of a free Gospel, and adorned its doctrines by their lives.

It would not be easy to describe the loving harmony existing between my father and his fellow-labourers, nor the blessing which this union of heart brought into their work in the parish.

When one of his daughters was spending a few days with Mr. Sandys and his beloved wife (who is now in the presence of the Saviour, to whose service her whole life was devoted), Mr. Sandys mentioned that the hymns which were sung on the Sunday evenings at Colchester were still his favourites for his own fireside. They recalled the time of his blessed intercourse with my father and mother, which seemed to him like a foretaste of the communion of saints in glory.

As there was no third service in St. Peter's Church on Sunday, my father preached in the evening for the incumbent of another church in the town, who, from delicate health, needed more assistance than he was able to procure. To those services he was accompanied by my elder sisters, while my mother remained at home with her younger children, making Scripture lessons delightful to them, and also to some children about their own age, of the upper and middle classes in Colchester, who thankfully came to share this privilege. In winter we gathered in a large circle around the fireside; and in summer weather we sat in the pleasant garden, around my mother's chair. When the rest returned from church, the elder children were allowed to sit up to a later hour; and the Sunday evening with their parents was the happiest time of all the week. The youngest, who was on special occasions allowed to remain, well remembers her joy on being placed by her father's side, and hearing him sing with her sisters the hymns with which he loved to refresh himself when the labours of the day were over. Kelly's hymns were amongst his chief favourites, 'because,' as he said, 'in the closing verse he always takes us up to heaven.'

The hymns which we remember as most frequently sung were those beginning :—

> 'Why those fears ?—behold, 'tis Jesus
> Holds the helm, and guides the ship.'

> 'Jesus, immortal King, go on !
> The glorious day will soon be won !'

> 'Hark, a voice, it sounds from heaven !
> Happy in the Lord who die.'

> 'Hail to the Lord's anointed,
> Great David's greater Son.'

And especially this—

> 'For Zion's sake I will not rest,
> I will not hold my peace
> Until Jerusalem be blest,
> And Judah dwell at ease.'

The following letter from the Rev. John Sandys, for whom my father ever cherished the warmest regard, gives a contemporary view of this period of his life :—

'To express the feelings with which I have ever looked back to the time when I was your dear father's curate at Colchester, is no easy matter. To have been associated with such a man in the early part of my ministry, I have ever regarded as a ground for special thankfulness. I have known more or less intimately not a few of the most eminent servants of God, of that generation; but by none, as it seemed to me, was the lovely image of the Saviour so fully reflected. The loveliness of your dear mother's character I was almost equally struck by. On one occasion, when your father and mother were sitting on the sofa in the drawing-room, Mr. Simeon, who was on a visit to the vicarage, remarked to me: "To see such a couple it would be worth while to walk from Cambridge to Colchester barefoot." When I was leaving Colchester for a permanent post, I remember saying to a friend, "I have now been with my vicar nearly four years, and almost daily with him during the time, and I have never known him do a thing which one would wish undone, nor say a word which one would have wished unsaid."

'He was in those days, you will recollect, in the habit of walking for nearly an hour before dinner. It was my privilege, very commonly, to accompany him. Some passage of Scripture was generally the subject of our conversation, and I was wont to avail myself of the opportunity of asking explanations of various passages in which I found difficulty.

'His knowledge of the Scriptures surprised me. My difficulties he rarely failed to remove. Never did I refer to a passage that he evidently had not thoroughly thought out; and no one that I ever met with equalled him in setting forth in each passage the mind of the writer. His expositions at family prayers were peculiarly interesting and instructive. They were not, as is often the case, detached explanatory thoughts, which, however useful, do not really open out the passage. The cart and the horse were not left thus detached, nor was the cart put before the horse. The leading point was always duly prominent, the subordinate kept subordinate; and the whole was made so beautifully clear and simple, that one was tempted to think that to do the like would not be difficult, but, on making the attempt, it would soon be discovered that without that clearness of head, that facility of expression, and that rich indwelling of the Word of Christ, which he possessed, it could not be accomplished.

'He was, too, the most unselfish man I ever met with. Those who would be followers of the Lord Jesus have to deny self; but it seemed to me that in him there remained no self to deny. The things that are Jesus Christ's, the things of others, were ever first with him. His own things, his own ease, comfort, interest, credit, never seemed for a moment to be thought of. All the various branches of Christian love, as set forth in 1 Corinthians xiii., seemed in a surpassing degree embodied in him.

'I recollect, in illustration of his benevolence, the following trifling but characteristic little incident. On one occasion, when ill and confined to his bed, a troublesome fly kept buzzing about his face; and though again and again driven away, it kept perpetually returning. It was at length proposed to kill it. This he would not hear of, but directed that a saucer of sugar and water should be placed for it. Thus he not merely prevented the destruction, but provided for the enjoyment of the troublesome little enemy of his peace.

'The cheerful character of your dear father's piety, I used also greatly to admire. Delightful indeed was the atmosphere that pervaded the vicarage. The sky was ever serene, the sun ever shining; no clouds ever gathered there.

'The hospitality exercised was almost unlimited. The frequency with which, week by week, I used to partake of that hospitality, I feel almost ashamed to think upon, though really the fault was with your dear father rather than with me. When conscience made me decline what was so pleasant to me—"Oh, I want to speak to you after dinner about parish matters," or some such reason, would be found to overcome my scruples. Not only was he ever doing kindnesses, but the kind way in which he did them surpassed anything I ever saw.

'A like sweet spirit was widely diffused among his people. Indeed, wherever he was, a heavenly atmosphere seemed to be generated. When, some years after, I was presented to the rectory of St. John's, Islington, he used to spend a week or so with us every year; and by all of us, parents, children, and servants, the visit was ever hailed with the greatest delight. He helped us to understand what it was to entertain an angel.'

When my father was obliged to leave home for change of air, he seldom allowed himself to rest. Like his Divine Master, in his measure, his meat, when weary, was to do the will of God, and to finish the work appointed for him. Devoted as he was to his parish, and the town in which he lived, his love was not confined within geographical limits, but overflowing all such conventional boundaries, it led him to seek, wherever his steps were guided, opportunities to preach the Gospel to every creature.

He travelled in many parts of England, Scotland, and Ireland to make known the objects of the Bible and Church Missionary Societies, but chiefly in the cause of the London Society for promoting Christianity amongst the Jews. His frequent companions were the Rev. Lewis

Way of Stanstead Park, Middlesex, and the Rev. Charles Simeon of King's College, Cambridge. The expenses of these journeys were defrayed by the three friends themselves.

In letters from my mother we read of his preaching in churches, and giving addresses to large meetings, and to assemblies in private houses, twenty-eight times in one week, and again of his preaching fifty times in forty-seven days, and other accounts of a similar nature.

In one of those journeys he visited Dublin in company with Mr. Simeon in the year 1822, and spoke in the Rotunda in behalf of the Church Missionary Society in support of a resolution proposed by the Earl of Roden. The Archbishop of Armagh was in the chair. Lord Roden's resolution urged upon his young countrymen, and especially upon graduates of the University of Dublin, to offer themselves as missionaries. My father, after describing the mental and moral qualifications which were requisite, added, 'they must be men of God, epistles of Christ, filled with the Holy Ghost, full of faith, heavenly wisdom, and well-tempered zeal, men who will go forth in a simple dependence upon the grace and providence of God, and by daily fervent prayer, seek the blessing from Him alone. Then the systems of Bramah and of Buddha will vanish before the luminous and illuminating truths of our holy Religion. Then shall Christianity accomplish that in the moral world which the fabled Buddha is said, when first he was born, to have produced in the natural world, wherever he placed his foot, a rose-tree sprang up in full leaf and flower. Of this we are certain, wherever the

Gospel is sent, accompanied by a blessing from above, "instead of the thorn will come up the fir-tree, and instead of the briar shall come up the myrtle-tree. The wilderness and the solitary place shall be glad, and the desert shall rejoice and blossom as the rose." In addressing the missionary students, I would remind them of a shrewd observation I lately met with in reading a history of Ceylon. The Cingalese say, "Three things prove a man to be a fool: If he attempt to execute without means, if he wrestle without strength, and if he dispute without knowledge." Now, my Lord, our Society will endeavour to furnish them with as suitable means as it can. Let them never go forth to the contest without prayer for strength from above, and let them study the languages and prejudices of the people, and especially be daily and diligent students of the Bible,—a book that is suited to all lands, and speaks to every heart. In alluding to the want of more labourers, perhaps I may be allowed to speak of home. I have an only son. What his father might say, if the hour came, I cannot answer, but that son has a mother who says, dearly as she loves her boy, she would cheerfully yield him, if called by the providence of God, and prepared by the Spirit of God, for the work of missions to the heathen or the Jew. Parents under such circumstances may be permitted to feel much, yet God forbid that the patriotic zeal of Grecian and Roman matrons should excel that of Christian matrons now; the one was for the welfare of their country, the other is for the welfare of immortal souls.'

It was in reference to these separations that my mother used to say, 'His Master's work leaves him less of his time to give me upon earth, but I shall enjoy him the more when we reach our home.' Yet was her society ever his sweetest earthly joy, and no father could have taken more tender delight in his children; whilst to them his presence and that of their mother was a pleasure which they never willingly exchanged for any other. It was dull work to be sent away from it, even to the merriest of childish playfellows.

Some letters written about this time to his daughter Louisa, who was at school, show his tender anxiety about his child, and his sympathy with her feelings and interests:—

'LONDON, *May* 18, 1826.

'DEAREST LOU,—Though I cannot be with you on your birthday, I can write a line to you. God bless you, dear Lou, with health and peace, and, above all, with that portion which I read this morning in Psalm xci.: "Because he hath set his love upon me, therefore will I deliver him: I will set him on high, because he hath known my name. With long life will I satisfy him, and show him my salvation." These are promises which belong, indeed, in their primary application, to our Lord as the Messiah, but in their secondary and spiritual application they belong to all who believe in Him for salvation. This is the portion I should choose for you and your dear sisters and brother, above everything the world could give; and for a plain reason,—the world corrupts its favourites, and leaves them when they most need comfort, and passes away; but these blessings are substantial, and in their tendency, effects, and duration *eternal*.

'I am going this evening to the Lord Mayor's, for a meeting at the Mansion-House for the Jews' Society. He remembers attending my ministry with pleasure, and I hope with profit, many years ago. Expect me, therefore, when you see me again, to be a large fat man, from turtle-soup and such fattening things as Mansion-Houses give. I certainly may need something to fatten me, having preached fifty times in less than fifty days, and yet I am rather better than usual.

'Give my kind regards to Miss Burman. I hope it is all peace in the eastern Burman empire now as well as in the Ipswich.

'I am looking forward to the holidays, as perhaps you are.—Ever your affectionate father, W. M.'

'*Nov.* 25, 1826.

'DEAREST LOU,—Some folks say "you must take the will for the deed." If *you* do, you have what is equal to a large bundle of letters from me. But now I sit down to write *indeed*. What a comfort it is to know that our Great Master does really in very many things take the will for the deed (2 Cor. viii. 12). If there be a willing mind, it is pleasing to Him. Let us therefore pray that, by His grace preventing us, we may have a good will, and that it may work with us when we have that good will. (10th Article of the Church of England.)

'We shall have many curious things to relate concerning the Jewish missionary Wolff when you come home. He arrived here in the middle of the night. They will make Christmas tales sweeter than Christmas cakes. I am glad Christmas is coming. But the work of school makes the holidays the more delightful; and absence makes presence even more sweet, and it is the same in higher things. Services and sufferings here will make rest and pleasure more delightful hereafter. God grant, dear Louey, that you and your sisters and brother may all serve the Lord and enjoy that final rest.—Your most affectionate father, W. M.'

'The Catechisms I purpose sending you in a parcel on Monday. I have promised the Jews a week's journey now, as well as a month in August, as they need pleaders, and the time to favour Zion is come. Jerusalem must rise, and Rome must fall, however violent her last struggle may be. And happy are they who are delivered from the latter and care for the former (Rev. xviii. 4; Isa. lxvi. 10). The history of the Jews, and of the Church of Rome, or apostate Christendom, are irrefragable proofs of the truth of Scripture. None but God could thus have declared the end from the beginning.

'May we be found among those in whom all His gracious promises will be fulfilled. Then shall we explore His works, adore His attributes, be employed in His service, and be filled with His love, during an unspeakably happy eternity.

'My kindest regards to all at Ewell.—Your most affectionate father, W. M.'

'1828.

'My dearest Lou,—Your absence from home will but

render home more sweet on your return. We are affected by contrasts, and it is necessary also that we should experience changes. We are in a world of trial, and our nature is fallen. If everything went smoothly, we should be in greater danger. I hope you will derive much profit from being at school. Pay attention to all the rules. Apply to your lessons. Do nothing contrary to conscience. And if you should see anything very thoughtless, or contrary to religion, in any school-fellow, say within yourself, I have been taught better, and take heed that you are not drawn aside by it. Satan is a bad master. He deceives, and tempts, and accuses, and leaves persons to suffer for their folly. The wages of sin is death. But by attending to God's Word and our duty we may be happy: yea, we may be cheerful and have our recreations. You know I like to see young people happy, but nothing that is wrong in itself can produce true happiness.

'Pray to God daily to give you His Holy Spirit.—Ever thy most affectionate father, W. M.'

'I am glad you have spoken your mind freely. In our family, where love is the rule and motive, I trust, there should never be any concealment in any matter.

'Dearest Lou, pray daily to God to graft in your heart the love of His name, to increase in you true religion, and of His great mercy to keep you in the same. The only pang I have respecting any of you is lest you should fall short of the kingdom of God. I know the world, its emptiness, its folly, its vanity, its deceitfulness, its absolute moral madness with respect to spiritual things; and

I pray God you may all discover it, and pass through it as the disciples—the happy disciples of Christ.'

Mr. Marsh's mother had followed him to Colchester, and lived in the next house to the vicarage. It was no common affection which bound them together; and this power of being able to minister daily to her happiness during the last ten years of her life was deeply prized by her son, and scarcely less by his wife, of whom Lady Marsh said, 'Had she been my own child, I could not have received more devoted love or more constant attention than I have always experienced from my beloved daughter-in-law.'

The following letters show the close bond of union between this beloved mother and her son:—

'Devizes, *June 11th*, 1823.

'My dearest dear Mother,—I am now actually on my way home, though I shall not reach it before Saturday night. Whether Matilda has received a letter from me as well as Mary, I cannot tell, but I have received another from each, and very welcome they were. I must now tell you about two ladies with whom I have lately travelled. The first, a Roman Catholic, who tried hard to make me one, and I tried softly to make her a Protestant. After a drive of forty miles, I walked with her another mile to see her safe to her friend's house in Sion Place, and we had scarcely finished our discourse by the time she arrived there.

'To-day I have had for my fellow-traveller a celebrated actress and singer. Poor thing! I pitied her much; her employers are killing her by excess of fatigue. The world is a hard master. She received my tracts thankfully, and said she would attend to any book or advice I would forward her at any time. Who can tell whether she may not become a true Christian?

'Some friends have suggested that I should charge the expenses of these journeys to the Societies. But I would rather leave the account with their PATRON. I am quite satisfied with the confidence that He does repay.

'Last night I slept in your favourite city, Bath. It is three times as large as when you knew it, and as gay as ever. But your favourite city, *now*, is a much gayer one. There are continual rejoicings in it, and one great advantage of its atmosphere is that weariness is unknown. Oh, what a hope is that of the Christian! It leaves all care, and sin and sorrow behind, and fixes our affections on things which never weary and never cloy. You are now travelling the last stage, perhaps the last mile; I would stop your carriage a little if I could; if I cannot, I must in desire and expectation hasten after you. It is a sweet thought that soon they that sleep in Jesus will be re-united, and be for ever in each other's society, as well as with the Lord. This last constitutes their heaven, but the former is a pleasant ingredient in their cup of bliss.

'I have been remarkably well on this journey, and success has attended it. Yet I really object more and more to leaving home. It is a conviction of duty that compels me, and I generally find what appears to me to be a proof of our great Master's approbation, in it. You may send in as much love as you can to the vicarage, and there is some Christian affection also to spare for the friends under the roof with you, and all others. Remember me to Keeling.—Ever thine own son in duty and affection,

'W. M.'

Lady Marsh died on Friday the 17th of September 1824, in the eightieth year of her age. Up to the time of her last illness, her brightness and cheerfulness continued to make her society as charming as her deep and fervent piety made it profitable. Within a few days of her death, Mr. Marsh drew the following brief sketch of her character:—

'Possessing an uncommon share of natural wit and vivacity, and with a mind improved by an extensive reading of the best English authors, my mother's conversational powers were such as will not easily be forgotten by those who had the happiness of her acquaintance; her wit being as devoid of satire as her heart was of pride and selfishness. She was beloved by the young for her cheerfulness and pleasantry, and revered by the more advanced in life for her piety and resignation.

'From circumstances over which she could have no possible control, she was at a late period of life involved in great difficulties and misfortunes; but as in prosperity she had exhibited a rare example of urbanity and kindness to all classes, so in adversity she displayed that contented acquiescence in the dispensations of Providence, which proceeded not from the cold indifference of the Stoic, but from the pious resignation of the Christian. For firmly she believed with the Apostle, that "our light affliction, which is but for a moment, worketh for us a far more exceeding and eternal weight of glory;" whilst her sole reliance for eternal salvation was on the merits and atonement of her Redeemer.'

The following letter to Dr. Hooper of Reading shows how deeply her loss was deplored by her son:—

'MY BELOVED FRIEND,—My dearest mother has been declining for some months—more so for some weeks. On Friday last we thought her very ill; on Sunday she revived and expressed a desire for some animal food. We thought it a good symptom, but it was the reverse. On Wednesday she became sensibly worse, and this morning her happy spirit took its flight, through the mercy of God in Christ, to the realms of peace. I have written a line to French, as one of her oldest acquaintance, but my spirits are too far gone to-day to write to any more.

'I have been with her for forty-nine years. I cannot consider that we have ever been parted. The last ten years (when in Colchester) I spent two hours and had a cup of tea with her every afternoon.

'She has manifested a great and Christian mind under many severe trials, and in this last one, patience seemed to have its perfect work. She trusted in her Saviour, and none can do this in vain. I wrote to my dear brother on Friday (having no idea of danger before), and again on Monday, to say that she was rather better, and on Wednesday to say how dangerously ill she was then. I have directed these letters to Hatherdon, and hope to see him to-morrow. But perhaps he is at Reading; if he be, have the great kindness to call directly and break it to him. He loved her dearly. My dear friend, pray for me, for I am wounded to the heart, and acknowledge it ought not to be so. I should think more of her gain than my loss. She died in perfect peace.—Your ever obliged and affectionate

'WM. MARSH.'

For a year after his mother's death he never awoke in the morning without tears, as the remembrance that she was gone broke upon him. He resolved to preach her funeral sermon himself, and when a brother clergyman suggested that the effort would be too great for him, he simply said, 'My Saviour may glorify Himself by it, and win some fresh jewel for His crown.' He gave his testimony to the grace of God in her, nor did his voice falter until he came to the close, when, describing the joys of heaven, he said, 'There the mother shall regain the long lost child, and the child his long lost mother.'

On the same day he and my mother received a summons apparently to the deathbed of their only son, who was seized with inflammation of the lungs, but, by God's blessing, he was restored; and thus the rough wind was stayed in the day of the east wind.

Well remembered still is the rejoicing when the only brother, then a child of nine years old, was brought home recovering.

The following letter, written a little later, to Miss Dornford of Brighton, shows the interest which my father was already taking in the study of unfulfilled prophecy :—

'COLCHESTER.

'MY DEAR FRIEND,—I like your plan much. It is a search after truth in its own field. As the Divine plan is to begin with the seed and carry it on to perfection, according to the nature of the plant, whether it be a diminutive flower or the oak of the forest, so, I conceive, man, redeemed man, will be carried on to perfection, according to his nature and capacity. But who shall set bounds to a rational nature made partaker of a divine, and a nature assumed by the Deity in the person of our blessed Lord? His people are called to the obtaining of His glory. I therefore believe that the Church will ascend to still higher degrees of knowledge and glory at the end of the millennium. But I have some doubts whether the parables extend to that period; yet I have no very strong objection to your application of Matt. xiii. 43. '*Upon,*' in John i. 51, refers, I conceive, to the image of the ladder. But the truth contained in it is simply this, that our Lord is the medium of union and communion between the heavens and the earth.

'I rejoice in the stir among the Jews in London. It is among the many and great signs of the times.

'If all the living saints are caught up, according to your last question, the converted nations will worship the King, the Lord of Hosts, especially Egypt and Syria (Isa. xix. 23-25).

'Many useful, happy returns of the year to you. As Mr. Drummond of Albury writes to me, "If you live as long as I wish you to live, you will be *changed,* but will never see corruption," so say I to you. May the hope become so lively in the Church of Christ as to set her more and more at liberty from the trammels of time and sense, from the chains of sin and unbelief.

'May the Saviour, atoning, interceding, returning, be your constant peace and hope.

'Kind regards to your sister.—Yours very truly,

'WM. MARSH.'

The warm interest which he felt in the Jewish nation, 'beloved for the fathers' sakes,' secured to him personal regard from numerous Jews, both English and foreign, whilst his evident sympathy made many of them not only willing to listen to his explanation of Christianity, but confide to him their doubts and difficulties.

At this time he became acquainted with two intelligent young Jews, first cousins to each other, who were then residing in Colchester. Both held sceptical views. Relying upon the power of that Word, the entrance of which giveth light, he induced them to begin reading the Old Testament Scriptures with him, and led them to seek proof of its authenticity as their minds became interested in its statements. Every day he prayed for them, until they became willing that he should pray *with* them. Gradually they were led on from the darkness of infidelity, through the twilight of inquiry, until the Sun of Righteousness arose upon their souls with healing in His wings. The genuineness of the Old Testament having been satisfactorily proved to them, their desire was raised to study the New. Type and antitype, shadow and substance, prophecy and its fulfilment, read, commented upon, and prayed over, by the power of the Holy Ghost took the veil away from their hearts, fold after fold, until 'the light of the glorious gospel of God in the face of Jesus Christ' shone into their souls, and showed itself in their lives. When once He was seen and loved as their own Saviour, they were resolved to confess Him before men, and at all costs to receive Christian baptism. This was administered to them by my father in St. Peter's Church. They were subjected from this time to considerable persecution from their own family. When one of them returned to his home, in a town at some distance from Colchester, a servant dressed in deep mourning opened the door. With a trembling heart, he asked which member of the family had died. It was scarcely a relief from suspense to learn that mourning was worn throughout the house for him, because he was considered as dead, and his existence was to be forgotten.

A benevolent physician in the town heard the story, and finding the poor young Jew ill of low fever in a small lodging, 'he had compassion upon him' and brought him to his own house, 'and took care of him.' The young convert sought to repay the generous kindness of his host and hostess by the only means in his power. He proposed that they should daily read the Scriptures together, with prayer,—thus endeavouring to reveal to them, by the teaching of the Holy Spirit, the unsearchable riches of Christ. Nor were his prayers fruitless. One after another, the younger members of the family received into their hearts the gospel of the grace of God.

A few months later, two of the number, a son and

a daughter, were called away to their heavenly home. They died witnessing to the living power of a Saviour to comfort and sustain them in their last hours; and bearing testimony also that the guide who had led them to His feet was this Christian Jew.

Not long afterwards a mutual attachment was formed between him and one of the daughters of this physician, which was heartily sanctioned by both her parents. But a cloud soon arose over this prospect of earthly happiness. Dr. W. became seriously ill for many months; and the circumstances of the family were so altered by this calamity, that his young daughter felt it to be her duty to seek a situation as governess.

My father and mother invited her to come to St. Peter's vicarage on her way through Colchester; and during her visit my mother often prayed with her, and gave her tender and wise advice with reference to the trials and difficulties of her new path. Miss W. went on her way, strengthened and comforted; but returned to the vicarage, only a few weeks afterwards, dangerously ill. Her parents and sisters were sent for, and remained in that home of hospitality and kindness until after the death and burial of their beloved one. With her, all was well. Her peace flowed like a river. Yet the sympathy of her friends at the vicarage provided one other source of consolation for her last days on earth—the society of that friend who had led her to the Saviour, and whose wife she would have become, had her life been continued.

Still can my sisters and I recall the beautiful face of the sufferer, as she lay in perfect calm upon her deathbed, surrounded by her family and our own; while by her side knelt the Jew, repeating, in her dying ear, 'O Death, where is thy sting? O Grave, where is thy victory? The sting of death is sin; and the strength of sin is the law. But THANKS BE TO GOD, WHICH GIVETH US THE VICTORY THROUGH OUR LORD JESUS CHRIST!'

Soon after her funeral, Mr. —— commenced his academical career at Cambridge, where my father's aid enabled him to carry on his studies. This he did with considerable success, winning, amongst other honours, the Hulsean Prize. He was afterwards ordained by the Archbishop of Dublin; and a bright career of usefulness seemed opening before him; when it was suddenly brought to an end by an illness affecting his mental powers, from which he never recovered. The other cousin is still living, and labouring as a clergyman of the Church of England.

The following extracts are from letters addressed to the two young Jewish friends above alluded to:—

'... As to the subjects to which you refer, I also rejoice that you are not *ultra*. One of Satan's methods of counteracting truth is by leading its friends to be partial in their statements, to carry them beyond scriptural bounds, and to give to some parts an undue preponderance.

'From a careful and repeated perusal of the Scriptures, I have long made up my own mind to the following conclusions:—

'That salvation is of grace, through Christ, by faith "which worketh by love" and manifests itself in obedience.

'That there is an election of nations to privileges, of persons to offices, and of individuals to special grace; but that the Gospel is free to *all*, is to be preached to *all*, and *all* are to be invited and exhorted' (Prov. i. 20-23; Matt. xxii. 3, 4).

'That God is a *merciful* SOVEREIGN and a *righteous* JUDGE; and that every act of sovereignty is an act of mercy, and every act of punishment an act of justice; and that, in the final states of men, there will be "a revelation of the righteous judgment of God;" and that every man will be "rewarded according to his works."

'That all men are to be treated by the ministers of the Gospel as rational and responsible beings, and, as far as their preaching can go, to be made to feel that they are such, and consequently, that there is no excuse for self-righteousness, or profaneness, or sloth, or lukewarmness, or neglect of so great salvation.

'And finally, that the grand design of the Gospel is to bring men into a state of peace with God through Jesus Christ, and thereby to lead them to love God and one another. It is a glorious display of the Divine character as light and love, and of the Divine government as just and good (2 Cor. iv. 6; iii. 18). Jehovah is not served because He is not loved, and not loved because He is not known (Ps. ix. 9, 10). Oh happy time, when the knowledge of the Lord shall cover the earth as the waters cover the sea, and Isaiah xi. shall be fulfilled! I merely add, that the peculiarity of the Gospel is, that it exhibits everything in the Person and Work of Christ. There the Divine perfections and government are displayed. There is the hope, and the strength, and the motive, and the model of man. A Christian is a man in whom Christ is formed the 'hope of glory;' who relies on Christ for strength; who is constrained by the principles of love and gratitude; who desires to be conformed to his Saviour's image! to whom, in short, Christ is made "wisdom, and righteousness, and sanctification, and redemption." Such Christians may we and our families and our congregations be, and leave controversialists and disputants to find a better way, if they can. . . . I shall always feel interested in your Christian walk and warfare, and hope to rejoice with you in the final victory. . . . .

'I have found salvation in Christ from the false hopes and delusive vanities of this world, for myself; therefore, if I have done you any good, you and I also are wholly indebted to Him. May we abide in Him, and then we shall not be ashamed before Him at His coming (1 John ii. 28).

'I do not wonder that you have met with stumblingblocks. I have long learned, thank God, to look for Christianity in the *Scriptures*, and there I find it in such a form as commends itself to my conscience and heart, as a Divine system suited exactly to the state and wants of man. As to imperfection in Christians, I am learning to make allowances for different habits and constitutions, and the different light in which two men will see the same object. At the same time, I am aware that Christianity itself does not allow me to offer any excuse for indulged and habitual evil. If Christ dwell in the heart by faith, His precepts must be manifested in the life, or our faith is fancy, and our hope delusion. May we grow in grace, and in the knowledge of Him, and may all His followers more and more walk even as He walked. This is the strongest recommendation of their principle.

'In all cases, means, and the diligent and persevering use of them, are ours. So the Lord has ordained. But in the use of the most Christian means we can employ, we must simply rely on Him,—He only has the key of the heart. He "openeth, and no man shutteth." But He never has yet, for 5826 years, suffered His servants to labour in vain.

'I hope churchmen and dissenters are now reading the Scriptures with reference to the people of Israel. Surely they should unite in prayer and exertion for their benefit. Do they profess to be "the Lord's remembrancers?" Then let them "give Him no rest till He establish, and till He make Jerusalem a praise in the earth" (Isa. lxii. 7). They ought also, on the general principle of Christian benevolence and zeal, to labour and pray for individuals who are dying in unbelief, and cannot partake of the privileges which await the nation.

'I sometimes fear the enemies of the Christian Church (Romanism and Infidelity) must be permitted to prevail for a season, to teach that Church the lesson of brotherly love and simplicity. By-and-by, though not *now*, our Lord's kingdom will be of this world, because "the kingdoms of this world will be His." They are His by redemption, and will be His by possession. When Rome sinks, and Jerusalem rises, "All the ends of the earth shall see the salvation of our God." (Ps. xcviii.)

'I was glad to see your handwriting and to hear of you

proceedings. "As I was with Moses, so will I be with thee; I will not leave thee, nor forsake thee," is a promise not worn out, however ancient. St. Paul thought it as fresh in his day as it was in the days of Joshua. "He hath said, I will never leave thee, nor forsake thee" (Heb. xiii. 5). How great is our privilege in believing a word which endureth for ever! May that word *dwell* in you *richly* in all wisdom, and be the joy and rejoicing of your heart. To communicate it to others is our great honour. May you be very successful in this also.

'The approbation of man, of every good man, is indeed desirable. But the Christian must learn to say, "With me it is a very small thing that I should be judged of you, or of man's judgment; yea, I judge not mine own self. For I know nothing by myself; yet am I not hereby justified; but He that judgeth me is the Lord" (1 Cor. iv. 3, 4). Let him walk with God, and study to show himself approved unto God, and all must be well. Matters are generally cleared up in time; but they shall be more than cleared up in the kingdom of our Lord, "Therefore judge nothing before the time, until the Lord come, who both will bring to light the hidden things of darkness, and will make manifest the counsels of the hearts, and then shall every man have praise of God" (1 Cor. iv. 5).

'Though I love all who love our Lord, and admire those who are seeking the greatest conformity to Him, I am increasingly convinced that there is nothing superior to the steady, zealous, loving, and fruitful Christianity to be found among the true servants of Christ in the Church of England; and no means of usefulness more enlarged than theirs. Unnecessary divisions must be evils. But no one can control conscience, and I do not expect union till John xvii. be answered, and Isa. xi. be fulfilled.

'I rejoice that your experience of the truth and excellency and suitableness of the salvation which is in Christ grows. However tried inwardly and outwardly, the more you know of the Redeemer, the more you will perceive reason to trust in Him, and to be stedfast and unmoveable, and always to abound in His work so far as strength and opportunity may be afforded. . . . We must not forget the Divine name, Jehovah-Jireh: "in the mount" (perhaps after ascending high, and with difficulty) "it shall be seen."'

The anniversaries of his favourite Societies were made great occasions at the vicarage, where the deputations were always welcomed with more than friendly hospitality. Hugh M'Neile of Liverpool (then rector of Albury), Legh Richmond, Edward Irving, Edward Bickersteth, Haldane Stewart, Basil Woodd, Lewis Way, Simons of Paul's Cray, Hawtrey, Simeon of Cambridge, Archdeacon Hodson, Hughes of the Bible Society, Gerard and Baptist Noel, with others whose names are still revered in the Church of God, were amongst the loved and honoured guests.

At the anniversary of each Society, three sermons were preached on behalf of the cause, on the Sunday, in St. Peter's, and collections were made after each. On Monday evening a meeting was held in a large room in the town, for the schools, and for those who were prevented by business or work from attending in the day-time.

Well remembered still at Colchester are the demonstrations of delight from a large foundation-school of boys when my father appeared on the platform on these occasions. The morning song of joy and praise which his spirit sang throughout life was in tune with the spirits of the young; and, indeed, he seemed to be the life and soul of the whole anniversary festival. His remarkable gift in speaking was perhaps more evident on the platform than in the pulpit, where his manner was more chastened, and where he would not allow so free a scope for his varied powers.

As many of the clergy and laity who were interested in these societies came in from the country to attend the afternoon meetings on the second day, and to remain for the service in the church, a dinner was provided by my parents in the infant school-room, which was close to the vicarage garden. At these dinners about sixty or seventy persons were usually present; and grace was sung before it, and at its close.

These 'high days' were concluded by an evening service and sermon in St. Peter's, after which the last collection was made; and when the sum-total which had been given to the good cause throughout these days had been named in the vestry, my father, and those assembled with him there, sang, with one heart and voice—

'Praise God, from whom all blessings flow,' etc.

And the anniversary was ended.

On the first occasion of my father's pleading for the Church Missionary Society from his pulpit in St. Peter's the sum of £670 was found in the plate. Sir William Pulteney and Lady Bath had been so much interested by the statements in the sermon, that they sent for pen and paper from the vestry, and drew cheques for £600.

But it was not only in public that my father testified his interest and delight in the great objects of these now time-honoured societies. The days on which the anniversary meetings were held were in a manner consecrated to the occasion. The choice of chapters in the Bible at family worship, his prayers, his conversation, enriched with anecdote, all bore upon the subject. His children learned to look forward with delight to such seasons as to a festival; and my mother's bright and earnest spirit was in tune with his on these, as on all other, occasions. She saved him from having any thought or trouble in making the necessary arrangements, and took her own part in the duties and privileges of each day with her usual courtesy of manner and thoughtful kindness for all.

When my father first went to Colchester, it was a garrison town, and a large number of military officers were quartered there. It was amongst these that the first-fruits of that spiritual harvest, afterwards extending through the town and neighbourhood, sprang up. The colonel of the regiment, and his wife and eldest daughter were, by the blessing of God upon my father's ministry, brought to the knowledge and love of the Saviour. The wife of one of the majors in the regiment was led through deep waters of domestic sorrow into peace and joy in the Lord. Several of the subalterns were invited to meet my father at the house of the commanding officer; and, charmed by his countenance and manner almost as much as impressed by his words, they were led to attend his church, where, in the faithful preaching of Christ crucified, they found life for their souls. Their Christian conduct afterwards, bore evidence of a change of heart.

It was soon known that my father wished only to visit as an ambassador for Christ, and many became anxious to secure him at their homes for an evening of reading the Scriptures and prayer. Not a few have dated their conversion to God from those evenings, while others have felt that they were thus built up on their most holy faith.

It cannot be supposed that such a work of grace could proceed without exciting much opposition. Bitter hostility sprang up. Satirical verses on these engagements appeared in one of the county newspapers; and many absurd stories were invented to bring the movement into contempt.

A clergyman in London, whose family at that time resided in Colchester, published a pamphlet containing various false statements about my father, of which he took no notice.

Shortly afterwards, on some public occasion, the benefactors of the county hospital were required to walk together in a procession. My father was one of them, and the clergyman who was appointed to walk with him was the one who had attacked him. My father had heard his name, but the other did not know that his companion was the man whom he had been persuaded to calumniate. He became so charmed with him in the course of their walk, that at the end of it he said to a friend who resided in the town, 'Tell me, who was my delightful companion? He seems to me the *beau-idéal* of a Christian and a gentleman.' 'He is the man about whom you have written in no measured terms,' was the reply. The clergyman was hurrying away, when my father hastened after him, took his hand, and expressed his cordial good wishes for him. The other was deeply touched, and at once went to his publisher to buy up the remaining copies of his pamphlet, that he might commit them to the flames.

Thus, in the spirit of the proverb, 'A soft answer turneth away wrath,' my father changed, by the help of God, enemies into friends; and gave the silver lining to the cloud.

But it was not only in things spiritual, but in things temporal, that he endeavoured to promote the welfare of the town.

Self-interest appeared to have no place in his heart; so that the Divine rule, 'Look not every man on his own things, but every man also on the things of others,' was carried out by him to a rare extent. On one occasion, during a commercial crisis in the country, a panic occurred on a market-day in Colchester, which seemed likely to prove ruinous to a highly respectable banking-house in the town. The farmers, and many other depositors, who had assembled for the market, rushed to draw out their money, and the run on the bank was great.

At this juncture, one of the clerks ran across to the vicarage to confide the alarm to one who, by his readiness to sacrifice himself to the temporal as well as spiritual interests of his fellow-townsmen, had already earned the title of 'the friend of Colchester.' It so happened that a large sum of money, subscribed for a charity, was in the house. My father was silent for a moment, and then drew a cheque for the amount on his London banker, and sent it at once to one of the churchwardens, thus rendering the cash his own. Without another moment's delay, putting the gold into one bag, and the silver into another, he walked across the crowded street to the bank, holding up the bags for the people to see, and saying, 'My friends, here I am! going to put my money into the bank!' They exclaimed, in much excitement, 'Oh, sir, don't put it there! The bank is just breaking.'

'I am not at all afraid,' was the cheerful reply. 'I shall find it all right when I want it;' and so he carried his money into the bank.

The crowd fell back from the doorway. Courage and kindness had done their work. Only a few men who had deposits there slowly stole in and demanded payment.

'Here is your money,' said my father, as he stood by the counter, handing the gold from his bag.

'No; not that, sir. That's yours, sir.'

'Yes; but you may have it. I shall be repaid in good time.'

Touched, and taking heart, one by one, they went away. Mr. Marsh remained until the closing hour. Confidence was restored, and the bank was saved.

Towards the beginning of the year 1829, my father's incessant labours in Colchester had begun to affect his health. They had extended, in one form or another, throughout the town and into various parts of the county; and the continual calls made upon him for counsel or comfort, added to his regular parish work, deprived him of all leisure and quiet. His medical adviser, who was a personal friend, was constrained, however unwillingly, to urge a pastor so beloved to exchange that post of duty for one less laborious.

After this had been represented to him as apparently a condition of prolonged life, my father still paused for Divine direction. For six months, from the first warning of approaching illness, he and my mother waited upon their God together for His guidance. At the end of that time, a threatening of disease in his chest and heart was observed; and, at the same time, the English Church in Guernsey having been offered to him, he consented to make a trial of it for three months.

The beauty of the island charmed his taste, and the warmth of Christian kindness with which he and his family were welcomed gratified his heart. He called it 'the land of friendship, fruits, and flowers.' During his short residence there, much blessing rested upon his ministry, and upon private intercourse with members of his congregation, especially amongst the young people, to whom he was always peculiarly attractive. In after years, several of them wrote to express their thankfulness for the benefit they had received.

In a letter of very recent date, a lady writing on business connected with a charity, thus expresses herself:— 'Mrs. G——, as well as myself, had the privilege of being under your revered father's pastoral care during his stay in our little island. Often have we listened with delight, and I trust with edification, to the words of Life, as they fell from his lips. His heavenly countenance, also, can never be forgotten by us. We had also the pleasure of the acquaintance of your sweet and blessed mother, and your three elder sisters. Those happy days, thirty-seven years ago, are still fresh in my memory. You will excuse my writing thus familiarly to one personally unknown; but my heart warms when I recall the fervent and earnest manner in which the love of God in Christ Jesus was set before us by him "whose praise was in all the churches."'

After fulfilling the duty for three months, he became convinced that the climate would not suit my mother. About this time he was pressed by his friend Sir Thomas Baring to accept the living of Mitcheldevor, but he felt that, with his health renovated, he was called to make trial of another and larger sphere which had been proposed to him. It was a far more extensive field than his own parish in Colchester; but the claims of a new place, he knew, would be fewer, and the arrangement of his time and of his duties would be more under his own control.

Still the thought of severing ties so woven into their very being was deeply painful both to himself and my mother. The final decision was delayed for a time, and when at length it was taken and became known, the blow went to the heart of Colchester. The town mourned as one man; and letters of grief and love distressed and yet gratified the tender feelings of my father and mother.

It was thought better not to return to Colchester at that time, and indeed they both dreaded to encounter the pain of personal leave-taking. The strength and constancy of this grateful attachment of young and old was proved by the enthusiastic welcome given to him on his first return to the town, nearly twenty-three years afterwards.

A noble presentation of plate, with a still more substantial expression of respect, in the shape of £1000, was sent by these grateful and warm-hearted townspeople. Their object was to repay to him a portion of the capital which he had expended in charity there. But the greater part of it was quickly devoted by him to the service of his Lord. For this only, and to make others happy, was money of value to him. Often have we known him deny himself new clothing, or give away the last suit left in his wardrobe, which more than once happened to be the best, that 'he might give to him that had none.'

The self-denials of his daily life, from no motives of asceticism, but from simple love to God, and to his brother man, were the unconscious fruit of his steadfast abiding in Christ. He seemed moulded into the image of Him whom his soul loved, 'who pleased not himself,' and 'went about doing good.'

A letter from a member of his congregation at St. Peter's, Colchester, to one of his daughters, shows the grateful and reverent love in which he was held there :—

FROM MRS. MACINTOSH TO LOUISA MARSH.

'COLCHESTER, *September* 17, 1829.

'. . . It was an every-day satisfaction, that we were perhaps hardly sensible of, to know that the vicarage held you all, and that if you left, it was but for a few Sundays at the most, and then we should see you all again taking your accustomed places at church. And there, too, *he* stood, the light of whose countenance is never perhaps to beam on us again,—the blessed medium of our spiritual light, he who shed so clear and softened a radiance upon the word of truth, that the glorious Gospel itself seemed better tidings than when it came from any other lips. We can hardly yet realize the thought, that one who has been the means of remodelling the place, who has lived down opposition and prejudice, and so established himself in the hearts of all,—good, bad, and indifferent,—one whose influence is felt through the moral atmosphere of the town, is really gone from amongst us. It is a thought too painful to bear and dwell upon. . . . Mrs. Paske is returned; I sat with her this morning sorrowing over our loss. Where is it I can go that it is not a theme of deep regret? The church here has lost its brightest ornament; the dissenters lament it far more than if one of their own ministers had gone. The poor, and all those in every class who have found your dearest mother a constant and consoling friend, are deeply grieved indeed. And some in higher stations who were just daring to do right,—oh how will *they* miss the sanction of your father's character and example to bear them out in the face of the world!"

CHAPTER IV.

LETTERS.

'Those fallen leaves that keep their green—
The noble letters of the dead.'

TENNYSON.

LETTERS TO SIR THOMAS BARING, 1816-1827, DURING THE TIME OF DR. MARSH'S RESIDENCE AT COLCHESTER.

'COLCHESTER, *July* 4, 1816.

'MY DEAR SIR THOMAS,— . . . I am thankful that while you have been led to experience the liberty wherewith Christ makes us free, you have not been led to suppose there is greater liberty out of our Establishment than within its walls. When a member of the Church of England lives a life of faith in the Son of God, I conceive, both for personal religion and extensive usefulness, he has the advantage over others. Yet I rejoice that, to a dying world, Christ is preached by others, as our Church cannot supply the wants of the world. May your eye be single and your whole body full of light, to the end of your mortal career.'

'COLCHESTER, *July* 19, 1816.

'MY DEAR SIR THOMAS,—If it was my duty to beg, it must be also to return thanks. Most sincerely do I discharge it in the name of poor dear S.

'I would to God that every member of our Church were so convinced of sin as to make Christ his only refuge

—and so united to Christ as to bring forth fruit unto God. The personal union of the Divine and human nature in Immanuel—the perfection of His righteousness and atonement—the suitableness of His offices as Prophet, Priest, and King—and the blessing of His salvation, are the darling themes of revelation, and the support of our Church and of our souls. There is no mercy or grace or love from the eternal Father but in Him, and from that love in Christ Jesus nothing can separate the believer. There is no influence from the Holy Spirit but as derived from Him. "The Father loveth the Son, and giveth not the Spirit by measure unto Him." Having finished the work, which in the Divine counsel was given unto Him, "He ascended on high, and led captivity captive, and received gifts for men, even for the rebellious, that the Lord God might dwell among them." Never had any of Adam's race been saved if Christ had not died for the ungodly, and never had any been useful on earth, or qualified to enjoy heaven, had not His salvation made them "the temples of the Holy Ghost." Happy are they who thus know the grace of our Lord Jesus Christ—the love of God—and the fellowship of the Holy Ghost. May it be the portion of your family as well as of yourselves.

'I hope, with your permission, when I have an opportunity, to converse with you on these things. They warm and cheer the heart.

'It has occurred to me that among the various methods of doing extensive good, that of purchasing advowsons in populous and important stations stands very high. They are sometimes to be obtained for small sums. The most useful stations have frequently the poorest livings. The late Mr. Thornton perpetuated the gospel in this manner. Witness the good effect for fifty years in this town. Should I hear of anything of this kind peculiarly eligible and reasonable, perhaps you would allow me to mention it?

'The friends of evangelical religion, particularly the clergy themselves, still want some point of union. If 2000 of them could be associated, we all know that twenty shillings each would produce at any time £2000 for any special purpose. We are to be wise as serpents. The enemies will unite to injure, though they cannot ultimately succeed; the friends should unite to conquer, because God works by means. We see what God has wrought by the Bible Society; and the nation, without feeling it, is capable of ten times that exertion, yea, the evangelical members of the Church alone. May Zion prosper, is, I know, both your certain expectation and your prayer.—I am, my dear Sir Thomas (with best compliments to Lady Baring), your obliged and affectionate W. M.'

'Colchester, *20th January* 1817.

'My dear Sir Thomas,—Many thanks for your kind letter, and the very interesting little tract. It is an excellent answer to Mr. O'Callaghan's pamphlet, which proceeds on the principle that the poor are incompetent to understand the Scriptures, and will therefore abuse them. He forgets the doctrine of Divine teaching, and the declaration that the poor are "chosen," "rich in faith." This was indeed beautifully illustrated in "Churchman."

I shall thankfully accept more of these tracts for circulation.

'My letter reached Roe safely. His address is awakening. The manner of expressing ourselves is something like our countenances; scarcely two men would do it alike. I have also thought that some ministers are called to one part of the work of the Lord's vineyard, and others to another. Some to gather and awaken; others to confirm and establish. But *all* to preach Christ crucified. There is nothing but darkness, barrenness, and misery without the sun. Christ is the sun in the moral firmament, giving light, life, and fruitfulness. He is perpetually testified of in Scripture as our Righteousness—the Propitiation for our sins,—our Advocate,—our Example,—our Motive,—our Strength. The glory of God is seen in the face of Jesus Christ. And beholding that glory, the enemies of God become His friends, and believers are changed into the same image from glory to glory. The Spirit of the Lord thus blesses the preaching of Christ crucified to the increase of the Church, and to the peace and devotedness of such as have believed, through grace. Where Christ is not all in all, and where He is not exhibited in the glories of His Person, the riches of His grace, and the suitableness of His salvation; where He is not set forth in all the offices and characters He sustains for the present and eternal benefit of His people, there, I conceive, "the whole counsel of God" is not delivered. Wherever the Apostle went, "he testified both to the Jews, and also to the Greeks, repentance toward God and faith toward our Lord Jesus Christ,"—the former, because all have sinned; the latter, because none can save themselves, in whole or in part. In thus preaching, he kept back nothing that was profitable. When converted to the faith of Christ, he led them to a knowledge of their safety for eternity. The Father had loved them with an everlasting love. The Son had obeyed and suffered in their stead. The Spirit had drawn them to Christ. They walked with God, and were kept by His power through faith unto salvation.

'In instructing the people of God, however, he does not confine himself simply to privileges. He employs those privileges as motives to devotedness (Rom. xii. 1). He also particularizes duties, that they might adorn the doctrine of God our Saviour in all things. Man is so formed that he must have motives, and so fallen that he must have the most powerful motives, such as redeeming love contains, or all the rules will be fruitless. But in a state of grace he must have rules, as well as motives, or he will make many great mistakes. The religion of the Scriptures, therefore, is exactly suited to man. It is doctrinal, experimental, and practical. In the most systematic part of Scripture, I mean the Epistle to the Romans, this is evidently shown. How doctrinal the four first chapters. How experimental the 5th, 6th, 7th. What a union of both in the 8th. In the 9th and 10th the apostle shows the just judgment of God in rejecting the Jews, and His sovereign mercy in adopting the Gentiles. In the 11th, the final union of both in one Church, and from the 12th to the end, how practical! This is the whole counsel of God.

'If our brethren state matters thus, it is wicked and unchristian to represent them as having departed from the faith, or as partial in their statement. Perhaps they may have dropped expressions which have been misunderstood; or, in their zeal to establish some grand point, they may have quoted texts which were not designed for that purpose. At any rate, we all ought to be tender of each other's characters as ministers of Christ; and those who differ on some points which do not affect the foundation, should make allowances for those who cannot see with their eyes. May your Christian wish be fulfilled in us all, "See that ye fall not out by the way."

'Probably I might differ from some in my views of Heb. xii. 14. I am quite certain the Apostle is not speaking of that righteousness which alone justifies before God, but of that personal religion which true believers follow. He had been declaring that they were chastened of the Lord for their profit, that they might be partakers of His holiness, and he exhorts them to follow *peace* with all men, and *holiness;* and then contrasts this with immoral ties (16th verse). Yet some minds, from their zeal for that blessed truth, that we are made the righteousness of God in Christ, will have the meaning to be, that without the holiness of Christ imputed, no man shall see the Lord. It is a truth, but not the meaning of that text.

'I remember many years ago reading Crisp, and adopting all his expressions, but I found, the more I examined the Scriptures, they did not authorize me so to speak. The statement led to unscriptural inferences from scriptural premisses. St. Paul, under Divine inspiration, guarded against the abuse of blessed and consoling truths, and so must all ministers, or they are answerable for that abuse. I think the expression "God sees no sin in His people" requires explanation, especially when we are told that the thing which David did "displeased the Lord exceedingly;" and that the Corinthian believers were chastened of the Lord, that they might not be condemned with the world. God the *Judge* sees no sin in His people so as to condemn them. It is God that justifieth. Who is he that condemneth? Will Christ who died for them condemn them? But God our *Father* sees sin in His children, and makes them to feel that it is an evil and bitter thing.

'Though believers will never speak of holiness in themselves,—I mean the holiness which the Spirit of God imparts—(though St. Paul indeed could speak of "the testimony of our conscience" as to "simplicity and godly sincerity"),—yet ministers must speak as the Scriptures do, or they omit the gold, silver, and precious stones which are to be built on the foundation. But they who talk of human merit, strength, etc., are building only wood, hay, stubble.

'Do the offices which our Lord is generally considered as sustaining,—I mean particularly those of Prophet, Priest and King,—appear to be fanciful, or are they founded in truth? If in truth, He exercises them for the good of His people, and each office and its fruits should be distinctly set forth.

'I have written this in great haste, after preaching; as I am so occupied during the day, I do not know when I can sit down for ten minutes to write a letter.

'Probably much of the difference between many of the Evangelical clergy and our friends to whom you allude is in appearance only, or in misunderstanding each other, or in false reports. May the Spirit of truth and love be with us. Happy are they who can say with the Apostle (Gal. ii. 19, 20), "For I through the law am dead to the law, that I might live unto God. I am crucified with Christ: nevertheless I live; yet not I, but Christ liveth in me: and the life which I now live in the flesh, I live by the faith of the Son of God, who loved me, and gave himself for me." To this the Holy Spirit has brought you. Blessed be His name. May He bring all your family to the same blessedness.—Yours, ever affectionately,

'WILLIAM MARSH.'

'1821.

... '"THE secret of the Lord is with them that fear Him; and He will show them His covenant." It is ordered in all things and sure; and as it is all our salvation, so it may well be all our desire.

'I thank His name for the mercy and grace bestowed on you, and pray that He may preserve you from those ten thousand snares which the foe lays for believers as well as unbelievers. They are, indeed, of a different nature, but are sometimes more subtle for the former. He dare not appear to them but as an angel of light. He suggests some new discovery which neither prophets nor apostles made. He leads us to draw unscriptural inferences from scriptural premises. We become wise above what is written, or seek to know more than God has revealed. We are satisfied with a part instead of the whole, and desire and expect less than God has promised. Thus he keeps men in sin, or draws them from duty, or deprives them of peace, or impedes their usefulness. What necessity there is for that gracious advice, "Watch and pray!"

'I cannot but think this adversary has taken an advantage of some of our dear brethren. If certain expressions do not perpetually recur, they seem to think neither the service nor the sermon to be truly evangelical. Are not words signs of ideas? And what ideas are those petitions in the Litany—"By the mystery of thy holy incarnation," etc.—calculated to convey but those of acceptance in Christ alone? And is not this the tenor of the whole? The Scriptures themselves are sparing in certain expressions though not in ideas as to certain truths. I hear also that it is asserted that we are not only justified in Christ, but so sanctified in Him at once, that we are not to go on receiving out of His fulness. But I cannot believe this, while an apostle says, "If any man have not the Spirit of Christ, he is none of His:" that Christ "gave Himself for us, that He might redeem us from all iniquity, and purify unto Himself a peculiar people, zealous of good works;" and that believers have "put on the new man, which, after God, is *renewed* in righteousness and true holiness." But, I think, there must be some misunderstanding in reporters, or that some incautious, unscriptural expressions are used, which lead to false reports and a perversion of truth in the ungodly. If it be so, I am persuaded a little time will convince our brethren that they have erred. He who has been their teacher, who has convinced them of sin and led them to Jesus, Immanuel, God with us, will deliver them from expressions, as well as ideas, which the Scriptures do not authorize. *No one is wise at once.* Even Divine teaching, as to many points, or the right use of them, seems to be gradual. It appears to be a part of the Divine plan that everything which has life should admit of growth. We see it in the vegetative, the animal, and the rational world. It is so in the spiritual. Even angels may make progress in knowledge, and in capacity for greater manifestations, though at every period their knowledge is without error and their nature without sin. Thus *we* may grow in grace, and in the knowledge of our Lord and Saviour Jesus Christ.

'There are two passages which convey to my mind the Gospel and its effects :—

'"God, who commanded the light to shine out of darkness, hath shined in our hearts, to give the light of the knowledge of the glory of God in the face of Jesus Christ." And "we all, *beholding* as in a glass the glory of the Lord, are changed into the same image, from glory to glory, even as by the Spirit of the Lord." The view which is given us of the Divine perfections in the person and work of our adorable Mediator lays an immovable foundation for our hopes.

"Till God in human flesh I see,
No comfort can I find."

This view supplies us with the highest motive to obedience. It actually leads the believer also to an imitation of the moral attributes of Deity. The Gospel is the ministration of the Spirit. It is *therefore* complete, because it conveys free pardon, justifying righteousness, and renewing grace.

'I wish I could be at your elbow for a few minutes, to ascertain what it is which gives rise to certain rumours. If our brethren have found a more excellent way, they must expect us to require satisfactory proof from Scripture; because it does not appear probable that the Lord Jesus should have left His Church in the dark on essential points, from the Reformation to this hour, except in the case of a very few,—some ten or twelve ministers in and out of the Establishment, who have light which others have not. Were Jones, Romaine, Cadogan, and other revivers of evangelical truth in our Church, still in the dark on essential points? It may be so; but surely the most evident proof must be given.'

'COLCHESTER, *May* 11, 1827.

. . . 'WILL you believe it, that I wish to think with you on the Catholic Emancipation question? I have conversed with many who are of opinion that if the Court of Rome would make a public declaration that it does not expect, in any form, allegiance in civil matters from any foreign member of the Church, it would not only deliver English Catholics from a dilemma, but satisfy English Protestants in granting them all civil power. The dilemma of the Catholics is obvious. They are good subjects of the British Constitution, and would not act contrary to it;

but they or their successors may be called upon in conscience to do that in obedience to their Church, and for her benefit, which would interfere with the British Constitution. Then they must either be heretics or rebels. The fear of English Protestants is that they must then choose the latter. Has anything of this nature ever been proposed to the Court of Rome? The opinion of all Catholics, as individuals, is nothing. The opinion of universities is nothing. It must be diplomatic. It must be from the Court of Rome itself.

'I do not say I have not other fears of a religious nature, but I do say this would stop the mouths of many, in a civil point of view.

'You have probably read Faber's work on the Difficulties of Romanism, and have admired the spirit in which it is written. On this subject I know that you cry as loud as any man, No Popery!

'Let us get our Jews back to Jerusalem! That will soon settle the whole matter.—Your obliged and affectionate W. MARSH.'

CHAPTER V.

THOUGHTS ON GREAT QUESTIONS.

'In the thick of the ancient battle,
  Where the strong bear down the weak,
With the flaming sword of living words
  He fought for the poor and meek.

'Where'er were wrongs to be righted,
  Or sick to be soothed and upheld,
Or a generous deed lay hidden,
  Or a generous purpose quell'd,

Or a noble heart lay sinking
  For the want of a cheering word ;—
The music of his earnest voice
  Above the din was heard.'

The Three Wakings.

THOUGHTS ON GREAT QUESTIONS.

THROUGHOUT the whole agitation, on the subject of giving the blessing of freedom to the slaves in our West Indian possessions, my father took a prominent part. Mr. Wilberforce was one of his dearest and most valued friends; and he was in strong sympathy with many others who led the van in the prolonged series of attacks on that standing national crime. My father visited several of the largest and most influential towns in the kingdom, to deliver lectures on the evils of slavery; and even at this distance of time his children can recall the kindling eye and mounting colour, mingled with an expression of indignant horror in his face, as he alluded to the manifold cruelties of slavery, and pleaded with fervent eloquence for the liberty of the chained African.

'Up now for freedom!—not in strife,
  Like that your sterner fathers saw
The awful waste of human life,
  The glory and the guilt of war;
But break the chain—the yoke remove,
  And smite to earth oppression's rod
With those mild arms of truth and love
  Made mighty by the living God.'

No other subject, save one, called forth from him such impassioned earnestness and high sense of wrong and injury done against his fellow-creatures. That one was the slavery of the human soul, which he believed to be more complete and enthralling in the Church of Rome than in any other communion on earth.

During the years 1827 and 1828, his mind was much occupied with the proposed measure for Roman Catholic emancipation. With all his breadth of heart, enlarged views, and tenderness for individuals, he still felt that toleration and political power were distinct considerations, —that whilst rulers, if actuated by the spirit of Christianity, would feel that toleration, in its utmost expansion of religious liberty, is due for every creed, political power could never with safety be intrusted to those who are pledged to render higher obedience to a foreign prince than to our own Sovereign, nor any degree of ecclesiastical equality be safely bestowed upon a Church whose priests are the sworn vassals of that supreme and alien power.

He also considered, with regard to the admission of the teachers of that religion, by our Government, into any posts of trust, that as the Church of Rome has never proclaimed a truce in her war with Protestantism, nor mitigated her persecuting spirit, it is contrary to the rules of war to invite the belligerents of an opposing force to take possession of our strongholds.

In addition to this, his conviction was so deep that Rome is the mystic Babylon of the Book of Revelation, and that to no other city upon earth could its descriptions and definitions possibly be applied, that he held it to be a national sin to 'give power unto it,' for which, as a nation, we must suffer, unless as a nation we should repent.

Gladly as he went all lengths in the removal of 'the penal code,'—for persecution for creed was abhorrent to his whole nature as well as to his religious views,—he foresaw, from the time of the passing of the Roman Catholic Relief Bill in 1829, and the consequent admission of members of that Church into the Houses of Parliament, and into situations of high public trust, that there would be a steady rise of the Papal power in this country, which he feared would never cease until it had extinguished, by persecution, the light of truth, unless it should be arrested in its progress by the special intervention of Almighty power. But this impression never paralysed his exertions on behalf of Protestantism, nor abated the fervour of his prayers. From that time, until the hours of his last illness, he ceased not to bear his witness, on every fitting occasion, whether from the pulpit or the platform, in school-room services or in expositions of Scripture within the house, in the language of our Church,[1] against 'the blasphemous fables and dangerous deceits,' as well as the persecuting spirit, of the Church of Rome, whilst ever advocating the utmost tenderness towards the members of that communion, and firmly believing that multitudes of them, rising superior to the errors of their Church, and trusting in Christ alone for salvation, would be numbered amongst God's saints in glory everlasting.

The following letter briefly expresses his views on this subject:—

[1] Art. xxxi. of the Church of England.

'*Feb.* 10, 1829.

'As a man of liberal views, you probably agree with the King's Speech. I cannot approve of Mr. Peel's policy. He acknowledges that he acts through fear. But what is this fear? Is it not the fear of man, and the want of trust in God? If he still saw—and he declares he does—the same danger as ever, he ought not to have yielded to expediency for a moment. If we displease God by the act, judgments await us. The argument of all the speakers contains no more than this: "If we grant not the boon, the (Irish) Romans will take away our (Irish) kingdom, place, and nation." But what if this very act should eventually lead to it? Human policy is very short-sighted. I hope I may be mistaken in my views, but I confess I feel anxious, as a Briton, to preserve the Constitution unimpaired, and, as a Christian, to enter a national protest against a Church whose principles and character are as clearly denounced in the volume of inspiration, as unbelief or ungodliness may be.'

With his mind thus awakened to discern the most insidious advances of the foe, he was one of the first to detect the leaven of Romanism which, within two years from that date, began to work in Oxford.

Tender as his heart was to persons, he was from first to last uncompromising in his opposition to those 'principles,' 'earnestly contending for the faith once delivered unto the saints.' Neither was he slow to exhort, on this subject, those of his brother clergy with whom he had the opportunity of intercourse, warning them of the end to which the views set forward in the *Tracts for the Times* unmistakably tended—namely, nothing short of union with a fallen and apostate Church.

Efforts were made by some of the leaders of 'the Oxford Movement,' as it was then called, to secure his countenance and aid; and his family have in their possession a document of Mr. Newman's, inquiring of a mutual friend whether there were 'any chance of persuading Mr. Marsh of Birmingham to join them.' But not for a moment was he beguiled. He never permitted himself to use the party phrases 'High Church' and 'Low Church.' He recognised only the distinction of a *sound* and *unsound* Churchmanship, considering that a sound Churchman was one who, firmly believing in the doctrines of his Church, was conformed to her order, holding her Articles in their natural sense, and fervently entering into the spirit of her beautiful and devotional Liturgy.

He was himself a most loyal son of our Protestant Church, and was devotedly attached to her communion. And he held all those to be her foes who would undermine the pure doctrines of the glorious Reformation, upon which she had taken her stand. Wickliffe, Cranmer, Latimer, Ridley, and other not less honoured names, enrolled in the noble army of martyrs of our Church, were spoken of by him as amongst the foremost benefactors of the human race; together with such as John Knox, Melanchthon, Huss, Zuinglius, and last, but greatest, Martin Luther, whose memory is a still living possession of the whole world of Protestantism and freedom.

'They climbed the steep ascent to heaven,
Through peril, loss, and pain:
O God, to us may grace be given
To follow in their train!'

Early in the days of the Oxford movement, my father corresponded with some of its chief leaders on the subject of justification by faith, the key-note of the Reformation; and in a letter addressed to the Rev. Dr. Pusey on this subject, to be forwarded to the other leaders, he stated his own creed with regard to that cardinal doctrine in the following words:—

That we are justified—

FREELY, by Grace (Romans iii. 2).

MERITORIOUSLY, by CHRIST (Romans v. 19).

INSTRUMENTALLY, by Faith (Romans v. 1).

EVIDENTIALLY, by good works (James ii. 26).

To the third clause of this, objection was made; and the sentence, 'Instrumentally, by the Sacrament of Holy Baptism,' was finally substituted on the paper, before it was returned to him.

My father always considered that belief in the theory of spiritual regeneration, as a necessary accompaniment of baptism, was the foundation of that sacramental system which has led so many into the Church of Rome; and, therefore, that baptismal regeneration, in this sense, could never be held with safety, as it is a part of that system in which the priest arrogates a power which belongs only to the Spirit of God; who, as the wind that bloweth where it listeth, 'waiteth not for man, nor tarrieth for the sons of men.'

At the same time, he felt no difficulty, on his own account, in the Office for Baptism. He considered that the services of a Church must be made for believers, and that no confession of faith could be framed, or form of prayer composed, except for those who would believe in earnest, and pray in spirit and in truth; and therefore, that a church, in her formularies, must of necessity assume that those who take part in her services, and share in her rites, are sincere in their use of them.

But the practical argument of the ungodly lives of so many of the baptized, was one which he felt told most strongly against the whole theory of grace being of necessity imparted in the sacrament of baptism.

At the same time, he rejoiced in the service himself, as an expression of strong faith on behalf of the infant. For he held that the act of obedience to the Divine command, 'Go ye into all the world and teach all nations, baptizing them in the name of the Father, and of the Son, and of the Holy Ghost,' would not be performed in believing prayer without a blessing. It was enough for him that the Master had said, 'Whatsoever things ye ask in prayer, believing, ye shall receive.' Nor did he find anything stronger in the language of assurance, used in the thanksgiving prayer after the baptism of the infant, than the words of St. John, 'And this is the confidence that we have in Him, that, if we ask anything according to His will, He heareth us: and if we know that He hear us, whatsoever we ask, we know that *we have* the petitions we have desired of Him.'

In after years, he wrote the following paper on this

subject for a young friend, in prospect of his taking orders :—

'Baptism was never designed to be the agent in regeneration, only the sign and seal. It was *never intended that a minister* (when *he pleased*) *could regenerate a soul.* Our Lord said, "Go, *teach* all nations" (make disciples), and *then* baptize. Our Church, therefore, will not receive any person into communion until by baptism a profession of faith has been made. But a confession of faith, if sincere, implies regeneration *before* baptism,—only the Church cannot pronounce a soul to be regenerate till the faith has been confessed. Our 27th Article declares, *not* that grace is *first given* by the act of baptism, but that faith is *confirmed*, and grace is *increased*, in *answer to prayer.*

'The Church, not being finally satisfied, adopts confirmation, that the child, when of age, may confess his faith in Christ; and this she requires before granting admission to the Lord's Supper. If a child at that time were to say, "I do not believe," the Church must say, Then you were not a regenerated person at your baptism.

'Finally, "*Except a man be born of water,*" *that is, baptized,* he cannot be received *as a member of the Church of Christ on earth.* If he be not baptized *of the Spirit,* he cannot enter into the Church of Christ in heaven.'

'The baptism of infants is to be maintained by—

'1. *Analogy.*—Circumcision of infants. If infants of eight days old were admitted into the Jewish covenant, why may they not be admitted into the Christian covenant? Converts among the Jews would naturally expect it, except it were prohibited.

'2. *Inference.*—Households are supposed to contain infants. Whole households were baptized: we naturally infer that some of them must have included infants.

'3. *Antiquity.*—From the most ancient date, it appears to have been the custom of the Christian Church.

'4. Under the Abrahamic covenant, by Divine command, infants were to be dedicated to God by a sacramental rite, —a rite which is called a sign and a seal of that covenant. But the Abrahamic covenant is nothing more or less than what we term the covenant of grace. We therefore are under the Abrahamic covenant, which is plainly asserted in Rom. iv. and Gal. iii.

'(1.) Under the Abrahamic covenant, infants were to be dedicated to God by a sacramental rite;

'(2.) We are under the Abrahamic covenant;

'(3.) Therefore we are bound so to dedicate our infants.

'There shall be no more shedding of blood, since the Redeemer has shed His blood, and made an atonement for sin; therefore the sacramental sign is now by water.'

The following letter was written in reference to proposed changes in the constitution of the British and Foreign Bible Society:—

'BIRMINGHAM, *April* 2, 1832.

'DEAR SIR THOMAS,—I should indeed rejoice to see a measure introduced for the relief of tender consciences, if, at the same time, it would preserve union. It would be very much against my conscience to join the Sackville Street Society.

'Have you read Gurney's *Terms of Union?* Can it be answered?

'I fear whether *vocal* prayer, at the public meetings will be adopted by a society formed of Episcopalians, Independents, Baptists, and Friends, otherwise I should *greatly* prefer it. But to say prosperity cannot be expected without it, is to contradict a fact of twenty-five years' standing. It is true that trouble from within has arisen, and the Society may have accomplished the principal part at least of its glorious work; but this is no more a proof of the Divine displeasure, than the difficulty in finishing the Temple in the days of Ezra and Nehemiah.

'I fear a test, in such a Society, is contrary to the simplicity of its object, and injurious to its operations; but, if anything can be done to restore harmony, I shall greatly rejoice, and most readily unite. But if there must be a breach, I conscientiously remain with the British and Foreign Bible Society.

'Pray favour me with another line, when you have read Joseph John Gurney's pamphlet, and as soon as you can see the least opening that may lead to union, or prevent further division.

'Might it not be left to any of the auxiliaries that pleased, to commence with prayer, without its being binding on *all*, as a rule of the Society? Except the 67th Psalm and the Lord's Prayer were adopted, could any other form be prepared in which all would unite?

'You see I am obliged to borrow an eye to finish this letter,[1] but, thank God! I have been able to go through

[1] Written when suffering from a severe ophthalmic attack.

my public duties during the last week, and I have also great reason to express my gratitude for the cheerfulness afforded me during the discipline. May your peace flow like a river, and your life be preserved to promote peace amongst others.—Yours, dear Sir Thomas, very faithfully,

WM. MARSH.'

In allusion to a secession which subsequently took place from the Bible Society, partly through misapprehensions and unintentional mis-statements, my father thus wrote:—

'So Satan smiles, if smile he can. But the Lord reigneth. Happy are they who are not ignorant of Satan's devices, and are not carried away by his dissimulations or wiles. We must be ever on our guard. Watch and pray. We pray, but do not always watch, and the Lord will not encourage idleness, no, not an idle religious life. "What I say unto you, I say unto all, watch," is the Master's charge to the end of time. And the watch must *begin within.*

'The disciples knew not what manner of spirit they were of, when they thought themselves very zealous for their Master. We seldom fail by LOVE. What a subject for daily prayer is the 13th of 1st Corinthians.'

ON CONFESSING CHRIST.

'I REJOICE that you have had an opportunity of declaring the love that was in your heart towards the truth as it is in Jesus, and His blessed cause, in our world. It may give temporary offence, and yet afterwards recur with a power that shall leave the conscience without rest till there be the same love and the same zeal. When I see a man not only following conscience, but pursuing truth, I cannot but hope that all will end well. Yet something like despair creeps over one when years pass on, and no progress is made. Still we should "pray, and not faint." When God's vivifying Spirit effectually works either through the fear or the love of God, or both, the man will be in earnest and break through impediments, caring little for the opinion of the world, acting for God and man, and leaving all reproaches to a future judgment. God grant more of this spirit to all His ministers and people, and add to their number this year a hundredfold! . . . How strange is the idea of not being of a party! Every man is of a party; Abel, and Noah, and Abraham, and Moses, and the prophets and the apostles were all "party men." "He that is not with us," said the Lord Jesus Christ, "is against us; and he that gathereth not with us scattereth abroad."'

THE CHRISTIAN'S SECURITY.

'ALL of you have a certainty, by faith in our Redeemer. You are begotten to a lively hope by His resurrection. The inheritance that fadeth not away is yours by promise, by oath, by purchase. What can render it more secure? Love the Giver, serve Him, suffer His will; and yet a little while and possession shall extinguish every doubt for ever.

'Nevertheless, if needs be, ye may experience heaviness at times from many causes; but that very trial of faith shall be found unto praise, and honour, and glory at the appearing of Jesus Christ. Be "looking for that blessed hope." Read again, with reference to all creation as well as to yourself, Rom. viii. 18-23.'

DECISION ON THE LORD'S SIDE.

'The Lord makes more allowance than we do. Nevertheless, I think no great blessing in our age will attend a trimming policy or a refusal to aid the general cause. The Lord calls for decision and devotedness on His side, before His return; especially when the hosts of infidelity are mustering to the battle. Half measures will not much longer please either God or man. The wisdom of the serpent is indeed most desirable, but it should not interfere either with the innocence of the dove or the zeal of the Christian.'

ON ASSURANCE OF FAITH.

'I think a well-grounded assurance, which is always accompanied with humility, has a very holy tendency. The Church of Rome opposed it. Some Protestants misrepresented it or abused it, and this has led others to reject it. But the inspired Apostle prays for the Romans, that "the God of hope would fill them with all joy and peace in believing, that they might abound in hope through the power of the Holy Ghost."

'May this blessing be on you all. Amen.'

ON THE SECOND COMING OF OUR LORD.

'*Feb.* 4, 1831.

'It is long since I read Frere's *Combined View.* I thought I differed a little from him at the time, but I found much information. I am an eclectic on that subject. I am also a sober Catholic. I collect more from a council than I do from a Pope. But, after all, I am a sound Protestant; for I derive more light from the Scriptures, by comparing one part with another, than I do from all Popes and councils.

'As to the coming of our Lord, I simplify it thus. There is no intervening period of a millennium between Daniel's "Son of Man" coming in glory, and the destruction of the fourth empire. Nor in our Lord's prophecy of the fall of the civil and ecclesiastical sun, moon, and stars, and His own return. Nor in the apostle Paul's revelation of the man of sin (2 Thess. ii. 1-8), and the Lord's return to destroy him. *Ergo*, the millennial period succeeds, not precedes, the Lord's return. The prophecies in the Old Testament proceed on this plan. As to the signs of the times, without fixing days and years, they are most remarkable; I cannot but regard them as latter days—last days. There is scarcely a sign wanting, as far as an evident preparation for the whole is concerned, except a movement of the Jews eastward.

'Let us, therefore, believe, and watch, and pray, and hope. And "yet a little while, and He that shall come, will come, and will not tarry. Now the just shall live by faith." And the just by faith *shall live.*

'God grant our nation to repent, and our Church to be zealous, and we shall be spared till the Day dawn. Oh! what a blessed hope the humble believer in Jesus has, whatever may happen to kingdoms or churches."

ON THE SAME 'BLESSED HOPE.'

'You ask me to answer the question, "How you reconcile the series of signs of our Lord's coming with its supposed suddenness? How can people be taken by surprise when His approach is announced?" 1. It will be sudden when it arrives, notwithstanding preceding signs. "Of that day and hour knoweth no man;" and the majority will not regard the signs of the times as bearing upon that event. 2. The signs of the times were clear at the First Advent; yet who were ready to welcome it but Zacharias, and Elizabeth, and Mary, and Joseph, and Simeon, and Anna, and a few more? To the five wise virgins, the coming of the Bridegroom is sudden—to the foolish, unexpected.'

After studying the subject of unfulfilled prophecy for some years, he embodied the views he had drawn from Holy Scripture in a small volume entitled *Plain Thoughts on Prophecy*, which, from its simplicity and comprehensiveness, has proved a valuable guide to many.

From the year 1829, he gathered together annually at his own house many of the clergy and laity from different parts of the country, who were most deeply interested in that subject. Many have borne testimony to the practical tendency which he gave to these views. He sought for himself and for others that they should lead to more separation from the world, more entire consecration to God, to deeper humility and more exalted holiness.

Often did the prospect of the return of his Lord and Master, to be crowned King over the earth, where once He was crucified, cause his joy to rise into triumph. Well can his children remember the brightness of his face, and the exulting tones of his voice, as he sang one of his favourite hymns—

> 'Jesus, immortal King, go on!
> The glorious day will soon be won;
> Thine enemies prepare to flee,
> And leave a conquered world to Thee.'

CHAPTER VI.

WORK AT BIRMINGHAM.

'Yet despite your earnest pity,
   And despite its own smoke and din,
I cling to yon crowded city,
   Though I shrink from its woe and sin.

O'er the fields of earth lie scatter'd
   Noble fruitage and blossoms rare;
Yon city the store has gather'd,
   And the garner of hearts is there.

And the home to which I am hasting
   Is not in some silent glen;
The place where my hopes are resting
   Is a city of living men.

The crowds are there; but the sadness
   Is fled, with the toil and pain;
Nought is heard but the song of gladness;
   'Tis the city of holy men.'

H. Bonar.

WORK AT BIRMINGHAM.

A YEAR or two before the time that my father decided to leave Colchester, the attention of the Church Commissioners had been drawn to the large and rapidly increasing population of the town of Birmingham, and to the very small number of its places of worship. Accordingly, it was arranged that several new churches should be built; and at the same time, the young rector of Birmingham, the Rev. Thomas Moseley, came to the noble determination of not only rendering them independent of the mother Church, by dividing a large portion of his parish of 120,000 souls amongst them, but also, after requisite arrangements had been made, of giving up to each new parish its share of the rectorial tithes. One of these churches was offered by Mr. Moseley to my father. It was consecrated in the month of October 1829, and on the following Sunday it was opened by its new incumbent for three full services.

The majority of the congregation had never entered a church before, a great portion of the town having been left in a state of lamentable ignorance, and disregard of the barest externals of religion. In consequence of the disorderly manners and conduct of many who, attracted by novelty, now flocked to the church, a strong body of police was for some time required to be in attendance. But within six months, two constables only were needed, and even they could take their places quietly as worshippers. In the meantime, there were doubtless some difficulties to be overcome. Boys would bring mice, which they held in long leading strings, and let them stray about to the inconvenience and disturbance of those who were within reach. Other boys, and even grown-up persons, would bring packs of cards to play. But these extraordinary acts of levity in a place of worship, rose to a climax on the first evening of gas being substituted for candles. Owing to some accident, after each attempt at lighting, it went out, leaving the church in total darkness. Peals of laughter resounded through those consecrated walls. The curate expostulated in vain, until my father, appearing from the vestry with a lamp in his hand, with calm and quiet dignity ascended the pulpit stairs. Placing the lamp by his side, he knelt in silent prayer for a few moments; then raising from the cushion his serene and beautiful face, he stood before his congregation, and said in tones of mild solemnity, 'Remember, my young friends, whose house this is, and in whose presence you are assembled—the presence of the King Eternal, Immortal, Invisible; and remember that "the darkness is no darkness with Him, but the night shineth as the day." The darkness and the light are both alike to Him.'

He said no more. No further sound was heard. Then,

after a silence of some minutes, he gave out a hymn, well known already to the children in the schools:—

> 'Almighty God, Thy piercing eye
> Strikes through the shades of night,
> And our most secret actions lie
> All open to Thy sight.'

It was sung in the darkness by almost the whole congregation. At its close, sufficient light was obtained for the service to be continued, and reverent attention prevailed throughout the church.

From that day, he was master of the field. Devout and almost universal joining in the responses of the prayers, and breathless attention to the sermons, with faces all turned towards the pulpit, like a field of wheat blown in one direction, characterized the multitude who thronged St. Thomas's. There was accommodation for 2200 persons, besides the numbers who stood in the aisles and corners every Sunday evening, yet crowds often turned away from the doors, in despair of entrance. When, after years of labour, my father had begun to feel the pressure of the place overwhelming, the sight of those Sunday congregations seemed always like a reviving draught to his wearied frame. Individual cases of conversion frequently came to light; but of the bread cast upon those wide waters, with open hand and praying heart, for ten years—who shall calculate the return, when it is seen again 'after many days!'

At the time my father opened his church in Birmingham, great excitement prevailed there with reference to the proposed measures of political reform. This continued to be on the increase until the passing of the great Reform Bill in 1831. Meetings were held in the suburbs of the town, on 'Newhall Hill,' then a name of terror to the country, where heads might be counted by scores of thousands. They gathered like a torrent, in tributary streams, from all the manufacturing towns within reach; and their language and threats were fierce enough to occasion reasonable alarm. The barracks were filled with soldiers, who were every day expecting to be called out, as at Bristol just before, to fire upon the mob.

By this time, my father's exceeding benevolence of character had become pretty well known in Birmingham, and an unexpected bond of sympathy was discovered.

It had been spread about that he held hopes of an approaching millennium, which the uninstructed amongst the Radicals and Chartists of that day, who formed the vast majority, took for granted to be of a similar nature with 'the golden age' which they had been led to expect. Thenceforward 'Millennial Marsh' became the name by which he was known amongst them. This fancy brought numbers to his church, to hear him expound his views; and there, as he read to them from the Book of Revelation, they listened to the promise of a city, paved with gold and built upon precious stones,—

'Such a city, such a glory,
Far beyond the highest story
Of the ages old and hoary,'—

'whose builder and maker is God.' And many a man left that church determined, by God's help, to make sure of a home there, by asking at once for his name to be 'written in the Lamb's book of life.'

On one occasion, a monster-meeting had been assembled in the great Town-Hall, by the Protestant Association. Some persons of opposing religious views had engaged a large number of the 'rough-and-ready' class to be present, in order to prevent the speaker from being heard. Meanwhile my father was quietly reading in his study at Edgbaston, two miles away, for he was suffering from a severe sore throat. Suddenly a fly drove up to the door, and a messenger brought in an entreaty, that he would come and pour oil upon the troubled waters. Not a moment was lost. He knelt for a brief prayer to God for wisdom and power, and then stepped into the fly. A private entrance afforded access to the platform. A child who accompanied him, can even now recall the first sight of that sea of angry faces, and the sudden change in their expressions, as her father was recognised almost immediately on his advance to the front. The hall rang with shouts of 'Here's Millennial Marsh! Hear him! He's a good one!' with a variety of similar plaudits.

Not a sound escaped his lips, for his voice was lost with the severity of the attack in his throat. But the sight of that familiar face, radiant with love and peace, was sufficient to turn the tide of feeling, and to change frowns into smiles on the countenances of the numbers who knew him. Order restored, he pointed to his painful throat and speechless lips, and then signing for an interpreter, made him ask in his name for 'fair play,' by giving the appointed speaker a hearing. Silence and attention repaid him for the risk he had run. Nor could he bear to leave the generous hearts which had yielded to him so trustfully, without writing words of heavenly entreaty, love, and blessing, to be read to them after he had gone home. He was kept a close prisoner for several days, by the accession of illness which he had willingly risked, for the sake of restoring peace and good feeling.

At the time when my father accepted the charge, the population of the parish of St. Thomas's was reckoned at 16,000 souls; but a later census made it 18,000. Machinery was immediately set to work to reach the masses; Scripture-readers and Bible-women had not then been thought of; but a band of earnest district visitors, from all ranks in the place and neighbourhood, was soon gathered, and had work given them to do, while they were diligently superintended, assisted, and encouraged in it. The weekday and Sunday schools soon became very large and extremely interesting. My father offered up a prayer, and gave a short address to teachers and children every Sunday morning; and held a teachers' meeting at stated intervals, to which my mother often gave additional zest by turning it into a tea-party. Shoe, clothing, blanket, and coal-clubs for the poor soon sprang up, and the moral effect of this care for their temporal comfort was very beneficial.

But it was not only amongst the working classes that my father's influence was felt and acknowledged. Mr. Moseley's testimony to him is,—'A more heavenly-minded man I never knew. As far as I can recollect, I never spent half an hour with him, or received a note from him, which did not breathe of that kingdom on which his affections were supremely set. And this was the more remarkable, as he had evermore a fund of playful wit and pleasantry at his command,—such a combination of spirituality and vivacity I never saw in any other man.'

To his curates, here as elsewhere, he was as a father. His heart and his home were ever open to them. Indeed, not only to every Christian, but also to those who desired to become Christians, most especially to inquiring Jews, he used "hospitality without grudging," on a scale which his income could hardly have met, but for the careful, though generous, economy and simplicity with which my mother ordered her household, for the sake of never narrowing the margin of her husband's numberless gifts to the needy, in various classes, and in his Master's service. Scarcely one-third of their income was consumed by their household expenses.

On every Saturday afternoon, my father and his curates never failed to be present at the prayer-meeting which took place at the rectory of the mother parish, nor were they less regular in their attendance at the clerical meeting, which was held once a month for the clergy of the town and neighbourhood; 'and into them,' said Mr. Moseley, 'he pre-eminently infused a spirit of peace and love. He kept us all together.'

It was no slight addition to his happiness, in making a home in the neighbourhood of Birmingham, to have the opportunity of renewed intercourse with a friend of former years whom he greatly valued, Mr. Hodson, archdeacon of Lichfield, and incumbent of Christ Church, Birmingham, 'a man full of faith and of good works,' of accomplished mind and much learning. His lovely and gifted wife had been a still earlier friend of both my father and my mother, and the children of the two families grew up in daily intercourse, and formed ties of mutual friendship, which time and absence have never broken. Archdeacon Spooner, of Elmdon Rectory, was another valued friend in the neighbourhood, with whom my father had frequent and refreshing intercourse. The late Archdeacon Garbett and the Rev. G. Breay, and last but not least, one over whose head fifty winters had passed whilst he was incumbent of St. Mary's, Birmingham, and who went by the venerable name of 'Father Burn,' were other labourers in that field, —labourers, who all wrought for their Master in heaven with such manifest blessing, that besides numbers of individual souls being brought to the knowledge and love of a Saviour, it has been publicly stated more than once that it was mainly owing to their efforts, with those of their successors, that Birmingham, from being the scene of Chartist riots, has become a peaceable and well-ordered town.

The following letters were written at this period of his ministry:—

GODLINESS BEFORE ORDER.

'*Feb.* 15, 1830.

'THE question to which you refer is a difficult one, and the answer must depend on circumstances, in some cases, and on the view conscience takes of it in all cases. I am disposed to think that the mere law of convenience, I mean that of dividing the kingdom into parishes, though most useful in itself, does not bind conscience in all cases to attend the parish church. The Church of England is one and the same everywhere; but if in some parishes the very principles of that Church are opposed from the pulpit, or a system taught very different in spirit and statement from the Prayer-book, I cannot regard it as inconsistent with the conduct of a true member of our Church, to testify against it, by attending at the same services of the Church of England in another parish. I believe the Reformers in general would have authorized this. It is not an infringement of unity, in my view; and others, instead of being injured, might be led to inquire, and cease to be satisfied with error. If a few can listen to error without injury, the many cannot. As to such a minister being over us in the Lord, I doubt it. The Lord never yet put a man ignorant of his Gospel, as a minister of that Gospel, over any people; though He may permit it in judgment. As to the question, 'Who art thou that judgest?' it relates to non-essential matters, in the observance or non-observance of which every one should have credit for sincerity; but we cannot but judge when we hear what is contrary to Scripture, that it is error; or when we see evil conduct, that men do not gather thorns of vines, or grapes of thorns—the tree is to be known and judged by its fruit. Oh! let us never forget to pray that it would please God to "send down upon our bishops and curates, and all congregations committed to their charge, the healthful Spirit of His grace." All that the Church of England wants to make her the glory of all Churches, is the spirit of her own services.'

'*September* 27, 1830.

'I HOPE your new member is an anti-slavery man, and that the town will petition. I have no hope for our nation during the storms which will agitate Europe, except we show mercy to our slaves, and kindness to the Jews, and reverence the sabbaths and oracles of Jehovah. Scriptural knowledge—the nation wants; more scriptural knowledge—we all want. We can never have too much of that light in our understandings, or of the love it reveals, and enjoins, and produces in our hearts. The character of God, as revealed in the Scriptures, the designs of God as therein made known, and the salvation of God, as fully developed, are comparatively little known and understood. Darkness covers the earth; but when the sun shines forth, all will be light.'

TO MRS. MARSH.

'SHREWSBURY, *Saturday, August* 27, 1831.

'EVER DEAREST ONE,—Thank God we have had a safe and very pleasant journey, save and except that we left behind some most valuable articles by the sea-side, and that Lou had never travelled seventy-six miles by land in one day (and fourteen hours upon the road) before. She was, however, very well, and in the breakfast room before myself. The people at the Talbot are now acquainted with us, and they gave us good rooms. We are now going to see Shrewsbury, and hope to be home early in the evening. It has been a most pleasant journey to us, when we recollect your extreme illness, and your present recovery. Now take care of yourself, and be quiet the remainder of the time.

'We remember our fellow-worshippers. And now and then run over the Epistle, as we would the strings of a harp. If we can enter into its tones, we shall, ere long, be found among "the harpers harping with their harps." May God Almighty carry on this work in us, and perform it in the day of Jesus Christ. I can believe that there will not be a single beloved one missing then. Lord, help my unbelief. In prayer we must seek to realize this, "I will not let Thee go, except Thou bless me," and bless A. and B. and C. and D.

'When dining at Llanidloes, some were speaking of the wreck. Matilda read a part of Catherine Austen's letter, and they were much affected. The death of Christians is often the means of life to survivors. The sufferings of the present time, therefore, are not worthy to be compared with the glory which shall be revealed. But it is difficult, while the temporal cloud is passing, to behold the eternal glory. Lord, increase our faith.

'Christian love attends so many, that I can only say give it to all. W. M.'

TO SIR THOMAS BARING.

'*January* 18, 1832.

'The Jesuits are recovering and exerting their baneful influence. Nevertheless, yet a little while, and it will be said, "Babylon the great is fallen, is fallen." And at the same moment the warfare of Jerusalem will be accomplished. No man can behold religion, as in Catholic countries, reduced to a form, and the pastoral power to priestcraft, and not feel thankful for a Protestant Government and a Protestant Church, if he have any knowledge in his head and grace in his heart.

'. . . Let me, in conclusion, wish you and Lady Baring the blessings of the season, a believing, happy New Year. Faith's view of the Cross, Hope's expectation of the Crown, and Love's grateful obedience.'

ON THE PURIFICATION AND PRESERVATION OF THE CHURCH OF ENGLAND, AND OUR COMING STORMS.

'I CANNOT but fervently hope the Church of England will be preserved. To her purification from anything which impedes her usefulness, what Christian will object? But her destruction must open a flood of ignorance and insubordination throughout the kingdom. The Nonconformists could not supply her place; nor could they stand their ground against mutual foes without her.

'The increase of faithful labourers is a token for good. Mr. Berridge, in his quaint way, said, "I am sure my Master is not going to give up housekeeping, because He is hiring more servants."

'Nevertheless, the whole Church of Christ, in all kingdoms, may be preparing for a storm, which shall purify her, and destroy the wicked, by giving them a tremendous opportunity of filling up the measure of their iniquities. Yet how we ought to pray that "to-day men may hear

His voice," and come out, that they receive not of His plagues.

'I send you my Sunday morning text and subject in one, "God is love." Proved, as manifested in His works, revealed in His Word, and, above all, as exhibited in His Son. Oh that Calvinists and Arminians, Churchmen and Dissenters, Romanists and Protestants, reformed churches and unreformed, kept more to this grand point,—the exhibition of the Divine character in the Christian dispensation. Would it not, as believed from the heart, accomplish all things? "God is love; and he that dwelleth in love, dwelleth in God, and God in him."'

In 1831, some meetings were held in Birmingham for discussions upon articles of faith, between Roman Catholics and Protestants, which were conducted with remarkable temper and spirit on both sides. The principal speakers were the late Captain Gordon, R.N., M.P. for Dundalk, a man endued with 'the spirit of power, and of love, and of a sound mind;' the Rev. Nicholas Armstrong, a young Irish clergyman, endowed with thrilling eloquence, and great warmth of heart; and the Rev. Edward Irving, whose rare genius had not then been altogether entangled with those imaginations which afterwards obscured the clearness of his evangelical teaching. My father took part in these meetings, with his habitual candour and tenderness towards those who held opposing views. Whilst he was valiant for the truth, his motto was always, 'Let us attack principles, not persons; measures, not men.'

These meetings were convened and conducted in the

spirit of earnest prayer, which was publicly offered at the commencement of the meeting, those who objected to it remaining outside until the prayer was concluded. Mr. Falvey, a Roman Catholic barrister, and the Rev. T. M. Macdonnel, the only Roman Catholic priest then resident in Birmingham, with one or two priests from some neighbouring place, were the chief speakers on the other side. Mr. Macdonnel had an undisguised admiration for my father, which remained unshaken by the antagonism of these occasions.

A young man, who was preparing for the Romish priesthood, attended one of these meetings. Before its close he was convinced of the errors of his Church, and sought interviews with my father; but shortly afterwards he was sent away to Dublin, and from thence to Spain. Once, and once only, he succeeded in forwarding a letter. Its purport was to implore his friend to pray that whatever he might have to suffer, he might be kept steadfast in the faith once delivered unto the saints; and that the Holy Spirit would bring to his remembrance all things necessary to salvation; for, in punishment of his heresy, he was in strict custody, and had been already deprived of his Bible. From that hour my father heard no more of him, yet long and anxiously was he remembered in prayer.

But the more extensive benefit which arose from these meetings, my father believed, was the better instruction of Protestants in their own faith. The principles of the blessed Reformation were proclaimed; and those who held them were provided with sound arguments against the errors of the Church of Rome, in case they should at any time find an effort made to attack or undermine their faith.

TO THE BISHOP OF CALCUTTA, ON HIS APPOINTMENT TO THE SEE.

'*May* 31, 1832.

'DEAR BISHOP WILSON,—Beloved brother,—More or less, above thirty years, have I traced your steps, and now I will try to follow you, in heart, over the seas. Your rise among men has not been so sudden as to endanger your humility. You have been already in most important stations, and you have "purchased to yourself a good degree, and great boldness in the faith which is in Christ Jesus;" and being thus trained, by the providence and the grace of God, you may fill the highest office with advantage to others, and no injury to your own soul.

'You are neither a novice in self-knowledge, or the knowledge of Christ, or the knowledge of the Church, or the knowledge of the world; and, while your mind may still enlarge and grow in acquaintance with all these, so may your spirituality be preserved, and your usefulness be made to abound.

'Happily, you are not a man for extremes; and yet you know the importance of warmth, and energy, and perseverance, in such an object as that of promoting the glory of Christ's name, the increase of His kingdom, and the benefit of His Church. In love there can be no extreme; but how happy it is when there is wisdom profitable to direct love in its actions—when the minister is never ashamed of the Gospel of Christ, and never exposes it to shame.

'Oh, what a charge did the "Bishop of souls" give to His first ministers, as recorded in Matt. x. "Search the Scriptures," good Mr. Cadogan used to say, "and you shall be wise as serpents; *keep* them, and you shall be harmless as doves."

'I can easily conceive you may come into circumstances which may exceedingly try either faith, or patience, or prudence, or zeal. But you know, experimentally, what Nehemiah did (Neh. ii. 4), and how Jehoshaphat acted (2 Chron. xx. 12), and how they both succeeded. I never expect your Lordship to be circumstanced as the apostle was (2 Tim. iv. 16); because you will find many in the East, thank God! both clergy and laity, who will stand by you with prayer, and example, and influence, to promote the Christian cause. Yet you may meet with false brethren, and weak brethren, and erring brethren, and may have to exercise patience and long-suffering towards them—but "*omnia vincit amor*." Your text in my pulpit at Colchester (2 Cor. v. 14, 15) will carry you through all. Your labours will be in love; your preaching and living will be in love; your reproofs and advice will be in love; you will "dwell in love;" and "he that dwelleth in love dwelleth in God, and God in him." And what may not this man do!

'Dear Bishop Wilson, beloved brother, we meet no more, in all probability, till we meet in the presence of our blessed Lord. May I be found, as you will be, among those described in Luke xii. 35-44. I can guess how you are hurried. Do not write to me now, but give me a line, some time or other, after your arrival. I must not even ask you to pray for me, except in the *general petition*, "Bless my friends and their families."—Ever your most affectionate WM. MARSH.'

In the year 1833, the vicarage of St. Peter's, Hereford, was offered to Dr. Marsh, and a strong appeal was made by the parishioners to induce him to accept it; but the earnest entreaties of the parishioners of St. Thomas's, and even more, considerations of the vast importance of that sphere of duty, prevailed with him to remain. Amongst the testimonies from various quarters which had touched him the most, was that of Joseph Sturge, a well-known member of the Society of Friends, and a strong Radical. 'Friend Marsh,' he said, 'if thee leavest Birmingham, the Friends will put on crape.'[1]

During the three years or more that he had now lived in Birmingham, he had met with many professed Unitarians,—for the benevolence of whose characters he had a great regard. His peculiar gentleness of disposition, and large-hearted sympathy for those who were tried with doubts and difficulties, combined with the strength and simplicity of his own faith, made him well qualified to discuss with them the great points of difference. The following letter was written to a member of his congregation, with whom a Unitarian acquaintance was in

[1] At that time mourning was inadmissible amongst Quakers.

the habit of conversing freely upon their religious differences:—

ON THE DIVINITY OF THE 'SON OF MAN.'

'*January* 21, 1833.

'DEAR MISS RICHARDS,—The manuscript you lent Louisa is a fair and candid statement of Unitarian views, and every man should think for himself, and state his opinions candidly. Nevertheless, truth is not necessarily what A. thinks, or what B. thinks, but what the inspired volume asserts. Truth is immutable, and does not depend on the opinions of men. On the subject of revealed truth, we must therefore appeal to prophets and apostles, and not to reason. They indeed never assert anything contrary to reason, but they make known many things which reason would not have discovered, and which are above its comprehension when discovered. Indeed the first principle of all religion contains the deepest mystery, and is perfectly incomprehensible. The existence of a Being who never had a beginning, is an ocean which the human mind cannot fathom. "Who can by searching find out God?" It is equally impossible for us also, *a priori*, to determine how that great Being exists. "Who can find out the Almighty to perfection?" We are at sea without a compass. We absolutely know nothing correctly but in the light of revelation. Now it is admitted by Trinitarians that the Scriptures are exceedingly jealous on the subject of the unity of the Divine Nature, and it forms an article in their faith. But they infer from this, that in the scriptural mode of expression there would not be the least ambiguity of language, or possibility of supposing anything contrary to the idea of One Person in that Unity, if there were not something mysterious in that nature analogous to a plural, or, as Trinitarians express it, a Tri-une Existence. But leaving this out of the question, and taking no advantage of the peculiarity of the Mosaic idiom, "Let *us* make man in our image," "after *our* likeness." "Remember now thy *Creators* in the days of thy youth." "Thy *Makers* are thy husband, the Lord of Hosts is His name." "Jehovah our *Elohim* (gods) is one Jehovah," and similar expressions in the Hebrew; yet is it not evident that Divine perfections, works, and worship are ascribed to a Being in some sense not the same person as the Eternal Father? Who was that Angel of the Lord that called unto Abraham out of heaven? (Gen. xxii. 11, 12, 15,) that "redeemed Jacob from all evil?" (Gen. xlviii. 16, compared with Hosea xii. 4, 5.) Who was that Man that demanded the same reverence which Moses paid to the God of Abraham, Isaac, and Jacob, when He appeared as a flame of fire in a bush? (Joshua v. 13-15, compared with Exod. iii. 2-6, and Acts vii. 30, 38,) and concerning whom Manoah said, "We have seen God"? (Judges xiii. 6, 13, 17, 18, 21, 22.) Was it not the same who "was in the beginning with God, and was God," the only-begotten Son, who was in the bosom of the Father, and hath revealed Him to us"? (John i. 1-4, 14, 18.) Was He not the resplendent out-beaming of the essential glory of God? The radiance of the eternal light, radically and essentially the same as the inherent splendour? The very character of the Divine Substance, by which all the likeness of the original became manifest?

'Read Hebrews i. throughout. And if Deity thus exists in a mysterious nature, and will thus manifest Himself for our happiness, shall we reason on the mode of the Divine existence, and say this is impossible? Well may we exclaim with *adoration*, "Will God in very deed dwell with man on the earth!" But so to say in *unbelief* is to mar our best foundation of hope and joy. To prevent this, may "God, who commanded the light to shine out of darkness, shine continually into our hearts, to give us the light of the knowledge of the glory of God in the face of Jesus Christ" (2 Cor. iv. 4-6).

'There is no truth in all Scripture that contains more encouragement to a fallen race than those words of our Lord, "He that hath seen Me, hath seen the Father." Was not the Apostle therefore fully authorized to call Him "over all, God blessed for ever;" and is it not the "great mystery" of godliness, that "God was manifest in the flesh"? It is not a mere speculative point, but it contains the most powerful motives to gratitude, obedience, and to all godliness. The knife of criticism, however keen, can never excise it from the sacred page. As to the human nature of our blessed Lord, we are all agreed that Jesus Christ had a reasonable soul and human flesh. It is not fair, therefore, to quote passages which relate to His human nature, and oppose them to those which speak of His Divine. And why should it be thought a thing incredible and impossible, that God should thus manifest His love? He became a worm to converse with worms, and to redeem worms, and will He not by this manifest His glory to the universe? We read in Eph. iii. 9, 10, not only that all *men* may "see what is the fellowship of the mystery, which from the beginning of the world hath been hid in God, who created all things by Jesus Christ;" but also that it is "*to the intent* that now, unto the *principalities and powers in heavenly places*, might be known by the church the manifold wisdom of God." Is not this worthy of God? worthy of Him whose name is love? Oh, let us pray, "I beseech Thee, show me Thy glory!" Nothing can be better calculated to win the heart than such a display of grace and condescension—nothing better to encourage the soul in prayer, or to lead it to abound in praise (Heb. iv. 14-16), or to strengthen it in temptation (Heb. ii. 17, 18), or to influence it to aim at the highest standard of Christian dispositions and benevolent conduct (Phil. ii. 5-7; 1 Pet. ii. 21, 25). It is the "*love* of Christ which constraineth us." It is to Him we are to live, who died for us. Nor can we wonder if this be the rule of heaven. "Grace be with all them that love our Lord Jesus Christ in sincerity;" and, "If any man love not the Lord Jesus Christ, let him be anathema maran-atha."

'With respect to our Lord's humiliation, have you never noticed the shining forth of His proper glory through the cloud? Is He a babe in Bethlehem? He is called Immanuel. Has He not where to lay His head? By a miracle He feeds thousands. Is He charged as a sinner? He forgives sins. Does He die an ignominious death? He promises a malefactor eternal life. Is He laid in the silent grave? According to His own saying, "Destroy this temple, and in three days *I* will raise it up," He rises from the tomb.

'Have you never noticed not only the authoritative style of His preaching,—"I say unto you," but the peculiar manner of working miracles, as from underived power? And that while prophets of old wrought them in the name of Jehovah, apostles wrought them *in the name of Jesus Christ?*

'The incidental proofs of His Divinity are also very numerous. Prayer is made to Him, providential acts are perpetually ascribed to Him, and not less frequently divine grace. St. Paul writes, "I besought the Lord thrice. And He said unto me, *My* grace is sufficient for thee. Most gladly therefore will I rather glory in my infirmities, that *the power of Christ* may rest upon me" (2 Cor. xii. 8, 9). In Romans x. 9, we read that confession of the Lord Jesus, and belief in His resurrection, is salvation; and in the 13th verse, that "whosoever shall call upon the name of the Lord shall be saved." Hence St. Paul, in the dedication of his 1st Epistle to the Corinthians, addresses "all that in every place *call upon the name of Jesus Christ our Lord.*" And well he might! for that same Lord had promised to be *wherever* two or three were gathered together in His name (Matt. xviii. 20). The Lord, whom we are not to tempt or provoke to jealousy, is the Lord Jesus, and is called the same Jehovah as He who sent the judgment of fiery serpents on the Israelites that spake against Him (1 Cor. x. 9, 22), and in whom St. Paul trusted to send Timotheus to the Philippians (ii. 19). And by the providence of the same Lord, he trusted that he himself should come shortly (ver. 24). If then the names and attributes and works of Deity be applied to our blessed Saviour,—if Creation, Providence, and Redemption, be ascribed to Him,—if He partake in common with Deity in the adoration of angels and of men,—if works and words bespeak His majesty, and if this truth be full of consolation and of practical influence,—why should I oppose my puny reason to the mighty proofs of Revelation, because I cannot conceive the mode by which God and man can be united in one person?

'I have written in great haste, on the eve of a journey, and have not time to revise or add, but I shall be glad to do so on my return.

'Your amiable friend will not wonder that I am surprised at his calling St. John's words "an interesting but metaphorical mode of expression." "Interesting" indeed; but the Scriptures of God would not have used titles and words metaphorically which might lead to so great an error as the worship of a mere man, albeit the noblest of mankind. "See thou do it not!" was the adjuration of one like unto an angel, the bearer of messages and revelations from God, who called himself to St. John in Patmos, "one of his fellow-servants and of his brethren the prophets." "See thou do it not! Worship GOD!"

'I am alarmed for your friend when he appeals to the justice of God for safety while he rejects the Divine method mentioned in Rom. iii. 23-26, "For *all* have *sinned*, and *come short of* the glory of God: being justified *freely* by His *grace, through the redemption which is in Christ Jesus;* whom God hath set forth to be a *propitiation through faith in His blood,* to declare His righteousness for the remission of sins that are past, through the forbearance of God; to declare, I say, at this time His righteousness, that He might be just, and the justifier of him which *believeth in Jesus.*"

'Grace and peace be with your friend and with you and yours. Remember that one great end of all divine discoveries is to mortify pride and self-sufficiency, and lead us to live by faith in the Word of God and in the practice of every grace and virtue.—Yours affectionately,

'WILLIAM MARSH.'

CHAPTER VII.

BEREAVEMENT AND CONSOLATION.

'Still one in life, and one in death,
One in their hope of rest above,
One in their joy, their trust, their faith,
One in each other's faithful love.

Yet they must part, and parting, weep;
What else has earth for them in store?
These farewell pangs, how sharp and deep,
These farewell words, how sad and sore!

Yet they shall meet again in peace,
To sing the song of festive joy,
Where none shall make their gladness cease,
And none their fellowship destroy.'

H. Bonar.

BEREAVEMENT AND CONSOLATION.

For several months in the year 1833, my beloved mother's health had begun to fail. Her unwearied and self-sacrificing efforts in the service of her Divine Master had far exceeded her strength, and at length a long-latent disease of the heart developed itself. This produced occasional depression of her spirits. It was then that the peculiar tenderness and sympathy of her husband's disposition manifested itself to the uttermost. His prayers—his study of the Scriptures—seemed to be expressly for her. That mine of hidden wealth, from which he brought forth such riches for others, yielded peculiar treasures for her, in her hour of need. By the recommendation of her medical adviser, he took her to Leamington, to try the effect of the mineral waters, and whilst there he thus wrote to a friend:—

'I have been here for some days with my beloved wife, who is worse rather than better. She is trying these waters, but we are not yet sure that they will be the means of restoration. That is indeed alone in the power of our Lord; and power and compassion were ever united in Him in the days of His humiliation, and power and compassion are His nature, and will remain with Him for ever. "We have not an High Priest which cannot be touched with the feeling of our infirmities." "Let us therefore come boldly unto the throne of grace, that we may obtain mercy, and find grace to help in time of need."'

'In infinite wisdom, and undoubtedly also in infinite love,' wrote my eldest sister, not long after our mother's death, 'the Lord saw fit to withhold the healing power of those waters, for she for whom it was sought was soon to be led beside those still waters that rise beneath the tree of life.'

On Saturday, July the 20th, his birthday, my dear father felt extremely reluctant to leave her, as her weakness had greatly increased; but, knowing that his people expected him to preach on the following day, and that there would be great difficulty in getting the whole duty supplied, he hesitated as to what he should do. With her accustomed and beautiful self-denial, she determined it for him, saying she thought the congregation would be disappointed, and added, 'Do not think of me.' He therefore consented to go, purposing to return early on Monday. When he took leave of her she said, 'I hope you will have a good Sabbath to-morrow. The Lord bless and strengthen you.' He repeated to her the passage, 'Looking for the mercy of our Lord Jesus Christ unto eternal life.'

When the Sunday came, however, her kind physician, Dr. Jephson, thought it best at once to convey her to Edgbaston, fearing that any delay might make it too late for her to return home, where she had expressed her wish to die, surrounded by her family.

On the following Wednesday, she 'fell asleep in Jesus.' Early in the morning, as she watched the sun rise, she exclaimed, 'Arise, O Sun of Righteousness!' adding, shortly afterwards, 'My flesh and my heart faileth, but God is the strength of my heart and my portion for ever.' Almost her last words were, 'Hear me, all of you, I die in the faith of Christ. He has followed me with loving-kindness all my life, and He will not give me up now.'

The following sketch was drawn up by my father shortly after her death :—

'My late beloved wife, from a very early period, was remarkably attentive to the wants of the poor in the neighbourhood, but without very distinct views of religion. Mr. Wilberforce's work on *Practical Christianity* had a great influence on her mind; and on reading Hervey's *Theron and Aspasio,* her views were much changed with reference to the mode of our acceptance with God, as through the merits of Christ alone. She began then to take great delight in studying the Scriptures, and reading the works of some of our best divines. Her whole life was now devoted to her God and to her neighbours, paying the strictest and most affectionate attention to every relative call. When she entered upon the duties of a clergyman's wife, the poor and the children of the parish were as her own family; and no means were omitted by which my ministry at home, or the cause of Christianity at large, might be promoted by her. Growing more and more acquainted with the Divine character, as revealed in the Scriptures and exhibited in the Saviour, she attained a solid peace. She lived in the spirit of prayer. Her time was wholly occupied with private devotion, domestic duties, social Christian intercourse, and public ordinances. She gave much time to the religious instruction of her children. No duty was omitted. Yet her self-abasement was as great as if she had omitted every duty. She was indeed remarkable for unaffected humility, habitual self-denial, tender kindness, peculiar courtesy of manner, and fervent Christian love. She has been greatly honoured in leading many, by her conversation, advice, letters, and example, to seek the kingdom of God, to love their Saviour, and to promote the welfare of others, as responsible beings who should live for eternity. Though her path on the whole was smooth, yet it pleased God that she should have her day of trial, and walk through the valley of humiliation to her rest.

'The disease under which she laboured for some time, occasionally depressed her spirits. The only effect was to lead her to the most humiliating views of herself. Her hope had been, for many years, only in the mercy of God in Christ, but now she felt herself to be the chief of sinners. As she approached her end, a sweet calm ensued, with the exception of a momentary interruption. Near the close, she requested that all her family might be assembled, and, turning towards them, she said, "I die in the faith of Christ. His goodness and mercy have followed me all my days, and He will not give me up now."

'She had listened with pleasure during the previous night to Psalm xxiii. and John x., and every now and then she finished the passage herself. She said to one standing by, "He hath loved me with an everlasting love, therefore with loving-kindness hath He drawn me." Shortly before her death she said to me, "Give my beloved children my blessing, as I have not strength." Thus fell asleep a single-hearted and sincere Christian;

one qualified to shine in any rank of human society, and yet delighting to attend the lowest; and, like the Lord and Master whom she loved, "to go about doing good." Loving all, and beloved by all, every one who came within the sphere of her acquaintance will lament their loss; but their loss is her gain. She has left behind that good name which is better than precious ointment; and the day of her death was to her better than the day of her birth. Such were the effects of a scriptural faith in God our Saviour, Jesus Christ, as manifested in the life and death of one of whom it may be said, "She hath done what she could;" and, having "washed her robes and made them white in the blood of the Lamb," is now "before the throne of God, and serves Him day and night in His temple."'

So blended was her spirit in all his highest interests, that just after he left the chamber of death, my father said to us, 'I feel as if my ministry were ended;' and, at a another time, when we had gathered around him, and our eyes fell on her vacant place, in the warmth of his wrung heart he said, 'We thought we had loved her as much as it was possible to love; but now, if we had her back again, we should be almost tempted to place her on a pedestal and worship her.'

After her funeral, he left home, with his mourning family, for a fortnight; and then returned to throw himself at once into the work of the Lord, as the best solace, next to 'fellowship with the Father and with His Son Jesus Christ.' At that well-head of consolation he drank hour by hour; and every grace shone out with a fuller lustre, from this time of his deepest earthly sorrow. Frequently has he said to other mourners, that 'submission and occupation were the true remedies for a wounded spirit.' 'But submission,' he said, 'was not enough for the Christian—it must melt into a perfect acquiescence with the Divine will, under the contemplation of the character of God—for GOD IS LOVE.'

But one blessed hope bore up his spirit—the hope of eternal re-union in the presence of the Lord.

'Poor comfort,' he said, 'would there have been in the stress St. Paul laid on the promise to the bereaved Thessalonians, that they should be caught up *together* with those whom they were mourning—at the coming of the Lord—if they were not to recognise each other in that company!'

The prospect of the comparatively near approach of the Second Advent of our Lord was, indeed, his most joyful theme. For years it had been the subject which called forth his highest eloquence, and his most exulting praise. But now a tenderer tone was added. The hymns which touched upon the glorious prospect became his chief favourites—and his countenance lighted up with more than usual radiance as he clearly and succinctly explained to inquirers, his scriptural grounds for believing that 'the day of glory nears.' Although not thinking it right to fix on any dates with definite certainty, he looked forward to the closing years of the present decade as a time which would probably usher in 'the beginning of the end.'

The following letters were written to a lady who had been brought up in Unitarian doctrine, but who had, under my father's ministry, embraced the belief of a Triune God:—

'Heavy trials are, to the Christian, clouds full of fructifying showers; and the darkness of midnight does but declare the dawn of approaching day. If we can but apprehend the Divine character, as revealed in the Scriptures, and particularly as exhibited in our Lord and Saviour, we shall know where to go at all times, and shall find peace. He loves us; He forgives sins; He bestows peace; He fulfils promises; He "will do exceeding abundantly above all that we ask or think."

'... Gratitude without a repining thought, and obedience without a flaw, will constitute a great part of our happiness in a future state.'

'Here we groan, being burdened. Here we suffer by sympathy with others; but there, no one effect of sin remains, nor one sight or sense of woe. Let us ever, when they are of a grievous nature, place our present trials beside our future prospects.

"Fear not, ye saints, fresh courage take;
The clouds ye so much dread
Are fraught with mercy, and shall break
In blessings on your head."

'Trials either prepare us for greater usefulness or greater joy on earth, or train us for our station of service and glory in heaven. They shall be abundantly sanctified through Him who was "a man of sorrows, and acquainted with grief;" and who is "a merciful and faithful High Priest," an atoning Saviour and a sympathizing Friend:

and "He sits as a refiner and purifier of silver." May His peace rest upon you!'

OUR SORROW AND CONSOLATION.

'*June* 6, 1833.

'ARE we rational creatures? God commands us to love Himself, the fountain of all perfection and goodness; and also to love one another. Are we sinful creatures? He commands us to believe on a Saviour, and be at peace, and expect everything needful for everlasting happiness. Are we believers? He commands us to rejoice in His salvation, and to let our light shine before men, that they also may be led to seek and to find the same eternal good. Thus in humility, in faith, in love, and in peace, may we pass our days; but not, indeed, without trials from within as well as without. It is through faith and patience that we are to inherit the promises,—and the great enemy will try to harass us—and our own hearts will fail us—and our animal spirits will sink—and circumstances will arise to prove us—but "*all* things work together for good;" and it is only "for a season, if need be," that the heaviness shall last. "Heaviness may endure for a night, but joy cometh in the morning." And what must that joy be which cometh in the morning of the resurrection! when we shall be equal to the angels in love, purity, wisdom, and strength; and superior to them in some privileges, because the Son of God took not on Him the nature of angels, but He took on Him the nature of the seed of Abraham.'

ON HIS OWN BEREAVEMENT.

'BIRMINGHAM, *Aug.* 15, 1833.

'DEAR FRIEND,—Your letters of sympathy are very acceptable. These are dew-drops; but "times of refreshing" must come from the presence of the Lord to fill up in any measure the tremendous vacuum. Adam is turned out of Paradise, and he may well weep. Yet let him remember the many years in which he was favoured with so rich a gift. Yes, my dear friend, *you* knew something of the value of the departed saint, and *I* never saw so striking a union of apparently opposite graces. She lived in the element of love. "The law of kindness was" indeed "upon her lips," and ever flowed from her heart.

'A murmuring thought, thanks be to God, has not arisen, but the heart has bled. Pray for us all, that we may profit for eternity by this heavy trial in time. Yet how greatly have we been favoured, and how many and great mercies are left! My beloved children do all in their power to comfort me, and try to conceal their own anguish. May the consolations of heaven, the comfort of hope, descend and dwell in them. Willie left us this day for his tutor's. It was a trying day to him. Dear fellow, his trials commence early in life. But our heavenly Father knows our several dispositions and circumstances, and what is best for us with reference to our future state.

'May we follow her example, realize her joy, and live

and die like her; and then be ever like, and ever with her Lord and ours. These events do indeed teach us the uncertainty of all things below the skies, and should teach us our entire dependence on God for happiness. Let us enjoy God in all things, and all things in God. We all unite in kind love to dear Mr. R. and yourself. Your letter was, I think, the last she read.—Ever your affectionate friend, WM. MARSH.'

ON DESIRE FOR CONFORMITY TO THE WHOLE WILL OF GOD.

'REMEMBER that the changeableness of our feelings does not alter the unchangeableness of Divine love; and our very inability, at times amounting, as we think, to indisposition for spiritual exertions,—if it do not wholly arise from physical causes, the state of our health, or our nervous system,—may yet be *permitted*, to show us what we should be if it were not for the grace of God. Let any such experience but humble us and cause us to renounce all confidence in ourselves either for merit or strength, and bring us with the publican's prayer to the throne of grace, and it shall not injure us or impede our spiritual progress. But, oh! how unspeakably delightful it will be to find ourselves in a world, and in a nature, where neither doubt, nor fears, nor deadness, nor the least want of conformity to the Divine will, can be feared or felt for ever! May we be "looking for the mercy of our Lord Jesus Christ unto eternal life."'

TO LIEUTENANT RHIND, R.N., ON RECEIVING HIS PICTURE OF A MARTYRDOM IN THE REIGN OF QUEEN MARY.

'DEAR RHIND,—John Bunyan was mistaken when he thought that "Giant Pope" was disabled for life. He has cut teeth since that time.

'"Pictures of martyrdom," writes Dr. Arnold, who expects another day of trial, "are very wholesome, not to be sneered at, nor yet to be looked on as a mere excitement, but a sober reminder to us of what Satan can do to hurt, and what Christ's grace can enable the weakest of His children to bear."

'Send me five. By exhibiting them the orders may multiply.

'I send you and dear Mrs. Rhind my Christmas wish. May faith in the First Advent and hope in the Second be in lively exercise, and love will not then be far off; and love to Christ's person, confidence in His work, and devotedness to His service, are the best evidences of Christianity. —Yours most truly, WM. MARSH.'

Not long after the marriage of his third daughter, Louisa, to the Rev. William Knox Marshall, incumbent of St. Mary's, Bridgnorth, my father was appointed official of the 'royal peculiar' of that place. The only emolument connected with this ecclesiastical office was from a surrogateship attached to it; and this small income he devoted entirely to the benefit of the eight parishes in the peculiar.

Mr. Marshall—now Vicar of Wragby—explains, in the

following letter, the nature of the office, and the manner in which his father-in-law filled it:—

'Early in the year 1837, Dr. Marsh was appointed, by the late T. Whitmore, Esq. of Apley Park, Shropshire, to the office of "principal official and commissary of the royal peculiar of the deanery of Bridgnorth."

'This ancient office had its origin in a gift from the Crown in the reign of King William III., which gave to the lay dean of Bridgnorth the power to appoint an official, who should have plenary jurisdiction, as well in things spiritual as in things temporal. The peculiar comprehended eight parishes and about 10,000 inhabitants. Over these the official exercised ecclesiastical jurisdiction, independently of any bishop or archbishop. One of the duties belonging to the office was to hold yearly visitations, to which the clergy and churchwardens were summoned. On these occasions Dr. Marsh assembled the clergy, officers of the court, and churchwardens, for divine service, and delivered to them a charge. The text he chose for his first address was from Malachi ii. 7,—"For the priest's lips should keep knowledge, and they should seek the law at his mouth: for he is the messenger of the Lord of Hosts." It was delivered with his usual earnestness and affection, and it produced a deep impression on the hearts of those who heard it. These visitations he continued to hold each year until he removed to a considerable distance, which, together with increasing age, rendered his attendance too great an effort for him, in addition to the manifold other claims on his time and strength.

'His last sermon, as official, was from the words, "For

what is it wherein ye are inferior to other churches?" (1 Cor. xii. 13.) In it he dwelt on the pure and scriptural character of the Articles and Liturgy of the Church of England, and warned all of the dangers that were then threatening the nation from the inroads of Popery and Rationalism.

'He held this office until the year 1855, when he resigned it in my favour,—as I was then incumbent of St. Mary's, Bridgnorth. But his interest in the clergy and people never ceased until the day of his death. Each year he sent to them his message of Christian affection and regard, accompanied by some useful book suited to the times and circumstances of the Church.

'The remembrances of his visits, his holy influence, and his words of living counsel and warning, were cherished and valued for years after his personal ministrations had ceased.'

During his frequent visits to his son-in-law and daughter, he had many opportunities of renewing intercourse with the patron of the living, Mr. Whitmore of Apley Park, Shropshire, who, with Mrs. Whitmore, had long been within the circle of his attached and valued friends. A touching proof of the steadfastness of his regard for them was given in his last illness, when he mentioned that for thirty years, he had never missed for a day praying for them by name, and for their family. It was then we learned, for the first time, what a long list of friends and relatives had shared the same privilege.

On one of his visits to another country-place in that neighbourhood, the family circle had gathered round him with loving veneration, to ask him questions on scriptural subjects.

A thoughtless man of the world who was present, perhaps hoping to break up the conversation, asked him, in a scoffing manner, a question of much levity concerning the Evil Spirit. Without losing his gentle composure for a moment, and yet with more than his usual dignified seriousness, my father said, 'To some questions one would reply, That is above me. But to this I can only answer, It is *beneath* me.' The questioner was abashed, and withdrew. In the later part of the evening, my father sought him out, and conversed so kindly with him that his heart softened, and he went away impressed by the dignity and tenderness of true holiness.

ON THE KEEPING OF THE LORD'S DAY, ETC.

To the Rev. Peter French.

'BIRMINGHAM, *February* 7, 1834.

'MY DEAR FRIEND,— . . . Now for a long pull, and a strong pull, and a pull altogether in favour of Sir Andrew Agnew's Bill. If it pass, it may be "a lengthening of our tranquillity."

'I hear to-day that our patriarch Biddulph is dangerously ill. His last sermon was upon "Now lettest Thou Thy servant depart in peace." How happy to depart in peace! How honourable still to be in the field of battle! May we fight skilfully and manfully. May the Lord teach our hands to war. Love to you all.—Your ever affectionate, WILLIAM MARSH.'

On the mode of keeping the Lord's Day, his views were at once stringent and liberal. None could make larger or tenderer allowance for the poor, with their six days of weary toil, and especially for those who are shut up in factories, workshops, or alleys. But he argued that to cause hundreds or thousands to work through the seven days alike, with a bare chance of half a Sunday for themselves once in three or four weeks, for the sake of providing change of scene or amusement for others, was unfair, even when viewed only as a matter between man and man; and that, as regarded man and his Maker, it left him no time for prayer to Him, nor chance of 'entering into His courts with praise.' With regard to the habit of railway travelling in particular, on the Sunday, he had ascertained that comparatively few of those who most need recreation, could afford to take it in that form.

In his own home, secular employment was laid aside as by law, but the law was more enforced by his example than by his precept, and perhaps the home of which he was the centre was scarcely a fair specimen of strict Sabbath-keeping. For he rose every Sunday morning with such a fresh spring of spirits, that his hallowed joy seemed to spread to every inhabitant of the house, nor could visitors escape the contagion. At the beginning of the day, he would be singing

> 'Fly abroad, thou mighty gospel,
> Win and conquer, never cease;'

and at the close of the day he was sharing in the joy of angels over sinners repenting; and catching, as it seemed to us, fresh light from the flashing of new jewels just set in the Saviour's crown.

Seldom was the evening closed without his voice being heard in the hymn—

'Thanks we give, and adoration,
For Thy gospel's joyful sound;
May the fruits of Thy salvation
In our hearts and lives abound;
May Thy presence
With us evermore be found.'

Once, when travelling abroad, he had fallen into discussion on the Sunday question, with a learned Professor of a German University. The Professor argued that the views of most English Christians on that subject were legal. My father replied by reading these words from the prophecy of Isaiah:—'If thou turn away thy foot from the Sabbath, from doing thy pleasure on my holy day; and call the Sabbath a delight, the holy of the Lord, honourable; and shalt honour Him, not doing thine own ways, nor finding thine own pleasure, nor speaking thine own words: THEN SHALT THOU DELIGHT THYSELF IN THE LORD.'[1] Closing the book, he said, 'If this be legality, may I be legal!'

'And may I!' added that Christian Professor; 'for the utmost liberty of the gospel can carry me no higher!'

ON IRVINGISM.

'EDGBASTON, *Dec.* 3, 1834.

'MY DEAR FRIEND,— . . . I am now in full controversy with the Irvingites, in consequence of having sent to one

[1] Isa. lviii. 13, 14.

of them the following alternative for prayerful consideration. I should be glad of the opinion of wise and good men on the best means of recovering our erring brethren. To some it is a plausible delusion. They are "beguiled," and know it not.

'*Alternative.*

'If the Spirit of God do not speak by those whom you have joined—

'1. They who affirm that He inspires them to prophesy, commit *a* sin against that Holy Spirit.

'2. They set up another standard than the Oracles of God.

'3. They create another and unnecessary division in the Church.

'4. They cast a stumbling-block in the way of the weak.

'5. They employ their talents and influence in a wrong cause.

'6. When the delusion is discovered, though some will be mercifully restored, others will be driven to infidelity. Therefore they ought to possess evidence as clear as the *various* and *indisputable* miracles of the first age of Christianity, to warrant them in propagating such a system.

'Three of their ministers met me, and we had seven hours' conversation. I have since sent for their consideration ten protests against their scheme. Would you wish to have them? I have long believed it to be a delusion, but I begin to think there is more of the Evil Spirit in it than I supposed. The Lord deliver them from his crafts.'

ON BEREAVEMENT AND CONSOLATION.

To the Honourable Emily Powys.

'BIRMINGHAM, *July* 4, 1835.

'MY DEAR FRIEND,—The paper has just announced your loss, and your dear sister's gain. She is indeed beautified with salvation. In vain our fancy strives to paint the bliss of departed believers. Is it not probable, that in addition to the certainty that their own happiness is eternal, they can see how safely those whom they have left behind will follow them, and thus their joy in the Lord be increased? Oh, what a difference there is between faith and sight! The latter beholds nothing but sickness and weakness, and pain, and death, and corruption—a transitory scene, soon closed. But "faith" sees good in all, and life and incorruption and immortality; and where "sight" views death, faith beholds a present paradise, and eternal glory. And all this, because "Jesus died and rose again." Your dear sister, therefore, is not dead, but sleepeth. She is only gone before to yonder world of light.

"To them we'll follow on,
Leaning on Jesus all the way,
Who now and then lets fall a ray
Of comfort from His throne."

May He send down many such rays into all your hearts; and bring to your minds every alleviating thought, that your spirit may say those tranquillizing words, "It is the Lord," 'the Lord gave, and the Lord hath taken away; blessed be the name of the Lord."

ON THE USE OF MEANS FOR DOING GOOD, IN THE SPIRIT OF PRAYER AND FAITH.

'BIRMINGHAM, 1837.

'WITH respect to the essays called "Mammon" and "Anti-Mammon," I think both are right and both are wrong. The former has used expressions very liable to be misunderstood, and the latter has been too severe, and attributed to the first, sentiments which it neither expresses nor indicates. I think also that the author of "Mammon" is right, *as far as means are concerned, and our duty* also, when he asserts that it is the fault of the Christian Church—its supineness, and want of self-denial and self-sacrifice—that the Gospel has not been proclaimed throughout all the world.

'Money given to God's treasury is nothing—a Bible is nothing—preaching is nothing—sacraments are nothing, IF THE BLESSING BE WITHHELD. Money is everything (in the order of means for procuring agencies, if good); a Bible is everything—preaching is everything—sacraments are everything, if the blessing of Heaven accompany them. And what right have we either to expect the blessing without the means, or to doubt the blessing if we use the means in faith and prayer? Are not both these statements equally correct? I would stand up with Paul for the doctrines of grace. I would stand up with James for the fruits of them.'

ON BOOKS OF THE DAY, AND THE BOOK OF ALL TIME.

To the Same.

'*Feb.* 24, 1838.

'. . . HAVE you seen Mr. Hough's letter to Dr. Wiseman, in answer to his Jesuitical attack on Protestant missions? It is a complete refutation of the former, and a great encouragement to all the friends of the latter. This book, and Dr. Turton's answer to the same author on the Eucharist, seems to be quite unanswerable. Faber's work on Justification makes a good trio with the above.

'But I am reading a book again this year which answers all errors, confirms all truth, reveals all mysteries, administers all comforts, gives all rules, is the friend of all missions, and, like the charity it inculcates, "never faileth." May it be engraven more deeply than ever on my heart.

'I leave you to guess what book it can be.'

ON DIVINE GUIDANCE.

To Miss S. Hooper of Reading.

'*July* 16, 1835.

'ALL hearts are in the hands of Him who is infinite in wisdom and in love. He calls upon us, however, to think as reasonable beings, having prayed to Him for direction, and submitted all to His will. Yea or nay then ends well.'

ON THE ATTENDANCE AT PUBLIC WORSHIP.

To the Same.

'In listening to sermons, you say the benefit seems not so great as formerly. This may sometimes arise from the state of the animal spirits, but may it not also arise from the effect of the novelty of the subject having subsided? I think it a great mercy that the truth and essence of religion do not depend on feelings, but on principle leading to action.

'But though other means may be more enlivening, yet the duty is evident, as an example to others, and also as being the prescribed path for ourselves. And now and then a seed is sown, which afterwards springs up, though we knew not of it at the time. As to past experience of the Lord's goodness in blessing with good, or delivering from evil, the Psalmist often refers to it, and so does the Apostle, and therefore we may derive consolation from it, and be encouraged still to "look again towards His holy temple."'

ON 'IRVINGISM.'

To a Member of his Congregation.

'*March* 5, 1835.

'My dear Friend,—I should not have commenced this year with a clear conscience, if I had not warned my friend H. D. of his danger. That conscience has sometimes smitten me because I have not requested you to warn your cousin, and to take warning yourself. The delusion, into which the followers of poor dear Irving have fallen, is most dangerous. They make the greatest pretensions without authority, and follow the voice of man for the voice of God. They are little aware that they are committing a sin against the Holy Spirit, and are setting up another standard besides the Holy Scriptures. They are also creating an unnecessary division in the Churches of Christ, and are casting another stumbling-block in the way of the world. They bring the truths they do hold into disrepute. And when the delusion is discovered, some of their disciples will probably be driven into infidelity, though others may be mercifully restored.

'. . . On these, and many other grounds, nothing short of *numerous* and *indisputable* miracles should induce any Christians to countenance the system. That they will have many followers I doubt not. They may "deceive the hearts of the simple," and "draw away disciples" for a time; because anything new, strange, or mysterious, or which presents, as Satan presented to Eve, an apparently greater good, will be followed. The holiness of some of the party is no proof of the correctness of this system. They cannot be more holy than Eve was; and yet she was beguiled from the simplicity that is in Christ. You have formerly derived benefit from Mr. D.'s ministry, therefore will naturally wish to think that he cannot be deceived, but I entreat you to weigh the subject well. I pray God to preserve you from that snare. In my view, the risk they run is tremendous. Indeed, I have no doubt that it is a daring attempt on the part of Satan to mislead the Church of God. I do not hesitate to say that they are misinterpreting and misapplying Scripture, and following their own fancies.

'Some have happily been recovered. I pray, and hope, and wait for the dear D——ns, that they may be also. But while in the error, I dare not countenance them.

'Have you seen M'Neile's *Letters*, and Goode on the *Modern Claims to the Gifts of the Spirit?* If not, will you read them if I send them to you?

'You once said, "Warn me." You will therefore not be displeased that I do warn you in the spirit of love, lest your usefulness be drawn from the Church of Christ, and your zeal be expended upon a mere imagination.—Believe me to be, your affectionate pastor, W. MARSH.'

TO SIR THOMAS BARING, WITH REFERENCE TO THE ANNIVERSARY MEETING IN LONDON OF THE JEWS' SOCIETY.

'BIRMINGHAM, *May* 1, 1835.

'... IT is my day of triumph, while I greatly rejoice in all the other anniversaries. But the whole cannot triumph "till the kingdom shall come to the daughter of Jerusalem." How little are Christians aware that hatred or neglect of that people is very displeasing to God; but that kindness shown them meets with His approbation. Then what kindness so great as that which speaks comfortably (to the very heart) to Jerusalem, brings the glad tidings that her Redeemer cometh, that her God reigneth! Many individuals will now believe and be saved, and anon the nation will repent and be restored.'

ON TRUST IN CHRIST.

'BIRMINGHAM, *May* 22, 1835.

'DEAR MRS. WILLIMENT,— . . . You say you were dull and heavy at the Lord's table when you last attended. What a mercy it is that our safety depends not on frames and feelings! True religion consists in principle and practice, not in frames and feelings, however desirable joyful feelings may be. There is however a calm, a peace, which accompanies a simple reliance upon Christ, even when joy may be altogether absent. "Thou wilt keep him in perfect peace whose mind is stayed on Thee, because he trusteth in Thee" (Isa. xxvi. 3).'

MILLENNIAL HOPES.

To the Honourable Emily Powys.

'BIRMINGHAM, *Nov.* 1, 1836.

'MY DEAR FRIEND,— . . . The absence of dear Mr. Biddulph must have excited some strong feelings at the last Jewish meeting. A star indeed has set at Bristol, but the Sun of Righteousness will shine, and that Sun can kindle clods of earth into stars, and that Sun alone can preserve the splendour of any. . . . How many are the devices of the enemy to keep us from our God and Saviour, or to impede our progress and peace! I am forced perpetually to cry out, "Come quickly, come quickly!" So you see I am a determined Millennarian. I have no hope for the Church at large, or the world at large, but in the return of its lawful King. But for this very reason I would be diligent in the preparatory work, and earnestly pray for the increasing success of all missionary work, both among Jews and Gentiles, at home and abroad. . . . With respect to the aspect of the times, we have been delivered from as great, if not greater, dangers, and there is a test that may comfort believers: "It may be ye shall be hid in the day of the Lord's anger." Oh, how gracious and tender is the advice of our redeeming Lord! "Take no thought for the morrow." If we followed His directions, our peace would flow like a river. One reason why I wish to go to heaven is, that I may "follow the Lamb whithersoever He goeth." How often am I in thought, word, or deed going in a different direction! But this we know, that when He shall appear, we shall be like Him; and to be with Him will be heaven indeed.'

The following is addressed to the widow of his brother-in-law, General Chowne (afterwards Lady Dukinfield):—

'WATLINGTON PARK, *June* 14, 1836.

'DEAR MRS. CHOWNE,—I write from the house of mourning. As I had to preach before the University, I could not arrive till Monday.

'Dear Tilson[1] had fallen asleep on Sunday morning. Latterly he could say little more than "MY SAVIOUR!" But how much that contains! You will have heard particulars from our brother James, as he and William Langford have been with him of late. What sympathy and prayer there should be for his dear little orphaned child!

[1] The eldest brother of my mother.

Oh what a scene of desolation this place is now! My heart sinks within me.

'But the thought of the rest of those departed, and the hope of meeting in a world where death is unknown, casts a beam of light upon the surrounding gloom.

'How soon, and to all of us, life will be as a tale that is told. Yet uncertain and short as human life is, and therefore in itself a mere vanity, a vapour that appeareth for a little season and then vanisheth away; yet, I say, how infinitely important as connected with our eternal state!

'I have been making a few remarks at family prayer here this morning, on that comprehensive petition, "So teach us to number our days, that we may apply our hearts unto wisdom." Indeed this needs prayer; we cannot thus apply our hearts without Divine grace. We rest satisfied without religion, or in a mere lifeless form, until taught of God, and influenced by His Spirit. May that Holy Spirit comfort and strengthen you, and lead you daily to the throne of grace for all you need to direct you in time, and to prepare you for a happy eternity. Keep that eternity in view. It will sanctify the trials of time, and by no means diminish the enjoyment of those mercies God bestows.—Ever yours affectionately,

'WM. MARSH.'

CHAPTER VIII.

CORRESPONDENCE.

'The heart of the righteous studieth to answer.'
'The lips of the wise disperse knowledge.'

KING SOLOMON.

CORRESPONDENCE.

TOWARDS the close of the summer of 1837, my father went to Ireland, accompanied by his family, to spend there his usual weeks of recreation. His first visit was to his friends Mr. and Mrs. Bourke, now Lord and Lady Mayo, at Hayes, in county Meath; where the kindly warmth of an Irish welcome made no passing impression on his heart. Owing to the postilion losing his way, and finally entangling the carriage inextricably in the branches of an oak in a wood not far from the house, the travellers arrived on foot, at eleven o'clock at night. As soon as their steps and voices were heard, a shout of welcome from the house roused their slightly depressed spirits, and its echo reaching the nursery, some of the younger children, who had been ordered to bed, as no arrival from England had taken place at a reasonable hour, appeared wrapped in shawls and cloaks, to add to the unforgotten pleasantness of that welcome.

In addition to the enjoyment of Christian intercourse at Hayes, my father was much interested in the asylum, established within the grounds, for persecuted Protestants;

and in meeting with many of the Irish Scripture-readers, whose warm and simple piety delighted him, whilst their cheerful confidence in God, amidst the risk to which their calling perpetually exposed them, in the more bigoted parts of the country, enlisted his heartiest sympathy.

Accompanied by Mr. and Mrs. Bourke and some of their pleasant children, he and his family next visited Lord and Lady Roden, at Tollymore Park; and in their most congenial society he found refreshment to his mind, whilst his health and spirits were recruited by the pure air and beautiful scenery of Tollymore and its neighbourhood. To him—as he listened to the sound of the waterfall, mingled with the breaking of the sea waves on the distant shore—the almost tropical luxuriance of shrubs and foliage, the wooded hills and the barren mountains, had the crowning glory of being the handiwork of One with whom he walked day by day in blessed fellowship. He delighted in claiming the goodness of creation for his 'Master and only Saviour.' 'All things were made by Him, and without Him was not anything made that was made!' he would exultingly exclaim; 'and for Thy pleasure they are and were created,' was the ascription of praise in which he delighted.

He accompanied Lord Roden up the mountains to a little nest of cottages, where he held a meeting every week for reading and prayer: and to the Sunday schools, where my father enjoyed the bright intelligence of the children and the eager manner in which they received religious instruction. An answer given by a little child in one of the Government schools in the neighbourhood was quoted by him, more than once afterwards, as a definition 'worthy of one of the Schoolmen.' A clergyman found the children reading the Douay version of the Testament, and on noticing a passage in the chapter which was translated 'Do penance,' where the English version rendered the same word by 'repent,' he asked them if they knew the difference between penance and repentance? A short silence followed, and then a little girl asked, 'Is it not this, your reverence: Judas did penance, and went and hanged himself; Peter repented, and wept bitterly?'

He was the centre and life of the daily Bible readings, held in the drawing-room, at eleven o'clock, each morning. In the course of one of them he told the story of the blessed change which took place in the views of his old schoolmaster, Dr. Valpy, repeating a verse he had written as his confession of faith, not long before his death. Lord Roden requested my father to write out the lines for him, and then fastened the paper over the mantelpiece in his study. It hangs there still, yellow with age, its firm and legible characters bringing to memory with almost painful vividness the beloved one who traced them.

Some time after Lord Roden had adopted this verse for the motto of his study, one of the old heroes of Waterloo, General Taylor, came to visit him at Tollymore. He had not, at that time, thought much on the subject of religion, and preferred to avoid all discussion of it. But whenever he came into the study, to talk with his friend alone, Lord Roden remarked that the eyes of the old soldier invariably rested for a few moments upon the motto over the mantelpiece. At length he broke the ice by saying,

'Why, general, you will soon know that verse by heart.' 'I know it now, by *heart*,' replied the general, with emphasis and feeling.

From the time of that visit, a change came over his spirit and life. No one who was intimately acquainted with him could doubt its reality. During the following two years he corresponded regularly with Lord Roden about the things which concerned his peace, always concluding his letters by quoting the favourite motto.

At the end of that time, the physician who had attended General Taylor wrote to Lord Roden to say that his friend had departed in peace; and that the last words which fell from his dying lips were those which he had learnt to love in lifetime—

'In peace let me resign my breath,
And Thy salvation see,
My sins deserve eternal death,
But Jesus died for me.'

It happened, in after years, that Lord Roden told this story at the house of a near neighbour. A young relative of the family, an officer in the army who had recently returned from the Crimea, heard it, but turned carelessly away. Some months later, Lord Roden received the intelligence that his young acquaintance was in a rapid decline, and was desirous of seeing him without delay.

As he entered the sick-room, the dying man stretched out both hands to welcome him; at the same moment repeating those simple lines. 'They have been God's message,' he said, 'of peace and comfort to my heart in this illness, when brought to my memory, after days of darkness and distress, by the Holy Ghost the Comforter.'

It had long been my father's custom to take his family, once in the year, for five or six weeks, to travel or visit in some of the loveliest parts of the United Kingdom. No buoyancy of spirits, or power of enjoyment, surpassed his own amongst the happy travellers on these occasions. His delight in nature was intense. 'What beauties are still left in our fallen world!' he remarked one day. 'What then will it not become when the curse shall be uplifted!' But in the midst of his enjoyment, he seemed never to forget to be on the watch for opportunities of doing the work so dear to his heart. However tired with a long day's journey, he made a point of inviting not only the landlord of the hotel and his servants, but also any visitors who were willing, to attend family prayers in his sitting room. The day's fatigues were forgotten in his fervent desire to persuade his hearers to choose those ways of pleasantness and paths of peace for which his own countenance and manner, no less than his words, pleaded so eloquently.

At one time, during an excursion in the northern Highlands, when he spent a couple of days at the little inn of Glengarry, the whole household, and some of the servants' friends, came in for morning and evening prayers. On sending for his bill, he found that no charges were made for a carriage and ponies, of which free use had been made. My father pointed out the omission, but the grateful landlord declined to give any other answer than that it would spoil his pleasure if he might not lend his ponies to the minister who had spoken such good words to him and his household.

On another visit to Scotland, he found that whenever he and his family travelled by the steamboats belonging to a Glasgow company, no payment was accepted. At first he was rather perplexed by the refusal, being so much more in the habit of giving than receiving; but upon further inquiry he found that the head of the firm was one of a large number of guests who used to assemble in his room for family prayers when travelling in Switzerland the year before; and that on hearing of my father's intention of spending a little time at Dunoon, and visiting the Western Highlands, he had generously given orders that all passages on board Burns's steamboats should be free to Dr. Marsh and his family.

The following letter is addressed to the Hon. Emily Powys, at the time of the last illness of the Rev. W. Biddulph:—

'*May* 21, 1838.

'MY DEAR FRIEND,—And is it true that the dear patriarch is dangerously ill? The Church of England never had a more enlightened minister, or the Church of Christ at large a more sincere friend. He will go to his grave, or rather to Paradise, with the blessing of multitudes on his head, but I know also with deep humility in his heart. His religion was of that growth which dear Mr. Simeon described as that which he most desired to possess,—the humility of a penitent prodigal, and the faith of a received child. What a loss he will be! . . .

'I send you my Easter wish. May a dying Saviour's love, a risen Saviour's power, an ascended Saviour's intercession, and a returning Saviour's glory—be the comfort and hope of your heart.'

Extract from a letter written about this period:—

THE WHOLE COUNSEL.

'*March* 11, 1838.

'I FEAR some of our brethren conceive that "the whole counsel of God" consists in preaching election and justification. These are but parts of that astonishing scheme of salvation which exhibits the glory of God. St. Paul applies the expression, in the 20th chapter of the Acts, to "repentance toward God, and faith toward our Lord Jesus Christ." In his Epistle to tho Romans, it is declared fully. But not one of the chapters must be left out. The whole counsel relates to doctrines, and privileges, and duties. He who takes either alone does not preach the whole, and he who does not give each its proper place and proportionate importance, does not speak according to the analogy of faith. May the Spirit be poured upon ministers, from on high, that they may speak "as the oracles of God." May the blessings of the everlasting covenant be richly showered down on you and yours. Lift up your heart for me.'

The following paper was written in answer to questions which had arisen at the daily gatherings of parents, children and guests, for reading the Scriptures, at Chilham Castle, Kent, during one of his visits to his beloved friends, Mr. and Mrs. Wildman; under whose hospitable roof he and his family spent many happy days, in the enjoyment of affectionate and congenial intercourse with that bright family circle:—

'The revealed character of God is that of a merciful Sovereign and a righteous Judge.

'Any favour bestowed on sinful man is an act of sovereign mercy. Any punishment inflicted is only righteous judgment on sin. As to salvation, "Of His mercy He saved us" (Tit. iii.) As to punishment, "Thy way and thy doings have procured this unto thee" (Jer. iv. 18). This is the constant language of the oracles of God. A few (and they are very few) particular passages, which appear to convey other ideas, should be interpreted according to the general tenor of holy writ. For instance, Proverbs xvi. 4, "The Lord hath made all things for himself, even the wicked for the day of evil." The day of evil is the day of war or calamity (see Amos iii. 6). Wicked men are fit instruments for the day of evil (Isa. xxxvii. 26, 27). "The staff in their hand is mine indignation" (Isa. x. 5-7).

'Again, 1 Pet. ii. 8 may be thus understood,—They were appointed to stumble at the Word, being disobedient, or unbelieving; not, they were appointed to that disobedience or unbelief. The passage in Jude (verse 4) declares that they were ungodly men who abused the gospel, and then denied our Lord, who were ordained to the condemnation there referred to; but the expression in the original seems to convey the idea of their being forewritten, as if referring to the prophecies which foretell that in the last times such characters would arise (2 Pet. iii. 2, 3).

'It is worthy also of remark that when St. Paul is speaking, in Rom. ix., of the righteous rejection of the unbelieving Jews, and of the merciful calling of the idolatrous Gentiles, though he would stop the mouth of the man who would reply against God, by asserting God's authority, yet he proceeds to show a reason for the Divine procedure (ver. 22). The vessels of wrath also fitted themselves to destruction, while the vessels of mercy were prepared of God for glory. In the same chapter, when the question is asked, Wherefore Israel did not attain to the law of righteousness? the answer given does not refer to a divine decree, but to their unbelief, "they sought it not by faith."

'We therefore infer from these passages, interpreted according to the analogy of faith, and still more from innumerable other passages, that there is a *sufficiency* in the atonement for all, and that the gospel is to be preached to every creature. No soul, therefore, sensible of its need of mercy, and willing to receive it through Christ, should ever be discouraged under the idea of rejection, but should turn the very doctrine of election into prayer. "Remember me, O Lord, with the favour which thou bearest unto thy people," etc. (Ps. cvi. 4, 5). And no statement can be perfectly scriptural which does not admit the responsibility of man as well as the foreknowledge of God.

'On these subjects men should not reason, but act at God's command. Effort is ours, though the strength be His. The withered arm therefore was stretched out, and behold it was made whole.

'It is very encouraging to observe that no one who believed in our Lord's power was refused a blessing, though His willingness might be doubted. "If thou wilt, *thou canst* make me clean." "I will, be thou clean."

'But when His power was doubted, there was a pause. "If thou *canst* do anything, have compassion on me and help me." "If thou canst believe, all things are possible to him that believeth."

'May we come to Him as sinners, and we shall not be cast out.

'May we serve Him as believers, and our poor services shall be acceptable.

'To Him be glory for ever and ever, Amen.

'Salvation is—of Grace; through Christ; by faith, which worketh by love, and shows itself in obedience.

'We are justified—Freely, by Grace; Meritoriously, by Christ; Instrumentally, by Faith; Evidentially, by Good works.

'God is love, in His own nature. This is proved as—manifested in His works; revealed in His word; exhibited in His Son. By this love may we be constrained to give up ourselves to His service. Amen. (1 John iv. 9, 10, 11, 16.)'

The following letters were written during the latter years of his residence in Birmingham:—

TO A. GORDON, ESQ.

'I HAVE been lately enabled to give comfort to a poor heart or two, by showing that the full assurance of faith, mentioned in Heb. x. 22, is not a peculiar degree of faith as to our own state, but a full confidence in the *sacerdotal work of Christ.* This is the subject the Apostle is discussing. "Having boldness to enter into the holiest by the blood of Jesus." "Having an high priest, let us draw near." Several books have been written on this subject, which might have been spared if the context had been consulted.'

TO H. V. TEBBS, ESQ.

'PERHAPS you have heard of Mr. S—r's case: he has joined the Church of Rome. I do not wonder at it. After some conversation with him, I feared it would be so. . . . Oh what a Church would the Church of Christ even now be, if she would let prophets and apostles speak for themselves, compare diligently their writings with each other, and neither add nor diminish, but have a creed large enough to contain all in its proper place, and small enough to reject even inferences which the Scriptures do not reveal! I believe it will be found at the last that Christianity is a religion of common sense; for is it not common sense to believe what God says, and expect what He promises? But alas! this sense, on the subject of religion at least, is not common to men.'

To the Same.

'Oh what a Friend we have in our Lord and Saviour! His wisdom, His power, His grace, are all exercised in our trials, and comforts, and duties, and concerns, and will be magnified. May our trust in Him more resemble the unchangeableness of His love, which will be the same for ever. It was for us that in human nature He lived, and died, and rose again. For us, He lives at the Father's right hand. For us, He will return. In the faith of it, may we live for Him! "Ye are not your own;" (sad if we were!) "Ye are bought with a price." Then how safe as His property! Therefore glorify Him. Amen, and amen.—Yours affectionately, W. MARSH.'

TO MISS LEYCESTER.

'BIRMINGHAM, *December* 23, 1835.

'MY DEAR COUSIN,—Now for an answer to November queries.

'1. I do not think the two witnesses are slain. No past event seems to fulfil such a silencing of the truth.

'2. I do think the description of Pharaoh and of Sennacherib may be regarded as typical of the destruction of the future antichristian power.

'3. I doubt the accuracy of their views who think all the book of Revelation still remaining to be fulfilled, and I am very jealous of drawing off the attention from that remarkable opposer of truth for so many ages, the Church of Rome. If the Church of Rome be not described in the Revelation, she has imitated, with the utmost accuracy, the character there delineated. And neither Hardman nor De Burgh can fairly answer William Cunningham's *Protestant Interpretation of St. Paul's Prophecy of the Man of Sin.*

'4. You will perhaps be surprised when I say I believe Rev. xiv. 4 refers to converted Jews, and beyond a doubt Rev. vii. 4 does. (The overlooking of the Jewish nation, and of the converted remnant, has occasioned many misinterpretations of Scripture.)

'5. God's people, as citizens in this world, may *taste* of the cup which will be put into the hands of all nations, but *not drink the dregs* thereof. When those dregs are poured forth, God's children will find that their redemption is come.

'6. I think there will be new heavens as well as a new earth, and that the former will rule over the latter, but the mode of reigning, and all particulars, the event alone can declare.

'Accepted in the Beloved, and renewed by the Holy Spirit, may we be found meet for that inheritance. Do not hesitate to ask questions at any time. It is a pleasant occupation to answer them, as far as I can.'

TO HIS DAUGHTER, MRS. KNOX MARSHALL.

'*March* 2, 1836.

'DEAREST DEAR LOU,—. . . . On Sunday morning I took up the subject of evil spirits, from Eph. vi. 12, and in the evening the antidote, from Heb. ii., last verse. To what evil is not that atoning Saviour and sympathizing Friend an antidote? If the law condemn us, He justifies us by His blood; if sin pollute us, He sanctifies us by His Spirit; if Satan tempt us, He succours us by His grace; if the world give us trouble, He gives us peace; if death destroy the body, He raises us triumphant from the grave; if eternity be dark to us, He brings life and immortality to light. Glory be to thee, O Lord! "When Thou hadst overcome the sharpness of death, Thou didst open the kingdom of heaven to all believers. We therefore pray Thee help Thy servants, whom Thou hast redeemed with Thy precious blood. Make them to be numbered with Thy saints in glory everlasting."'

TO MISS LEYCESTER.

'*Tuesday, February* 16, 1836.

'I ADMIRE Mr. S—'s charity. I can exercise it with him to the same extent towards some of the members of the Church of Rome, and approve, as he does, of some sayings from their writers; but neither he nor I would justify the Council of Trent or the Creed of Pope Pius IV., and these are the authorized doctrines of that Church. It is probable the writer from whom he quotes was found fault with. They made the blessed Fénélon and Quesnel, though faithful sons of the Church, to renounce their *Scriptural* principles. In that, their men of power have too much resembled the same class in the Jewish Church, who made "the commandments of God of none effect through their tradition." Mr. S— is a little mistaken about prayers for the dead by the "chosen and *taught* people of God." It is true the Jews did this, but therein they departed from what God had taught them by Moses and the Prophets. There arose a very curious resemblance between the Church of Rome and the Jewish Church, at the time when each had forsaken the simple declaration of Holy Writ.

'There can be no union for the Church of England with the Church of Rome till the points referred to are given up. (But will an *infallible* Church give up anything?)

'See Articles 6, 11, 13, 19, 21, 22, 24, 25, 28, 30, 31, 32, 35. The Homilies are equally opposed to the doctrines of Rome.

'The 6th Article shows that the Church of England does give a right of private judgment. She requires no man to believe what may not be proved by Holy Writ.

'The objection I have to the mode of a sinner's justification, as stated by the Church of Rome, is that it resembles the advice of an architect to build a house partly on a rock and partly on sand.

'The 11th and 12th Articles of the Church of England place faith and works in their proper position.'

To the Same.

'BIRMINGHAM, *March* 18, 1836.

'MY DEAR COUSIN,—The best metaphysical writer I have seen on the points to which you refer is a Dr.

Williams. His book on Equity and Sovereignty gives a view of the Divine character as "a merciful Sovereign and a righteous Judge." Acts of mercy are acts of sovereignty. All punishment is righteous retribution. I like, however, poor Joseph's reasoning: "Jesus Christ came into the world to save sinners. Poor Joseph is a sinner; therefore Jesus Christ came into the world to save poor Joseph."

'I fear many readers would understand dear Dr. Malan as pressing the point of particular redemption. It is a beautiful tract. But if the Holy Scriptures state that point in another way, comfort should not be communicated in this form.

'As a whole, the tract is admirably calculated to reach some hearts; but it appears to me that many weak believers would be discouraged by it. The first thing for a convinced sinner is not to ascertain that he is elect of God, but that there is salvation for him, however great his sinfulness, in the work of Jesus Christ. Then, that God hath given eternal life as certainly in Christ as He gave natural life in Adam; and that this eternal life is the portion of every believer. I rest upon this truth; I am a believer; I am saved; I will love my Deliverer, and live to Him. But the idea that the atonement is only sufficient for a limited number, would create insuperable doubts in some minds that ought not to doubt. The great question however is, What saith the Scripture? Why, the Scripture saith *both*—He loved the *Church*;[1] He loved the *world*;[2] and that "*whosoever* believeth in Him shall not perish but have everlasting life." The latter draws

[1] Eph. v. 25. [2] John iii. 16.

the unconverted; the former establishes the man who knows himself to be a believer. We must therefore preach both,—the *sufficiency* for all, the *efficiency* for the believer. I think, therefore, as Malan dwells on one of these views, only a little explanation in a note or two, or the omission of certain expressions, is required. What think you of this? The inspired writers never treat these subjects metaphysically, or, I had well nigh said, theologically, but in a consolatory, experimental, and practical way; not in so exact a manner as some divines would write.'

To the Same.

'BIRMINGHAM, *May* 3, 1836.

'MY DEAR COUSIN,—The Easter work has so filled my hands, that I have long delayed answering yours of the 4th of April, though I wished to do it sooner.

'Ask your friend if Deut. xxviii. do not include the present dispersion of the Jews. If so, Deut. xxx. 1-6 must refer to their future restoration, not to that from Babylon. Moreover, only about 40,000 returned from Babylon, with 7000 stragglers of the ten tribes, but not one whole tribe of the ten. Would such a restoration fulfil the glowing language of the prophet? Isa. xi. and lxii.; Jerem. xxxi. and xxxii. 26-41; Ezek. xxxvii. (The 37th of Ezekiel does not belong to the Christian Church; and Isa. lxii. 11 calls upon the Christian Church to do her duty towards the Jews.) If Zion be the spiritual Church, who is intended by "Say YE to the daughter of Zion, Behold, thy salvation cometh"?

'The God of all grace may do above all that we ask or think, or *more* than He has promised in His word; but He will never do *less*.

'Let your friend consider also what a poor thing was the deliverance from Babylon, as far as the Jews as a nation were concerned.

'It was immensely important with reference to the tribe of Judah and the coming of Messiah. But the *nation* saw little prosperity. The 150 years under the Maccabees were passed sword in hand. Then they kept declining till the Romans came and took away their place and nation, and they have been eighteen centuries in captivity since. The real fact is, that some of the prophecies, even the latter prophecies in Isaiah, do not refer to the Babylonish captivity at all. They refer to *gospel times*, and to a restoration of the Jews *after those times*. But there is a veil upon the Gentile Church on these subjects, as much as there was on the Jewish Church, with reference to the coming in of the Gentiles. The Gentile Church, however, is happily opening her eyes with reference to present duty toward the Jews as sinners perishing in unbelief; and it is well she begins to rise to her duty, for she has been guilty of a great omission of it. I have asked for a turn in the University pulpit that I may state my views on this subject. If they be correct, our sin will be great as a Church, should we continue indifferent to the subject.

'The covenants are forgotten. There was a *national* covenant with Abraham, a *regal* covenant with David, and a *covenant of grace* with both Jews and Gentiles.

The former are not set aside by the last, as to the Jews; but, happily, we Gentiles are included in the last, which is for eternity. The very name of Israel is kept distinct even in the New Testament (Gal. vi.) Who are described by "*them*," as distinguished from the Israel of God? Certainly the believing Gentiles. With any of the peculiarities of the Jewish nation the Gentiles have nothing to do. This is the Apostle's argument. And peace will be upon them, and mercy, without Jewish ceremonies (Gal. ii. 14). But the Jews, as children of Abraham, may retain Abrahamic distinctions without acting contrary to the gospel of Christ. The apostles did so, and the primitive Jewish believers (Acts xxi. 20-26).

'It was not necessary for Malachi to speak on these points. But are we sure that Mal. iv. 1-3 has been fulfilled, and that the fifth verse is the same coming of Elijah as that mentioned in chap. iii. 1? I am not.

To the Same.

'*July* 8, 1837.

'The absolution in the Visitation of the Sick is not a whit stronger than John xx. 21-23. I think not so strong; because our Church requires first such a confession of faith as will prove the person to be in a state of acceptance, and therefore pardon may be absolutely pronounced in the name of the Lord. At first sight, John xx. 21-23 may appear to have no limitation; but the fact is that our Lord had limited it to penitent believers (Luke xxiv. 47; Acts ii. 30; iii. 19). Our general service opens with a declaratory absolution. The service for the sick and dying *penitent believer* is absolute, and not without cause. *But the power is not in the priest.* After all, it must be declaratory or conditional in his mind. That is, he can only pronounce it on the persuasion or evidence he possesses of the Christian state of the individual. But the Church of Rome conveys the idea of saving power in the priest. This is a crafty and wicked device, and whoever believes it is miserably deceived. Mr. —— would not say that no man can be pardoned who is not absolved by a priest. We cannot follow Scripture too closely; but, off that ground, Protestants should be very jealous. Their Master's glory and the Church's true peace are concerned.

To the Same.

'BIRMINGHAM, *June* 10, 1839.

'HAS —— entirely joined the Plymouth Brethren? Oh that Christians would but learn that true religion consists in principle leading to practice, rather than in excitement; and that it is a perfectly rational as well as spiritual service. It is like the sun, sending forth light and heat without noise. It is like the moon, reflecting the light of the sun without noise.

'I confess, when I think of Cranmer, Latimer, Ridley, and Hooper, and then put —— on the other side,—or when I think of Romaine, Venn, Cadogan, and Biddulph, and put —— and —— on the other side; or when I think of Episcopalians, Presbyterians, Independents, and Wesleyans, and then think of a *new* church to be formed, I cannot but feel that those who are forming it require *very strong* proof of a divine call so to do. Oh for the time when in mind and heart all will be one! But the Jews must be converted first.'

TO A WIDOWED FRIEND.

'DEAR MRS. C.,—What shall I say to comfort you? I have just heard of the deep sorrow to which you are called. It is the Lord. His ways are all in wisdom, and righteousness, and love. Submission is therefore our duty and our privilege. Nevertheless, submission does not mean want of feeling. We are intended to feel. We may sorrow. We cannot but grieve. And over the death of a friend even "Jesus wept." Time only can so far heal the wound as to relieve its piercing smart. Such is the will of God. I pray Him to communicate to your mind every alleviating and consoling thought. May we all learn from these events the deep importance of being prepared for our great change. "So teach us to number our days that we may apply our hearts unto wisdom," is a suitable petition for each day of our lives. And our Heavenly Father will hear it, and will sanctify his providences, as well as His ordinances, to that great end.

'Your letter contains a question I must immediately answer. "Need I doubt his happiness?" No. The Christian rule is to be anxious for the living, that they may afford every evidence of a renewed state; but always to be hopeful for the dead. It is not for us to judge, even in very doubtful cases. God only knows the heart. But where there has been "the fear of God," and "the faith of

Christ," why need we doubt? We also are bound to make allowances for early habits and associations, and circumstances under which persons are placed, and not to expect equal degrees of spirituality from all.

'The house of mourning is always painful, but it is often very profitable. It is difficult to realize the change for eternity till it comes very near us. But to be prepared for that change should doubtless be the principal object of life. Nor is this any impediment to true pleasure. I never knew real peace till I became acquainted with the way of salvation by Jesus Christ, and could approach God as a Father.

'In our fallen nature, and in our thoughtless world, no doubt there are difficulties, but our Heavenly Father will give the Holy Spirit to them that ask Him, by whose grace the warfare may be maintained until the victory be won.'

In the course of the year 1838, a gradual failure of health forced upon my father the conviction that he would no longer have strength to fulfil the arduous duties of his post at Birmingham. The effort of preaching twice on each Sunday to a congregation of about 2200 people, in addition to two week-day services in the church, and the manifold duties involved in the charge of a parish numbering 18,000 souls, began to tell seriously upon him. His eyesight also became affected, partly from the general strain upon his nervous powers, and partly from his habit of pursuing to a late hour of the night those studies which he could not make up his mind to forego, and which the multiplicity of his engagements left him little time for, by day. Thus the necessity was admitted of seeking a smaller charge, though it could not be without much pain that he contemplated severing the ties that bound him to that most animating and engrossing sphere; and to the circle of friends with whom he and his family had frequent and agreeable intercourse. Foremost amongst those friends might be named his kind and skilful physician, Dr. Birt Davies, whose venerable Christian mother and delightful sisters had been amongst the first to welcome him as a pastor; his valued friend and churchwarden Mr. Chance and his admirable wife, whose intelligent and pleasant family were always amongst the most welcome of the young guests at my father's house.

It was not with less pain that his congregation learnt that there was a prospect of parting with their beloved rector. Warmly did they urge him to reconsider his decision, offering to secure to him £1000 a year, to enable him to provide the fullest clerical assistance, that he might himself take a lighter share in the duty. He listened gratefully and affectionately to their pleading; and although he had little hope of ever again being able to fulfil, as he would desire, the duties of such a parish, he consented to try, before finally relinquishing the charge, what a lengthened season of comparative rest would do for him. For this purpose he removed to Leamington Spa, in the same county, in the month of July 1839.

With the assistance of a few friends, he had built a church there, in order to meet the need of a rapidly increasing population: and to secure to that town, as far as human means could, the preaching of the gospel of Christ in its simplicity and fulness, he vested the advowson in the hands of carefully selected trustees. He removed to Leamington in time to be present at the consecration of this church. It was at first held by his son, who had previously been ordained to his curacy in Birmingham, and who had delighted him by preaching the truth clearly and ably in his pulpit. My father for a time retained St. Thomas's, no less by the desire of his parishioners than by that of his diocesan. It need scarcely be added that he placed the church and parish in the hands of excellent substitutes, until his decision was finally made to resign it.

CHAPTER IX.

LIFE IN LEAMINGTON.

'COME as a teacher sent from God,
  Charged His whole counsel to declare;
Lift o'er our ranks the prophet's rod,
  While we uphold thy hands in prayer.

Come as a angel, hence to guide
  A band of pilgrims on their way;
That safely walking at thy side,
  We fail not, faint not, turn nor stray.'

JAMES MONTGOMERY.

LIFE IN LEAMINGTON.

No sooner had my father arrived in Leamington than he was sent for to visit a dying lady. Her husband had brought her thither in the fond hope that the skill of its celebrated physician might yet rally her sinking health. But it proved to be only to learn that her case was hopeless. Still young and beautiful, with everything that this life could give to make her happy, and without any definite idea of how to find acceptance with God, it was not wonderful that she dreaded the approach of death.

As the unknown pastor, whose visit she had desired, entered the room, her sweet dying face turned towards him with an anxious, inquiring expression; and it was a beautiful picture to see him standing by her side, 'looking,' as she said afterwards, 'as if he were "an angel sent to speak unto her, and to show her these glad tidings," and what those friends would be like who would be sent to carry her home.' Whilst he remained there 'preaching peace by Jesus Christ,' no parched ground ever drank in refreshing showers more readily than that thirsting soul received a draught from the fountain of living water. Before the interview was concluded, she had seen and believed that she was 'accepted in the Beloved.'

On the following day he gladly granted her request, that he would administer to her the Sacrament of the Lord's Supper; in his brief address beforehand, helping her to see clearly with what holy thankfulness she had the right, as a believer in the sacrifice made on the Cross, to receive the memorials of that sacred body broken and blood shed for her. Before the next day's sun arose, she had passed away in humble and peaceful trust, from a world of shadows and symbols to the world of realities, and of joys that never fade, in the presence of Him 'that liveth and was dead, and is alive for evermore.'

During the twelve years of his residence in Leamington, a series of deep and hallowed interests, such as the foregoing, were given him in visiting the numerous invalids who were brought thither, as a last resource; or for mitigation of their sufferings, if hope of recovery were vain. Amongst several who are remembered, as having distinctly spoken of him as the means of bringing them to their God, were General Hunter Blair, and a young daughter of Lady Catherine Bernard.

It would be difficult to say which remembrance is the more affecting; that of the gallant veteran, taking his place with the humility and love of a little child, and the penitence of a pardoned sinner, at the Saviour's feet; or the passing from agonizing doubts and fears, of the lovely Margaret Bernard, into a foretaste of the raptures of the glorified, as she triumphantly sang the praises of her Redeemer, whilst passing through the valley of the shadow of death.

Although his work in Leamington was on a smaller scale than that in Birmingham, and therefore was more within the compass of advancing years, his time was still fully occupied; and the duties connected with the district, shortly afterwards formed into a separate parish, were fulfilled with his usual energy, whilst he also took a general interest in the welfare of the town, and in the promotion of every good cause.

On the 21st of April 1840, Dr. Marsh married the youngest daughter of the Earl Cadogan; thus linking himself afresh to the associations of his early days at Reading, which still shed their hallowed lustre over his life.

Like her sainted brother, Lady Louisa Cadogan united to clear views of salvation through Christ alone, an earnest, prayerful, and watchful spirit, with fervent desires for entire consecration to her God. Blended with this devoted piety was a nature of no common charm. The transparency and truthfulness of a little child were mingled with quickness of penetration, delicate tact, and playful humour. Her memory was so retentive, that it made its own the most amusing, or the most striking points in the character and history of the many remarkable persons with whom she had been thrown. Her powers of conversation, added to the freshness about her winning manners, might have proved a gift as ensnaring as it was delightful, had she not laid it, with all she possessed, at the feet of her

Saviour, to be used by Him as should best promote His honour, and serve the interests of His kingdom.

Amongst many pleasant friendships into which my father was brought by this marriage, was that of his brother-in-law, the Honourable and Reverend Dr. Gerald Wellesley: an intimacy which ripened with increasing similarity of religious feelings, until his death, and was also cemented by frequent and most affectionate intercourse with one of Dr. Wellesley's daughters, who, with her husband, the Rev. George St. Quintin, was frequently at his house, and ever regarded by him with tender esteem. The following extracts from a letter of Mrs. St. Quintin's, written after he had been taken from us, show her appreciation of his character:—

'May God help you to lift up your eyes and see, as it were, that buoyant and joyous spirit enter into the fulness of that Presence which, more than any one I ever knew, he seemed to delight in, here on earth. He was one of the very few to whom Christ seemed so precious, that he could enjoy nothing thoroughly unless he felt He was present with him. It seems presumptuous to speak as if he had wholly rested from sin here, and yet to us it appeared as if he had—as if his spirit had become so one with his Lord that ere he left the earth he had entered into the rest which remaineth for the people of God.'

Amongst Lady Louisa's most intimate friends were a few with whom he was brought frequently into contact, and to whom he especially attached himself,—Mrs. Kingsley, the wife of the rector of Chelsea, Mrs. Courtenay

Thorpe, the Misses Waldegrave, sisters of the late Lord Radstock, Lady Henrietta Fergusson, and her daughter, afterwards Mrs. Bruce of Kennet, who, from the time of her first visit to Leamington, was regarded by him, to the end of his life, with fatherly affection.

Mrs. Kingsley loved to lay aside the burden and the cares of a large metropolitan parish and to come to the more quiet yet ever cheerful home of her friend at Leamington. She was accompanied at one time, on a visit of some weeks' duration, by her eldest son, then a youth at college, whose high mental gifts, force of character, and generous nature made him a most welcome guest to all at Lansdowne House, and attracted my father's interest in no common degree.

It so happened that they met no more, save for one brief interview, in after years; but that length of absence and difference of view have not lessened Mr. Kingsley's respectful admiration of him, may be gathered from the following extract from a letter, written more than twenty years afterwards:—

'I recollect him now—a man who had been peculiarly graceful and handsome; tall, delicate-featured, with the air noble of the old *régime;* with a voice and manner full of suavity, even to tenderness, which you felt to be sincere, from the earnestness of the voice and the honesty of the eye. Belonging to the old evangelical school, to which all later schools owe their vitality, he seemed to me no bigot, but ready to welcome, or at least patiently to hear, novel thoughts, which did not interfere with fundamental truth.

'He belonged, in thought as well as in manner, to a

class of ministers which is growing, alas! more rare among us; he fulfilled rather my notion of what the purest German evangelicals of the last century must have been like, —those who, with Spener and Franke, re-awakened vital Christianity among a dry and dead generation, given up to the letter of Lutheranism and forgetful of its spirit.

'In his goodness, there was no severity; on the contrary, a gentle benignity, which made his presence always a source of happiness to his relatives and friends.'

In the autumn of 1840, my father took his family for change of air to Malvern, where they were joined by his married daughters and the infant children of Mrs. Knox Marshall. The whole party arrived at the end of the week; and on Sunday morning they attended service in the fine old parish church, which was so crowded that they were separated in finding seats. For a time he stood in the aisle with one of his daughters, when a lady in a large pew noticed his venerable appearance, and sent to offer seats. As he entered, another lady, accompanied by a little boy, also came in. Before the service began, her eyes rested intently on my father's face, then tears gathered, and at last she said to his daughter, with much emotion, 'Is not that gentleman Dr. Marsh? May I speak to him after the service is over?'

The opportunity was, of course, afforded her, as the congregation went out of church; and she told him that, although no rumour had reached her of his having come to Malvern, she had dreamt the night before (and had mentioned it to her husband at breakfast), 'that she had gone into a church where she was placed in the same pew with Dr. Marsh. And in my dream,' she added, 'you spoke words which comforted my soul. Deeply do I need such comfort.'

Struck by the coincidence, which looked like a providential direction, and by the troubled earnestness of her manner, he, after a short conversation, invited her to join his family worship at the close of the day.

She came half an hour before the time, and asked to see him alone. She then told him, that eight years previously she had heard him speak at a meeting for the British and Foreign Bible Society at Walsall, in Staffordshire. Some words which he had spoken about the blessedness of diligently studying the Scriptures every day, had then taken possession of her heart, and she began that study earnestly; but after a time, her husband, an officer in the army, had taken her to Italy, where they occupied themselves entirely with gaiety and amusements. 'I forgot my Bible!' she exclaimed in an agony of remorse; 'I forgot my God! and now He has forgotten me, and I am lost!'

Then was the dearest of all joys granted him,—to persuade a wandering sheep that the Saviour of the lost had come to seek and to save *her*,—to persuade a broken and contrite heart that One stood at the door and knocked,—saying, 'If any man hear my voice, and open the door, I will come in to him and sup with him, and he with Me.'

These words of comfort sank deeply into that troubled heart. At family prayers, my father read 2 Cor. v.;

and when touching on the words, 'We must all appear before the judgment-seat of Christ,' he suddenly broke off, and said, 'Behold an Advocate with the Father! —our Advocate—Jesus Christ the righteous; pleading that in His own person is the propitiation for our sins; pointing to the one sacrifice once offered for the sins of the whole world, before He sat down at the right hand of God. Behold Him well! Then, when you see His face upon the judgment-throne, and recognise your Advocate,—oh thou of little faith, wherefore shouldst thou doubt?'

After family worship was ended, she said fervently, 'God reward you, Dr. Marsh! This will be a memorable day in my life.'

Four days afterwards she died.

She left Malvern on Monday, caught cold on her journey, which turned to a fatal attack of inflammation of the throat. She was delirious during the greater part of those days; but in more than one lucid interval she was heard to say, 'I should have died in misery, but for what Dr. Marsh told me on Sunday night at Malvern. But he led me to my Saviour; and now that Saviour is with me, and I fear no evil—for He has saved me!'

'In the morning sow thy seed, and in the evening withhold not thy hand; for thou knowest not which shall prosper, this or that, or whether both shall be alike good.'

Towards the close of this year, the dimness which had betokened serious injury to his sight for some time past, was discovered to be cataract; but it was found necessary to postpone the operation requisite for the restoration of sight, for another twelvemonth. In the interim of increasing darkness, his cheerfulness was unabated. His step scarcely lost its buoyancy; nor did his natural independence, which led him often to walk about the immediate neighbourhood of his house by himself, ever bring him into trouble. There was nothing about him suggestive of blindness; the sweet and sunshiny smile came as readily as ever; and his acuteness of hearing and delicacy of touch prevented him from meeting with the small accidents which often occur under such circumstances. Once only, he met with a slight *contretemps*, which, however, resulted in a pleasant renewal of old acquaintanceship. Leaving a bookseller's shop before the rest of his party, he stepped by mistake into a stranger's carriage; but, on discovering the blunder, made himself so charming to the young people whom he found there, that, on the return of their mother, who proved to be an old friend just arrived in Leamington, it became a doubtful matter whether he was to be restored to his own family or not.

Throughout this year of darkness, he regularly continued to perform his public ministrations. From his long familiarity with the words he loved so well, he was able on occasion to go through the whole service of morning or evening prayer; and constantly took the chief part in the administration of the Lord's Supper. And never was his preaching more clear, consecutive, and beautiful than it continued to be during these days of blindness.

At length he was considered to be ready for the operation, which was performed in the month of November 1841, at a house which he took for the purpose, in Albemarle Street. He had placed himself in the hands of the celebrated oculist of that day, Mr. Alexander. On the day before the cataract was removed, one of his daughters read to him the story of the blind man, to whom it was said, 'According to thy faith be it unto thee;' and reverently inquired, 'Have you faith that your sight will be restored, beloved father?' He paused for a moment, and then replied, 'I leave sight and health with perfect peace in this assurance—THE ONLY WISE GOD!'

He walked into the room where the operation was to be performed without the slightest appearance of nervousness, and, pointing to his eyes, said, 'I have brought two *pupils* for a tutor.' Then he gently declined the proposal of the assistant to tie his hands according to the usual practice, saying, 'I think you will find it to be unnecessary; although, if I *should* tremble, I shall not be the first person who has quaked before an *Alexander*.'

So calmly and cheerfully did he undergo an operation by which he incurred the risk of total blindness, that he won the entire admiration of the skilful operator under whose hands he had placed himself. 'I could not bear giving him any pain, or chancing the loss of his sight,' he said afterwards. 'It was as bad as having to do it for an infant. He is as sweet as a child, and yet so wise and good.'

But it was not alone the composure and brightness of his patient's spirit which won Mr. Alexander's regard.

My father's sympathy and consideration had had its share. He had postponed, for some weeks, the time previously arranged for the operation, at considerable inconvenience to himself, in order to set Mr. Alexander free to attend upon a beloved son who was dangerously ill at Brighton.

Owing to the peculiarly delicate nervous structure of his eyes, the success of the operation remained for some days extremely doubtful. When at length it was time for the bandage to be removed, he was placed by Mr. Alexander with his back to a window, and the light was rather suddenly admitted. 'Now, sir,' inquired the anxious oculist, 'what have you to tell us?'

There was a pause for a moment, which seemed long to those whose hearts were trembling between hope and fear; and then fell the solemn yet joyful music of their father's words upon their ears, 'Thank God, I see!'

But the joy of returning sight was to be checked for a time by severe illness. Inflammation of the optic nerve set in, threatening to affect the brain. It was the opinion of Mr. Alexander that only the singular self-control of his patient, and the perfect peace in which his mind was kept, preserved the sight and warded off the danger, under the blessing of God.

For many nights he could only obtain even the short relief of an hour's sleep, by listening to the reading of the Bible in a low voice. The last chapter was read through, from beginning to end. Well does one of his children remember, after she had closed the New Testament, saying, 'What can we do now that our book has come to an end?' the characteristic playfulness of his reply—'Send to Hatchard's for a second volume!'

His animated delight in listening to the Word of God, and the beautiful thoughts which it elicited from him, made those vigils far more precious than repose to the watchers by his side. Yet was he ever on the alert to persuade them to rest. In sickness as in health, self seemed to have no place in his thoughts.

When, at the end of several weeks, he recovered and returned to Leamington to resume his duties, Mr. Alexander expressed a wish to be present at his first sermon, and came down to spend the Sunday with him. The sermon was preached from the story of the blind man in Luke xviii. 41-43, 'What wilt thou that I shall do unto thee? Lord, that I may receive my sight.'

Mr. Alexander was deeply impressed by it, and towards the close of his life he wrote that neither had the precious truths taught in that sermon been forgotten, nor the lessons of Christian faith and love which he had learnt whilst his patient was under his care. They had led him up, he added, to the Fountain of that goodness which he had so truly admired and appreciated.

My father's return to Leamington, with restored sight, was to him an occasion of renewing the consecration of every power to his Redeemer's glory. With fresh zest he not only entered upon all his former plans and duties, but also added new ones; and whenever they were such as a wife could share, Lady Louisa was his ready helpmeet.

Her large family connexion and numerous friendships

brought many influential persons within reach of his hallowed influence; and by not a few since that time has the testimony been borne, that at his house they first learnt the way of peace.

His hospitality continued to be on its old scale of liberal simplicity. Many may still remember the charm of the quiet social evenings at that pleasant home in Leamington. Lady Louisa retained the loveliness of voice for which she had been remarkable in her youth; but now she exercised it chiefly in singing sacred melodies. The soul she threw into the words she sang has often moved to tears the little circle of friends around her.

But perhaps the chief interest of those evenings was found in the play of animated conversation, elevated to the highest subjects with so much tact and grace that no strain was felt, even by those to whom the turn it took was a new thing. Lady Louisa's chief aim, in the success of which she was singularly happy, was to call forth the powers of her husband's mind, for the benefit of those whom she had brought under his influence. It would be impossible to put into words the peculiar charm of his conversation. There mingled with the stores derived from his incessant reading in almost every branch of literature, a certain flexibility of thought, which could turn from the gay to the grave without effort, and then again would relieve the strain of prolonged religious conversation by some ready illustration, pointed anecdote, and touches of holy playfulness, which his profound reverence for sacred themes preserved from being ever out of season. They sparkled like sunlight upon the sea, relieving the depths of feeling which lay below. His talent for calling forth the information and intelligence of his more gifted guests was scarcely so much to be admired as his unwearying patience in listening to the most prosaic talker, the benevolence of his nature enabling him to take a real pleasure in that which gave pleasure to the speaker.

The evenings at Lansdowne House were invariably concluded by family worship at ten o'clock. This was commenced with a hymn, after which my father read and explained a portion of Scripture, and concluded by short, fervent, world-embracing supplications, holy aspirations, and most humble and hearty thanksgivings, which none who were privileged to hear could lightly forget.

At this time he had morning service in St. Mary's once in the week, and an evening service in the school-room. Throughout Lent there were morning services on Wednesday and Friday, and on every day in Passion week. True to his old principle, each service was followed by a short sermon; and the week of fasts was indeed a 'week of feasts' to the members of his congregation.

None could more vividly realize than he, the facts of Gospel history; and during Passion week he lived amidst the sacred scenes brought before him, in an especial manner, by the services of the Church at that season. He sorrowed in Gethsemane, he mourned at Calvary, he felt a relief in a sense of the quiet of the grave on the day following the burial; but not less by natural temperament than by religious faith, his imagination passed with a bound, after the painful sympathies of the week, 'through the grave and gate of death,' to a joyful resurrection. It was by an evident restraint upon himself that he closed Easter even's reading without forestalling the glories of Easter Day. And when set free for the 'kindred rapture' of that 'day of days,' with the dawn of the morning he awoke to read the narratives told by the four Evangelists of that event, the tidings of which must have rolled fresh waves of happiness across the universe, and have caused the morning stars to sing for joy—

> 'Captivity is captive led,
> For Jesus liveth—that was dead.'

Easter Day was scarcely long enough for all my father found to go through, in its course. He walked with the women to the garden where the grave lay; he stood with one who lingered weeping by the empty tomb, and listened with her to the thrilling tones of the voice which carried in a tide of joy upon her soul, with the one word, 'Mary!'

He met his children every Easter morning with the customary salutation of the early Christians—illuminating his face, as well as uttered by his lips—'He is risen, HE IS RISEN!' It is needless to say that his sermons on that day caught the same strain. 'The Resurrection, as the keystone of the arch of our Faith,' was the subject, first, of substantial evidence, then of eloquent description and triumphant exultation. No preaching of his ever rose so high as those Easter-day celebrations of the conquest of death and the grave.

When wearied at night, he loved to listen to Cowper's paraphrase of the walk to Emmaus, and to dwell upon the subject of the two disciples' converse; and on the gracious condescension and heavenly tenderness of the Friend, who drew near, and went with them on that blessed evening of the first 'Lord's day.'

Easter Sunday was invariably closed with the hymn which best expressed the overflowing of his thankful heart for the blessing it commemorated, and the blessing it promised :—

'LOVE's redeeming work is done,
Fought the fight, the battle won!
Lo, our sun's eclipse is o'er;
Lo, He sets in blood no more!

Vain the stone, the watch, the seal,
Christ hath burst the gates of hell;
Death in vain forbids his rise—
Christ hath opened Paradise.

Lives again—our glorious King;
Where, O death! is now thy sting?
Once he died—our souls to save,
Where 's thy victory, boasting grave?

Soar we now where Christ hath led,
Following our exalted Head;
Made like Him, like Him we rise—!
Ours the cross, the grave, the skies!'

The near neighbourhood of Leamington to Rugby brought my father acquainted with Dr. Arnold's remarkable work amongst the boys of the school which he rendered so celebrated. Deeply did my father regret that he had not earlier known him. They met but once; and differing upon some points as they did, it was but the lovelier to see how their hearts sprang to meet each other —drawn by the mutual sympathy of their noble natures, and by the yet stronger attraction of love to the Saviour. The academic and the pastor not merely discovered enough of common ground for cordial intercourse, but each entered with keen interest upon the subjects of the other's field of duty; and both again rejoiced together in the prospect of employment being granted as a reward by that Master whose 'servants shall serve Him,' whilst they 'see His face.'

A few years later, when my father had read with his family Mr. Stanley's record of his friend's life and character, as he closed the book he said, with tears filling his eyes, 'I am like those boys of Arnold's—I know not how to bear his loss!'[1] The impression upon his mind, after reading that beautiful biography, was (as he expressed it), that 'Dr. Arnold was evangelical without knowing it; and that he disliked evangelicals because he did not know them.'[2]

[1] When the news of Arnold's death reached Leamington, my father was standing at the door of Lansdowne House, watching two of his children mount to ride with friends to the ruins of Kenilworth Castle. Two Rugby boys—one of whom has since met with the reward of merit and talent in high position in India—the other with the guerdon of the brave—a soldier's death, were to have been of the party; but when those heavy tidings reached them they went away sorrowing, and were seen no more that day. My father's tender nature was melted by their grief,—whilst at the same time he felt its cause to be no less than a public calamity.

[2] Possibly Dr. Arnold might have come in contact with some of the narrower and more unreal, who might be found in any party.

Well were they agreed in the painful apprehension that, in the nineteenth century, the battle of the Reformation would have to be fought over again. They held alike that the belief in the necessity of a 'succession' lay at the root of the errors already corrupting a large body in the Church; involving, as it does, the invalidity of the sacraments as administered by the Presbyterian, Lutheran, and other Churches; and carrying with it the doctrine of a priestly and mediatorial power.

My father felt the full value of the noble protests against the sacerdotal system, borne by Arnold in letters cclviii., cclxxiii., and others, in Vol. II. of the Life and Correspondence, in which such passages occur as the following:—'That the Church system, or rather the priest system, is not to be found in Scripture, is as certain as that the worship of Jupiter is not the doctrine of the gospel.' . . . 'That the great enemy should have turned his very defeat into his greatest victory, and have converted the spiritual self-sacrifice, in which each man was his own priest [explained above as 'the spiritual sacrifice of each man's self to God'], into the carnal and lying sacrifice of the mass, is, to my mind, more than anything else, the exact fulfilment of the apostolical language concerning antichrist.' And again (in Letter cclxxiv.), 'Now that the two systems are set front to front, I do not think that a middle course is possible. The priest is either Christ or Antichrist. He is either our mediator, or he is like the man of sin in God's temple. The church system is either our gospel, and St. John's and St. Paul's gospel is superseded by it, or it is a system of blasphemous falsehood, such as St. Paul foretold was to come—such as St. John saw to be "already in the world."'

Often has my father referred to Dr. Arnold's delight in the book so dear to himself, *The Pilgrim's Progress;* and especially to the anecdote of his being unable to trust himself to read aloud that exquisite passage which describes Christian and Hopeful, as they pass through the river up to the Celestial City; and in his own last illness he quoted those words of Arnold's, which seemed a presage of the nearness of his Lord's call to him, that 'within the last few days he had felt quite a rush of love in his heart to God and Christ.'

With the distinctness of Dr. Arnold's view of all blessings coming to us through our Lord Jesus Christ, especially as shown in the journals of his last few weeks, he had a strong sympathy. It was one of his own sayings, that whilst the mercy of God was like the light scattered throughout the universe, that light, for our world, is all concentrated in the sun; so God's mercy is all gathered up for us in Christ Jesus, 'the brightness of His glory.'

In the early part of my father's life at Leamington, the Honourable and Reverend Montagu Villiers, then vicar of Kenilworth, afterwards bishop of Durham, formed an almost filial attachment to him. He was by my father's side at every anniversary meeting for a religious society, and frequently sought both his public instructions, and private counsel and prayers. In after life he used to refer to him as 'his father in Christ.'

The happy temperament, and frank, genial nature of the younger man were peculiarly attractive to the elder, and their friendship continued to be cultivated even when their paths had diverged. On almost every visit to London my father was Mr. Villiers' guest, and delighted in seeing something of his untiring labours in his large London parish, and his fearless faithfulness in the cause of truth. Nor did he hear less thankfully of his apostolic manner of using his episcopate at Carlisle; preaching in the open air, visiting from cottage to cottage, praying with the dying, exhorting the living, elevating to a wonderful degree the tone of morality amongst the working classes in the neighbourhood; besides throwing open his house to the younger clergy, and especially to the candidates for holy orders.

When Bishop Villiers had been promoted to Durham, and a storm of public opinion was directed against the appointment of his son-in-law to the living of Horton-le-Skerne, my father, who had watched his disinterested course through his ministerial life, stood by him manfully, feeling convinced that the bishop believed that in the sight of God, he was putting the right man in the right place. To his chivalrous nature, the fact of a friend being misunderstood or misrepresented, only made him stand up for him the more heartily, when he was himself convinced of the integrity of his motive.

In the summer of 1843, Lady Louisa's delicacy of health increased. Headaches, from which she had long suffered, became severer and more incessant, so much so as to prevent her sleeping more than an hour or two in the night.

She expressed a desire to consult Dr. Birt Davies, an eminent physician in Birmingham, who had for many years attended my father and several members of his family. To enable him to gain an insight into her case, my father took her to Birmingham, where they were affectionately received by Mr. Moseley, at the rectory. But all efforts of skill and kindness proved to be unavailing. Although three doctors, who met in consultation, saw no cause to apprehend immediate danger, she grew more ill, day by day. Yet no suffering could concentrate her feelings upon herself, or even depress her bright spirits for any length of time. Their elastic spring rose up at the slightest relief, and she was as ever, thoughtful for the comfort and pleasure of all around her. Even during her drive with her husband and his daughters on the last evening of her life, she was planning little gifts for the children in the rectory, and ordering a supply of good books to be given away amongst the poor of the town. During the drive, she conversed with almost her usual animation, and amongst other subjects dwelt on the one so dear to her heart, the return of our Lord in glory. 'I think,' said she, 'if I were in the world of the lost, but could just see the Lord Jesus coming in triumph to this world, it would bring me a ray of happiness even there.'

After her return, she had a slight spasm of the heart. One of her step-daughters, who was with her at the moment, entreated to be allowed to sit up with her that night. The severity of suffering produced by pressure on the brain caused her mind to wander slightly, for a time; but it was evident throughout that her heart was occupied with heavenly subjects. She seemed to fancy that several members of her own family were present, and earnestly addressed them upon the importance of seeking salvation through Jesus Christ. After a time the mist passed away, and her mind became again quite clear. She felt conscious that death was approaching; and seemed to be taking her measure of herself by the side of Divine requirements—and her spirit shrank from the view. 'It is an awful thing,' she said, 'to go into the presence of a Holy God! What if He were to condemn me?'

She was reminded of the words of Rom. viii. 1, 'There is therefore now no condemnation to them which are in Christ Jesus.' But she solemnly rejoined, '"Who walk not after the flesh, but after the Spirit." What a life of holiness, of rising above the world, must not that imply?'

It would have been worse than vain to remind her then of her own fervent pressing after closer and yet closer conformity to the mind and will of her Saviour, and her readiness to give up anything and everything for His sake. It was therefore urged that she should look away from herself entirely, to 'behold the Lamb of God, which taketh away the sin of the world.' The history of the brazen serpent in Numbers xxi. 19 was then read to her, with the parallel passage in John iii. 14-16. In a moment her eyes brightened, and with her accustomed genuine simplicity she said, 'I see it all again, darling, how could I forget it? They looked unto Him and were lightened, and their faces were not ashamed. I look to Jesus, and He saves me—precious, blessed Saviour!'

At three o'clock, my father was told that she seemed to be seriously ill; he came at once, and remained by her side from that moment till she died at noon-day. Once, when looking at him with that unutterable tenderness that one sees from time to time in the eyes of the dying, she said, 'Oh what happiness I have had with you and your children! Now, it is passing away, but it will return in the presence of our God. Before I go, give me your blessing, my husband!'

He commanded his voice enough to say calmly, 'The Lord Jesus, who came to save sinners, bless thee.

'The Lord Jesus, who died for thee, bless thee.

'The Lord Jesus, who ever liveth to make intercession for thee, bless thee.'

'Again!' she exclaimed, with clasped hands, 'oh, give me that blessing again!'

To her chief medical adviser she said, 'Devote yourself to God, dear Dr. D—; there is no happiness but in devotion to Him.'

'None can depend more entirely upon the goodness of the Deity than I do,' was the reply. 'I believe it,' she said fervently; 'but we must depend in God's way, through His Son. It was incomprehensible to the Israelites that looking up to a brazen serpent should cause them to be healed of their wounds; just as it is incomprehensible to mere human reason that looking to a crucified Saviour should be sufficient for salvation; but those of the Israelites who looked were healed, because it was God's appointment; and those who look to Jesus now, will find Him to be the power of God unto salvation.'

The nearer she drew to her heavenly home, the brighter flashed the lights from its windows. Yet her joy was as simple and natural as that of a child leaving school for the holidays, and whose dear companions were to follow in a very little while. 'If I may have the lowliest place in heaven where I can see my Saviour, how happy I shall be,' she said. Then smiling at us, 'I shall look about for your dearest mother, and tell her how I have loved her children. We shall all *soon* be meeting in our Saviour's presence.' Then shortly afterwards, she asked for her favourite hymn, 'Jesu, Refuge of my soul.' At its close she softly said, 'Beautiful!' and her gentle spirit fled.

She was buried, in accordance with her dying request, beside my mother, in a vault in the chancel of St. Thomas', Birmingham.

Amidst the members of her family and connexions who attended her funeral was her brother-in-law, the Marquis of Anglesey, who was so much impressed with the holy resignation in my father's countenance, that he wrote of him afterwards, 'We beheld his face as it had been the face of an angel;' and a younger relative, alluding to the dignity of his quiet sorrow, said, 'No one ever made me realize before what it could be even on earth, to be made a king and a priest unto God.'

Several years afterwards, when Lord Anglesey was drawing near his death, he sent word to my father that 'during his latter visits to Beaudesert, when they had read the Bible together daily, he had first been led to seek pardon through the atoning blood of the Saviour, in whose mercy he had at length been enabled to place a humble confidence.'

Between my father and Lord Cadogan there was, to the last, a most tender tie : his letters never varied in their expressions of reverence and regard; and on one of the last visits that he was able to make, nearly twenty years afterwards, he also bore testimony to the blessed effect both of his beloved sister's and of my father's holy life and conversation upon his heart.

My father returned to Leamington, after this heavy blow had fallen, to find again his comfort in serving and holding communion with his Lord and Saviour. It was a solace to him also to have the society of Lady Louisa's beloved niece, Mrs. St. Quintin, and her husband, for some months under his roof. No one could be more accessible in grief than he was, nor more alive to sympathy and consolation. Not only could his sorrow never harden into sternness, but his tender and unselfish nature, filled as it was with Divine grace, grew even tenderer and more unselfish under the discipline; yet he showed little of that sorrow, as his manner was, to strangers, and only now and then spoke freely, out of the depths of his grief, to those around him who were so keenly sharing it.

The following letter was written shortly after his bereavement, and when he had been alarmed by hearing of the illness of his eldest daughter, who some years previously had married the Rev. Francis Trench, eldest son of the late Richard Trench, Esq. of Freehills, Hampshire.

His heart was most tenderly united to this beloved

daughter; and she ever retained for him the most devoted attachment. After her marriage he enjoyed frequent intercourse both with her and her husband, and always took the warmest interest in their earnest and untiring labours of love for their Divine Master.

TO MRS. GORDON.

'FREEHILLS, *near* SOUTHAMPTON,
August 30, 1843.

'MY DEAR FRIEND,—Your kind sympathizing letter has just reached me here, whither I came in haste, accompanied by my youngest child, on hearing of the illness of my eldest daughter. I thank God she is better, so that I may be spared "sorrow upon sorrow."

'You have touched a string of comfort,—the happiness of the departed. Her humility, her faith, her hope, her readiness to every good work, leave me no doubt; and if Tully, on the loss of his daughter, and after deep grief, said, "When I thought of her happiness, my joy was greater than my grief had been before;" my Christianity would fall short of his philosophy, if I did not take comfort from the same. Nevertheless, the wound is deep, and is intended so to be: despise it, I cannot; faint under it, I would not. Yet I must look to my Saviour to preserve me from both. My dear children feel, in their measure, as much as myself. But our health is preserved; I pray we may look backward with humility and gratitude, forward with desire and expectation, and upward with faith and prayer; then we shall be supported, and all will be well.

'I trust you and dear Mr. Gordon and your family will derive benefit as well as pleasure from the scenes through which you are passing.

'"An eye for nature and a soul for God" constitute much gratification and the highest happiness; and "if such," said pious Bishop Horne, "be the prison-house, what must the palace be?"

'Let us look forward to the Palace, and may every dispensation of Providence be among the means of preparing us for it.—With kindest regards, I am ever your obliged and affectionate friend, W. Marsh.'

TO HIS DAUGHTER, MRS. KNOX MARSHALL.

'... As to present clouds, I must recollect many years of sunshine, and be thankful for the past. And as to the future,—" It cannot last a hundred years," an old nurse in our family used to say. Besides, we may trust for the future, even a future eternity, and there

"sing Hallelujah
With them that are gone before."

"Oh, that will be joyful,
When we meet to part no more!"

'... Seducing spirits are abroad. Happy are they who abide by the good old way of Scripture, and the good old customs which our Church has followed for above two hundred years. They who do not are schismatics. Do you know my definition of schism? An unnecessary separation, or divergence, from a Church of Christ, in which I have scriptural instruction, the means of grace, and opportunities of doing good.'

Previously to his late bereavement, his second daughter had become engaged to be married to Captain Chalmers, who had recently returned from holding a high civil appointment in India. He had long been earnestly employed in the Lord's service; and having, for some time past, felt a strong desire to devote himself to the work of the ministry, he took his degree at Cambridge, and was ordained to the curacy of St. Mary's, Leamington. Soon after his marriage to my sister, in the following winter, they came to reside with her father, and their presence added, in no common measure, to the comfort and happiness of his daily life.

TO MRS. RIO.

'*Dec.* 7, 1843.

'MY DEAR MRS. RIO,—. . . We all love you for your own sake, and for your affectionate remembrance of one ever dear to our memory,—the thought of meeting whom again adds another ray of light to futurity. I have been passing a second time through a dark cloud; but resignation and occupation are means of relief; and "there is a silver lining to the darkest cloud."

'I have great reason to be thankful for my beloved Matilda's marriage, as dear Chalmers is a true servant of Christ; and they will remain under my roof; so that the old saying is true in my case, I do "not lose a daughter but gain a son."

'I am weeping over the Tractarians. I corresponded at one time with some of the leaders. They have departed as much from the scriptural faith as those had of whom St. Paul speaks (Gal. i. 6-8), "I marvel that ye are so soon removed from him that called you into the grace of Christ unto another gospel: which is not another; but there be some that trouble you, and would pervert the gospel of Christ. But though we, or an angel from heaven, preach any other gospel unto you than that we have preached unto you, let him be accursed." Their own souls are in danger, and they are drawing others into the snare. I tremble for them, because God is jealous for His truth; and these are men who might have known it, or knowing it, have departed from it. They do not appear to be at all impressed by such powerful refutations of their system as are given in Goode's *Case as it is*, Bishop O'Brien's Charge, Bishop Wilson's, and the many warnings that have now been given by several of our English bishops, and others. But the blackest mark is their own 90th Tract, fit only for the pen of a Jesuit. The Spirit of God must have departed, when such a perversion of common honesty and truth is advocated, whatever be the outward appearance of piety left. Yet that holy and gracious Spirit may return: and for this the lovers of truth and of immortal souls should pray. The system is founded on pride,—the pride of self-righteousness, and, more especially among the younger clergy, the pride of office.

'These novelties show us the necessity of keeping close to the oracles of God and to the throne of grace, that we may abide in the truth. There peace is to be found, and the promise of eternal life.

'For your own comfort, remember the distinction between the faith of adherence and the faith of assurance. We may exercise the former when we have not the comfort of the latter. But we are still to pray,—"Lord, increase our faith."

'The best wishes of all here attend you both.—Ever your affectionate pastor and friend,

'WM. MARSH.'

TO MRS. GORDON.

'LEAMINGTON, *Dec.* 2, 1843.

'... I HAVE been much struck lately with the thought of the privileges to which we sinful creatures are called:—

'He hath called us to *peace.*

'He hath called us to *holiness.*

'He hath called us to the *fellowship of His Son.*

'He hath called us to His *kingdom and glory.*

'This is the calling, according to His purpose of grace and mercy given us in Christ Jesus our Lord.'

TO HIS FRIEND THE REV. PETER FRENCH, THE SON OF HIS FRIEND OF EARLY DAYS.

'LEAMINGTON, *July* 1844.

'MY DEAR FRENCH,—Thy son liveth, and will live for ever. Yet he is gone before. His loving parent must grieve, and he may grieve. The saints of old wept. Jesus Himself wept. But how great the alleviation to know that there shall be a reunion. "Them that sleep in Jesus will God bring with Him." And how great the comfort to know that he believed in Jesus. Though not spared for further usefulness, yet the end of life was answered. And what may be the service in another world, who can tell?

'Have you ever met with Meek's *Recognition of Departed Friends*. There are some sweet thoughts in it.

'But may "the Comforter" Himself bring every soothing reflection to your mind, and fill your heart with joyful hope. I have heard the most delightful accounts of the dear departed. Well, he is gone out of a world of sin and sorrow, and in an age of danger and division, into a world of light and love, and uninterrupted, though *increasing* bliss.

'We all sympathize with you both. Amidst the great company of the redeemed, "the Lord hath need of him." "Blessed be the name of the Lord."—Your ever affectionate WM. MARSH.'

CHAPTER X.

LAST YEARS IN LEAMINGTON.

'My spirit seeks its dwelling yonder;
  And faith fore-dates the joyful day
When these old skies shall cease to sunder
  The one dear love-linked family.

Well pleased I find years rolling o'er me,
  And hear each day time's measured tread
Far fewer clouds now stretch before me,
  Behind me is the darkness spread.

My future from my past unlinking,
  Each dying year untwines the spell;
The visible is swiftly sinking,
  Uprises the invisible.'

H. Bonar.

LAST YEARS IN LEAMINGTON.

TOWARDS the close of the year 1844, my father was tenderly interested in ministering daily to the spiritual comfort of his beloved young friend, Lady Augusta Dalzell, who was to have become the wife of his only son, in the following year. But consumption had begun, almost unperceived, to do its work of destruction, and whilst she was expecting to recover for her bridal, the watchful eyes of affection—and even his who hoped on longest—could not fail to trace the near approach of death.

Yet no sooner was she told that there was no prospect of her recovery, than she yielded her will without a murmur to that of her Father in heaven, and raised her hopes of happiness to the world where

> 'Disappointment cannot fling
> O'er its joys her darksome wing.'

During their constant intercourse with his family, from the time of my father's residence in Leamington, he had loved both her and her sister, almost as if they had been daughters; and now his quick sympathies and fatherly tenderness, blended with the clear vision of his faith as to eternal joys, made his presence at once soothing and strengthening to the sweet and gentle sufferer.

On the 27th of December she died. On the night of Christmas eve, when it was thought that she could not live till the morning, whilst her brother, Lord Carnwath, with her devoted sister, was tenderly watching by her side, she asked him to read to her the 8th chapter of Romans. As the dying one was listening to those glorious words, uttered with deepest earnestness by a voice so dear to her, her face was suddenly irradiated, while her musical tones echoed through the room,—'For I am persuaded that neither death nor life, nor angels nor principalities nor powers, nor things present nor things to come, nor height nor depth, nor any other creature, shall be able to separate us from the love of God, which is in Christ Jesus our Lord.'

It need scarcely be told how deeply the heart of the father felt for the son in his bereavement; nor how tender was his sympathy with each of the mourners—thenceforth to have a more sacred claim than that of mere connexionship upon his affections and prayers.

The following extracts are from letters written

TO MRS. GORDON.

'LEAMINGTON.

'. . . I AM to speak on Friday night on "the re-union of all the people of God." Oh, what a world that must be, and what bliss that must be, where all are the people of God, and all reflect His light and His love. I long to be there! and when "I can scarce connect myself and heaven in one thought," I call to mind this truth, and am comforted,—"I am the DOOR, by ME if any man enter in, he shall be saved." Therefore, with apostolic authority I say to you, "Rejoice in the Lord always, and again I say, rejoice."'

'LEAMINGTON, 1844.

'. . . I ALMOST wish some expression of respect for Lord Ashley's noble, humane, and Christian conduct could be given by that part of the community which can appreciate such a character. But his commendation is on high. The servants of God must not expect to pass through this world with its approbation. But how wonderful is the thought that any of the human race should ever receive the plaudits of heaven!

'In one thing we ought to differ from Heaven. God in Christ forgets our sins, but remembers our services; we should remember our sins, but forget our services.'

In the summer of 1845, my father accepted an invitation to spend a few weeks at Huntly Lodge, in Aberdeenshire, with the late Duchess of Gordon, whose friendship he had long enjoyed. Her devoted piety, dignified simplicity, and sweet sunshiny temper, blended with remarkable truthfulness of character, were in strong sympathy with his own; and the refreshing intercourse of these days deepened a friendship which had existed for some time past. The Duchess was at that time a member of the Church of England, and had built a chapel within her grounds, in which he preached, with his usual loving earnestness, to as large a congregation as the walls would hold, drawn from a variety of communions; for all who loved the Lord Jesus Christ were attracted by the spirit of love in His servant.

He also gave several addresses at the Lodge, and in the town-hall of Huntly; and this visit was long referred to, not only by the Duchess herself, but by ministers and laymen of several denominations, as a time of refreshing, from which an abiding blessing was left in the hearts of many.

To his friend, the Rev. George Acklom, who was undertaking the senior position in the charge of St. Mary's Church and parish, during his absence in Scotland, he writes,—

'HUNTLY LODGE,
ABERDEENSHIRE, *July* 17, 1845.

'MY DEAR FRIEND,—I leave the duty with great comfort in your hands. God has taught you, and is with you, and will bless your message. . . . You must not be surprised at the thoughts and feelings which you mention. "My son, if thou wilt serve the Lord, prepare thine heart for temptation." This is apocryphal, yet it is true and sound advice. But whatever may be our thoughts and feelings, we must persevere in preaching that which we believe to be the truth of God, and in praying for a blessing upon it. We shall find that our labour has not been in vain. Our Lord most graciously passes by our infirmities; and where power has failed, accepts the will for the deed. Yea, and accepts the deed, however imperfect. "If there be first a willing mind, it is accepted according to that a man hath." . . . I am endeavouring, as to preaching, to act upon Mr. Simeon's advice, "Leave off, whilst your congregation are still hungry. That will bring them back again for more." But it is difficult. I was so long expounding last evening, that I sent one of the servants into a sound sleep. Poor fellow! he had probably been too wearied with his day's work to be fit to listen for more than a few minutes. Dear Simeon said, "If you pour a bucket of water to fill a pint bottle, how much you spill!" But then, what to leave unsaid, is the question. However, "Wisdom is profitable to direct," and I must continue praying for it. It is generally some text of Scripture, or some pointed saying, which is the appointed arrow.

'The poor dear Sherers! The good Lord comfort them under the loss of their sweet daughter! What should we do without "that blessed hope," be it realized when it may—a thousand years sooner or later—though I prefer, and *look* for the "sooner."

'We are all delighted with our visit here. Our Christian hostess has "a single eye" to her Master's glory; and a large heart—to promote the spiritual and tempóral welfare of her fellow-creatures.

'Light in the understanding and love in the heart, how blessed the combination!

'Our love to dear Mrs. Acklom and Miss Williams.[1]—Yours ever affectionately, WM. MARSH.'

'OBAN, *July* 9, 1845.

'MY DEAR FRIEND,—Our journey, as far as this, has been both safe and pleasant. At Liverpool, we had an interesting meeting for the Foreign Aid Society, with Merle D'Aubigné and Roussel present. Romanism is losing ground abroad, though, alas, gaining ground here! It is a judgment on Britain, because we have not employed our talent as we might have done. Nevertheless, I trust we are rising to the occasion, and offering up many prayers for the continuance of His mercy, and for supplies of His grace, that we may defend the truth, and live under its influence.

'Our good friends at Largs, Mrs. Speirs and her family, gave a most kind and hospitable reception. In the morning I went to the kirk. In the afternoon I gave an English service to the English Episcopalians, at Mrs. Spiers', and in the evening attended at the Free Church. Sound doctrine and evident piety in both the churches. The next morning, I delivered a lecture on the Jews, and got about one hundred persons together, who had nothing better to do.

'We are now at Oban, a quiet harbour, and proceed (*D.V.*) this evening to Fort William.

[1] An aunt of Mrs. Acklom, residing at Leamington, who had been blind from her nineteenth year; and who bore the privation with Christian fortitude and cheerfulness. Her animated and intelligent conversation, and warmth of heart, made her society sought by a large circle of friends.

'Heaven's best blessing rest on you and yours; on Dr. Wright and his; on my churchwardens, and congregation and parish; on all Leamington; and, speedily, on all the world.—Yours affectionately, WM. MARSH.

'Remember us to our servants.

'I think an allowance of ten shillings per week for poor —— would be safer, and more for his real benefit, than the whole sum at once. Might I trouble you to call upon him, and tell him I have sent a post-office order for £5, and that you will pay him ten shillings per week till my return? If it would really be of essential service, I could give him more, or all at one time. I fear he has been a slave of bad habits. Sorrow may have driven him in the wrong direction. Here is an opportunity, in Providence, which may turn to good account. If abused, he will only, poor fellow, treasure up wrath. What a dreadful captivity is that of sin! But we must not despair (as some seem to do in this case). "Is anything too hard for the Lord?" Perhaps you may insert a lancet, concealed in a sponge wet with the oil of love.'

The 'charity that hopeth all things, that suffereth long and is kind,' was indeed his, in no common measure. Years before, at a clerical meeting in Birmingham, he had felt himself constrained to mention the name of a person who was asking assistance very generally, as 'on his suspicious list.' 'What, Dr. Marsh! have *you* a suspicious list?' exclaimed Archdeacon Garbett. 'Then those who are on it must be confirmed rascals!'

From Huntly Lodge my father proceeded to make some other visits in the neighbourhood, where courteous and cordial welcomes awaited him. The beauty of Logie-Elphinstone, with its picturesque Benachie, and the meeting of the waters at its foot, peculiarly charmed him.

On his way back to England, he visited Belmont, the residence of Lord Mackenzie; where he greatly enjoyed the genial society of his gifted host, with that of his noble and devoted Christian wife; whose presence, wherever she went, was a centre of blessing and delight. In that bright and intellectual family circle might have been seen Christianity in its most attractive form; adding zest to every interest and innocent amusement provided for its younger members, and supplying them with an animating motive in every varied occupation for their own improvement, and for the good of their fellow-creatures.

Since then, the father, the two sons, distinguished alike for mental and moral excellence,[1] and, but recently, the loving and beloved mother, have joined the Church triumphant.

Not long after his return from Scotland, my father preached a sermon on the signs of the times in connexion with the hope of the coming of our Lord. Rarely was he heard to speak of dates with reference to that subject, without extreme caution. But in the course of this sermon he stated his own strong impression, that within about five-and-twenty years from that time (1845) Antichrist would be revealed, and then the Second Advent of the Anointed King would be at hand.

[1] See *Memoir of Francis Lewis Mackenzie*. By Rev. C. P. Miles.

In the month of October of the same year, he was visited by another severe affliction in the death of his daughter, Mrs. William Knox Marshall. The shock of hearing by express, one Sunday afternoon, that she had died suddenly that morning, was a blow which it required faith and grace in full exercise to enable him to bear without a murmur.

Brilliant in intellectual gifts, no less than in her personal beauty, with a flow of spirits which was almost inexhaustible, and a warmth of affection which made her cleave to her father with as strong an attachment after she had left his roof, as when she was a child at home, his frequent intercourse with this beloved daughter—ever warmly promoted by her husband—bringing, as it always did, mirth and gladness to his home, could not thus suddenly cease, for ever on earth, without plunging him into deep waters of affliction. But he had long learnt to realize that trial, however keen, is but 'the severer aspect of our Father's love.'

Not leaving himself time to recover from the first stunning effect of the blow, he hastened with his daughters to the desolated home, to be the support and the comfort of those whom this affliction had visited still more heavily. The first sight of the little motherless children, weeping bitterly as they threw themselves into his arms, completely overwhelmed him. But a short time of communing with his God restored his self-possession. Assembling the family of his bereaved son-in-law—to him always a son in dutiful affection—he read aloud a part of 1 Cor. xv., speaking a few short words of powerful consolation, and then poured out his soul in prayer for comfort and support for all, and for grace to profit by so severe a chastening.

His little grandchildren clung to him, in this their first knowledge of sorrow, as if they learnt something of a heavenly Father's pity and tenderness from the reflection of it which they saw in one so loved and revered.

On the following Sunday he preached a funeral sermon for his beloved child. When it was urged that the strain would be too great for him, he replied, 'Some one may be present whose heart, opened by sympathy, may listen to the things which are spoken by a sorrowing father, and thus be led to seek the Saviour whilst there is yet time.'

A few days before preaching this sermon, he had received a letter from a clergyman whose young daughter had been beguiled, whilst on a visit to a relative, into the views set forth by the Oxford Tracts, and who had been led by that too well-trodden pathway into the Church of Rome. In the course of his sermon, after briefly describing the simple faith in Christ Jesus which had been given to his own beloved child, together with clear, enlightened views of evangelical truth, and earnest dread of innovation upon it, he said, 'Great as the pang of separation is, I would rather have followed my child to the grave, than have seen her leave the pure light of truth, to become a member of the Church of Rome.'

Towards the close of his sermon, when alluding to her affectionate and unwearying care of the poor of the parish, and to her tender devotion as a mother, his voice faltered for the moment. But he was enabled to go through the trying ordeal with calmness, and earnestly to beseech his hearers to prepare to meet their God, by seeking the knowledge of Him who is 'the way, the truth, and the life.'

The last letter my sister had written, only the night before her death, was addressed to an acquaintance of former days, then apparently an earnest believer in revelation, but who had afterwards sunk into a dreary scepticism. The grave had just closed over his young wife, and he had written to my sister as if he had no hope beyond this passing, dying world.

Gently she sympathized with him in his great sorrow, and then appealed to his old faith, closing with those glorious words of the Redeemer, so tenderly chosen by the compilers of our Liturgy for the first words which shall fall on mourners' ears as they draw nigh to the burial-place : 'I am the resurrection and the life; he that believeth on me, though he were dead, yet shall he live; and whosoever liveth and believeth on me shall never die. *Believest thou this?*'

Whether that message from the dead—for she who wrote it had ceased to breathe before her letter had left the town—was the means of any permanent blessing, can never be known upon earth. But 'she had done what she could;' and perhaps is now rejoicing over the harvest of that small seed-sowing, in the world

> 'Where some for whom thy spirit grieves
> Will re-appear among thy sheaves.'

Some time afterwards, the following letter was found set apart as one of her choicest treasures. It had been written to her when she was a young girl of fifteen, and still at school. In later years she had referred to it, as the means of having turned her heart from desiring, or, at all events, from seeking, the amusements of the world.

'DEAR DARLING LOU,—I thought I could not love you more than I did, but I assure you your open candid letter will make me. I do remember what such feelings are, and do not wonder at them in the least. I recollect Mrs. Keysall telling me that she informed her sister "that her heart was in the world, so might she not as well be there herself?" But her sister's answer was, "Keep your person away, and God in due time will take your heart away."

'Continue to pray, dearest Lou, that the Lord would graft in your heart the love of His name, and give you a taste for spiritual things, and make you happy in present duties, and you will be heard. The young friends who have conversed with you, have as yet known nothing of the importance of vital religion. Nor are they aware that, as the hours and atmosphere of those places of amusement are injurious to health, so their tendency is equally unfriendly to Christian morals. An inspired apostle has said, "She who liveth in pleasure is dead while she liveth." Recreations are lawful and desirable; but those pleasures are diversions, and have in many respects a bad effect. I was not taught the evil of them when young, but afterwards I learned it from the Scriptures and from reflection. When you feel the temptation to be strong, and do not feel the power of religion at the same time to oppose it, call in aid even your love to your father and mother, and then the temptation may be turned into an act of self-denial, perhaps for the Lord's sake, and certainly for ours.

'Always speak your mind freely, dearest Lou, and tell me anything in which I can promote your happiness consistently with your highest and your future good, and you will always find your dearest mother and your father ready and glad to do so.

'Willie has written a most loyal letter, and quite witty. I must keep it for you to see. I long to hear that your cough is better.—Ever thy loving father, W. M.'

Never was promise better kept than that one given in the close of this letter, to promote his children's happiness. His very presence made it. And every rational pleasure, which was within his reach, was provided for them with open hand.

The following letters were written not long after the death of this beloved daughter :—

TO THE REV. GEORGE ACKLOM.

'LEAMINGTON, *Oct.* 30, 1845.

'MY DEAR ACKLOM,—Thanks for your kind sympathizing letter. Resignation, occupation, hope, and the sympathy of friends, and especially as shown in prayer, are great alleviations. Oh that it may be a sanctified sorrow to us, and a warning voice also to the neighbours! What sources of consolation are 1 Thess. iv. 13-18, and 1 Cor. xv. I might add Rev. xxi. and xxii.

'We are mercifully supported. I always think it my duty to throw myself into my usual clerical occupation as speedily as possible. It does not benefit us to dwell upon sorrow; yet the floodgates will open at times; but the Lord is righteous in all His ways, and holy in all His works,—yea, and very gracious; for His name is Love.

'May a great blessing attend your ministrations. There is nothing worth living for but to glorify God, and do good to man. May you long be spared for this.

'I have Owen *On the Spirit;* and if William has not taken it to London, it shall be much at your service, or any other of my books.—Yours, ever affectionately,

'W. Marsh.'

TO MRS. GORDON.

'*November* 1845.

'My dear Friend,—The stroke was indeed sudden, and the wound deep; but the Bible has taught us from whence it comes, and we have the assurance that every dispensation is ordered by infinite wisdom and love. ... My dear child was saved the great trial of taking leave of her little children. Her sainted mother had taught her to love her Bible and trust in her Saviour, and God had blessed it. She also taught the same to those of her children who were capable of learning. Oh, how great is the mercy of having the Book of Life in this world of death! I have been going through 1 Cor. xv. and 1 Thess. iv. 13-18. They are always new, especially when death enters our homes. The dark valley is illuminated. A bright prospect is visible. May that word have free course and be glorified. (Thank God, four copies every minute issue from Earl Street alone.)

'Lift up your hearts, that we may meekly bear and duly improve this dispensation. The pain of the surgeon's knife should be accounted nothing if life and health may be preserved or improved.—Your affectionate friend,

'WILLIAM MARSH.'

TO MISS DORNFORD.

'MY DEAR FRIEND,—You and your dear sister have indeed been the subjects of sorrow, but, thank God, you have also been the subjects of joy. The sorrow will soon flee away, but the joy is a foretaste of that which will be eternal. I have also passed through deep waters; and have found but little relief except in present duties and future prospects. It answers no good purpose to pore over our trials, or to be too inquisitive as to the reason or design of them. It is enough to know that the Lord is righteous, that we suffer infinitely less than our iniquities deserve, and that they are sent in love to make us partakers of His holiness, and increase our future happiness. "It is the *Lord*, let Him do what seemeth Him good,"

"Who nothing does, or suffers to be done,
But thou thyself wouldst do, couldst thou but see
The end of all events as well as He."

'I am glad your sister has undertaken the Jewish and Moravian causes. They are both the Lord's. I greatly rejoice that you have both been preserved from those deep snares which Satan has laid to divide the churches of Christ, to separate the hearts of Christians, to lay another stumbling-block in the way of the world, and to bring the subject of prophecy into disrepute. Well, in the midst of all these mistakes, the foundation standeth sure; and the solid piety of true religion in the Church of England does but the more commend itself. Tell your dear sister, she is journeying to the land the inhabitant of which shall no more say, "I am sick;" but in which there will be knowledge without error, holiness without sin, and happiness without alloy; and how infinite our obligations to Him who, having overcome the sharpness of death, opened the kingdom of heaven to all believers.

'When you happen to write, give me an account of things at Brighton. I am more than commonly interested in that place. Remember me to our mutual friends.—Yours most truly, WM. MARSH.'

'. . . WHAT has sin not done? But, thank God, we may add, what will the Saviour not do? Exceeding abundantly above all His Church thinks,—not, perhaps, above what she asks, when she says, "Thy kingdom come. Thy will be done *in earth, as it is in heaven.*"

'In the prospect of the glory to be revealed, may you both be comforted. Christ died, rose, revived, rules, and will reign. Here is the Christian's hope and glory.'

TO MISS LEYCESTER.

'The signs of the times call for—

'1. A close adherence to the Word of God.

'2. The exercise of faith, hope, and love.

'3. Watchfulness and prayer.

'4. A diligent use of all available means of grace for ourselves, and a zealous endeavour to propagate revealed truth among others, both at home and abroad.

'The complete victory of truth I do not expect until the Second Advent of our blessed Lord. I have *no* hope of a general or universal spread of Christian knowledge "till He come." When He has "taken out of the Gentiles a people for His name," and called "a remnant of the Jews, according to the election of grace," then He will return and convert the Jewish nation, put down all rule, authority, and power opposed to His gospel, and cause the knowledge of Himself to cover the earth.

'So I read in very many passages of Holy Writ, and long for the day; for then Satan will be bound, and creation will cease to groan.

'As to the darkness which has covered the earth, I should say: Sin separated human nature from God: but the Most High intended to teach the universe an important lesson by that fall, and to display His glorious perfections by the method of recovery.

'Nevertheless, as all His Divine works are small in their beginning, and gradual in coming to perfection, so it would require six thousand years to teach human nature what an evil and bitter thing it is to depart from God, and to bring to maturity the fruit of redeeming love. And not *only* to teach *men:* "Which things the *angels* desire to look into." "That unto the principalities and powers in heavenly places might be known by the Church the manifold wisdom of God." And God in all things will be glorified through Jesus Christ. An upright universe will join in praise. "Thou art worthy, O Lord," etc. (Rev. iv. 11). "Great and marvellous are thy works" (Rev. xix. 3, 4).

'From Rom. ii. 5 we read that there will be the revelation of the righteous judgment of God. Wrath is now revealed against all ungodliness and unrighteousness of men; but it does not necessarily follow that all will be lost who have not an *explicit* knowledge of Christ, though none will be saved but *through* Him.

'The number of the saved, including infants and the millennial world, may very, very far exceed the number of the lost.

'It was a striking thought of Lord Bacon, that the Redeemer is the head of preservation to angels, and of restoration to men.

'During our time of probation we must give credit to the wisdom, and goodness, and faithfulness of God. Whatever clouds and darkness may be round about Him, righteousness and judgment are the basis of His throne.

'I like this view of the complex character of Jehovah, "He is a merciful Sovereign and a righteous Judge."

'Do these thoughts give any answer to your questions? If not, put them again;—as well as any more which may occur to you, adding your own meditations and views.'

TO MR. TEBBS.

'LEAMINGTON, *March* 11, 1846.

'WE must work while it is day; but work not *for* Life, that is too hard work for us, that is impossible; but *from* Life we shall work, and then it will not be in vain in the Lord.'

FROM A RELATIVE OF HIS FIRST WIFE.

'I WELL remember what extreme pleasure as well as edification Dr. Marsh's visits used to give to us, now thirty years ago and more, at our dear old country-place. They were joyfully welcomed by the whole family, from the father at the head to the youngest child, then a bright sunny Eton boy.

'Dr. Marsh's expositions of Scripture, prayers, and conversations were all delightful; full of power and life, with a peculiarly reverent tenderness when he spoke of his Saviour.

'Once, I recollect, he met there a very clever Oxford scholar, with whom he had a great deal of intercourse, and who was very much struck by his conversation. After Dr. Marsh had left, the scholar used to say of him in his own emphatic way, "A very remarkable man indeed!"

'When sickness and sorrow hung over that home, Dr. Marsh took what was then a long journey to see the youngest daughter on her dying bed. She had a firm trust in the Saviour, who was her stay under severe, sometimes agonizing, sufferings, and her Hope for eternity; but the dark valley was at times dreary to her, and she dreaded leaving those near and dear, especially a beloved tender young sister, friend, and nurse. I remember her saying to me, after Dr. Marsh had been with her, "He has opened a door in heaven for me."

'My last recollection associating him with that home, is his friendly coming again to the old place on a joyful occasion—the christening of the first son of the "Eton boy," before alluded to. His venerable figure, whilst baptizing the lovely babe in his arms, remains in my mind as a beautiful picture, and his sermon afterwards was very striking. He made a speech the following day at the entertainment to tenants and labourers, and I can recal now the open-mouthed surprise and delight manifested, for they had never heard such speaking before, so bright, yet so tender and so solemn.'

In the summer of 1846, my father went abroad for a few weeks, and spent most of that time in Switzerland. He was accompanied by his much-valued friend Miss Leycester, a cousin of his first wife, and by his youngest daughter, and the eldest of his little motherless grandchildren, to whom he was tenderly attached, and who resided much with him after her mother's death.

Amidst his exceeding enjoyment in the glories of the mountain scenery, he seemed never to lose any opportunity afforded him of working for his Master. At English chapels, or failing any chapel, at hotels, he offered his services readily; and his sitting-room, at the time of family prayers, was always open to any who were willing to be present.

At Interlachen he had great delight in the companionship of the Rev. Charles Girdlestone, whose acquaintance he had first made when in Birmingham; Mr. Girdlestone having been appointed vicar of Sedgeley in that neighbourhood. His clear intellect, deep earnestness, and firm scriptural views, made his society most congenial to my father. 'Dear Girdlestone!' he wrote, just after they had parted in Switzerland, 'what a pleasant thing it is to see so much talent, and such an interesting character, wholly consecrated! It has been one of the indulgences granted us in our holidays to have met him again with his dear, Christian wife.'

For about a fortnight my father was detained at Basle by the serious illness of his grandchild. During this time he frequently visited the Missionary institution from which our own Church Missionary Society has largely recruited its ranks. With the joyful sanction of the heads of the College, he gave addresses to the young men, and held Bible-classes for them. In after years several have written of it as a time of much blessing.

In almost every large town which he visited in Germany, he found that the converted Jews had been apprised of his intention of coming, and were on the outlook for him—their leaders hastening to welcome him with respect and love, as one whose devotion to the best interests and general welfare of their nation had been long known and appreciated. In one place the chief Rabbi, still a rigid Jew, visited him, to express gratitude, in the name of his people, for his efforts to alleviate their trials, and to promote their temporal advantage.

In the year 1847, my father had the happiness of welcoming the Rev. James Haldane Stewart, his beloved friend, and former helper in the ministry, at his house in Leamington. Mr. Stewart came to undertake the office of sponsor for the first-born son of Mr. Chalmers and my sister, an office which he filled with double pleasure, as he had been godfather to the mother of the infant.

Mr. Stewart's spirit of prayer and praise was in delightful accordance with such occasions. In the evenings several friends were invited to meet him, and the conversations—chiefly sustained by himself and my father—were most animating and edifying. One of those conversations, on the subject of death as the gateway of life, and on scriptural indications of the varied sources of happiness in the land beyond the 'gateway,' produced such an effect upon a man of the world who was present, that he said, as he left the room, 'That is the religion I would give all I have to possess! Now, for the first time, I realize what a happy thing it is to be a Christian!'

TO MRS. RIO.

'We need Luthers in these days. The Church of Rome is proceeding stealthily and vigorously, and many see nought of the danger. Great is our mercy who have and study and believe the Bible. May it yet have free course, and be glorified among fallen churches! . . . Yet a little while, and all and everything will be well, if we be "looking for the mercy of our Lord Jesus Christ unto eternal life."

'Christian love is beyond all price. Thanks for your expression of it. What cause I have to be thankful for the love I have experienced from the disciples of Him whose name is Love! It should make me both humble and grateful. What may we not expect from Divine love? "I have loved thee with an *everlasting* love; therefore with loving-kindness have I drawn thee. . . .

'When shall we be out of debt if love be always due? But what a pleasant debt it is, and always being incurred, and always being paid. If thus in debt to one another, how much more to Him whose name is love, whose law is love, whose gospel is love, whose providence is love in all His dealings with us!

"Eternity will seem too short
To utter all His praise."

'WM. MARSH.'

'MY DEAR FRIEND,—Your "Charity"[1] has arrived. Charity is always beautiful, and "never faileth;" and, I doubt not, President Edwards has described it well. He had a powerful mind. Not *many* wise men are willing to become fools (in the estimation of others), that they may be wise for eternity; but he was one of those happy souls.

'The subject of love is the great subject of Scripture. It makes known God as love. He is such, as manifested

[1] President Edwards *On Charity*.

in His works, as revealed in His word, and, above all, as exhibited in His Son. "He that hath seen me," said our Lord, "hath seen the Father."

'Jesus invites all, and casts out none. He particularly invites the "weary and heavy laden." He told the woman of Samaria there was nothing between her soul and the water of life, but a prayer. "If thou hadst asked, He would have given." All this is love, but the highest expression of it was on the cross.'

'How great is the mercy which renders what is essential (in the Bible) plain and simple. I am a sinner! There is a Saviour! He casts out none who come to Him! He gives the Holy Spirit! He promises heaven! It is my privilege to confide in Him! It is my honour to serve Him! It will be my heaven to be with Him! God in Christ is all in all!'

Foremost amongst the numerous Christian friendships that cheered his life at Leamington, was that which bound him to one who, whilst ably occupying the position of Accountant-General, had been a leader in every good cause in Bengal. Mr. John Walter Sherer, brother-in-law to the late excellent Bishop Corrie, was a man of a kindred spirit with my father, possessing the same happy buoyancy of disposition, and single-minded devotedness of life to his Master's glory. They were united in their fervent interest touching everything that concerned the kingdom of Christ; and in their hearty support of every plan to promote its increase upon earth. As Mr. Sherer lived, so he died, 'rejoicing in Christ Jesus, and having no confidence in the flesh.' Just as his last hour drew nigh, he sent for my father, and said, 'I am a dead man; but in Christ Jesus alive for evermore. . . . You were at the Bible Society meeting yesterday, beloved friend, and I was with you in spirit. How I have loved that Society! How I love everything that helps to spread the knowledge of the everlasting gospel! "GOD IS LOVE." I know it. I feel it. It is no cunningly devised fable.'

Just before his eyes closed in death, the face of the aged saint caught a ray of the glory about to be revealed to him, as with clasped hands he said, 'He that hath the Son of God hath life; and he that hath not the Son of God hath not life.' But 'this is the record, that GOD HATH GIVEN TO US ETERNAL LIFE, AND THIS LIFE IS IN HIS SON.'

TO THE REV. GEORGE ACKLOM.

'LEAMINGTON, *Nov.* 18, 1846.

'DEAR ACKLOM,—I rejoice in your appointment. May the Spirit of power, of love, and of a sound mind, rest on the vicar and yourself, and all your brethren. Great is the honour conferred on those who are called to preach the Truth; and great the happiness of those who, through grace, believe it. Such was the portion of our dear friend Mr. Sherer. A life of usefulness terminated in a death of peace. Christ was his all. Religion was therefore in him a well of water springing up to everlasting life. What a double sorrow for the family—dear Mr. Corrie dying at the same time in the next room! O blessed world, where there is no more death.

'You will see a second letter from Chalmers. I think conclusive. But Popery can evade anything, and assume any shape. It is, in itself, an awful judgment of God upon men—2 Thess. ii., "strong delusion." We must, however, do what we can to save some. It is a part of our ministry (1 Tim. iv. 16).

'If God bless the efforts now being made, we are safe. But we are late in the field. However, we must work while it is day, and "at evening-time it shall be light."

'All send their love to you both.—Yours affectionately,

'W. MARSH.'

'MY DEAR FRIEND,—How wonderful will be the state of the human mind when free from all error, prejudice, and mistake. "In Thy light shall we see light," will then be fulfilled to the utmost. "When that which is perfect is come, then that which is in part shall be done away." In the meantime, in as great a degree as can be obtained, and as, in fact, including all true religion, three things are to be sought,—right beliefs, right affections, right practice. Right beliefs received into the heart produce right affections, and right affections constrain to a right practice. We know—we love—we serve. But by-and-by all these graces will be in perfection. And all this is open to us through our blessed and adorable Redeemer.'

'WHERE is the *uninspired* book of which one can say, "I can never tire of reading it?" There *is* a Book which I think I must have read fifty times, and I have not done with it yet. In a sense, I doubt whether I shall have done with it in *time*, for it is in *eternity* we shall know fully its wondrous contents.'

The following letter is in reply to a friend's questions on some observations concerning the resurrection, in the *Protoplast*:—

'I AM aware that some critics have thought that our blessed Lord took His departure to glory on the evening of the resurrection-day (see Luke xxiv. 26). I believe He did ascend to heaven, but frequently appeared to the disciples during forty days after the resurrection. But His *public* and visible ascension did not take place until after those forty days. As on the mount of transfiguration, He would appear in glory on the day of the resurrection; but, as when He came down from that mount He appeared as he did before, so He would appear to His disciples during those forty days.

'Comparing one passage with another, I confess I draw the inference that He did ascend *privately* on the first occasion, and *publicly* on the last occasion. When He had finished His work of humiliation—that work of unutterable love,—time and space, as to Him, were no more.

'WM. MARSH.'

Early in the year 1848, my father married the Honourable Louisa Horatia Powys, seventh daughter of Lord Lilford. She was, with the exception of one married sister, the only surviving member of a family of sincere and earnest

Christians, whom, with their excellent widowed mother, he had known and valued for more than forty years.

Though often suffering from feeble health, Mrs. Marsh devoted herself, with untiring and affectionate assiduity, to ministering to his comfort to the end of his life.

'DAWLISH, *Mar.* 15, 1848.

'I VALUE your congratulations, my dear friend, because they are not a mere compliment, but sincere. Nor would you congratulate me if you did not hope the event might be connected with eternal good. Nothing in time is worth a thought that is not in some way connected with a future eternity. And how wonderful it will be when we shall see all the connecting links of that chain which, being let down *from* heaven, draws us up *to* heaven. "Thou shalt remember all the way which the Lord thy God led thee." What must be the results but deep humility and unfeigned gratitude!

'Solemn indeed are the warnings to nations, and these should be improved by individuals. I fear our expediency plan greatly endangers our peace. Popery and Infidelity must receive the due reward of their deeds; and no nation that favours them will long enjoy peace. The earth is burdened under them, and the heavings of that earthquake which will swallow them up are now sensibly felt. But, as Luther would say, "Let us sing the 46th Psalm."

'There is an American judge of high repute who has sent forth a "trial of the witnesses,"—quite unanswerable.[1] It was intended for the legal profession in particular. I

[1] Witnesses for the truth of Christianity.

have read it with great pleasure; and also a little book, containing great matter—*The Philosophy of the Plan of Salvation.* The Religious Tract Society sells it for sixpence or eightpence. Of course these books are designed for doubters and unbelievers.'

'5 CATHERINE PLACE, BATH, *March* 28, 1848.

'DEAR MRS. GORDON,— . . . Mr. Gordon and yourself, and all of us, are looking for the things which are coming upon the earth; and are praying, if it please God, that the British Isles may be spared. The Divine patience appears to be nearly exhausted as to Popery, and Infidelity will be the scourge. Our hope as a nation lies in having been mercifully employed in sending forth the Holy Scriptures, and propagating the gospel of Christ. But our danger lies in apathy and lukewarmness, in neglect of our great privileges, and unthankfulness for them.

'The time for the beginning of the end appears to have arrived. How long it may last till the end, no man knoweth. I recollect reading many years ago Fleming's *Apocalyptical Key,* written in 1701 or 1704, which professed to foretell the downfall of the King of France in 1794, and the commencement of the downfall of Popery in 1848. The former we know took place. If the present revolutions end in Infidelity, the latter will begin to take place. But Popery will make great exertions, and die hard.

'It is our privilege to be looking upward for all the mercy and grace we need, and forward, to the rest which shall never be disturbed—either by error, or sin, or sorrow. It is "a kingdom which cannot be moved."'

'SYMPATHY is soothing; we must prize it in our fellow Christians. Then how ought we to prize it in our great High Priest! (Heb. ii. 17, 18; iv. 15, 16;) and you have well applied the subject in the line—

"*Our* feelings—once *His* own."

Yes, "Jesus wept," though he could raise the dead. And finally, "He will *wipe away* all tears." There is something beautifully tender in the expression.

'I quite understand you as to the pastor's duty. "We are not sufficient of ourselves to *think* anything as of ourselves, but our sufficiency is of God." Yet, as He does not work miracles now as to time or strength, it appears to me that the extent of duty in many parishes prevents that important part of it, the strictly pastoral work. It also requires peculiar wisdom from above, not to break the bruised reed, not to give strong meat to babes, not to treat all characters alike, but to discern natural and constitutional differences; but, above all, to be the sincere, tender, sympathizing friend; the wise and loving parent; "but who is sufficient for these things?"

'Still one man has one gift, another man another gift; but by-and-by all gifts will be accompanied by all graces, and there will be only a world of light and love.

'Lamented unbelief is very different from wilful unbelief. As much as possible let the mind rest on the great truth, that "God *hath given* to us *eternal life*, and this life is in His Son." As certainly as life was given us in Adam, and he lost it, so is life given to us in Christ, and *He preserves it* unto life eternal. When we have no sensible comfort, we have authority to rest on the Word. Its great Author is "the same yesterday, to-day, and for ever;" and "the promises are yea and amen," "faithful and true." Though not essential to our final happiness, yet Christianity would have us be cheerful by the way. So thought St. Paul, when he prayed for the Romans (Rom. xv. 13), yet simple faith may be in high exercise when there is little feeling."'

TO MISS LEYCESTER.

'*June* 3, 1847.

'. . . DEAR Dr. Chalmers!—Gone to his rest without a word, and without a witness. Yet there was something grand in his death! Leaning on his pillow, with his Bible and his papers by him, ready for the duties of the next day. Alas, we cannot spare such witnesses, unless we call to mind with whom is the residue of the Spirit. But we should be thankful for the gifts, and grace, and usefulness which have been so abundantly bestowed upon him.

'. . . As to the only object of worship, that is made plain by Scripture, and by our being dedicated to the Father, the Son, and the Holy Ghost. "Worship God," and none other, is the language of Revelation. It appears, as to prayer, that we approach the Father in the name of the Son, as led by the Holy Spirit (Eph. ii. 18). But it is equally true that prayer directly to the Lord Jesus is heard; indeed it is characteristic of Christians, that they "call on the name of our Lord Jesus Christ" (1 Cor. i. 2); and St. Paul, anxious to be delivered from a great trial, prayed to the Lord Jesus, and received the encouraging answer, "My grace is sufficient for thee." And St. Stephen dies committing his spirit by prayer into the hands of our Redeemer. We cannot therefore err in prayer, whether to the Father or to the Son, for so the Spirit leads.

'Our Collects in the Church of England are usually framed on the model referred to in Eph. ii. 18; but in the Litany we have both views :—

'1. The prayer to God the Father.

'2. The prayer to God the Son.

'3. The prayer to God the Holy Ghost.

'4. The prayer to God the undivided Trinity.

'If at the close of any prayer we give glory to the Father, Son, and Holy Spirit, we cannot be wrong.'

TO HIS EARLY FRIEND, REV. T. TYNDALE.

On Infant Baptism, etc.

'SOUTH MALLING, LEWES, *Aug.* 13, 1849.

'MY DEAR TYNDALE,—Your letter finds me here attending the baptism of Matilda's little girl.

'The circumcised child among the Jews was called one of the people of God—the children of God—the holy nation, etc., as being brought into covenant with God by an appointed ordinance. Nevertheless, St. Paul says, "He is not a Jew which is one outwardly; neither is that circumcision which is outward in the flesh: but he is a Jew which is one inwardly: and circumcision is that of the heart, in the spirit, and not in the letter; whose praise is not of men, but of God" (Rom. ii. 28, 29). We are under the Abrahamic covenant, therefore our children may be called " members of Christ, children of God, inheritors of the kingdom of heaven," in the same sense.

'I think with you, that the term is not used in the Christian sense, *i.e.*, of true regeneration, but would gladly have it altered to prevent a misunderstanding. Is it not singular, that —— never referred to the Church's own explanation in the Catechism on the Sacraments?

'Namely—" What is required of persons to be baptized? —*A*. Repentance, whereby they forsake sin; and faith, whereby they steadfastly believe the promises of God made to them in that sacrament. *Q*. Why then are infants baptized, etc.—*A*. Because they promise them," etc. She does not say, because they are certainly and necessarily regenerated at baptism.

'The language here and in the Articles, and then in the Service, presents an apparent contradiction or dubious sense which should be avoided. But I cannot think that the multitude imagine they will enter the kingdom of heaven because they have been baptized; when they think at all, they know they must repent and be changed, if they would be saved. I never met with any one but a clergyman, and an extreme party man, who really did say, "When I doubt my regeneration, I go to my baptismal register and am satisfied."

'As to ——'s view of two regenerations, and one amounting *almost* to justification, it is too learned for me. I cannot get beyond Scripture and the Articles of my Church. If I were presented to a living in Exeter diocese (and it is time I should be preferred!) I should say, "I am ready to subscribe, *ex animo*, to the Liturgy, Articles, and Homilies." If questioned again, or 149 times, I should only add, "I am ready to subscribe, *ex animo*, to each separately." Not a word more would I answer, and the law would be on my side. We must wait till "that which is perfect is come," before we shall find anything perfect.

'Hal is a sad fellow for writing, we can scarcely get a letter once a year. I fear Charlotte is too infirm to travel, but Hal is, I am sure, grateful for your kind invitation. He is now almost the age of man. But I must not mention that, or I shall make myself out an ancient! I hope never to die. I have heard that voice, "He that liveth and believeth in Me shall never die." But I should like to be of the publican's spirit, when the change comes,—"God be merciful to me a sinner!" and to offer St. Stephen's prayer, "Lord Jesus, receive my spirit;" and to exercise David's faith, "Into Thy hands I commend my spirit, for Thou hast redeemed me, O Lord, Thou God of truth."

'Gorham's expenses should be met. Every evangelical clergyman should raise at least one pound. That would do it. The whole opposition is to evangelical men and measures. Kindest regards to Mrs. Tyndale, and best wishes for you all.—Your ever affectionate,

'WM. MARSH.'

To his young friend Richard Nugent, Esq., who was actively engaged in promoting the interests of the Protestant Association, and who had been for some years one of his most attached hearers at St. Mary's, Leamington, he writes :—

My dear Nugent,—What stirring times we live in, and what need there is for prayer that those who have votes may be directed aright at the ensuing election; and that God "would be pleased to direct and prosper all the consultations of their representatives to the advancement of His glory, the good of His Church, the safety, honour, and welfare of our Sovereign and her dominions."

'England is asked to endow a Church which is now endeavouring (and with too much success) to beguile the unwary to a system opposed to Holy Scripture, and which, by the dark device of the Confessional, would injure the simplicity and purity of the minds of her daughters, and entice many of them into convents—those prisons without crime, over which Dante's words might too generally be inscribed with truth,—

"All hope abandon,
Ye who enter here."

'Nor will Rome rest satisfied with increase, nor with increase without supremacy, nor with supremacy without withdrawing toleration from all other churches. She is the same as she was in the days of Queen Mary, when she burned at the stake one archbishop, four bishops, twenty-one clergymen, eight gentlemen, eighty-four tradesmen, one hundred husbandmen, fifty-five women, and four children.

'The Earl of Arundel and Surrey—himself a Roman Catholic—stated in the House of Commons, by the report of the *Times* of April 15, 1847, that "the Church of Rome is antagonistic to Protestantism, and as long as the world lasts will continue so, until Protestantism be extinct."

'This statement is corroborated by various authoritative documents of the Church of Rome, amongst others, the notes to the Rhemish Testament, revised for the Irish Roman Catholics of the present day, and published in Ireland, under the sanction of the highest authorities of the Romish Church; one specimen of it will suffice:— "Where ill men (BE THEY HERETICS or other malefactors) may be punished or suppressed without disturbance or hazard of the public good; they may and ought, by public authority, either spiritual or temporal, to be CHASTISED or EXECUTED."

'We have lately seen this theory reduced to practice in Madeira. In the month of August 1846, thirteen British subjects (several of whom were women) were compelled to save their lives by seeking refuge in a British ship off Funchal; the only crime alleged against them was, that they had encouraged some of the inhabitants of Madeira in reading the Scriptures of God.

'The first object of this relentless attack, headed by a Jesuit priest, Canon Conego Telles, who had been educated in England, was Dr. Kalley, a benevolent physician, who gave his time and medical skill gratuitously for the benefit of the islanders. Upwards of two hundred Portuguese Protestants have since effected their escape from the island. English ships received them (many having managed to swim to these under cover of darkness), and conveyed them to Trinidad, where they were nobly welcomed and provided for by the Christian governor, Lord Harris,— houses, farms, and possessions having been taken from them, so that they escaped with only their lives.

'England, as has been well proved from history in *The Fortress of Christianity*, by Rev. G. Croly, LL.D., has risen in the scale of nations whenever she has upheld Protestant truth, as she has fallen whenever she countenanced the Papacy; and now, from treachery within her Church, and from the avowed enemy without, she seems to be standing again upon the threshold of her destiny—the blessing of freedom of conscience and of her open Bible not yet forfeited—the bondage of mental slavery, of priest-craft and priest-rule, impending once more.

'The battle of the Reformation must ere long be fought over again; and English Protestants will find that they must live as conquerors, or they may have to die as martyrs.—Ever your affectionate friend, W. MARSH.'

TO THE REV. G. ACKLOM.

'DEAR ACKLOM,— . . . People may bear the name of Protestants, but it is the spirit of Popery which objects to an exposure of the errors of the Church of Rome. The country needs men of the stamp of dear M'Ghee, in the days of his health, who would go from place to place, consecrating remarkable gifts of oratory to warning and exhorting Protestant Christians, and building them up on their faith.

'You have acted faithfully, and I thank God for it. Satan misnames things. It is one of his artifices. He calls speaking lightly of the errors of the Church of Rome liberality. They who think it such would find it to be the very reverse. I wish they could look into the nunneries. Prisons without crimes. Relatives not allowed to see the veiled nuns without a witness. This alone is enough to excite suspicion.

'I daily pray for myself and for all Christians: Give us clear judgments, tender consciences, and strength of will. Thus work in us to will and to do; and let us not be ignorant of Satan's devices.—Yours ever affectionately,

'WM. MARSH.'

TO A. GORDON, ESQ.

'DEAR MR. GORDON,—We have been praying for you all, and were anxiously waiting for a better account of the dear invalid.

'David says, "Twice have I heard, that power belongeth unto God,"—also, "Unto Thee, O Lord, belongeth mercy." That mercy employs that power in restoring our comforts from the borders of the grave; or (when Infinite Wisdom denies this) in sustaining us under our sorrow, and making it productive of present fruits and future joys.

'On that power and that mercy, as revealed in Christ, and secured by promise to the believer in Christ, it is our privilege to cast ourselves. O blessed sickness, sorrow, or fear of death, which proves instrumental in bringing the heart to the Redeemer! Messengers of mercy all, and conveying us in faith and prayer to Him who casts out none, who is the Resurrection and the Life, and who, having given the greatest gift of love, will withhold no manner of thing that is good.

'To His power and mercy I commend you all, and hope to be employed in giving thanks for the recovery of your dear child.—Yours, my dear friend, very affectionately,

'W. M.'

To the Same.

'SOUTH MALLING, LEWES, *Aug.* 9, 1849.

'DEAR MR. GORDON,— . . . On the 17th of St. John I sometimes startle my friends by asserting that our blessed Lord does pray for the world, notwithstanding ver. 9, and endeavour to prove it thus:—Consider—

'I. The persons for whom He prays.

'II. The blessings for which He prays.

'1. He prays for His apostles, and thereby consecrates them to their high office (ver. 9).

'2. For all who should believe through their word (ver. 20).

'3. Ultimately for the world (vers. 21-23). And this agrees with all prophecy. When Christ has perfected His Church (ver. 21), then the knowledge of the Lord shall cover the earth. Read Ps. lxxii.; Isa. xi.; Rev. xi. 15; Amos ix.; xi. 12, with Acts xvi. 17, and Rom. xi. 15, as connected with this subject.

'II. The blessings for which He prays.

'1. That His disciples might be kept from the evil that is in the world (ver. 15).

'2. That they might be sanctified through the truth (ver. 17).

'3. That they might be *one* (in love)—ver. 21—(one mystical body united in Christ, and so to the Father).

'4. That they might be with Him and behold His glory (a beautiful climax).

'The words "*believe*" and "*know*" are used in the sense of a saving faith and knowledge in the 8th verse. I therefore infer that they are used in the same sense in vers. 21-23.

'The world will not be converted till the Church be brought into that unity expressed in ver. 21. But our Lord prays for the world ultimately,—does He not?

'I like questions to be asked. They set me thinking. I am no more infallible than the Pope of Rome! But my Bible is.'

To the Same.

'BRIGHTON, *Sept.* 11, 1849.

'MY DEAR FRIEND,—You have truth in its origin. Beyond a doubt the next dispensation will be one of sight. Nor will Jew and Gentile be united, the Church be formed, or the world blessed, till He, who visited us in great humility, shall return in majesty and glory. As to the conversion of the Jew, nationally considered, St. Paul was a type (1 Tim. i. 16). "They shall look upon Me whom they have pierced" (Zech. xii. 10). The 98th Psalm gives the history to come. Substitute the word "rule" for "judge" in the last verse, and you see the cause of the universal rejoicing. He will then "put down all rule, authority, and power" opposed to truth, holiness, and peace. Who, therefore, would not say, "Amen, even so come, Lord Jesus"?

'I never knew an anti-millenarian give a satisfactory answer to 2 Thess. ii. 8. If the Man of Sin must be destroyed before the millennial period, the Lord must come before that period; for it is of His personal, not spiritual coming, that the apostle is speaking. Spiritual, indeed, that will be also, for there will be little spirituality till then. Judah will vex Ephraim, and Ephraim envy Judah.'

To the Same.

'LEAMINGTON, *Feb.* 6, 1850.

'MY DEAR FRIEND,—I thank you for your note to-day. It reminds me of what I ought to be. My family lesson this morning was the 73d Psalm. Simeon used to call it the old man's psalm. When we consider the mixture of motive in our actions, how truly we must say—

"The best obedience of my hands
Dares not appear before Thy throne."

This self-knowledge leads us to trust in a perfect righteousness, even the righteousness of Christ Jesus our Lord. He also, as our High Priest, bears away the iniquity of our holy things. Accepted in Him, our prayers, our praises, our services are put into His censer and ascend perfumed.

'The duties of old age are reflection, gratitude, humility, and a deep sense of nearness to eternity,—hope as to that eternity, and a cheerful recommendation to all around of the blessedness of the faith of Christ (Ps. xiii. 6; lxxiii. 26; ciii.; 2 Tim. i. 12).

'You must tell me any other duties that occur to you as belonging to that period of life, or as belonging to me in particular as a minister. Our duties are double.

'... A TRADESMAN said to me, "I have enough, and yet riches flow in. Should I not retire from business?"

'I answered, "*Yes;* if your heart be set on wealth, or if you intend to hoard it."

'I said, "*No;* if you intend to lay out your profits, in the service of God and man."

'Diligence in trade or profession is no real hindrance to religion: Adam was to till the ground and keep it, even in Paradise.

'Doubtless, as in other cases, watchfulness and prayer (a heart for prayer and an eye for the Bible) are necessary. But the heart may be with God, while the mind is given to the duties of the day.

'Though some profession or business be most desirable in this world, yet let us rejoice in the prospect of that world in which "His servants shall serve Him, and they shall see His face, and His name shall be on their foreheads."

'Activity, contemplation, and conformity will be there for ever united.'

TO AN INVALID.

On Divine Faithfulness.

'*April* 1850.

'MY DEAR FRIEND,— . . . I need not tell you that a change of employment, and even of reading, is necessary to an invalid. Christians—sinners believing in the Saviour—have need to give little credit to physical feelings as affecting their spiritual state.

'The covenant is ordered in all things, and sure. The

love of God is everlasting. The work of Christ is perfect. The promises of Scripture are yea and amen. Here we must rest. The enjoyment of divine truth may be much interrupted, but truth itself is unchangeable; and confidence honours its great Author.

'I am beginning my Bible again. When Mr. Cadogan was offered Tom Paine's works, he said, "I have not done with Moses and the prophets yet." We shall *never* have done with them.

'One more thought. Accepted in Christ, we have a title to heaven. In the spirit of love we have a meetness for heaven. Love contains in itself all holiness.'

Mr. Chalmers was offered the living of South Malling, in Sussex, in the year 1849; and, after some consideration, he accepted it. But it was not without deep reluctance that he made up his mind to resign the curacy of St. Mary's, Leamington,—involving, as it necessarily did, for his wife separation from a father so beloved, and for himself from one with whom he had lived and laboured, as son and curate, with the warmest affection and most entire sympathy.

My father keenly felt the trial; yet, recognising in the appointment a providential call, he advised the acceptance of the living. But before he parted from his daughter, whose tender devotion to him was, to the day of his death, an unceasing source of comfort and delight, he caused these words to be engraved for her upon a ring—'If two of you shall agree on earth as touching anything which they shall ask, it shall be done for them of my Father which is in heaven' (Matt. xviii. 19).

They had mutually agreed to pray that, if good in the sight of that all-wise Father, they might ere long be brought together again, to live under one roof. Within two years of that parting and prayer, their God had granted them their hearts' desire.

In the spring of 1850, my father, accompanied by his family, spent a short time in the Isle of Wight. The object of his visit was to be present at the marriage of his only son, then incumbent of St. James's, Ryde, to Rose, daughter of the late George Morgan, Esq., of Brickenderbury Manor, and niece of Lord Tredegar.

No man could throw himself more heartily into the hopes and joys of young hearts, and none could take a higher or more apostolic view of marriage—not only as God's ordinance for the happiness of man in Paradise, but even more so, as it sets forth the relationship between Christ and His Church.

For a heart like his, ever chivalrously alive to excellence in woman, that which he found in a gentle and attractive young daughter-in-law could not fail to have a peculiar charm. The affection between them was mutual, and remained unaltered to the last.

Towards the close of this year, my father began to feel that the various and incessant duties which had accumulated upon him in Leamington, had become overwhelming. It was not only the unfailing increase, year by year, of parish duties (in which he was ably assisted by his curate, the Rev. William Croker), but his help was sought as that of a father by the whole town. Every society, philanthropic and religious, claimed the boon of his benignant presence and gifted advocacy: for his powers as a public speaker had increased in charm by the mellowness gained in advancing years.

He had united with his beloved friends, Mr. O'Halloran, and that noble Christian sailor, the late Admiral Henry Trotter, and others, in the formation of a Scripture-Readers' Society for the town; and had been the mainspring in establishing branch associations for the support of the Society for promoting Christianity amongst the Jews, and of the Irish Church Missions, besides forwarding the cause of the Bible and the Church Missionary Societies which had been previously established in the place, chiefly by the influence of Mr. Sherer, and of Mr. Edwin Woodhouse, who in after years devoted himself to the circulation of passages of Scripture in large type, by placing them in railway waiting-rooms, workhouses, gaols, and other public places throughout England.

Amongst various efforts for the moral as well as spiritual benefit of his fellow-creatures, my father warmly befriended the Total Abstinence Society. Though himself, both as to food and beverage, one of the most abstemious of men, he gave up, in the year 1841, his daily glass of wine; because he could not bear to urge working men, whose comforts are few, to relinquish all use of alcoholic liquors, whilst allowing himself even the smallest supply. This practice was continued by him for upwards of fourteen years, until his health began to fail, and wine was medically ordered.

He felt convinced that total abstinence was in most cases the only remedy which could reach a confirmed drunkard, so as to render him capable of understanding the offer, the appeal, and the requirements of the Gospel. At the same time, he was most careful to impress upon all 'teetotalers' who came under his influence, that if 'total abstinence' were put in the place of conversion, or regarded in any other light than as the handmaid of religion, it would be a deadly injury to immortal souls.

The following statement of his gifts as a public speaker was written by Mr. Chalmers:—

'Nowhere was his eloquence more felt or appreciated than at public meetings. His radiant countenance was always greeted with welcome, and was equally hailed with acceptance whether the audience were the rich and refined, or the humbler classes of society; whether the subject were of public importance to the masses of the working men of Birmingham, or connected with the religious societies brought before the visitors of Leamington. His appearance on the platform seemed to exercise an immediate influence upon the assembly; and the influence was the effect both of his life and character, and of those personal qualities which so endeared him to all who knew him.

'Every one seemed to feel that they possessed in him a friend; speakers and hearers alike looked to the beaming countenance, and all were ready to catch the lively and loving words which were sure to fall from his lips. His speeches were exactly what his look and character betokened.

'The most striking felicity of expression and illustration, the most chaste and correct and simple language, the clearest and most distinct énunciation of his ideas,—these were the outward clothing of thoughts which always overflowed with love to God and benevolence to man. In the most stirring meetings at Birmingham, his voice was like oil upon the waters; and while he was able to bring out into prominence the principles of truth, wherever it was to be found, there was always a kindliness of feeling, and a judicial calmness, which gave the utmost possible credit to opponents, and disarmed hostility of its personality and bitterness.

'But it was in meetings for the furtherance of the great religious and philanthropic causes of the day, that he found his most congenial element. To listen to the most lengthened details of effort for the mitigation of suffering, or the promotion of what was good, seemed to produce no weariness in him. The subject swallowed up all lassitude; and every tiding of success which could be gathered from the humblest labourer or the most unpractised speaker, was manifestly received with a zest and avidity which his keen sympathies and overflowing benevolence turned into a real feast. For this reason he generally preferred, notwithstanding the remonstrances of friends, to reserve his own speech to the conclusion of the meeting. He would then, with the finest tact, string together anything worthy of notice which had fallen from preceding speakers; enrich all with the happiest comment or aptest illustration; frequently enliven the subject with some well selected anecdote; and wind up all with an appeal enforced by quotations or adaptations of Holy Scripture, which seemed to breathe his own loving spirit upon those who heard, and make all for the moment at least to be wiser, happier, and better men.

'Strong as his predilections were for our own Church, they were based upon his deep convictions of her scriptural wisdom, her scriptural moderation, and her studious honour of God's Holy Word. Every unsectarian society, therefore, which exalted the Word of God, claimed his sympathies; but they seemed more joyously to expand on two special subjects. The one was the conversion of the house of Israel, on which he never spoke but apparently under an absorbing sense of the Apostle's words, "of whom as concerning the flesh Christ came, who is over all, God blessed for ever." The other was the British and Foreign Bible Society, the magnitude of whose aims to send the message of a Saviour's love and grace to every nation and kindred and people and tongue reflected the wide benevolence of his own soul. Gentle as he was by nature, there were also two subjects which always roused him to an indignation which could not be repressed. The one was Slavery, the other Popery. The sordid cruelty of the one over the body, and the dark superstition, tyranny, and relentless bigotry of the other, exercised over both soul and body, called forth his strongest denunciations; and yet, even with regard to these, he was always careful to disarm his invectives of personal asperity; to make every allowance for the shackles of education, and to discriminate between those who were the deceivers and the deceived.'

CHAPTER XI.

ONE HOME AGAIN.

'O DAYS of Heaven, and nights of equal praise,
Serene and peaceful as those heavenly days
When souls drawn upwards in communion sweet
Enjoy the stillness of some calm retreat,
Discourse, as if released and safe at home,
Of dangers past, and wonders yet to come,
And spread the sacred treasures of the breast
Upon the lap of covenanted rest.'

COWPER.

BECKENHAM RECTORY

ONE HOME AGAIN.

EARLY in the spring of 1851, Mr. Chalmers was presented to the living of Beckenham, in Kent. The first letter which he wrote, after accepting it, was to my father, affectionately to urge him to resign a charge too heavy for his advancing years; and to come and take up his abode at Beckenham Rectory, occupying himself with any share in the services of the Church to which he might feel equal, without the constraint of necessity. My father felt the wisdom of this counsel, and after brief consideration he accepted the proposal so lovingly made, recognising it as the answer to the prayer in which he had agreed to unite with my sister. But he delayed his departure from Leamington for a few months, until a judicious and devoted Christian minister, the Rev. Robert Morgan, was found to succeed him at St. Mary's. When this appointment was made, he prepared with delight to share one home again with his beloved daughter and son-in-law. But his happiness in the prospect of this family reunion was not unmixed with tender regrets for the friends and parishioners whom he was about to leave. Within the large circle of his acquaintance in

Leamington, he had attached to himself in an especial manner, a small knot of friends, who, in addition to their value for his ministry, were bound to him by ties of warm Christian affection. Amongst these may be mentioned Mr. and Mrs. Earle of Newbold Firs, whose agreeable society, with that of their bright young family, he frequently enjoyed at his own house; the Rev. James Riddell, who with his devoted wife and daughters were ever ready to assist in works of piety and benevolence. Mrs. Paske, a beloved friend of Colchester days, who, with her daughter, had settled at Leamington, chiefly for the sake of being near their old pastor; and Mr. and Mrs. O'Halloran, who were linked with all his interests in the place.

Testimonies to the reverence and affection with which he was regarded, flowed in from all sides. Amongst others, an eminent Nonconformist minister, the Rev. Dr. Octavius Winslow, thus wrote: 'The religious associations in Leamington meet now with depression and a sense of loss. It would be impossible to describe how all of every shade of opinion miss the animated eloquence with holy unction, the youthful ardour and buoyancy with apostolical wisdom and tenderness, so happily blended in Dr. Marsh. We seem to have lost a uniting link. Wherever he was present, the Dove of Peace (we felt) was brooding overhead.'

On leaving Leamington, my father and Mrs. Marsh paid a short visit to her beloved sister-in-law, the late Mrs. Lyttleton Powys, and from her house he wrote that he hoped to arrive at Beckenham Rectory on Saturday the 19th of July, in order to give his children their earnest desire, that he should spend his birthday in his new home.

Children and grandchildren had been assembled from far and near to welcome his first arrival at Beckenham. The best suite of rooms in that charming rectory had been reserved for him and Mrs. Marsh, by the thoughtful love of its owners.

My father was expected by five o'clock, but six, and at length seven had struck, and no sign of his arrival was given. In the dulness of 'hope deferred,' the large family party sat down to dinner without his joy-giving presence.

Suddenly, however, a peal rang out from the belfry of the village church; and scarcely had they all reached the steps in front of the hall-door when the carriage was seen driving in at the gateway. Servants and lingering workmen, at that inspiriting call, hastily left their employments to follow the family; and almost as quickly my sister's little son climbed out of his crib in the nursery, to run down stairs and spring into the arms of his grandsire.

As he entered the house, the sweet voice of my eldest sister led the old and loved doxology—

'Praise God, from whom all blessings flow,
Praise Him, all creatures here below;
Praise Him above, ye heavenly host;
Praise Father, Son, and Holy Ghost'—

in which every one heartily joined.

At the first note of the song of thanksgiving, my father uncovered his venerable head; and he bowed it in reverence, when the last note had died away, as he prayed, 'Peace be to this house, and to all who enter here.' Then, with a look of radiant love around, he exclaimed, 'I dwell among mine own people!'

Immediately afterwards, he was led by my sister to see his own rooms. As he looked from the windows on the sweet English views of garden and lawn, and fields and wood and stream, his eyes were often lifted up in praise to God; and he said, 'I shall like to go from this paradise to the Paradise above.'

From first to last, he thoroughly enjoyed his residence in Beckenham. In addition to its own attractions, and the happiness he found in the large family circle, the easy access to London gave him the opportunity of renewing many of his old friendships, and of taking an active part in several of the religious meetings, as well as of sharing in other ways in the deep and stirring interests of the metropolis.

It was pleasant to see the welcome which, wherever he went, awaited him. In Exeter Hall, the sight of his silvery head was watched for, and his smile of recognition was sought both by clergy and laity on the platform, and by numbers amongst the audience in the body of the hall. His address was eagerly expected, and received with a general expression of warm interest and reverent affection.

At the meeting of the Society for Promoting Christianity amongst the Jews, he was peculiarly happy, and especially in his manner of addressing the Hebrew children educated at the Society's school in Bethnal Green, who are present on these occasions. Dearly did he love to listen to the rich melody of the national voice, in the anthems and hymns which they sang before the commencement of the meeting; and especially to the one with which they usually closed, beginning with this verse—

'When His salvation bringing
To Zion Jesus came,
The children all stood singing
Hosanna to His name.
Hosanna!
Hosanna to Jesus our King!'

Frequently at these meetings might be seen the last of my father's contemporaries and his first fellow-worker in the ministry, Mr. Haldane Stewart. They generally sat side by side, and their 'hoary heads' were 'crowns of glory' to those Christian assemblies.

He regularly attended also the meetings of the Bible, the Church Missionary, the Prayer-book and Homily, and the Soldiers' Friend Societies. The Protestant Association too had the benefit of his earnest advocacy; and on its platform he often met, with no slight pleasure, Dr. Hugh McNeile, the friend who from early manhood had been dear to him; whose warm sympathy had brought him from Liverpool to Birmingham, to speak words of comfort to my father in his deepest bereavement; and whose unwearied work for God, and unflinching courage in the front of the battle for Protestant truth, at all risks of loss of worldly promotion—had made my father continually thank God on his behalf.

Another of his pleasures, perhaps the dearest, in Exeter Hall, and elsewhere, was to meet on every platform where the cause of scriptural religion or philanthropy was advocated,—the man known and respected even in the dingy alleys of St. Giles's, and among the haunts of thieves--the friend of the friendless, the champion of the overtasked, himself working harder than any, to redress the wrongs of the poor and needy—the Earl of Shaftesbury.

But if meeting with valued friends on these occasions was a delight to him, it would be impossible to describe the happiness which filled his heart as he listened to the stories of territory after territory reclaimed from waste places of the earth for its lawful King—to whose final crowning, 'with many crowns,' His faithful servant was joyfully looking forward.

'PERFECT LOVE CASTETH OUT FEAR.'

'DEAR MR. GORDON,—. . . Oh, if the great day were kept in view, what different Christians we should be! "How will such a spirit or such a line of conduct appear then?" would be the great question. The more love prevails, the less fearful will be that day. "Herein is our love made perfect, that we may have boldness in the day of judgment" (1 John iv. 17). It may be understood thus—So that we have boldness in (reference to) the day of judgment. Because we are partakers of His nature, which is love. Again, "We know that we have passed from death unto life, because we love the brethren."

'More humility, and more love, would go far towards healing all divisions in the Church. We must pray for "all who profess and call themselves Christians."

'Love to you all.—Yours ever truly, WM. MARSH.'

'Ah, dear friend, if the Thracians wept over the cradle but rejoiced over the tomb, under the idea of the miseries of life being ended, how much more may Christians rejoice over the tomb of those who, like the beloved Henry, have entered upon eternal joys. The loss, indeed, must be felt by survivors, and especially by yourself; but in proportion as you can look beyond the grave,—for he is not there, —you will be cheered even in the gloom. His heart was overflowing with love. This arose from having known and believed the love that God had to him. And love is the true meetness for that kingdom which the blessed Redeemer, by overcoming the sharpness of death, has opened to all believers. I enclose my little tract on the loss of friends, but you need it not. May the Comforter bring to your recollection every soothing thought, and fill you with the delightful prospect of being ever with those you love, yea, ever with the Lord, the eternal fountain of joy to all His people.—Yours, dear friend, in true sympathy,

'Wm. Marsh.'

ON THE TESTIMONY OF SOME UNBELIEVERS TO THE EXCELLENCE OF CHRISTIANITY.

'Will the quotation from Lord Bolingbroke answer any purpose with Mr. —— ?

'Under such impressions as his, what deep research there should be as to the evidences of the Divinity of the Lord Jesus Christ, and what deep silence rather than speaking lightly of it, or inducing others so to speak.

'"He that believeth on Him is not condemned: but

he that believeth not is condemned already, because he hath not believed in the name of the only begotten Son of God. And this is the condemnation, that light is come into the world, and men loved darkness rather than light, because their deeds were evil" (John iii. 18, 19). Here He solemnly condemns wilful unbelief. But we must despair of none.

'That great philosopher, Dr. Mason Good, was an unbeliever, but he became convinced that Christianity must be Divine, from the effect it had produced on a person he had attended as a medical adviser. He then read the Scriptures with diligence, and prayed God to enlighten him, and became one of the most useful Christians of the day.

'Lord Herbert, a freethinker, calls Christianity the best religion, and acknowledges that its doctrines and precepts aim at the establishment of those very articles of belief in which he says all religion consists. Dr. Tindall, a freethinker, says, that Christianity is a most holy religion.

'Lord Bolingbroke asserts, that no religion has ever appeared in the world, the natural tendency of which is to promote the purest happiness of mankind, like the Christian faith; that no system can be more simple and plain. "It is," he adds, "a complete system, adapted to answer all the purposes of religion, natural and revealed." He thinks that it could not be opposed by thinking and rational beings, had it been propagated with the same simplicity with which it was originally taught by Christ. "Supposing Christianity to have been an invention, it had been the most amiable and the most useful invention that was ever imposed on mankind for their good."'

'My dear Friend,—I do not in the least wonder at your desolate feelings. We are not angels, but of the human nature, and sorrow is a part of our portion here. But your desolate feelings are no proofs that God does not love you. I often think of the wisdom of Manoah's wife (Judges xiii. 23). You have not only heard of salvation by Jesus Christ our Lord, but have believed there is no salvation in any other; and you will find it to be true, and will be enabled to rejoice in Him, notwithstanding the shrinking of nature from the sorrow under which you suffer. I lift up my heart while writing, that, though "walking in darkness," you may yet trust that all shall end well. . . . You say you "would, but cannot give your heart to God." "If there be first a willing mind, it is accepted." "He knoweth whereof we are made, and remembereth that we are dust," and has compassion on our infirmities. One of the Fathers said, "Take my heart, for I cannot give it to Thee. Keep my heart, for I cannot keep it for Thee; and save me in spite of myself."'

'If Christians would take common sense as their guide, they would make such discoveries as to the Divine character and the Divine purposes, as would astonish and delight their hearts. But we must be patient towards all men, and not unchristianize any because they cannot see with our eyes. As long as they hold Christ the Head, and derive an influence from Him as members, all will be well. Light increases as I read, yet I have nothing *new* to advance. It is the old truth, the everlasting truth, that God is light, and God is love.'

'If men had studied how time could be misspent, money wasted, temper injured, spiritual duties neglected, and religion be regarded rather as burdensome than as making the happiness of man, they could not have invented a better mode than the usual amusements of cards, assemblies, theatres, and such like.

'Where the treasure is, there is the heart; and where the heart, there the happiness; and where the happiness, there the God.'

ON THE TENTH ANNIVERSARY OF HIS SECOND DAUGHTER'S MARRIAGE.

'*Nov. 26th, for 27th,* 1853.

'Lost, ten years ago, a daughter, named Matilda Harriett Marsh. Gained, ten years ago, a son, named Frederick Courteney Chalmers. Both redeemed property, belonging to the Redeemer for ever; and, through Providence and grace, both, with all theirs, mine for ever.

'*Text for the day.*

' "In everything, by prayer and supplication, with thanksgiving, let your requests be made known unto God."

' "And the peace of God, which passeth all understanding, shall keep your hearts and minds through Christ Jesus."

'*My Text.*

'The God which hath fed me all my life long unto this

BECKENHAM CHURCH.

day, the Angel which redeemed me from all evil, bless them all. WM. MARSH.'

'Whoever will bring all "the property" here before Christmas shall have their carriage paid, and be handsomely rewarded.'

By the request of Mr. Chalmers, my father preached once every Sunday in the parish church; from time to time, also, he assisted some of the neighbouring clergy. There was a morning service every Wednesday in Beckenham Church, after which he regularly preached. Several of the clergy and laity from the surrounding parishes felt it to be a privilege to attend; gathering wisdom from his ripened experience, and deep Scriptural knowledge. Some of these friends would come to the rectory afterwards; and, whilst partaking of the ever-ready hospitality to be found there, enjoyed finding a place in the genial family circle of which he was the centre and the sunshine.

Children, grandchildren, and in later years, great-grandchildren gathered around him, delighting in the varied play of his pleasant wit, his store of anecdotes, told with brevity, point, and animation; his brilliant spirits, and inexhaustible sweetness of temper.

And none the less were they impressed by the manner in which he held every gift as a trust to be used for his Master; and consecrated every affection of that loving heart, by setting the Lord always before Him.

From the time when the Lord had called him, the language of his heart had been—

'Become my rejoicing, my stronghold of love,
My aim and my end;
My glory on earth, and my glory above,
O Jesus, my Friend!'

And now, in old age, the steadily increasing knowledge of his Saviour, rooted in ever-deepening humility, had ripened into a conscious and abiding 'fellowship with the Father and with His Son Jesus Christ.'

He sustained the freshness of his mind by diligent reading. From eight in the morning till twelve at night he was constantly occupied in reading, writing, or conversation. Works of literature or science, the press of the day, leading reviews, biographies, and writings on prophetical subjects, formed his recreation. But his studies lay amongst the works of the old divines. The writings of the Reformers, of Archbishop Leighton, and Bishops Jewel, Horne, and Hall were some of his especial favourites. In Owen and Erskine, also, he found much food for thought. Not less was his interest in continuing to hold communion, through their writings, with the fathers of his own early day—Scott, Newton, Romaine, and other leaders of the evangelical revival of the last century—men of whom he was wont to say, 'There were giants in those days.'

But far above all other books, did he read, mark, learn, and inwardly digest, the Word of God. A few years later, he told his children, that besides the constant study of the New Testament, he had read the Bible straight through more than fifty times. Rich was the harvest reaped from his meditation day and night in the law of his God, by those who conversed with him on Scriptural subjects, or who had the privilege of being present when he conducted family worship.

It would be vain to attempt, by any fragments preserved, to give an idea of the mingled brightness and wisdom of his conversations. But some of the following thoughts may recal to those who knew him happy hours passed in his society.

These words were noted down, from time to time, by his eldest daughter, Mrs. Francis Trench, whose mind was in such harmony with her father's that she was peculiarly happy in calling forth his views on scriptural subjects. She thus writes :—

'One Sunday evening, when he was delighting us by his presence at Islip Rectory, after I had been singing his favourite hymn,—

"There is a land of pure delight,"

he gave me another rendering of the last verse, which turns it into a prayer :—

"Place me, O Lord, where Moses stood,
The promised land to see;
Not Jordan's stream, nor death's cold flood,
Could keep me back from Thee."

'Then he added, "Do you know that Moses died of joy? He was not allowed to enter the promised land. There were reasons for this. Moses was typical of the law, and therefore could not enter the land of promise. Also, the Lord would reprove his conduct on one occasion; but though He could not allow him to enter Canaan, He would let him *see* it. 'Oh let me see that goodly land!'

So the Lord told him to go up the mount. When Moses was on the top of Pisgah"—(here he stood up and pointed out, in imagination, the various places)—"the Lord told him to look at the land. There is Bethlehem, where Messiah will be born; there is Galilee, where He will frequently teach the people; there is Jerusalem, where He will reprove the errors of the priests; there is Gethsemane, where will commence His dreadful agony; there is Calvary, where He will die a sacrifice for the sins of mankind; there is the grave of Joseph of Arimathea, where His body will be laid. From thence He will rise from the dead, and appear to many of His disciples. From Mount Olivet He will ascend gloriously into heaven. Then His gospel will be preached, and a way will be open to Jew and Gentile to have, through Him, eternal life. But, Moses, your people must pass through a fiery trial. They must be driven from their own land, and trodden under foot of the Gentiles, till the 'times of the Gentiles be fulfilled;' and when the tribulation is ended, they shall see Messiah in yonder clouds. They shall be converted to Him. They shall be more blessed than ever. From that period He will put His fear into them, that they shall never depart from Him. Jerusalem shall be the metropolis of the globe, and the holy of holies; Judea, the holy place; and the rest of the world the court of the Gentiles. Thus shall God be glorified in the final glory of your people!" And here he acted Moses fainting and dying—"'I can bear no more!' He had had such a wonderful view of the whole dispensation, that his heart burst with joy."

'Speaking afterwards about a testimony on a dying bed as not being *needful*, but *pleasant* when given, he mentioned that Mr. Cadogan had said, "Don't tell me what his death was, tell me what his life was."

'On another occasion, he remarked, "If I were to speak to a wilful infidel, who propagates his unbelief, I should say, You are both unreasonable and uncharitable. What do you mean? It is not the way of sound reason to take the side of danger. If this Book be true, where are you then? You take the side of danger, therefore you are unreasonable. And you are uncharitable. This Book has been the comfort of many a sorrowing heart in this world. They have drawn their comfort thence. It has given them a hope beyond this world and its trials, beyond death and the grave. If you take this Book from them, what have you to give in its stead? See how uncharitable you are."

'Speaking of views which would, in this day, be called Ritualistic, he said, "They put tradition in the place of Scripture; the priesthood in the place of Christ; and the Sacraments in the place of the Holy Spirit."

'"There are two things a man should do: Follow his conscience, and endeavour to get his conscience as much enlightened as he can."

'One evening he gave us a beautiful commentary on the Romans; and, at the last chapter, he said, "Who are those that may help in this work? 'Phœbe, our sister;' 'Tryphena and Tryphosa;' and you know the list. Women lent their aid then; and women, as well as men, may lend their aid now."

'Then, speaking of visiting the people at Islip, he gave me the following instructions: "In your visits, I would be short, not to tire the people, nor to take up too much of their time. You might say something like this: 'A soul, a Saviour, and a heaven.' 'Time is short, with all its trials. Eternity will be long, with all its blessings;' and then a text or two of Scripture. A soul: 'What shall it profit a man, if he gain the whole world, and lose his own soul?' A Saviour, who 'came to seek and to save that which was lost.' A heaven: 'In my Father's house are many mansions.'"

'He told me of an old woman, living by herself in an isolated cottage at Ashampstead, whom he asked one day, "Molly, are you not afraid sometimes of being alone all night?" to which she replied,

"My noonday walks He shall attend,
And all my midnight hours defend."

'One Sunday morning, he said, "May this Sabbath day be a *high* day to many souls," and then made the following verse:—

"May many troubled souls this day,
Like little Samuel, learn to pray,
'Speak, for thy servant heareth.'
And many souls, oppressed with guilt,
Hear of that blood on Calvary spilt,
Which the believer cheereth."

'Speaking of the passage, Heb. xi. 6, he said, "Two things to believe: His being, and His bounty."

'"Faith, hope, and love are the great privileges of our religion. Let us daily pray that God may give us the increase of faith, hope, and love.

"*Faith*, in the first Coming of our Lord; hope, in His second Coming; love, to Him who came into our world to save us,—who lived and died, and rose again, and ascended into Heaven, and ever liveth to make intercession for us.

"*Hope* of the second Coming of our blessed Redeemer. The Spirit of Christ in all the prophets testified beforehand of the sufferings of Christ and the glory that should follow. Not one book of the New Testament that does not refer to it. In the 1st Epistle to the Thessalonians, it is mentioned five times.

'"God is love; and he that *dwelleth in love* dwelleth in God, and God in him. Hereafter it will be inscribed on the skies of the universe, that 'God is Love.'"

'One of my sisters went with me to his sitting-room late one night to persuade him to leave off reading and retire to rest. He was kneeling, with his back to the door and did not see or hear us (from his deafness). We paused for a moment before noiselessly retreating. His hands were upraised, and we caught the words, "Hasten, Lord, the time when the kingdoms of this world shall become the kingdoms of our Lord and His Christ; when Thou shalt make Jerusalem a praise in the earth; when all shall sing, 'Salvation to our God and the

Lamb. Hallelujah! for the Lord God omnipotent reigneth. Hallelujah!'"

'At the close of Easter Day he said, "What an indulgence God has granted me in assembling so large a number of my children and grandchildren for Easter. All mercies come to us through Redemption.

> 'Every blessing, without measure,
> Flows to us through Christ the Lord.'"

'"An old clergyman once said, 'When I come to die, I shall have my greatest grief and my greatest joy; my greatest grief that I have done so little for the Lord Jesus, and my greatest joy that the Lord Jesus has done so much for me.'"

'"For a thrice threefold cord, look to FATHER, SON, AND HOLY GHOST, as the objects of faith, hope, and love, and this will enable you to live soberly, righteously, and godly. Yet a little while, and we shall find ourselves in a world where every thing will be to our hearts' content. I wish I could think of it morning, noon, and night, and of Him who became poor that I might be thus rich; a man of sorrows, that I might be thus joyful."'

'"WAITING for the adoption, to wit, the redemption of the body" (Rom. viii. 23). The idea is from ancient customs.

'"A private adoption. A public adoption. The Christian's private adoption (Gal. iv. 6). His public adoption, the Resurrection."

'"Christian friendship soon begins and never ends."

'"I am still able to preach twice a week, but I confess weariness; it is one of the few things in which we can be apostolic."

'"True science and true religion are friends,—the God of nature is the God of grace."

'"No effort in the Lord's service is ever in vain; but trust in the merit of any service is always in vain; and it is remarkable that those who do most good works are the last persons in the world to trust in them. 'What hast thou that thou hast not received?' is a text continually before their eyes."

'"What would this world be without the sun, and what would our hearts be without the Sun of Righteousness?"

'"I would not live in this world without a Providence, nor leave it without a Saviour."

'"Let us look to the antitype of the brazen serpent; to Him who uttered the words, 'It is finished.' Let us look at Joseph of Arimathea's empty tomb; let us go to the mount of Olives, and behold Him ascending to the Father's right hand. Oh, let us behold Him as ever living to make intercession for us; as offering up our poor prayers and praises, perfuming them with His merits, and see that we are accounted righteous in the sight of God for His sake, our sins forgiven, our poor services accepted. Let us pray that all unbelieving doubts and fears may be removed; regard all discouraging thoughts as coming from beneath, all encouraging thoughts as coming from above. Pray that you may thus overcome the evil one. Men are little aware of his great and mysterious power, but thus you shall not be ignorant of his devices. Look to Jesus to bring you safe to eternal life, and believe that nothing shall separate you from His love; 'neither death nor life, nor angels, nor principalities, nor powers, nor any other creature, shall be able to separate us from the love of God, which is in Christ Jesus our Lord;' and thus you shall have joy in believing."

'The following was written in a copy of Mr. Trench's *Life of St. John*, when presented to a friend by my father:—

" To believe with St. John,
To love with St. John,
To serve with St. John;
This is eternal life,
This is blessedness,
This is usefulness."

'"If I were to fall into a river and were just drowning, and some benevolent man jumped in and saved me, I should praise that man for what he had done for me; but if afterwards I heard that he was a very good and a very benevolent man, and did much good in the world, I should praise him for what he was in himself. So have we cause to praise the Lord for what he has done for us, and for what He is in Himself. 'Let everything that hath breath praise the Lord.'"

'One evening my husband spoke of a reason why some to whom he had alluded had taken réfuge in Romanism, namely, that they could not bear the thought of responsibility. My father remarked, "Then they choose a fellow-creature to be responsible for them rather than the Almighty Saviour Himself. I think," he added, "that reply of Judah to his father Jacob would be true and beautiful if applied to the Saviour, representing Him as saying to the Father touching every soul committed to His care, 'I will be surety for him; of my hand shalt thou require him: if I bring him not unto thee, and set him before thee, then let me bear the blame for ever.'"

'Mr. Trench quoted a saying of old Fuller's:—"He that falls into sin is a man; he that grieves at sin is a saint; he that boasts of sin is a devil." My father replied, "Only one thing more, He that forgives it is GOD."

'"We should endeavour to remember our mercies. We remember our trials, but we are too apt to forget our mercies. Among the greatest is the forgiveness of sins."

'Speaking of the blessings of salvation by Christ, he said,—

"If a person is a believer in Christ, what does he gain?
"He gains the pardon of all his sins.
"What more does he gain?
"He gains acceptance with God.
"Anything more?
"Yes, the Holy Spirit to sanctify him.

"Anything more?

"Yes, all things become blessings. The curse is turned into a blessing.

"Anything more?

"Yes, all the strength he needs by the way; and then an entrance into Paradise.

"Anything more?

"Yes, the resurrection of the body, made like unto Christ's glorious body.

"Anything more?

"Yes, to sit with Christ on His Throne; to reign with Him.

"Anything more?

"I will tell you at the end of eternity."

'In speaking on the subject of introducing religious conversation in society, without knowing the character of those present, or how it will be taken, he observed, "We are sometimes too ready to fancy that it will not be well received; but," he added, "it is very difficult at times, specially if there is nobody to support one. We have in the Proverbs, 'A word spoken *in due season*, how good is it.' The figure also is very remarkable, '*seasoned* with salt.' It must not be too much."

'On a visit of my dear father to us at Reading, in May 1854, he told us, "I was baptized, confirmed, ordained deacon, and appointed lecturer, all in one parish. Coming here," he added, "reminds me of all the way by which the Lord hath led me. A call for much humility and much gratitude. 'Thou shalt consider in thine heart, and remember all the way in which the Lord thy God led thee.'"

'Referring to the future state, beyond the millennial period, he said, "The mediatorial work having accomplished all that was intended, then the Triune God becomes 'all in all.'" He considered that the inhabitants of our earth in the millennium would be "a race of men preparing for a higher state, as Adam in Paradise, supposing he had lived a thousand years there in an unfallen state." Then he added, "It appears to me that the millennial world is to be distinct from the 'kings and priests.' Kings have subjects, and priests have services. *They* are to 'reign with Christ' during the thousand years; and to 'serve Him,' 'seeing His face.'

'"If we can only say Hosanna now, we shall sing Hallelujah then."

'"That is a fine expression, not only liberty, but '*glorious* liberty of the children of God.' There are two other things mentioned in that chapter (Rom. viii.), the 'manifestation of the sons of God,' and the 'redemption of the body.' They have not yet been manifested. 'The world knoweth us not;' but 'when manifested,' they will enjoy their glorious liberty in a redeemed body."

'He remarked, "Though the passages are not many, I think they are very decided as to the consciousness of the spirit in the separate state, and quite warrant the beautiful expression in our funeral service, 'With whom do *live* the spirits of just men made perfect.' The most clear, I think, is 'absent from the body, present with the Lord.'"

'Speaking of Romans v., he said, "It is a wonderful chapter. The contrast between the two Adams, the one bringing death, the other life. The one bringing evil, the other good. The whole of blessing, preponderating over the curse, will be 'much more' than we can tell."

'"The Law is subservient to the Gospel, by convincing us of our need of a Saviour, and the Gospel, when believed, becomes subservient to the Law, by producing in us the spirit of love."

'"Our remedy under the consciousness of sin is to be found in Christ's merits and atonement. Our comfort under trials and temptations is in His sympathy; but we do not want sympathy in *sin*—for *that* we have *His blood* that 'cleanseth from all sin.'"

'"The 'full assurance of *faith*' is a bounden duty. I have no right to doubt the Gospel. If I do not believe the record, I make God a liar. The 'full assurance of *hope*' is in our own perseverance to the end. There are many persons who have the full assurance of *faith*, who think they have no faith at all. They do not doubt the Gospel, but they doubt their own interest in it. You evangelicals," he playfully added, "make faith everything! —So we do. Believe and live; believe and hope; believe and obey; believe and love; believe and suffer; believe and serve; believe and go to heaven. I have only one thing more to say. There is a wonderful passage to encourage the lowest degree of faith (Heb. xi. 6): 'He that cometh to God' has only to believe two things, the being and the bounty of God, and then he will have a wonderful display of that bounty in the Gospel."

'"There was a serpent in the Paradise of man. There will be no serpent in the Paradise of God. That alone will make a vast difference."

'Speaking of Psalm ciii., in an exposition, he said, "David's harp was in beautiful tune when he wrote this, and he earnestly wishes to keep it in tune, and that to the best tune, the tune of praise, so he repeats it, 'Bless the Lord, O my soul; bless the Lord, and forget not all His benefits.' The memory is too often far too tenacious of what it ought to forget, and too easily forgets what it ought to remember."

'"As to religious reading, I am more than ever delighted with the four Gospels. I like daily to read something that our blessed Saviour said, or did, or suffered whilst on earth. There are four things remarkably noticeable in His character: Majesty and meekness, power and gentleness. The greatest man upon earth is he who is most humble. I remember an old hymn, speaking of searching for the Saviour when He was upon earth, having this line—

'Mark the lowest, that is He.'"

In the spring of 1852, Mr. Chalmers was requested to preach at Colchester; and on his return to Beckenham, he brought to his father-in-law such an urgent entreaty from his old flock, that, after an absence of twenty-three years, he would once more come amongst them, that his heart felt constrained to comply with it. It was therefore arranged that at the approaching anniversary of the Church Missionary Society, he should preach for it in the pulpit of St. Peter's, by the warm invitation of the vicar; and spend a few days amidst his old and faithful friends.

Accordingly, in the month of June, he went thither, accompanied by several members of his family. On arriving at the station, he found a crowd of well-remembered faces smiling their welcomes; whilst on some of the elder ones were tears of joy. Peals rang out from belfry to belfry of the distant churches, sounding softly across the river. On the road from the station to the town, groups of aged women were seen, waiting to catch a glimpse of their beloved old pastor's face. Windows had been engaged, for invalids to see him, in the street along which he was to pass; whilst a younger generation who had been trained to revere him, and to know his face by the portrait which hung in so many homes, blithely followed the carriage.

Opposite the door of the vicarage, a large number of men had assembled, who reverently raised their hats, but suppressed a shout of welcome, because one who had been no less dear to them, and who was by his side when he left that place, was no longer an inhabitant of this world.

On Sunday morning, St. Peter's was crowded with worshippers; and when the musical tones of that familiar voice, which had not sounded within those walls for so many years, were heard at the commencement of the Communion service, a suppressed exclamation of thankfulness was audible in several parts of the church. He preached Christ that day with even more than his usual tender earnestness. In the afternoon, he addressed the children and their teachers in the schoolroom; and, in the evening, again preached at St. Peter's.

The old beadle returned for the day to an office for which his strength had long been unequal, and followed his former vicar with watchful care, looking more than once into the pulpit to see that he had him safe at last. Several of the poor came long before the hour for service, in order to secure places between the vestry and the pulpit, that they might be able to touch his gown as he passed. Every foot of ground in the church was occupied; yet crowds were obliged to retire disappointed of entrance. A clergyman in the neighbourhood, and two Dissenting ministers in the town, had closed their respective places of worship that they might give their congregations the opportunity of attending at St. Peter's that evening, to hear words of 'truth and soberness' from the lips of one who had so long been 'esteemed very highly in love for his work's sake.'

Early in the week, my father pleaded the cause of the Church Missionary Society at the anniversary meetings. Wherever he went, his appearance was hailed with enthusiasm; and every word which fell from his lips was treasured by that grateful people. The old tie, never broken, was renewed in fresh strength; and year after year, from that time, until his health began to fail, he went to Colchester to preach and to speak for the Bible, the Jews, or the Church Missionary Society.

These visits afforded him the greatest pleasure; not merely from the gratification of the personal attachment of so many in different classes of life, but he had the joy, which an apostle counted unsurpassed, of seeing that his children walked in the Truth.

His excellent successor, the Rev. Samuel Carr, who, in his boyhood, had been led to the Saviour by my father's instrumentality, welcomed him with almost filial affection; and when, after his death, a stranger filled his place, it was with no stranger's heart that the Rev. Henry Caddell received the aged pastor. He opened his church and his home to welcome him, with loving respect, as a father in Christ, delighted that his parishioners should benefit by the experience of one so long and deeply taught of God.

On these occasions he visited many who had formerly been members of his flock and of the wider circle of his friends; some of whom during prolonged seasons of suffering and trial had been proving the truth of those Divine promises in which, in bygone years, they had been taught by him to trust. In the chamber of sickness his presence seemed to shed a tender radiance, as it was wont to bring a yet brighter glow to homes where health and happiness prevailed.

> 'When one who holds communion with the skies
> Has filled his urn where living waters rise,
> And once more mingles with us meaner things,
> 'Tis even as if an angel shook his wings.'

On leaving Colchester, my father usually went to

Birch Hall, the home of his long-loved friends, Mr. and Mrs. Charles Gray Round. It was his delight to attend their annual Church Missionary meeting, held in the spacious hall, where neighbours and tenants, to the number of three hundred, assembled to hear from him and others, stories of the gospel of peace in heathen lands. But he never allowed himself to plead for a society without remembering his ambassadorship, and its claims; bearing in mind to beseech those around him, in apostolic language, to 'be reconciled to God.' Nor did he forget to urge upon those who had found the way of peace, to 'press toward the mark, for the prize of the high calling of God in Christ Jesus.'

These visits to Birch Hall were always seasons of most refreshing Christian intercourse, not only with Mr. and Mrs. Round, in whom he delighted; but also from the enjoyment he found in the society of the rector of Birch (the Rev. William Harrison), between whom and himself there existed a peculiar sympathy of character and view.

In the year 1853, my father visited Terling Place, in Essex, the residence of his beloved and valued friend Lord Rayleigh. In former years Lord Rayleigh had been quartered, for a short time, in Colchester, when he had but recently received the message of life and peace. Lord Rayleigh not only made diligent use of his leisure in attending the public ministry at St. Peter's, but also availed himself of every opportunity of gaining help and strength in private intercourse and friendship with my father.

They met again, after many years, with undiminished

feelings of attachment; and Lord Rayleigh's welcome was cordially seconded by his attractive and warm-hearted wife, who, though until then a stranger, had ever after her own place in the affections of her husband's old and revered friend. Here also he met, for the first time, one whose manly frankness and noble simplicity of character, combined with his bright and fervent piety, at once gained my father's heart; and who, on his part, looked up to the aged Christian with a tender veneration, which rapidly ripened into a close communion of spirit rarely seen between two friends of such different ages. The young stranger was Lady Rayleigh's eldest brother, Captain Hedley Vicars, of the 97th Regiment, shortly afterwards to become well known as a devoted soldier of the cross and his country.

On my father's return to Beckenham, after the first of his visits to Colchester, he was deeply interested in a medical man, who had come to stay in the village in a hopeless consumption; and who was in deep despondency of heart, as well as sceptical in his views of revealed religion. Great was the joy to my father of watching the opening of the fine mind of the sufferer to 'the truth as it is in Jesus;' whilst to Mr. Reeve, the very sight of my father's face seemed to bring thoughts of peace and joy.

In the summer of 1853, the numbers of workmen assembling for the building of the Crystal Palace at Sydenham, and for the formation of the grounds, brought a great and long-lasting interest to Beckenham Rectory. My father shared in the whole, and in every detail of the work, with even more than his usual animation and wonderful power of sympathy. Although age prevented his going much amongst them, yet, whenever they were brought within his reach, his kindly looks and venerable appearance caused his words of counsel to be listened to with respectful interest. He always addressed them after their tea-parties in the grounds of the rectory; and not a man amidst those numbers would fail to kneel down when he led them in prayer.

Few things delighted him more than the mingling of rich and poor in these festivities. His birthday was anticipated in the parish as one of the high days of the year. All the old people were invited to drink tea on the lawn; and an easy spring-van went to and fro, from one end of the parish to the other, in the service of the most infirm.

On the first of these occasions, two old persons, who had been bedridden for years, found the use of their limbs for the day. In some cases, strenuous efforts were made to prove that the required age had been reached; and even elderly looks were now and then pleaded as a sufficient qualification. But with all due allowances for such cases, it was computed that the united ages of the members of the first 'birthday tea-party' amounted to four thousand years.

Many friends from the neighbourhood, and from London, besides parishioners, were invited to see and share the enjoyment of the poor and aged.

After tea was concluded, my father prayed for a blessing upon all assembled, before speaking to them in his own winning manner; and then the following hymn was sung:—

'There is a land of pure delight
  Where saints immortal reign;
Infinite day excludes the night,
  And pleasures banish pain.

There everlasting spring abides,
  And never-withering flowers;
Death, like a narrow sea, divides
  That heavenly land from ours.

Sweet fields, beyond the swelling flood,
  Stand dressed in living green;
So to the Jews fair Canaan stood
  While Jordan rolled between.

But timorous mortals start and shrink
  To cross that narrow sea,
They shivering stand upon the brink,
  And fear to launch away.

Oh, could we make our doubts remove,
  Those gloomy doubts that rise,
And see the Canaan that we love
  With faith's unclouded eyes:

Could we but stand where Moses stood,
  And view the landscape o'er,
Not Jordan's stream nor death's cold flood
  Should fright us from the shore.'

CHAPTER XII.

SHADOW AND SUNSHINE.

. . . .

'They have ended life's brief story,
They have reach'd the Home of Glory,
  Over death victorious!

. . . .

Are we not upon the river,
Sailing fast—to meet for ever
  On more holy, happy ground?

. . . .

Friends, who there await our landing,
Comrades, round the throne now standing,
  We salute you, and we come.'

LANGE.

SHADOW AND SUNSHINE.

In the midst of the consternation and intense excitement produced throughout the country, by the announcement of the first European war in which England had been engaged in the lifetime of this generation, my father took the deepest interest in the British soldiers called out—many of them for the first time—to fight the battles of their country.

No one could feel a more intense anxiety for British soldiers ordered out on active service than he did. He remembered that which younger men could only know from the calm pages of history,—the horrors of a great war. His thoughts, his sympathies, his prayers, were alike occupied with the subject; and he was the first to propose and commence a private subscription for providing every soldier with a pocket Bible or New Testament before the transports sailed.

Although unable personally to take any part in distributing them, he felt the warmest interest in having this desire carried out by a member of his family, in the first days of hurried departure of several regiments, and afterwards through the agents of the Soldiers' Friend Society.

He had been brought up amidst military associations from his childhood; not only was his father a gallant soldier, but his grandfather had been an officer in the 1st Life Guards, and many of his ancestors had been distinguished for their courage in the field. These things may have helped to quicken his ready sympathies on behalf of the army; but, apart from all associations, it would have been enough for him that men were going forth with their lives in their hands, and heroically to endure hardships and sufferings. Every plan of private benevolence for the relief of our brave and patient soldiers, during the terrible winter spent before Sebastopol, was joyfully forwarded by him, as far as lay in his power. At this time, he was the mainspring of the Soldiers' Friend Society, of which he was elected president, and for which he raised considerable sums of money by public and private appeals. He also united with the Duchess of Gordon in supplying funds for sending out, as one of the Scripture-readers to the soldiers, Mr. Duncan Matheson,—a man whose untiring energy and devotedness of spirit made him highly qualified for the work.

The tidings brought by Lord Raglan's despatch, on Good Friday, 1855, of Hedley Vicars' gallant death, at the close of his first battle, and in the moment of victory, pierced my father's heart with sorrow; and, in the depths of his tender sympathy with yet deeper mourners, he told us that he had said, in the language of David when lamenting over his son, 'Would God that I had died for thee!'

He preached the following Sunday on the subject, with

some effort at first; but Easter Day had as ever brought with it for him a vivid realization of 'that blessed hope,' the earnest of which it commemorates. Already his faith had grasped at the meeting on the resurrection morning; so that his sermon became almost as much a *Te Deum* of victory as a lament over the slain.

One of his hearers was his only surviving brother. He was in failing health at the time; but his deep and sorrowful interest in the subject of the sermon led him, at the risk of increased illness, to attend divine service that day (as it proved to be) for the last time on earth.

He was then, and for the remainder of his life, an inmate of the rectory. After the death of his wife, the beloved companion of fifty-seven years, which had taken place in the previous winter, Mr. Chalmers and my sister had brought him away from his desolate house to their happy home, where his rich and loving nature caused him to make his own the joys and sorrows of those around him.

He now became gradually weaker; and in a short time was only able to rise from his bed for a few hours in the evening. Yet, in the midst of illness and suffering, frequent flashes of his gay spirits and irrepressible wit and humour lent a charm to his sick-room. A sitting-room on the ground floor had been thoughtfully given up for his use by my sister; and from this time, it was arranged for him to sleep there, in order to save him the fatigue of going up-stairs, and as it communicated with the drawing-room he was able, almost every evening, to make one of the family party.

It was the delight of the two aged brothers to recall together the scenes and friends of their childhood, some seventy years before; and many a hearty laugh might be heard ringing from voices which never lost the melody of youth. Very lovely was it to the eyes of children and grandchildren, evening after evening, to look upon the living illustration of a hymn which their uncle had so often sung—

'How blest the sight, the joy how sweet,
When brothers joined with brothers meet,
In bands of mutual love.'

It has been mentioned in an earlier chapter, that there was a difference in their religious views. Never had the elder brother ceased to pray for the younger with a faith which refused to be discouraged; nor, as opportunity offered, to seek to remove his doubts and difficulties; and to guide him to that Saviour of whom Moses in the law, and the prophets, did write, Jesus, the Son of David,—perfect in humanity, and 'God over all, blessed for ever.'

It remained for the last few months of the younger brother's life to unfold a union with his elder brother which would endure throughout eternity.

It would be difficult to say in what manner faith stole into a heart so long sealed, until it took possession of his whole being, and opened a hitherto veiled heaven to his view. He could only tell us, that it arose through an inward conviction that those around him had found a happiness in the service of God, which he had never known in all his years of stirring interests connected with the things of this world. Long had his brother's holy life spoken to him like a message from heaven; yet it had been but 'as the lovely song of one that hath a pleasant voice,' touching his feelings for the moment, and then the impression vanishing away.

But now the Holy Spirit had begun to convince him of sin, in a life which to the world seemed almost blameless, and the need of a Saviour became the craving of his soul. 'Old things had passed away; all things had become new.' He clearly traced this work of a Divine hand in his own mind.

'I see things in a different light now,' he said; 'all things are vanity, apart from God. What a life your father has led; how different from mine! Though I have not been what the world calls a wicked man, I have lived to please man, and not to please God.'

It was suggested to him by my sister, who was tenderly nursing him, that he had come to Christ now, and wished to please God through Him; and that our Saviour has said, 'Him that cometh unto Me I will in no wise cast out;' and that God speaks to those who come to Him through His Son, as 'accepted in the Beloved.'

'Yes,' he replied, 'I say, God be merciful to me a sinner!' adding, with fervent emphasis, 'FOR JESUS CHRIST'S SAKE.'

That doctrine of the Atonement through Christ's sufferings and death was once a great stumbling-block to him; but now he was led to rejoice in it, as a drowning man would in a rock on which he had suddenly found a firm footing. 'I have no other hope,' he said, and then asked for this verse to be repeated to him—

'Other refuge have I none,
Hangs my helpless soul on Thee;
Leave, oh leave me not alone,
Still support and comfort me.'

At another time he said, 'Tell your dear father how I thank God for such a brother. He seems to me never to have had a fault—born beautiful within and without; I love him better every time I see him.' Just then his brother came in; and my uncle said, 'All my trials have been for the best, William; I have been brought into a different state, and to see things in a new light. I am a brand plucked from the burning.'

His brother clasped him tenderly in his arms, and my uncle kissed his hand again and again.

Frequently he alluded to the goodness of the Providence which had brought him to Beckenham Rectory for his last illness; and then would sing the refrain of a favourite psalm of his—

'For His mercies far extend,
And His bounty knows no end.'

The society of his young grand-nieces had a great charm for him. He loved to look upon their faces, and to listen by the hour to hymns which they repeated by his side. But he enjoyed the attention and affection of every creature who cared for him; and said, 'The family love me, the friends love me, the servants love me, even the dogs and cats are all amiable and friendly here.'

Communication, whether personally or by letter, with friends of his former days, was, to the last, a source of delight to him. His heart never grew old. Throughout his illness he was cheered from time to time by the thoughtful kindness of Mr. Walter of Bearwood, whose father and mother had been amongst his dearest friends; and he said, it had been one of the pleasures provided for his last illness to find the friendship which he had lamented at the death of the parents renewed by the son.

The last evening save one before his death, he was heard saying to himself, 'If I may but be a doorkeeper in the house of my God.' My sister saw that tears were filling his eyes, and said to cheer him, 'And a very pleasant place it would be, dearest uncle, to stand at that open door, and to say, "Come in," to every one.'

He caught the fancy with his usual brightness, and conversed about the happiness of seeing the beloved ones left behind coming across the river, 'through the flood, on foot,' to the celestial city. And then they spoke together of Him who has conquered death, and brought life and immortality to light.

This promise of the Saviour was quoted to him at parting, 'I will not leave you comfortless; I will come unto you.'

His faithful servant, who spent the night in his room, and nursed him with devoted attention, said that he heard him repeating to himself afterwards, 'Comfort, comfort! That *is* comfort!' "*I* will come unto you." "Behold the Lamb of God, which taketh away the sin of the world."

On the last night of his life, one who sat beside him heard the failing voice saying, 'In my Father's house are many mansions; if it were not so, I would have told you.

I go to prepare a place for you. And if I go and prepare a place for you, I will come again, and receive you unto Myself.' How delightful! 'Come quickly, Lord Jesus!'

At half-past twelve, he asked the hour, then closed his eyes with his own hand, as one might for another in the hour of death. But a gentle sleep followed, from which, without a sigh, his spirit passed, we doubt not, into the presence of his Saviour.

My father had seen the answer to the prayers of a lifetime, and amidst the keenness of his natural grief, 'was comforted concerning his brother.'

Mr. Chalmers' former connexion with the army, and the near neighbourhood of Woolwich, brought frequent and welcome visitors to Beckenham from amongst the numerous Christian officers quartered there. Foremost amongst these was the late revered and beloved General Anderson, of whose almost parental care of the young officers in 'the regiment,' together with his earnest interest in the welfare of the soldiers, my father never tired of hearing. And when he was able, from time to time, to spend a few hours at Beckenham Rectory, their conversation was almost exclusively concerning the increase of the Lord's kingdom on earth, and the joy of His presence in their hearts.

In one of his visits, General Anderson interested my father much in an account which he gave of his young friend Captain Vandeleur, then in the Crimea.

In the early part of the summer of 1855, Captain Vandeleur returned to England, and paid his first visit to

Beckenham Rectory. He came a personal stranger, but in heart a friend; one strong bond of mutual sympathy having drawn him to us—he had known and loved Hedley Vicars. A stronger tie still made the friendship there begun, one which will endure for ever—the knowledge and love of our Lord and Saviour Jesus Christ.

Captain Vandeleur accompanied my father and his family on a visit to Terling, not long after the great sorrow of Hedley Vicars' death; and it was comforting to the mourners to listen to one who had so recently delighted in personal intercourse with the beloved one now taken from them, and to hear another testimony to his life of holiness and self-devotion.

Captain Vandeleur's frequent visits to Beckenham, from this time, were a source of ever-increasing pleasure to my father, as he marked the deepening work of grace in that noble young soldier; and heard his simple yet animated accounts of the door of usefulness opened to himself and his brother officer, Captain Orr, amongst the men and boys at the arsenal, and of the Bible societies[1] and Bible classes which they had established amongst them. Captain Orr continued the boys' class after Captain Vandeleur

[1] This refers to a plan set on foot by these two young officers for inducing the arsenal workmen, who were in receipt of good wages, to become subscribers, by small weekly instalments, for M'Phun's valuable large-print Family Bibles, which they further encouraged by adding a small sum to each deposit. When a certain number of men had paid up their subscriptions, a tea-party was given; at which the copies were presented, and addresses delivered upon the blessing of a diligent study of Holy Scripture. It was found that many were thus led to search the Scriptures, and to begin the practice of reading them in their families.

had left the arsenal; and many received a blessing there which will be thankfully remembered in eternity.

In the spring of the following year, a young officer in the Grenadier Guards asked permission to bring with him, on one of his frequent visits to Beckenham Rectory, a friend of his, who had gone out (in the civil service) to the East at the same time with himself, and had been distinguished there for his gallantry in saving many lives at the risk of his own. From this time it would have been difficult to say which was the more welcome guest. My father delighted in watching the deepening decision of purpose in his two young friends to be wholly on the Lord's side, and their desire to be employed in His service; whilst they delighted in listening to his lucid explanations of Scripture, and to the words of wise and fatherly counsel which fell from his lips; and also in seeing his vivid pleasure and hearty sympathy in their young, ardent efforts in the service in which he had grown grey. The one was occupying himself in giving scriptural instruction to the men of his regiment; the other in hospitals, and in a Bible-reading for livery stable-men and domestic servants.

Not long after these two friends had believed and obeyed the words, 'Let him that heareth say, Come!' another interest connected with the army arose amongst the cadets at Addiscombe College. The work of the grace of God amongst these youths was at first gradual. A few began to desire to live in earnest as Christians; and then receiving, in its fulness, the message of eternal life by faith upon the Son of God, they were enabled, alike by their conduct and conversation, to recommend the faith which filled their hearts with joy, and spread a holy gladness over their young faces.

They were invited, by the hospitality and kindness of Mr. Chalmers, to spend their Sundays in the happy family circle at Beckenham Rectory. But as the numbers grew by degrees to nearly one-third of the whole college, it became necessary to divide; parties of eight or ten coming each Sunday. Beautiful was the sight of this gathering of young soldiers around the patriarch's arm-chair, listening to his animated illustrations and sacred anecdotes, singing with him his favourite hymns, and commended by him in prayer to God for His help and grace during the week's work and the week's warfare.

He was often as much surprised as gratified by the thoughtfulness of their questions on scriptural subjects, and on religious matters concerning the Church and the country. And the cadets were no less delighted with the manner in which he brought forth for their benefit, from the treasury of his memory, 'things new and old,' than with the sparkling freshness which eclipsed the mere youthfulness of years.

'What is the good of being young,' said one of them, as he lingered at the door for another smile and parting word from him, 'when one sees a man of eighty in better spirits than the jolliest of us?'

So quickly fled the happy hours of those evenings, that when the time arrived for the cadets to leave, it always took them by surprise; but so anxious was my father that military discipline should be preserved, and no encroachment made upon the kindness of Sir Frederick Abbott, the Lieutenant-Governor of Addiscombe (who gladly forwarded their intercourse with Beckenham), that he used to hold up his watch as it indicated the unwelcome hour, with a gesture of playful threatening, saying, 'Now I must turn you all out, or the gates will be closed.'

He was greatly interested in hearing of their meetings amongst themselves for reading the Scriptures, with prayer; and when they asked permission to come over to Beckenham Rectory from time to time, during the hours occasionally given them on a week-day for recreation, for a Bible-reading there, he delighted in coming in to conclude it with prayer.

After his earthly race was finished, they poured in their testimonies from the different provinces of India, to the blessing they had derived from his counsel and friendship, and beyond all, from the indelible impression left on their memories by the holiness and happiness of his life, and by the atmosphere of love which he seemed to diffuse around him.

The winter of the year 1856 brought dangerous and protracted illness, during which his severe sufferings were borne not only with patience but with perfect acquiescence in all the will of God, whilst every alleviation called forth his praises. No medicine was taken or refreshment received, without thanks being rendered. One of his children remembers well how with trembling hand the cup of cold water was held, whilst his faint voice said, 'Thanks for cold and refreshing water; and for the Water of Life—praise, praise be to Thee.'

His memory for the things learnt in his boyhood surprised us. He would quote long passages from Milton, Young, and Shakspeare, always contriving, by the spiritual alchemy of his mind, to give a sacred turn of thought to each quotation. When almost insensible to outward objects, from extreme suffering in his head, we heard him repeat Pope's lines,—

> 'Not bubbling waters to the thirsty swain,
> Not rest to weary labourers, faint with pain,
> Not showers to larks, not sunshine to the bee,
> Are half so precious as thy love to me—'
> 'My Saviour!'

Thus, the verse learnt in youth as an expression of natural affection, was consecrated in age to the Object of highest adoration and love.

During one night, when it was scarcely expected that he would survive till morning, his spirit seemed to be almost in heaven. We heard him picturing its blessedness and glory in glowing language; and amongst other things, which he gently murmured to himself, we caught the following verse:—

> 'Awhile they range the heavenly plains,
> Or sing His love in melting strains,
> Or, overcome with raptures sweet,
> Fall down adoring at His feet!'

Whilst his mind grasped the breadth of the promise, 'At His right hand there are pleasures for evermore,' and believed in their inexhaustible variety and extent, his heart was satisfied only with the words, 'In His PRESENCE is fulness of joy;' for it was the thought of the personal presence of his Saviour which gave the light, the bliss, the glory to all his visions of heaven.

He quoted at one time, with a voice full of emotion, the story of a little dying child, who had said with joy, that she was going to heaven to be with the Lord Jesus, and who, on being asked, 'What would you do if He were to go out of heaven?' replied, 'I would go out with Him.'

'You and I could claim His own promise,' he added, 'to be of that company; for the Lord has said, "Where I am, there ye may be also." There is a whole heaven in the promise, "I will come again, and receive you unto MYSELF."'

Prayer was made for him, during this illness, not only in many families, and social gatherings, but also in many churches, in places where he was known and loved.

Those prayers were heard. Our father was lent to us for nearly eight years longer.

TO REV. W. KNOX MARSHALL, ON THE DEATH OF HIS SISTER, LADY LAWRENCE.

'BECKENHAM RECTORY, *March* 2, 1854.

'MY DEAR MARSHALL,—I have just heard the melancholy news. I do greatly sympathize with you. I knew what it was to love an only sister. All we can say is, "It is the Lord." And He says, "It is I, be not afraid." No fear need be entertained for the dear departed. She knew and trusted in her Saviour. He who says, "Be not afraid," will also take care of survivors, and yet the loss must be grievously felt. Christians are no stoics; neither are they murmurers. The good Lord bring every alleviating thought to your mind, and to Sir Henry and the children.

'Yet a little while, and death shall be no more. May this enlivening hope relieve the gloom of the valley of the shadow of death, in which we are still, while some have reached its termination.

. . . . .

'Love to the dear children. Dear Agnes, Kennie, and I, and little Tom Thumb, are good playmates.—Ever most affectionately yours, WM. MARSH.'

'DEAR MRS. GORDON,—. . . You and Mr. Gordon have constantly prayed for your children.

'Prayer is always answered, but not always in the exact time and manner we expect. Believing parents have great promises. "The promise is unto you and to your children." "I will be a God unto thee, and to thy seed after thee."

'But what concern have we in promises to Abraham? St. Paul answers the question (Gal. iii. 14, 26, 29). I differ from that divine of the last century, who said, "It would have been well for the Church if St. Paul had never written his Epistles!" But I quite agree with a more ancient divine, Luther, who considered the Epistle to the Galatians to be a mine of immense wealth to the Church. Salmasius said, "If I could have my time over again, I would spend more of it in reading David's Psalms and

Paul's Epistles." Alas! for many of the modern German divines. They think the Psalms to be only a book of prayers and praises, and not of prophecy; while the second psalm opens with a plain prediction of "the sufferings of Christ and of the glory which should follow."

'I fear nothing will convince a certain class of minds but the actual appearing of the Lord; nothing short of it could convince Saul of Tarsus.

'Pray tell Mr. Gordon that the cultivation of Palestine is commencing. You see I must bring in the Jews, whatever be my subject.

'What does Mr. S. think of the intended Convocation? Are we to have another 1767? priests against bishops, and bishops against priests, and the people (who are the Church) against both. It appears to me to be perilous; but all will end well for the *true* Church, of which may all dear to us be living and lively members.'

'BECKENHAM, *Nov.* 23.

'MY DEAR FRIEND,— . . . The property men have is not their own, but the Lord's. They are but stewards. I am quite aware that the text you quote may mean that the Lord can provide silver and gold for the building of His temple; but I make a second application of the words.

'I doubt whether we who hold and maintain the doctrine of a perfectly free justification (the justification of the ungodly) through the redemption that is in Christ Jesus, have made sufficient use of the *rewardableness* of good works (2 Cor. ix. 6). How wonderful that it should be a part of the plan of mercy!

'Justified freely, adopted graciously, endued with the Spirit, and yet rewarded according to talents improved, services rendered, and sufferings endured; indeed, "Thou, Lord, *art* merciful;" for though it is the fruit of Thine own grace, yet "Thou rewardest every man according to his work" (Ps. lxii. 12).

'See how legal I become in my old age! yet my hope for *salvation* is *only* in the riches of Divine grace in Christ; not alone to blot out all sin, but also to bear the iniquity even of our holy things. W. M.'

'BECKENHAM, *Dec.* 6.

'MY DEAR MR. GORDON,—I am glad you give yourself a little more rest. The priests under the law might retire at fifty years of age; and under the Gospel, "Do thyself no harm" is a Christian rule.

'As to the profitable employment of leisure, something like a plan is desirable.

'1. A certain time for the Bible and prayer.

'2. A certain time for religious works.

'3. A certain time for correspondence, etc.

'4. A certain time for history, biography, philosophy, or lighter reading, such as reviews, poetry, travels, etc.

'The human mind is singularly assisted by variety. I have been tired after reading one book for a long time. But I could take another directly, and feel as fresh as ever for reading.

'I must not omit a certain time for air and exercise: and the family circle must have their portion.

'But oh how blessed will be the eternity, when (according to my text on Friday, Ps. xvii., last verse) we shall be without weariness, without imperfection! The works of God, and the ways of God, as displaying the perfection of God, will be our delight, with redemption as *the sunshine upon all.*'

TO THE REV. ROBERT KEMP.

'BECKENHAM, *May* 22, 1854.

'MY DEAR MR. KEMP,— . . . We live in ominous times, yet may hope that Old England will continue to be employed in making known the glad tidings to "Jews, Turks, infidels, and heretics." The prophets of 1829 are now proved to be true. Members of Parliament of the Roman Catholic persuasion must obey their priests, and will allow nothing to pass that appears to be opposed to their Church. We must grieve for them and pray for them, and faithfully tell them, as opportunity offers, that Popery is strong delusion. Great is the mercy which has instructed us by the only infallible standard, the Word of God. Grace and peace be multiplied to you and yours.—Ever affectionately yours, WM. MARSH.'

To the Same.

'BECKENHAM, *Nov.* 16, 1854.

'MY DEAR MR. KEMP,— . . . You are immortal till your work is done, and therefore have found yourself safe in the midst of danger. Yet a little while, and there can be "no evil occurrent." We "shall be like Him, for we shall see Him as He is," and that will be Heaven. How bright and wonderful the prospect! To be wise without error. To be holy without sin. To be happy without alloy, and that for ever and ever. We shall then begin to feel something of our obligation, and sing aloud, "Salvation to God, who sitteth upon the Throne, and to the Lamb, for ever and ever."

'We live in an age of agitation. But our path is plain. To preach the truth of God, to protest against error, and to endeavour by persuasion, example, and prayer, and by co-operation with the great institutions of the age, to bring our fellow-sinners to the all-sufficient Saviour. Remember me to Mrs. Kemp, and believe me, yours affectionately, WM. MARSH.'

TO HIS SECOND DAUGHTER.

'*January* 13*th*.

'TIME how short—eternity how long! "I paint for eternity," said a celebrated artist; but how much more truly may a preacher say, "I preach for eternity." May none of your words fall to the ground! Many happy and blessed returns of your birthday. It would be an Irish saying, but true, to say to you, "Very pleasant hast thou been to me, *my brother* Jonathan!"

'I give you the last four verses of the 90th Psalm. Love to dearest Frederick.—Your most loving father, W. M.'

TO ANOTHER DAUGHTER.

'TERLING PLACE, *June* 19, 1855.

'. . . "Many of the disciples went back, and walked no more with Him." "The servant is not above his lord." Let not sorrow overwhelm thee, if now and then a bud is nipped. There are those that will live, and bear fruit in the Paradise of God.

'Yet it is very painful to see that which was promising come to nought. But even in these cases the disappointment may be only temporary. "Return, O backsliding children,—I will heal your backslidings," is one of the many gracious sayings that proceed out of His mouth. Those poor fellows are exposed to great temptations; but there is grace enough, and to spare, to enable them to stand in the evil day, and having done all, to stand. We are glad that you stay till they sail,[1] though we long for your return.

'A large number besides the household were assembled by dear Lord and Lady Rayleigh for family worship last evening. I spoke from Luke xi. 13, and told them the story of "Praying Tom."

'Dear Mrs. Vicars looks back with Christian thankfulness, bears her present loss with Christian resignation, and looks forward with Christian faith.

'I will write to Mr. Matheson. He is doing wonders, by the help of God; but his soul is vexed within him, and no wonder, seeing the awful thoughtlessness of men on the verge of eternity. Yet there are many blessed exceptions.

'Shall I give you this morning's exposition? "As in Adam all die, even so in Christ shall all be made alive. We lost a *human* righteousness in Adam; we gain a *Divine* righteousness in Christ. We lost *human* power in Adam; we gain *Divine* power in Christ. We lost the paradise of *man* in Adam; we gain the Paradise of *God* in Christ. We were *driven out* of Paradise in Adam; we shall go *no more out* in Christ."

[1] A detachment of the Army Works Corps.

'Give our love to Diana and little Margaret Lawford, and great love to dear Uncle Hal. I am so glad that he is a little better; and I pray he may still improve, and be happy now in the thought of a Saviour, and of a heaven to come.

'Give our best wishes to dear Mina Holland and her husband. May they be happy in each other, and in the faith and service of the Lord.

'Take care of yourself, dear darling child, for the sake of us all, and of our soldiers, sailors, and navvies. Christians should pray for our army and navy, for our allies and our enemies, and, above all, for the final victory of truth, when men shall love war no more, nor be deceived by Satan, nor led captive by sin any more.—Thy loving father, WM. MARSH.

'The eternal love of the Father—the redeeming love of the Son—the renewing love of the Spirit—subjects for meditation this week, and for eternity.'

To the Same.

'*Short Praises.*

'I THANK God, through Jesus Christ our Lord, for as dear a child as ever father had.'

'*Short Prayers.*

'I PRAY she may be kept humble, zealous, active, useful, all the days of her life.'—This for September 15.

'THE Lord grant all her petitions. Prosperity can only be given to the work by devout prayers to that eternal Spirit, who can enrich with all utterance and knowledge, and send out the hallowed fire to purify the lips of whom He pleases, and kindle faith, hope, and love in the immortal souls addressed.'

TO A GRANDCHILD.

'BECKENHAM, *Sept.* 20, 1856.

'DARLING CHILD,— . . . We have had a pleasant little tour to Fredville, Chilham, and Tunbridge Wells. You have had a delightful tour among the Trossachs and Western Highlands. A quick perception of the beauties of nature is a blessed gift. Mr. Yorke says, in a wonderful book he has just published, *Researches in the Works of God*, that it acts like Elisha's minstrel—it soothes and elevates. It transplants us from a world of care to a world of grandeur, freedom, and peace. Ah! but that alone would not do; and no one more willing to acknowledge it than good Mr. Yorke. For repose, as sinners, we must look to the Saviour; for help against over-anxiety we must look to paternal love in God (John xiv. 1; Phil. iv. 6). Trials must come; comforts will come. When patience has had its perfect work, great is the reward of grace (James i. 3, 4; v. 8). There is a *Coming* in providence and grace as well as in glory.'

TO MISS EMMA LEYCESTER.

'BECKENHAM, *Oct.* 6, 1856.

'MY DEAR COUSIN,—I write by this post to Mr. Clay.

'He has had very lately a convert from the Church of Rome, who read his recantation in Mr. C.'s chapel.

'I rejoice over these cases. As to the perverts from our own Church to Rome, I quite agree with Dr. Hook, who says, "They expose their souls to peril." I *desire* their salvation, but there is no salvation *by* the Church of Rome, though we hope and believe there is salvation *in* the Church of Rome for those who have had no better teaching, and after all trust in their Saviour alone. How thankful we should be who are taught better, and how zealous that others should love the truth.

What is truth?

'We answer,—God and His glorious attributes; Christ and His great salvation; the Holy Spirit and His heavenly grace; the Bible in its revelations—the principles, the privileges, and the duties of a Christian; and the ample and glorious realities of a future state.

'I send you and your friends my usual wish: May you be happy in a Saviour's love, and useful in a Saviour's service.—Your ever affectionate WM. MARSH.'

TO HIS ELDEST GRANDCHILD.

'BECKENHAM, *Feb.* 12, 1857.

'DARLING LOUIE,—Our precious "Marny" left us on Monday. I sighed deeply when she was gone. No *man* will allow that he cried! And yet I was exceedingly glad, for her sake, as it would be a time of at least comparative rest. Neither the army, nor the navy, nor the working-men's corps, could call upon her at Cannes! I rejoiced also in the anticipation of your and darling Lucy's joy in seeing her dear face again. I am sure, likewise, it will be a happy time for all with the good Duchesses of Gordon and Manchester. If I could put myself upon the wires of the electric telegraph, I do think I should look in also.

'And now, dearest child, I am reminded that to-morrow is your birthday. Many happy and useful years to you. It is true that this is a world of sin and sorrow. But it is as true that we have an Almighty and ever present Friend, that we may enjoy His love in our many comforts, and know that He can sympathize with us in any trial. It is also the only world in which we can have the honour of serving Him, in the midst of difficulties; and the privilege of telling others what a Saviour we have found.

'Oh, to have been brought to some knowledge of Him, and to have any opportunity of serving Him, is worth being born into this world.

'We hope to see our Robert to-morrow. He is counting the days till the Cannes party returns.—Darling Louie's loving GRANDFATHER.'

TO HIS SECOND DAUGHTER.

'ISLIP RECTORY, *near* OXFORD, *June* 12, 1857.

'MY first look up to heaven this morning was in thanksgiving, before prayer, for the marvellous blessings I have had in my children. I may be allowed to feel anxiously for their health, yet I know that infinite wisdom and love consult our eternal interests, even in what is contrary to our present feelings and wishes. But pray I may, and must, for their ease and health, as well as Christian peace and usefulness. The latter God has graciously given in no small degree. Yesterday I walked with dearest Mary to see the village. I am much pleased, for I expected only a flat with stone walls, but there are some very pretty points and even rising grounds. I asked (you know my satirical spirit), whether a hill in the distance was not as Lebanon to the "goodly land," and whether the snow was upon it all the year round?

'I do not know any house where you could have been happier than at Birch Hall. Certainly, love to its owners would be an easy test of love to the brethren.

'My love to all. I have a sweet line from Frederick. —Ever your most loving and delighted father,

'Wm. Marsh.'

CHAPTER XIII.

MORE SOULS TO WIN.

'I ask no heaven till earth be Thine,
Nor glory-crown, while work of mine
Remaineth here. When earth shall shine
Amongst the stars . . .
Her sins wiped out, her captives free,
For crown—new work give Thou to me,
Lord, here am I.'

MORE SOULS TO WIN.

No sooner had my father recovered a measure of health after the illness mentioned in the last chapter, than he was anxious again to be employed in his Master's work. As he was still forbidden by his medical attendants to leave the house, he established a Saturday evening meeting at the rectory, with the hearty concurrence of the rector, for exposition of the Scripture and prayer, which the villagers were invited to attend.

After the opening of a railway station at Beckenham, several villas were built in the neighbourhood of the rectory; and some of the new parishioners thankfully availed themselves of the invitation to join the little band of those who had found the advantage of such a preparation for the day of rest.

The station-master, the sergeant of police, the schoolmaster and his 'staff,' and others in the parish who deeply valued his ripened ministry, were scarcely ever absent from their accustomed places on these occasions; and, besides the parishioners, old friends of my father's, and others from a distance, frequently came to hear his words, and to unite in prayer. Nor on that day of the week alone was 'open house' kept at the rectory. Friends before unknown, but ever after to be pleasantly remembered, came from America, France, Russia, Germany, and other countries, always meeting with a hospitable reception from the rector and his wife; and each carried away some instructive thought or wise counsel from the lips of the aged saint, sometimes written on the fly-leaf of some little book, often one of his own writing, which he kept by him in large supplies for such gifts. On more than one occasion the venerable Bishop of Ohio took part in these meetings,—speaking and praying with the fervour of a piety which had been devoted from early youth, but was glowing afresh with the warmth of that great work of God in America in the year 1857. Deeply were his hearers interested in his accounts of that time of blessing. 'Half a million,' he said, 'might probably be under the mark,' in speaking of the number of those who had been brought from darkness to light, and from the power of Satan unto God, in the course of a few months. He bore a delightful testimony, from his personal knowledge, as to the steadfastness of the religious character of many of these converts; and also of numbers of whom he had heard the same good report from the clergy of his diocese, and other reliable sources.

Bishop M'Ilvaine's visits to his old friend were delightful to the whole family circle, whilst the charm of his conversation, his perfect sympathy on doctrinal points, and above all the spirituality of his mind, made his society peculiarly attractive to my father.

Each united with a strong attachment to the Articles and Liturgy of our Church, a large-heartedness and absence of all bigotry and formality, which caused them to rejoice in the spread of the kingdom of Christ in any part of the world, and by any instrumentality.

On the last of these visits the Bishop gave an address in the barn at Beckenham, set apart for Scripture readings, with a simplicity and power which refreshed the hearts of his hearers.

Amongst several other visitors, from both the Northern and Southern States of America, was Colonel Henderson Smith, the head of the Military College of Lexington, Virginia. Whilst staying at the rectory he visited Addiscombe, and joined the cadets in their Bible-reading with lively interest and sympathy, having himself been engaged in fostering a similar awakening into spiritual life in his own college, where more than a hundred youths gave evidence of conversion.

The near neighbourhood of Beckenham to Addington Park, brought my father into frequent contact with his old and valued friend the late Archbishop Sumner. Between these aged servants of God there was an indescribable sympathy; their guilelessness of heart, their cheerful piety, and unfailing charity, causing them each to delight in the other's society.

Well remembered still in Beckenham, is the beautiful sight of these two venerable men, standing side by side within the chancel-rails of the old church, at the marriage of my father's eldest grandchild, on the 29th of July 1857.

When the service was ended, and the guests returned to the rectory, they found the school-children and many of the villagers assembled on the lawn, ready to show their sympathy in the happy occasion, and to welcome the young bride and bridegroom by singing a hymn of praise to the gracious Father, 'who giveth us richly all things to enjoy.' Many were the bright faces seen on that wedding-day; but none were more bright than those of the revered archbishop and the beloved grandfather; who, with hearts which never outlived their first freshness, rejoiced with them that did rejoice.

Later in the day, my father gave a short address to all present; and commended in prayer to God those who were just setting out together on the journey of life.

The months of August and September of the same year were spent at Malvern. In the midst of the enjoyment of that golden summer, so rich in foliage, fruits and flowers, like a black thunder-cloud came the terrible tidings of the Indian Mutiny. Deeply and painfully did my father share in the general distress occasioned by those dreadful despatches, which filled the press of the day with horrors —and hearts and homes with misery.

In common with so many others, my father had ties both of friendship and of relationship in India; and amongst the former, the great and good Sir Henry Lawrence stood foremost. Personally they were strangers, but Sir Henry's marriage with the sister of the Rev. William Knox Marshall had brought them into occasional connexion by correspondence, and more frequent letters to a member of his family, on the state of religion and general affairs in

India, had so deeply interested him in Sir Henry's mind and character, that when a telegram brought the fatal news of the death, at Lucknow, of that gallant chief, my father mourned for him as for a dear and personal friend, as well as for the blow to British India, in the loss of one of her noblest and most gifted sons.

The subject of the state of India entered frequently at this crisis into his sermons and addresses; as it was his habit to interweave present and public interests with his teaching. And gladly, both at Malvern, and at Beckenham on his return there, he promoted and joined in prayer-meetings on behalf of the English in India.

In the autumn of the same year, large numbers of railway men were assembled, in and near Beckenham, to construct the lines there. My father was not a little interested in hearing of their eager sympathy with the details of the war. He marked several passages to be read to them from the newspapers, narrating anecdotes of chivalrous courage and generosity, not alone of our officers and soldiers in the East, but also amongst civilians, missionaries, women, children, and the native Christians.

No story of brave readiness for self-sacrifice charmed him more than that of a clergyman, the son and grandson of two dear old friends of his own; who, after winning the highest honours at Oxford, had volunteered to go to India as a missionary in connexion with the Church Missionary Society, and who had, after a time, undertaken the presidency of their college at Agra, for training native missionaries. When the fort of that city was closed, in immediate expectation of a siege by the mutineers, five hundred native Christians, many of whom were members of his own congregation, came beneath its walls, entreating to be permitted to take refuge there.

The governor feared that the supply of provisions would prove totally inadequate to meet the wants of the numbers already within the walls; and thought it was his duty to refuse admission.

'Then,' said the faithful pastor, 'I will go out and perish with them. They shall not be left as sheep without a shepherd, in their hour of peril.'

But before he could fulfil the word, the eloquence of the intended self-sacrifice had prevailed, and the governor ordered the gates to be thrown open, saying, 'Mr. French has saved the native Christians.'

It had been arranged by the Society for promoting Christianity amongst the Jews that there should be a jubilee celebration of its fiftieth year in 1858, and an earnest request had been forwarded to my father—the last survivor of the founders of the association—that he would preach at the church of the Society's Home Mission Station, Palestine Place, Bethnal Green, on the occasion.

Although he was suffering from an attack of inflammation in the eyes, he joyfully consented to render his services on a day which called forth some of the warmest thanksgivings of his heart; for, in his devotion to the welfare of the Jewish nation, he might almost have said, with the royal Psalmist, 'If I do not remember thee, let my tongue cleave to the roof of my mouth; if I prefer not Jerusalem above my chief joy.'

The day appointed for the jubilee service proved to be bitterly cold, and we all felt anxious about the risk he was incurring for his eyes, in their suffering condition. But he never knew fear when in the path of duty; and about this duty, for him, there was all the glow of pleasure.

His text was taken from Romans xi. 33, 'O the depth of the riches both of the wisdom and knowledge of God! How unsearchable are His judgments, and His ways past finding out!' After a brief but powerful summary of God's dealings with His ancient people, and of the prophecies of their future glory at the return of the Lord, he besought his hearers to devote themselves to 'Jesus of Nazareth, the King of the Jews;' describing the character of our Lord, in His human nature, as a man might speak of the friend he most intimately knows and most devotedly loves, combined with the reverence of the creature for the Creator, and the gratitude of the sinner towards his Saviour.

As no serious increase of suffering resulted from this effort, he began to cherish the hope of being present once more at the May meetings in Exeter Hall. His long illness in the winter of 1856-57 had left him too much weakened to be able to attempt the exertion in the succeeding season. But now his spirits rose with a fresh spring, when he received the pressing invitations of the Church Missionary and Jews' Societies again to plead their cause. And cheering was the greeting which echoed throughout the Hall to welcome him, as once again he joined that vast assembly.

Never had he looked more radiant, or commanded the

attention and the feelings of the audience with greater power. But it was for the *last time* that his presence was to shed its mellowed light upon that platform. Standing on the brink of his eighty-third year, the last of the fathers left from that band of evangelical clergy—born of the Revival of the last century—who had nurtured, and worked, and preached, and pleaded for these Societies, had now taken his farewell of them, leaving them as a sacred legacy to the next generation.

In the course of the same spring, my father had the pleasure of welcoming a friend whom he had scarcely seen since the days when he and his brother, Mr. Lambart of Beau Parc, had been received in their early youth, almost as sons, into his family circle at Edgbaston. The Rev. Charles Lambart came to bring his only boy for my father's blessing, before sending him on a voyage round the world; and, at the same time, to tell his aged friend how deep was his own debt of gratitude for the spiritual benefit he had received from him in his youth.

A young friend, who spent some time at Beckenham Rectory in this year, wrote of him as follows:—

'. . . I AM writing to pay a last grateful tribute to the memory of Dr. Marsh. I do not know whether you will remember the first visit I paid at Beckenham. I was about seventeen; and when the happy time had come to an end, you said I might go up stairs into dear Dr. Marsh's sitting-room, to say good-bye to him. I explained that I was just going, and had come to take leave. "I am sorry you are going, my dear," was the reply of one who never spoke but in kindness, "but you know there must be partings here. I have a little book for you"—(giving me the Memorials of Archdeacon Brown's Son). "And now, never forget three words,—a Soul, a Saviour, and a Heaven."

'I shall always remember the impression of those words, with the beaming look of love yearning over a human soul. I felt as if God had told him to say it to me. I left Dr. Marsh to go and pray to the Saviour for the first time, that I might spend my life in His service. And now, may I be one of the hundreds who through a bright eternity will thank God they ever knew Dr. Marsh! That smile has often shone upon me as sunshine since. I cannot recal it without tears; and it will still be the same until I see him where all is sunshine. I have often tried to summon courage to tell him the blessing he had been to me, but shyness prevented me. Now it is a tribute which I owe to his sacred and lovely memory; and may many of his beautiful thoughts, repeated to others, by God's mercy, lead them to the feet of Christ. I shall never see any one else like him for his delicacy of kindness and goodness. I have watched him when any one happened to be sitting apart, perhaps, as it may have seemed, unnoticed, contrive to say a pleasant word, and bring him at once within the circle, without ever letting him feel that he did it for his sake. Time can never give again the joys he shed about him, and eternity only will show how broadcast were the blessings he scattered.'

This summer brought a new gladness to my father's heart, in the birth of his first great-grandson, and he expressed his wish that his own birthday should be kept on the day of the babe's christening.

Accordingly, the usual festivity was postponed until the young mother and her infant son were able to come to Beckenham. But in order that he might have some part of his usual enjoyment on his birthday, the school-children were invited to see him at the rectory; and, after hearing from him a few words of loving counsel, to receive plum-buns from his own hand. And not a little did they enjoy hearing from my sister a story of her having found her father feeding some swans on a piece of water in Leamington, on the afternoon of a snowy New Year's Day. He was returning from the town, wearied with his day's work, when the hungry birds swam towards him, and his benevolent heart could not resist the mute appeal. So, tired as he was, he had turned back again into the town, that he might get a bag of buns for them.

Not children only, but many a grown-up guest, will recall the regularity of his application for crumbs and broken bread all round the breakfast-table, morning by morning, that he might feed the birds, who soon began to know him as their friend, and took no alarm at sight of his face at the window. When he left home at any time, this office was always given into the hands of some one whom he could trust not to forget to care for his little feathered flock.

'When the day came for the baptism of little Ralph William Anstruther, the great-grandsire's heart over-flowed with prayer and praise. As Captain Anstruther's family had always belonged to the Church of Scotland, the child was baptized according to the form of that Church, by Dr. Cumming, in the drawing-room of Beckenham Rectory. After Dr. Cumming had given an earnest and beautiful address to the parents upon their new duties, my father took in his arms the infant already so dear to him for his mother's sake, and afterwards to be for his own, and adding a few tender and solemn words, concluded with prayer.[1]

Then followed the usual birthday gathering of the aged poor, whom he addressed on the subject of four great gifts of God to man:—His Son; His Spirit; His Scriptures; His Sabbath.

There were three appointed seasons of joyful family gatherings at Beckenham Rectory—Christmas, Easter, and the 20th of July. But every reasonable excuse, such as a wedding or a christening, which could be made an occasion for adding to the number of these happy reunions in this patriarchal home, was eagerly responded to by children and grandchildren. None more delighted in these cheerful seasons than my father; and at other times not the least of his pleasures was to see around him orphan or motherless boys, or children whose parents were in India, brought to the rectory by his son-in-law and daughter, to spend, amidst the cheerfulness of that happy home, the holiday time which would otherwise have been passed at school. Every school-boy sought his presence as the proper place for enjoyment, reposing his confidences in him

[1] Several years afterwards Dr. Cumming wrote, 'Well do I remember the noble and loving Simeon who blessed the child that day.'

concerning new riddles, small purchases (generally the outlay of a gift from him), and plans for boyish pleasure, as naturally as, in fitting seasons, he listened to the tender counsels and pithy sayings, full of common-sense and heavenly wisdom, which fell from the lips of the aged saint.

Amongst the guests at Beckenham Rectory, in the summer of 1858, was one whose frequent visits during the past nineteen years had been almost as welcome to my father as were those of his own absent children. Henry S— was the son of a valued friend, who had lived for the glory of his Divine Master, and died rejoicing in the assurance of His everlasting love; and he had been beloved for his father's sake, as well as for his own. He was a man of rare quality of mind, whose ready wit was ever softened by a tender consideration for the feelings of others, and whose high poetic gift was balanced by sound judgment and remarkable common sense. The ideal of a true and genuine Englishman, the very sight of his face, and the ring of his laugh, spread an irresistible cheerfulness throughout the house, whilst the shyest child, won by his bright smile, sought shelter in his strong arms. But one thing was wanting to give stability to his character and force to his purpose,—the union of his soul to his Saviour through the power of living faith. For years he had been pleaded for in prayer, yet prayer seemed still unanswered; but now the time was come to prove that it had not been unheard.

During the week he spent at the rectory he had many

conversations with my father on scriptural subjects, and there was a softened tone about his manner of speaking of these things; and, as the days went on, it was evident to those who anxiously observed him, that the impression, which seemed deepening hour by hour, was no mere passing matter of impulse. On Sunday evening it had been arranged that the Sacrament of the Lord's Supper should be administered at the rectory to a beloved guest, then an invalid, the young widow of my father's valued friend the late Duke of Manchester, who had expressed her wish to partake of that blessed feast. Several members of the family wished to join in the communion, and those who knew Henry S— felt that it would be a testing time with him, and that if he felt assured of the sincerity and truth of his present desire for a change of heart and intent to lead a new life, he would decide to join the little band about to commemorate their Saviour's dying love, and thus make an open profession of his faith in that Saviour. Throughout the day my father had been earnest in prayer for the son of his old friend, and when all were assembled, and the service was about to commence, I saw a look of heavenly joy in his face as his glance fell on Henry S—, kneeling amongst the number, his head bowed in earnest prayer.

That night was the turning point of our friend's history. The voice of God had spoken to his heart, and he presented himself as a living sacrifice to the Saviour who had loved him and given Himself for him. By the power of the Holy Ghost working in him, he escaped from the bands of sin, and through depths of penitence for talents wasted and time misspent, he rose up at length to walk in the light of his Saviour's countenance.

In the following month of October he became seriously ill; and during a temporary improvement he thus wrote:—

'I am afraid, even if it please God I should be cured, I shall never be strong again; but knowing my own miserable instability, I cannot pray to be led into the temptation of health and strength any more. My strongest wish as to *earth* is that I may be spared a little longer to tend the declining years of my mother, and in a very subordinate way do some work for God. I have done plenty for the devil.

'Continue to pray for me, that my sins, which are many, may be forgiven, and that I may therefore love much. If I am sincere now, as I sometimes hope, I could not stand a moment without the Spirit's *continual help.*

'I often think (with an earnest desire to follow in the same path, however far behind) of the simple, self-forgetting, yet fearless, way in which Hedley Vicars always went about with the name of Jesus on his lips, and His love in his heart; so that all who met with him "took knowledge of him that he had been with Jesus."

'The zeal and activity of dear Blackwood, too, so early in his Christian course, reprove the backwardness one feels when a word might be said in season.

'Your father, my father, and Joseph John Gurney, were remarkable for somehow always, whatever the conversation was, gradually drawing it towards their ruling subject.

'I hope, if I live to see you again, we shall be able to commune freely about the way of peace, and of Him who "is our peace." I never could before. Now, from down in the depths, I look up to Him who bore our sins in His own body on the tree, *and I dare not doubt* His power nor His will to pardon even me.

'Write to me as often as you can. Your letters are a great help and comfort. And dear Marianne Acklom writes me sisterly letters of Christian counsel, which I value highly.

'I must ever thank God for that last visit to Beckenham. . . . It is a beloved home; and your dear honoured father's presence sheds a halo around it.'

Within three short weeks after that letter was written, on the 26th of November, Henry S— died.

The following lines were found in a desk by his side, and were evidently written only a few days before his death:—

'A still small voice said unto me,
"Thou art so full of misery,
Wilt thou not now to Jesus flee?"

I am ashamed, my heart replied,
To flee to Him I have denied,
Yea, have betray'd and crucified.

"Yet," urged the voice, "thou art undone,
And other refuge there is none
But in the blood of God's dear Son.

Thy soul in its pollution lies,
Hideous and loathsome to the eyes;
There is but One that purifies.

In sadder plight thou could'st not be;
Thy Maker's face thou may'st not see,—
Thou hast no robe to cover thee."

Then did my troubled spirit groan,—
All that thou say'st I long have known;
My vileness and my need I own.

I know that in Love's sea I might
Cast my pollutions out of sight,
Nor stain those waters pure and bright;

I know the Spirit's quickening breath
Could raise my soul from sin and death;
But one dark shadow hindereth.

How can I hope to be sincere,
Should I, in trouble and in fear,
To the Redeemer's cross draw near?

Remembering the day of woe,
When to that Fount I seem'd to go,
Whose healing waters overflow.

Pardon and peace I seem'd to implore,
But soon, that sheltering sickness o'er,
Sin was triumphant as before.

Should mercy now the stroke remove,
Will not a heart so faithless prove
A double traitor to His love?

Once more that still small voice did say,—
"If thou from Grace didst fall away,
Haply thou didst not watch and pray:

But thy forgetfulness and pride
On something else than Grace relied,—
Leaned on some reed that pierced thy side.

Or, if thou *never cam'st* before,
All doors are closed but Mercy's door.
Thou shouldst *come now*, and sin no more."

(*Then*) "Just as I am, without one plea,
But that Thy blood was shed for me,
And that Thou bidst me come to Thee—
O Lamb of God, I come."'

The following letters were written by my father in the course of the same year:—

TO CAPTAIN ANSTRUTHER, GRENADIER GUARDS.

'BECKENHAM, 1858.

'MY DEAREST ROBERT,—Your handwriting is very pleasant to us, as well as darling Louie's. We rejoice that you have had such a pleasant time in the north, but we long to see you again in the south.

'Thank God, wherever you are, you have entered upon the narrow path, which not only leads to life, but honours the Redeemer by the way. If at any time any sacrifice be made in that path, there will be a proportionate, and more than proportionate reward. But, in the present day, few are called, as our forefathers were, to a conformity to their Lord in His sufferings. Yet I can remember, in my time, when a determined profession of religion, and consequent departure from former modes of life, gave great offence. My poor dear father (though one of the kindest of men) said at first of me, "I will cut him off with a shilling;" but he lived to say, out of the generosity of his heart, "He is the saviour of the family." Neither saying was right, but it shows what a change can take place in favour of the conscience of another. I did, thank God, live to see my dear mother and sister very decidedly on the Lord's side. You are privileged in having parents who know and love the truth. May you ever "*walk* in the truth;" and may you be happy in a Saviour's love, and useful in a Saviour's service!

'I can conceive no greater honour, and no greater happiness on earth, especially when those we love think the same.

'Mrs. Marsh begs me to give her love to you and Louie, and kind regards to Sir Ralph and Lady Anstruther, in which I heartily join.

'Bless you both, my darlings, WM. MARSH.'

'BECKENHAM, KENT, S.E., *July* 14, 1858.

'MY DEAR ROBERT,—What a treat you have sent me in the letter of M. A. S.

'I call that "ancient Christianity;" we want more of it in modern times. It is *whole-hearted.* May you and darling Louie ever with purpose of heart cleave to the Lord.

'I shall be pleased to have my name linked with the name of Ralph.

'I shall like much to be present with Dr. Cumming. You know my views of different churches. Every man has a right to a spirit of *preference.* No man has a right to a spirit of *exclusion.* Leave that to unhappy Rome.

'The accounts you send are very cheering. "Giving thanks always for all things" is our rule; a good man, Dr. Ring, used to say, "thanksliving is the best thanksgiving." But we must add, both are best! He also one day recommended a specific against murmuring. "I will bless the Lord at *all* times: His praise shall *continually* be in my mouth."

'Tell my darling "Marny" to rest as much as she can, that her strength may be renewed for future work.

'My best love to darling Louie, and my respectful

compliments to "The Stranger!"—Your most affectionate "Grandsire," WM. MARSH.'

'*P.S.*—You have answered my riddle quite correctly in the five letters of a certain little lady's name. Now I will send you my answer in verse:—

A Christian wife is cheering as the sun,
Her smiles all innocence, all guilelessness her fun;
Her speech like honey; shining as the light
Her life, warm as the day, and pure as moonbeams bright;
Soars like the lark, her soul; her form as slight,
And step as soft, as fairy's hid from sight;
Wise as the serpent, harmless as the dove,
Because she loves her God, and lives in holy love.'

TO HIS YOUNGEST DAUGHTER.

'ISLIP RECTORY, NEAR OXFORD,
Aug. 13, 1858.

'I HOPE you have received a line I enclosed to dearest Matilda, informing you of our prosperous journey, and of my blowing the trumpet on Sunday afternoon. The blast was on Rev. xxii. 12.

'To-day my memory is repeating a verse or two of a hymn I learned sixty years ago.

"In this world of sin and sorrow,
Compassed round with many a care,
From Eternity we borrow
Hope, which will exclude despair.

Thee, triumphant God and Saviour,
Darkly through a glass we see;
Oh! assist each faint endeavour;
Raise our earth-born souls to Thee."

'Nothing will go quite right, on a general scale, till the King returns; till He takes to Himself His great power, and reigns. Nevertheless, we may yet expect great things. The wonderful awakening in America shows us this. And "open thy mouth wide" encourages this. You know it by happy experience. "Cast not away your confidence, which hath great recompense of reward."

'Mrs. Marsh sends her love to you. What a delightful letter from Lady Maria Forester. How greatly God has blessed some of the members of that family! Dear Lord Roden will not come under the "*Woe* unto you when all men speak well of you." Yet those who attacked him must have felt in their consciences that he was right, and now they allow his light to be a true light. The disciple of Christ may well wait patiently.'

'Love from all here, to all at Chilham.—Ever your most loving father, WM. MARSH.'

To the Same.

'35 MARINA, ST. LEONARDS-ON-THE-SEA,
September 17, 1858.

'AN idle man has no time to write a *letter*. I am an idle man here, but I will sign my name to this bit of paper, and just say we have received your delightful letter. "Attempt great things; expect great things."

'I do not much wonder at that Christian lady meeting with opposition; for Satan is not yet bound. But it was certainly extraordinary in her case. It will be overruled. The enemy overshoots his mark. I trust she will not be discouraged.

'Send me a copy of the forthcoming Letters, especially the one to the prisoners; lest I should do something wrong to be sent to jail in order to get one.

'Dear little Katie Marshall is with us, adding to our fun.

'Great blessings attend all your words.

'We had a very pleasant visit at Bearwood. It is a charming place; and Mr. Walter is a most kind and agreeable host. The clergyman is author of an interesting biography of Jeremy Taylor. In reading it, I discovered a new relation. My great-grandfather[1] married Jeremy Taylor's third daughter.

'But I hope we are all related much farther back, even to Abraham (Gal. iii. 7).

'Dear William and Rose, and sweet little fair Rosamond, are well. St. Leonards seems to suit them, and is a fine field for work.

'China opened to the gospel, as well as to merchandise! We live in wonderful times. The crisis is approaching. In the meantime, may there be a great outpouring of the Spirit of God, to "accomplish the number of His elect, and to hasten His kingdom." I like the marginal translation of 2 Pet. iii. 12, 'Hasting the coming.' It should excite disciples to much prayer and great labour. For the elect's sake the days may be shortened: even the days of delusion and lukewarmness.

'. . . How great is the mercy that has brought us to abide by the evident meaning of Scripture, especially on the vital subject of the atonement—Death, that we might

[1] Archbishop of Dublin.

have Life. None can so forcibly feel the obligation to live to Him as the soul that knows it has been "bought with a price."

'Writing by owl-light, and almost as blind as a bat.—Ever thy most loving father, W. MARSH.'

In the month of October of the same year, my father visited his eldest daughter and Mr. Trench at Islip Rectory. He was delighted with all that he saw of their plans for the good of the villagers, who seemed to have learnt from his daughter's devoted and reverent affection for him to hail his visits as if they could not fail to bring a blessing. The society of his little grand-daughters was a great additional charm to him, for he never felt a home to be complete without a child in it.

In company with Mr. and Mrs. Trench, he went to Sandford Park, to visit his friend Dr. Guest, Master of Caius College, Cambridge, whose sisters had in former years derived great benefit from his ministry; and on leaving Islip, he spent a few days with Mr. Walter, at Bearwood, preaching on the Sunday in the village church. He next went to St. Leonards, to remain a fortnight with his son and daughter-in-law. Their only child, a lovely little girl of six years old, was then, and for the remainder of her brief life, a great delight to him. My father preached twice in his son's church during this visit, and spoke at a missionary meeting in the public hall; taking even more than his usual hearty interest in every plan for the benefit of the parish.

On his return to Beckenham, he shared with Mr.

Chalmers and my sister the happiness of welcoming their eldest son, then in the Rifle Brigade, back from India, after an eighteen months' campaign, during the suppression of the mutiny; and with a true old soldier's heart rejoiced in the high character for courage and steadfastness which he had won in twenty-seven engagements.

With his old delight in pastoral work, he cared for each of the various plans for doing good in the parish, continuing himself to preach and to give expositions of Scripture; with his heart, at the same time, going out to all the old world-wide interests connected with the spread of the kingdom of Christ.

It was towards the close of the same year that a last visit was paid to my father by his old acquaintance Mr. Fuller Maitland; at whose beautiful residence, Park Place, my father and his family had often, for many years past, enjoyed the Christian society and warm friendship of Mrs. Maitland and her gifted children.

The two aged men were comparing the number of their years, when Mr. Maitland said earnestly, 'I am not your equal in years; but I *wish* I were in wisdom and goodness.'

'We are both poor sinners,' replied my father; 'but both, I trust, looking to our Saviour, who hath said for each, "Look unto me, and *be ye saved.*"'

'I wish I were as sure of it as you,' was the rejoinder.

My father then spoke out of the abundance of his heart of the freeness and fulness of the offer of salvation through Jesus Christ to every sinner upon the face of God's redeemed earth, who will accept it. He quoted the words, 'Ho, every one that thirsteth, come ye to the waters,' adding, 'that call is to one wandering away, as you would call to a man at a distance, who, with his face set towards the opposite direction, does not perceive you. And how free the invitation, "Yea, come, buy wine and milk, without money and without price." "The Spirit and the Bride say, Come; and let him that heareth, say, Come. And let him that is athirst come; and *whosoever will*, let him take of the water of life, FREELY." We should come, just as we are, without a moment's delay, for it is a Divine command; without a moment's hesitation, for it is a most loving entreaty.'

He then quoted Dr. Valpy's lines :—

'In peace let me resign my breath,
And Thy salvation see;
My sins deserve eternal death,
But Jesus died for me.'

Mr. Maitland said, 'I must learn that;' so my father wrote down the verse for him: as he received it, he said, 'I shall wear it near my heart.' It was found there after his death.

TO HIS YOUNGEST DAUGHTER.

'BECKENHAM, *Jan.* 14, 1859.

'. . . I HAVE just finished Arthur's *Tongue of Fire.* It is a wonderful book. Some passages may be objected to, still he guards against being misunderstood. May it set many on fire, and raise up a bright flame amidst smouldering ashes.

'And shall we, Lord, for ever live,
At this poor dying rate!'

'I have a vain wish. I want to live my life over again.

'However, there is a fountain that washes away self-seekings and shortcomings, and all other blots.

'Our regularly returning comet, called Mary, has left our sphere again. She is brighter than ever.

'I prayed to-day for dearest Robert and Louie, that health may be granted, as well as their Christian labours be blessed; and courage and steadfastness ever be given them in serving our Lord and Saviour, that they may never be ashamed to confess Him before men, nor grow weary in well-doing.

'My kindest regards to all at Bearwood, from its hospitable owner to his youngest child.

'As much love, and more than words can express, to you and darling Lucy.

'I have just given dearest Kennie a wish, which I will give to children and grandchildren: A useful life; a peaceful death; a happy eternity. All come through faith in our Lord Jesus Christ—His Life, His Death, His Eternity.'

To the Same.

'ISLIP RECTORY, *July* 7, 1859.

'I SEND you a letter for you to forward to dear Leila. I might add to the subject by referring to the four daughters of Philip who did "prophesy." That word is used in the New Testament in the sense of preaching.

'I also send you a manuscript to read and comment upon. Try to do so *impartially*. He is no reviewer who cannot find fault. Yet we hope to be reviewed, and no fault found; not by the recording angel dropping a tear, and so blotting out a passage, but by the blood—inestimably precious blood—of the Angel of the covenant, which cleanseth from all sin.

'Dear William Marshall and Lizzy are here. She is a cheerful, pleasant creature. I have a heap of letters to write to-day, and can only therefore enclose in this the most weighty of all things—Love. Yet the law allows it to go for a penny.'

TO MISS WILDMAN.

'*December* 1, 1858.

'MY DEAR LEILA,—. . . I will now give you my views of 1 Cor. ii. It is taken for granted that a woman might pray or prophesy; and the decent and becoming manner of so doing is pointed out (1 Cor. xi. 5-10). It would appear as if some women, professing to be inspired, interfered with the appointed services of the minister (1 Cor. xiv. 34). A woman was not to conduct the regular public services, as if she were the minister. But this does not forbid Christian women from exhorting or praying, where persons might be assembled for a religious exercise. It would not come under the idea of a church. It is right that men only should be employed in the ruling of a church. Women were not to be in that office. Nor were they permitted to interrupt public worship by asking questions in the church.

'There have been some remarkable instances in which women have been employed by the Holy Spirit,—Miriam, Hannah, Huldah, etc., under the Old Testament dispensation; and there is a long list in Romans xvi., under the New Testament. When God gives seals to exhortation, who shall say nay? In our country, in modern times, we have had remarkable instances of this gift,—in Mrs. Fletcher of Madeley, Mrs. Stevens of Knaresborough, among members of the Church of England; and Mrs. Fry in the Society of Friends. Mrs. Stevens addressed any who attended her school-room in the afternoon, when the church was closed, and Dr. M'Neile was one of the fruits. Our best love to you all.—Your ever affectionate friend,

'WM. MARSH.'

His views of the Divine order concerning the agency of women in the work of the Lord, were further expanded in the following letter:—

'... ON the subject of your letter I will answer you scripturally with the sayings of a prophet and two apostles. Joel speaks of the outpouring of the Holy Spirit, and foretells that it would be upon *daughters* and *handmaids*, as well as upon sons and servants (Joel ii. 28,29). St. Peter concludes the primary fulfilment of this prophecy to have been at Pentecost. Women were there, and doubtless partook of it. In Acts i. 14, 15, we find the company consisted of the eleven apostles, the women, the mother of Jesus, and His brethren, and other disciples; the number of the names together were about a hundred and twenty.

'In Acts ii. 2 we find these were "*all*" with one accord in one place. They had been uniting in prayer and supplication for the promised blessing, and the tongue of fire descended alike upon the men and the women; for the text is emphatic,—"It sat upon *each* of them, and they were *all* filled with the Holy Ghost, and began"—(*not* the men alone to speak, and the women to keep silence) but *all* began—"to speak with other tongues, as the Spirit gave them utterance." This is additionally proved by St. Peter's reference to that prophecy of Joel.

'If some of the men among the disciples had interfered with the utterances of the Spirit through Mary, or any of the other women, and had questioned their right to speak in the assembly, asserting that it was unseemly, and out of the sphere of woman to proclaim a risen Saviour, in view of the fact that there were *men* mingling in the crowd of listeners, He who gave woman her commission on the morning of the resurrection, saying, "Go tell my brethren," would surely have disapproved of such an interference.

'An eminent commentator, in reviewing this text, "Go tell my brethren," says—"Behold what honour God puts on those who persevere in truth, and continue to honour Him before men. Thus these faithful women proclaim the gospel of a risen Saviour to those who were afterwards to be the teachers of the whole human race."

'St. Paul, knowing that women partook of the gift, was anxious that it should be exercised with discretion (1 Cor. xiv. 34, 35). It is plain that the "speaking" here referred to was asking questions, which might better be answered by their husbands at home. The word "women" here evidently means *wives*. This may tend to harmonize other passages in these epistles. In the Jewish synagogues it was a common occurrence for persons to interrupt the speaker with questions which frequently resulted in angry altercations. This practice, we have reason to infer, had been introduced into the Corinthian Church; and some women, doubtless devoid of spirituality, were disposed to take part in these debates. This unseemly practice St. Paul reproves, and says, "Let your women keep silence in the churches."

'With respect to prophesying (or preaching) as it is alluded to in 1 Cor. xiv., you will find its nature defined in the 3d verse. It was directed to be for "edification, exhortation, and comfort;" and St. Paul evidently admits of this prophesying of women in public assemblies, for he gives special directions respecting their conduct and appearance while engaged in this sacred duty,—the man praying or prophesying was to have his head uncovered, the woman to have her head covered. Again, this Apostle says, "I would that ye *all* spake with tongues, but rather that ye prophesied." The word "all" must comprehend every member, both men and women.

'Another passage, which is sometimes considered a difficulty, is 1 Tim. ii., from 11th verse to the end. But there again the command seems to apply to the relations between husband and wife.

'If its meaning were not to teach *at all*, no woman could teach in an adult school, or write instructive books. Some say, "It only means teaching face to face;" but St. Paul implies the contrary, by the directions he gives as to the mode of prophesying.

'Priscilla expounded the word to Apollos, and it would be difficult to prove that expounding was not teaching.

'"Aged women," says St. Paul, "should be teachers of all good things."

'With a few more examples from Scripture, some in the Old Testament dispensation, when women were in a far more subject position than they are now, I will close this letter.

'Miriam, who was joined with Moses and Aaron in leading Israel from Egypt to Canaan,—"I brought thee up out of the land of Egypt, and sent before thee Moses and Aaron and Miriam.'

'Deborah, who not only judged all Israel, but also led their armies to victory.

'Abigail, who counselled David, the Lord's prophet and the anointed king, and that in the hearing of all his followers, and David said, "Blessed be the Lord God of Israel, who hath sent thee this day to meet me, and blessed be thy advice, and blessed be thou."

'Huldah, to whom Josiah the king sent Hilkiah *the priest*, and others for advice in a time of much anxiety, when they feared the wrath of the Lord.

'Psalm lxviii. 11, reads in the original thus:—"The Lord gave the word, great was the company of women-publishers."

'Anna, the prophetess, spoke of Jesus to *all* them that looked for redemption in Jerusalem.

'The woman of Samaria preached Jesus to the people of her city, and many believed on Him for the saying of the woman.

'Tryphena and Tryphosa laboured in the Lord. The beloved Persis laboured much in the Lord. And women "whose names are in the Book of Life" laboured with Paul in the gospel (Phil. iv. 3).

'From these passages the scriptural view of the subject seems so clear to my mind that I have not a doubt about it left,—provided "all things be done decently and in order."—Your affectionate friend, WM. MARSH.'

TO THE REV. CHARLES BRIDGES.

'BECKENHAM, *August* 9, 1859.

'MY DEAR BRIDGES,—. . . I am glad that a new edition of the *Commentary on the Proverbs* is forthcoming. You know to whom to ascribe the glory, and therefore I do not mind telling you, that I know of no book better calculated to be useful to young men in particular. May your life yet be spared for continued usefulness. But, as *litera scripta manet*, great is the mercy that has employed your pen. Perhaps St. Paul, though careful of the "parchments," little thought that his letter to Philemon would be read nearly two thousand years afterwards, and especially on that island of pagans, which probably he visited only for a very short time. Colquhoun's *Life in Olden Times* represents Florence as the great and flourishing city; London not worth looking at. There were no Barings or Rothschilds to enrich it in those days; nor Bibles to bless it.—Yours ever affectionately,

'WM. MARSH.'

'BECKENHAM, *Nov.* 2, 1859.

'... PRAYER-MEETINGS are held in London for a shower of Living Water to descend there: we have them here also, that there may be a general outpouring. God honours united, fervent, persevering prayer. It may be that He is "accomplishing the number of His elect, and hastening His kingdom." ... I am in wonderful health, considering my age. Let us look upward continually for all the grace we need; and forward to the rest which will never be disturbed in the land of light and love.'

On the 5th of August, he baptized his first great-granddaughter, Mary Evelyn Anstruther, in Beckenham Church. As usual, friends flocked from far and near to hear him read a service of the Church in public, as well as to listen to his heaven-taught thoughts, with regard to it, in private. So correct was his taste in reading, and so earnest his spirit, that a friend who was no mean judge, who was present on more than one of these occasions, remarked, 'It is a rare enjoyment to hear a service thus read. Dr. Marsh has a soul in tune with our stately Liturgy, and the simplicity and fervour of his devotion could never offend the most critical taste.'

Towards the end of August he spent some weeks at Broadstairs; and whilst there, preached occasionally for the incumbent, the Rev. Frederick Newell, who was the son of one of his friends and parishioners at Colchester, and who had himself, as a boy, been instructed by my father in his catechetical lectures for the children of the upper classes in that town.

Now, as always, he doubled his pleasures by sharing them, and so assembled around him not only his children, grandchildren, and great-grandchildren, but also some of those cadets from Addiscombe who were prevented by distance from going to their parents for a summer holiday. To gather the young around him, to throw himself into their interests, and to plan for their pleasures, was as natural to him, as it was to sympathize with their trials and difficulties, and to persuade them to seek ever closer and closer union with their God and Saviour.

Whilst he was in this neighbourhood he met again Mr. and Mrs. Warre of Westcliff, who had been dear and early friends of his late wife, Lady Louisa Marsh, and whom they had visited together in the spring of 1840. The renewal of this friendship was a source of much pleasure both to himself and his family, who were welcomed with him to that lovely sea-side home with unbounded kindness and hospitality. Here also he met Archdeacon Davis, whom he had known and valued for years, and found refreshment in attending his ministry at Ramsgate.

TO HIS YOUNGEST DAUGHTER.

'BECKENHAM RECTORY, *Nov.* 17, 1859.

'DEAR DARLING,—You cannot think how well imagination has behaved since I gave it a stern reproof for its pictures of danger. Now it tells me of the kind American Consul; the good Captain of the vessel; the ease and safety of getting on board; the considerate conduct of the authorities; the silence of the audience; the tears trickling down some cheeks; the resolution formed in many hearts to think of and seek a Saviour.

'Just as imagination told me the above, I perceived a little hoarseness at the end of the tale; speaking in the open air at this season is trying to throats, so the sailors must be invited under some roof.'

'Mrs. Rio and darling Matilda are visiting the sick. I am trying to preserve my wits, as I am asked to write prefaces to three different works at one time. In one of them I intend to justify women in doing all they can to save souls. Oh, what a blessed work it is! But all the blessing in it cannot be known till "the Day shall declare it."

'My heart is just beginning to dance on learning that darling Lucy is a little better.

'I thank God for the report respecting our dear Charlie. He is a pleasant, affectionate youth. May the Lord stablish, strengthen, settle him. Our beloved Louisa's children have been greatly blessed, and not a little by your motherly love to them. . . . I pray your present efforts may be a blessing. You will raise the serpent on the pole. The sick will look and be healed. One look at the Cross, said Dr. Buchanan, is sufficient. But then he was dying. We who are living must be looking every day.

'We serve the best of masters. As sinners, He receives us graciously; as servants, He rewards us generously; as friends, He will make us partakers of His joys. . . .

'My love to dear Mr. and Mrs. Warre, with hearty thanks for all their kind care of my property.—Ever thy most loving and delighted father, W. MARSH.'

The following brief remembrances of some of my father's conversations are taken from notes written down at the time by his eldest daughter, during her visit to him at Easter, 1860:—

'On Easter eve, after speaking of the marvellous change from the Cross to Paradise, he said, "What a day this must have been for the penitent thief! . . . When Mr. Simeon was preaching on his prayer, he suddenly exclaimed, 'Heaven for asking for! Heaven for asking for!'"

'On Easter Day he spoke of the Saviour's tenderness in mentioning Peter by name, to reassure him of His love; "Go, tell my disciples, and *Peter*," (and the tears came to his eyes while thinking of the love of the Lord Jesus, the "overflowing of love," as he expressed it). "How he loved this earth, delaying his ascension forty days after His resurrection, and appearing frequently to His disciples."

'In talking with his medical adviser, Mr. Williams, on Heb. xi., he described the true translation of ver. 1 to be, "Now faith is the *certain expectation* of things hoped for." Mr. Williams quoted Luther's translation as being "the sure and certain confidence." "We all like to be trusted," my father rejoined, and so (pointing upwards) "*HE* loves to be trusted."

'At another time he spoke of the Epistles to the Romans and the Hebrews; "What wonderful epistles! The one exhibiting Christian doctrine, the other showing Christianity as the substance of the Levitical dispensation of shadows;" adding, "What a wonderful book the Bible is! what a variety is contained in it! History, prophecy, biography, poetry, doctrines, precepts, promises!" Alluding to Burke's habit of reading a chapter in Isaiah before going to speak in the House of Commons, and to the Speaker's comment on his remarkable speech at Warren Hastings' trial, recommending the House to adjourn that it might distinguish between the blaze of eloquence and the light of truth, he remarked, that "Isaiah possessed both the blaze of eloquence and the light of truth."

'He afterwards related one or two anecdotes of the Rev. Charles Simeon. He was told, that before he was appointed to his fellowship he must receive the sacrament. He felt he was unfit, and asked some one to lend him a book on the subject. Bishop Wilson's was lent to him, in which the type of the scape-goat is dwelt upon. He received the truth of the transfer of sin, and never afterwards lost it.

'He next told us Mr. Simeon's mode of describing a Christian's death. "Who are you?" (looking back)—"Sorrow." "And who are you?"—"Sighing." Then stretching his hands upwards—"And who are you?"—"Joy." "And who are you?"—"Gladness." "Then farewell Sorrow, farewell Sighing! Joy and Gladness, I will go with you!"

'The same evening he spoke on "the comprehensiveness of the testimony of John the Baptist to our Saviour. 1*st*, He is 'the Lamb of God that taketh away the sin of the world.' Hence guilt and condemnation are removed. 2*d*, He 'baptizeth with the Holy Ghost,' hence the power of Satan and the dominion of sin are destroyed. 3*d*, He is 'the Son of God,' and therefore is qualified to accomplish this great work; and finally, He will be the Judge, represented by gathering the wheat into the garner, and bestowing rewards of grace on His disciples; but punishing His impenitent foes, as it is written, 'burning up the chaff;' hence, in every sense, 'He must *increase*,'—Christ must be everything. 'Therefore, let no man glory in men; Christ must be all in all.' The Father says of Him, 'This is my beloved Son, in whom I am well pleased.' Happy is the soul that can say, 'This is my beloved Saviour, in whom my soul is well pleased.'"

The following letter shows that his interest in the welfare of the town of Bridgnorth continued unabated, after many years of absence:—

TO THE REV. J. BENTLEY, SHORTLY AFTER HIS APPOINTMENT TO ST. MARY'S, BRIDGNORTH.

'BECKENHAM RECTORY, *May* 2, 1860.

'REV. AND DEAR SIR,—From my long connexion with Bridgnorth, you will not require an apology for my writing you a line, though a stranger.

'I am very thankful for your appointment, and pray that your faithful labours may win many sinners to the Saviour, and lead believers to adorn His doctrine. I am sure that there are many there who will welcome your message. It greatly cheers the heart of my dear son-in-law to find that he is succeeded by such a faithful pastor.

'Your office is the most honourable and the most useful upon the face of the earth. It was but the other morning that I was reading Barnes' Commentary on 2 Cor., chapters ii., iii. They give a glorious view of the design of the Christian ministry, and its blessed results, as accompanied by the Divine blessing. And when the minister is a man of prayer, as well as a preacher, that blessing is not withheld.

'I have been long an upstairs-prisoner; but I find a sick-room a good library. I have read much of Barnes. I understood that his work was intended chiefly for teachers of Sunday-schools, but it is admirably adapted to the ministers of the Word. I am astonished at the extent of his research, and pleased with the independence of his own mind. On church government we shall differ from him, as he is not an Episcopalian, but on subjects essential for "edification, exhortation, and comfort," we shall agree with him.

'Dear Sir, it is a great privilege to escape superstition and rationalism in the present age, when the enemy appears to be making a desperate, because, perhaps, a last struggle. But ministers and people who keep close to the Throne of Grace and the Word of Grace are both safe and useful.

'Light, love, and usefulness attend yourself and Mrs. Bentley for many many years. And may your people know the time of their visitation.—Yours, dear sir, very faithfully, WM. MARSH.'

Towards the end of the month of May, just five years from the time of his first visit to Beckenham Rectory in joyous health and spirits, Arthur Vandeleur came for his last farewell.

Although he was within a few days of his death, his brave spirit bore him up above the infirmities of consumption, and he joined the family circle at meals, ready as ever for cheerful conversation. Whilst his soul was attuned to the highest solemnities, the bright sunshine of his spirit was as sparkling, and the music of his pleasant laugh almost as clear as ever.

He liked to have his chair placed every evening where he could best see my father's face. Earlier, he had written of him,—'How much of the Master's likeness do we see in your most beautiful and venerable father? The atmosphere of love and peace which seems ever around him is indeed a breath of Heaven's own air.' And still the sight of that countenance seemed to carry joy to his heart, although deafness on one side, and a failing voice on the other, prevented much communication. 'I cannot make my voice heard through his trumpet now,' he said, rather sadly; then brightening up suddenly, he added, 'but we shall have plenty of time for talking together when we meet in the everlasting Home.'

On the day when he and his beloved wife, who was nursing him with a devotion beyond her strength, left the rectory, he said, 'I should like to go to heaven straight from this dear home. I mean to go to Woolwich to-day to see my little children, and then Mary and I will come again in a few days, and stay to the end.'

That wish, however, doubtless for wise reasons, was not granted; probably, to give him the opportunity of bearing his last witness for his Saviour to his friends and brother officers at Woolwich.

My father keenly felt that parting. 'He will never come back,' he said. 'The hand of death is upon him. Yet there *is* no death for *him*, as he himself said, blessed soul! for his life is hid with Christ in God.'

CHAPTER XIV.

SUNSET LIGHT.

'Of life's past toils the fading trace
Hath given the aged patriarch's face
Expression holy, deep, resigned,
The calm sublimity of mind.
. . . . Yet his mien
Is bright with majesty serene;
And those high hopes, whose guiding star
Shines from eternal worlds afar,
Have with that light illumed his eye
Whose fount is immortality;
And o'er his features poured a ray
Of glory, not to pass away.'

HEMANS.

SUNSET LIGHT.

SOME weeks before this time, a subject of serious consideration had been brought before him, in the offer of the living of Beddington, a village in Surrey, within an easy drive of Beckenham.

Although still working ably in the service so dear to his heart, he had felt the comfort of having no responsible charge of his own, and he dreaded anything which would break up the happy home-circle at Beckenham Rectory. Twice, therefore, he declined the offer; but when an influential resident in Beddington came more than once to urge his acceptance of it, pressing him to consider the blessing that his presence and prayers would be in the parish, combined with the value of his well-known principles, and the power he would have to choose curates who would carry out all his wishes and plans in pastoral work, he felt it right to reconsider the matter, asking counsel of his God concerning it. He also consulted some of his friends, upon whose Christian judgment he could best rely. The late revered and beloved Archbishop of Canterbury, the Bishop of Winchester, in whose diocese Beddington is situated, the Rev. Charles Goodhart, and others not less valued, all alike concurred in telling him that, in their opinion, he would close a door of usefulness which the providence of God had opened to him, if he did not accept this charge. He was not a man to shrink from responsibility when once he could trace the Divine hand beckoning him to undertake it, and believing that his earnest prayers for guidance had been answered, he at length decided to yield to the request. Two other circumstances, which he looked upon as leading tokens, helped his decision. One was a visit from Mr. Hamilton, the venerable father of the late rector, who said that it would give him the greatest consolation to know that Dr. Marsh had consented to be the successor of his beloved and only son; whilst another and yet stronger call to him was that several poor people in the parish had united to plead in prayer that he might be made willing to become their pastor.

From the time he became rector of Beddington he determined to employ the whole of the income derived from the living in stipends to curates, in parochial and other charities, and the necessary additional expenses of a separate household, so as not to leave any surplus for his family or for his own gratification. The only indulgence he allowed himself was in doubling his subscriptions to several benevolent and Christian institutions, and in other ways giving even more largely than before towards the furtherance of the work of the Lord and the relief of distress. So heartily did he carry out the Divine command, 'Lay not up for yourselves treasure on earth, but lay up for yourselves treasure in heaven,' that,

FREDERICK HAY FORBES, PINX.

BEDDINGTON CHURCH.

knowing there was a sufficient provision for his children secured by trust-property and by his own insurances, he expended, almost every year, a considerable amount of capital, including legacies, in the service of his heavenly Master, and for the benefit of the poor. He felt it to be so important a duty for every Christian to provide for his family, according to his means, without being tempted to hoard, that he wrote several letters in the newspapers on the subject of insurance, and advised the married clergy to adopt the plan, even if they could only afford to insure for £100.

In his strong view of the error of accumulating money, he would say, 'I have read a melancholy thing in the paper to-day,—a man died possessed of £100,000!'

In connexion with this subject, he remarked to the Rev. Henry O'Rorke, one of his curates at Beddington, 'I wish I could write all across the sky, in letters of gold, the one word "Savings-bank."'

On the day of his induction to the living, he was accompanied by his three daughters, a grand-daughter, and two young friends, to Beddington Church. He was met by the Rev. George Hodgson, rural dean, and vicar of Croydon. It was a bright afternoon in July, and the sunshine lighting up the old grey tower of the church, and streaming through the stately trees of the park, at the entrance of which it stands, lent an additional charm to the beauty of the peaceful scene. The loving-kindness of the Heavenly Master had reserved this 'calm retreat' to be the last field of labour where His aged and faithful servant should expend the remainder of his strength, in the work he loved so well of gathering more sheaves for the Lord of the harvest.

After the usual ceremony was over, he returned from the church to the rectory; and, on entering the library, he prayed with us all that peace might be given to those who were leaving that home, and to those who were about to enter it, and for great blessing on the parish.

He deeply sympathized with Mrs. Hamilton, and was tenderly anxious in every way to consult her feelings, and to soothe, as far as possible, the severe trial of leaving a home associated with the whole of her happy married life, whilst she, on her part, putting aside her own sorrow, with thoughtful care arranged for his comfort on coming into the house.

The following day, he addressed about three hundred persons in the schoolroom at Beckenham, on the subject of 'Soul Prosperity,' from the words, 'Beloved, I wish above all things that thou mayest prosper and be in health, even as thy soul prospereth.' It was the last time that he spoke in that room; and the people listened to his parting words with even more than their usual reverent love. Their grief at his leaving Beckenham was great; but those who could walk so far, found a solace in going over, from time to time, to hear him preach, and the members of his Saturday-evening meeting were never forgotten amongst the numerous guests invited to be present at his birthday parties and other social gatherings.

On the 4th of August, 1860, he entered the last earthly home which was to be gladdened by his presence.

FREDERICK HAY FORBES, PINX.

BEDDINGTON RECTORY

His beloved friend, the Duchess of Gordon, had expressed a wish to hear his first sermon in Beddington Church. She came accordingly, to be the earliest visitor welcomed at the rectory; and her faithful spirit rejoiced in the hope that a rich blessing would be brought to the parish and neighbourhood by his coming there. It was the last time that they met on earth; and that meeting was a foretaste of the communion of saints in heaven. Many were their 'warm and joyful thoughts of the city not made with hands,' in which their dwelling was soon to be, amidst 'the general assembly and church of the first-born and the spirits of just men made perfect.' Above all, they communed with delight of Him

> 'Whom to serve and whom to know
> Makes the joy of saints below;
> Whom to see, and whom to love,
> Makes the bliss of saints above.'

He preached his first sermon from Rev. xxi. 25, 'There shall be no night there.' Before closing it, he alluded with tender sympathy to the sorrow of the parishioners in the loss of their devoted pastor; leading them on to thoughts of the world where, as he said, 'there shall be no night of ignorance, no night of sin, no night of sorrow, and no night of death.'

On Sunday, the 19th of August, he 'read himself in.' In the morning, he went through the usual service, and twenty of the Thirty-nine Articles, and in the afternoon, the service and the remaining Articles. There was no flagging of his energy in any part; but when the last sentence was concluded, we expected that he would be somewhat exhausted. However, to the surprise of every one, his voice was raised up with renewed power to address the congregation on the scriptural character of both the Articles and Liturgy of the Church of England. He showed how closely they were allied to the very language of the inspired Word; and ended this short extempore sermon with an earnest appeal to every one present to uphold, by the united testimony of life and lip, those blessed scriptural principles which had been overlaid by the errors of the Middle Ages, but brought to light again at the Reformation.

Adjoining the rectory grounds are excellent schoolrooms which had been built by Mr. Hamilton, with the aid of his parishioners and friends. At the head of the boys' school my father found an admirable master, who had been established there for many years, and who was particularly happy in gaining the respect and affection of the village lads. Mr. Price and his wife were much valued by my father, and he took a constant interest in their work in the schools.

The courtesy and kindness of his reception by the parishioners was very pleasant to him. Foremost to welcome him was Mr. Laurence, who had urged his acceptance of the charge; he, with his wife and family, became not only valued helpers in parochial work and in the schools, but were also delighted to minister to his happiness, with the never-tiring consideration of love, until the closing hours of his life.

It was a great addition to his enjoyment, in the newly-made friendships at Beddington, to find himself in the neighbourhood of some of the near relatives of his esteemed old friend 'Joseph John Gurney,' and several of the descendants of Elizabeth Fry.

With Mr. Samuel Gurney, M.P. for Falmouth, and his wife, he had a warm friendship, and through their thoughtful kindness he received many little pleasures. Often his library table would be adorned by them with a rare plant, a foreign fern, or a delicate water lily. Then, again, his mind would be interested by some memoir of one of the numerous philanthropists belonging to the Society of Friends, or his taste gratified by the loan of a portfolio of choice engravings. But beyond all these kindnesses to himself, fully as they were appreciated, was his heart rejoiced by the frequent sight, during the summer months, of bright faces of little children from ragged, orphan, and other schools, many of them brought from dark alleys and courts in the heart of London, to play in the hay-fields, and to row on the little river in the gaily painted barge, amongst flocks of beautiful waterfowl, and to spend a holiday in the park and gardens, which must have seemed to them like fairyland. But perhaps the happiest gathering of all was that of the poor women belonging to Miss Barlee's admirable institution for the employment of needlewomen. Many of those careworn faces, bearing the marks of their hard struggle to sustain an often suffering life, grew bright as they listened to the gospel story. At the close of the day, some Christian friend would, at Mr. Gurney's request, speak to them of the Lord Jesus and His free salvation, in the hope that those burdened hearts might carry to their dreary homes not merely the remembrance of lovely country scenes, but the assurance that for them was prepared 'a better country, that is, an heavenly,' where 'they shall hunger no more, neither thirst any more; neither shall the sun light on them, nor any heat: for the Lamb which is in the midst of the throne shall feed them, and shall lead them unto living fountains of waters, and God shall wipe away all tears from their eyes.'

The eldest son of the late honoured Mrs. Fry—that noble and tender friend of the suffering and oppressed—was amongst those who warmly welcomed the new rector; and, with his excellent wife and daughters, he shortly afterwards began a devoted work for the Lord in that part of the parish where he resided.

Another source of enjoyment which my father found in the neighbourhood, was in more frequent intercourse with his beloved young friends, Mr. Blackwood and Sydney Duchess of Manchester. From the time of Mr. Blackwood's first visit to Beckenham, early in the summer of 1856, my father had watched, with thankful interest, the steadfast devotedness of his walk with God. He always endeavoured to secure him, with other excellent laymen, to share with his clerical friends in addressing the assemblies on the lawn; for he was one of those large-hearted clergy of our Church who gladly give the right hand of fellowship to all who 'shine as lights in the world, holding forth the Word of Life,' not only because they labour in the service of a Master who said of one who was working miracles in His name without an official commission, 'Forbid him not; he that is not against us is for us;' but also because he clearly saw the scriptural authority for lay-preaching, in the inspired history of the early diffusion of tho Gospel, when its glorious message of life and peace was carried to many and distant lands by the agency of the laity, as recorded in Acts xi. 19, 20; and in the notices of Apollos, Aquila, Priscilla, and others. And he also felt strongly about the personal loss which must be sustained, of a large and loving Christian brotherhood, by those who withhold their countenance from evangelistic work.

Sedulous efforts, he knew, were frequently made to detach some of the best and most zealous laymen from the communion of the Church of England; and he deeply deprecated the injury to her should this be effected through a want of sympathy and sanction on the part of her clergy.

But beyond all, he marked how the Divine blessing rested, in a tenfold degree, upon parishes where the incumbents welcomed 'workmen' manifestly 'approved unto God,' giving them hearty encouragement in their labours, combined with the benefit of their own longer experience and deeper theological study.

Two young clergymen were offered a share in the work of Beddington. One, the Rev. Henry Willes Southey, had, a few years earlier, spent much time at Beckenham Rectory, before his ordination, where, while preparing for his future office, by laying up wisdom and experience under Mr. Chalmers's counsel and direction, his single-hearted and earnest piety had won my father's warm regard. The other, the Rev. Henry O'Rorke, by a chain of coincidences, had been ordained to a curacy at Burtonon-Trent, where he had enjoyed the privilege of intimate acquaintance with my father's old friend, the Rev. Peter French; had next assisted the excellent Vicar of Basildon, during the last months of his life, in his pulpit and parochial duties, and had gone from thence to the Rev. David Stewart of Maidstone, just half a century from the time when his honoured father, Mr. Haldane Stewart, had come to work with my father at Basildon. The incumbent of Maidstone had written to him that Mr. O'Rorke wished for duty in the country, and that he could not send him a greater comfort, or spare Beddington a greater boon.

My father found the parish in excellent order. Clothing and coal clubs, the dispensary, and district visiting societies, with Sunday and day schools, had been established, and each had a share in his attention and interest. He attended with pastoral care to the accounts of the state of the poor given by the ladies who visited districts in the parish, at the monthly meeting of the society at the rectory; and he always concluded it with an earnest and affectionate address, and a prayer. Each Saturday afternoon some time was devoted to the study of the Bible with his curates; and a Saturday evening meeting was established in the rectory, like that which had strengthened the bonds of union between the earnest Christians in Beckenham.

After the autumn 'treat' to the school-children, my father, who was anxious to make acquaintance with all his parishioners, resolved to have a somewhat similar gathering of the working men and lads in the parish, of whom there were a considerable number,—many being employed at a tannery, and at leather, snuff and paper, mills. Upwards of four hundred of these men and boys were accordingly invited to a tea-party. For this purpose the use of the large hall of the old deserted house in Beddington Park[1] was obtained, by the kind mediation of Mr. Gurney. This hall, in which Queen Elizabeth was wont to hold her banquets, was lent every succeeding year for the same purpose, by the courtesy of the absent owner of the place.

Several of the ladies of the parish gave their assistance in adorning the room, and Mrs. Laurence kindly lighted it with coloured lamps. Tea was provided in the hall for the working men; and in an adjoining room for other parishioners, with friends from the neighbourhood and from London. After tea was ended, my father addressed them. They could scarcely restrain their enthusiasm as they saw his spirit and energy, and listened to his heart-stirring words;—and shouts of grateful approbation burst forth when he promised, if life should be spared, to give a similar tea-party, in the course of the following summer, for their wives and daughters.

A Russian princess, who had requested to be present on the occasion, was charmed with the scene, but most of all with him who was its centre of interest; and a priest of the Greek Church, whom she had brought with her, after conversing with my father at the rectory, and listening to his address and prayer at the meeting, said, 'If there be a saint upon earth, this is he.' When returning to London by the train, he inquired of a young officer from Chatham, who had been staying in the house, 'Is that old priest always as happy as we have seen him

[1] Since sold to the Governors of the Lambeth Orphanage.

to-night?' and on receiving the reply, 'I never saw him otherwise,' rejoined, 'Then his religion must be a good one.'

This tea-party was made, as usual, an occasion for collecting absent members of the family, and friends from a distance. Amongst others who came to stay a day or two, were Mr. and Mrs. Acklom, who were then settled at the vicarage of Hemel-Hempstead.

One more opportunity of intercourse and happy fellowship of heart was granted us with these beloved friends before he, whose noble Christian character, fervent love to the Saviour, and judicious zeal in His service, my father so deeply appreciated, was to hear the Master's voice saying to him, 'Well done, good and faithful servant, enter thou into the joy of thy Lord.'

In the month of November, it was recommended by my father's medical adviser that he should pass the winter at Beckenham, on account of the much greater warmth of the house; the draughts and thinner walls of Beddington Rectory having brought on severe attacks of rheumatism.

Unfeigned was the joy with which the news of his intended return was received in Beckenham. 'To see him in the pulpit,' said one, 'would be as good as a sermon, even if he could not say a word;' and some, in their expressions of delight in the hope of soon seeing his face again, reminded us of the exclamation of an old woman who used to attend his ministry in Birmingham, 'He looks for all the world just like an old angel!'

As his carriage entered the village, cottagers with their children came out to welcome him, and the ringers ran from their work to give him a cheerful peal from the belfry.

During the following winter he was able to take family prayers every night, and to conduct the Saturday evening meeting at Beckenham Rectory. But whilst throwing his interest into all the service of the Lord around him, his heart and prayers were much concentrated on his new parish. His curates paid him regular weekly visits, and brought him full accounts of all the interests in their work, whilst every parochial matter was referred to him, so that his guiding influence was maintained unbroken in the parish.

The following letters, written in that year and in the early part of 1861, are published to illustrate the sympathy and affection which he manifested towards the members of his family, whether nearer or more remote:—

TO HIS YOUNGEST DAUGHTER.

'ISLIP RECTORY, *July* 13, 1860.

. . . 'I HAVE been appointed chaplain to the old ladies of Islip,[1] and am to preach to them this evening; so I must retire to search out the choicest treasures to display before them.

'I shall advise them to take *two looks*, which I would recommend to all Christians,—" Look *Upward*, for the grace needed now; and *Forward*, for the rest that remaineth."'

He received a visit, whilst staying at Islip, from his old friend, 'young Tom Tyndale.' The following words

[1] A large Bible-class of poor old women, who met at the rectory once a week for Mrs. Trench's instruction.

which he wrote on a slate carried by Mr. Tyndale on account of his deafness, are still preserved :—

'How glad I am to have another shake of your hand. It reminds me of former years, and reflection should always produce deep humility and fervent gratitude. But if such is the retrospect, what gratitude do we not owe for the prospect? Paradise, resurrection, perfection of our nature; knowledge without error; holiness without sin; happiness without alloy.'

TO HIS ELDEST DAUGHTER, NOT LONG AFTER THE DEATH OF HER LITTLE SON.

'BEDDINGTON, *Aug.* 28, 1860.

'MY DARLING CHILD,—Your letter was most welcome. The more you can look into Paradise the better. Every prospect there is pleasant; and dear little Richard is one of the plants in that garden. Oh, how he will grow, and bear fruit unto eternity! I wish I knew now as much as he knows, and enjoyed as much as he enjoys!

'Matilda is gone back to Beckenham for a few days. 'I do not know how I could have accepted this place if it had not been so near Beckenham.

'In ourselves we are all wrong for eternity. In our blessed Lord Jesus, in Whom is our trust, we are all right for eternity. "*It is finished;*"—the most blessed words that were ever uttered.

'Do not trouble yourself at present about inability either to think or pray. The dulness or difficulty is merely the effect of previous exertion and distress of heart. I wish we could always distinguish between what is physical and what is spiritual, and then we should not charge the latter with that which is due to the former.

'I knew an old Christian at Reading, who said, in every variation of circumstances, "It is all for the best. I am in the hands of a sovereign God." He knew that sovereignty is always exercised in the way of mercy. I could preach a sermon on that subject, and prove it.

'I preached yesterday with perfect ease; indeed I have never found any difficulty in making myself heard in this church; but I regard increasing strength as one of the evidences that I was guided here. K. reads with a large number of the working-classes in the schoolroom on Sunday evenings. The work seems to prosper. Let us be thankful and humble, and prayerful. Love to you all. WM. MARSH.'

TO THE REV. CHARLES BRIDGES.

'BEDDINGTON RECTORY, *Sept.* 9.

'MY DEAR FRIEND,—A thought has been for some time in my mind, and your pen could realize it. I have never seen any work on the subject. It is this—CHRISTIANITY AS TAUGHT BY JESUS CHRIST.

'All doctrines, promises, and precepts of true religion will be found in the personal ministry of our blessed Lord, while he was executing the office of "the Prophet that should come into the world."

'I would not introduce a single word more than we can find in the four Evangelists. I am disposed to think that the Apostles taught nothing but what may be found, seminally at least, in the Gospels.

'If it meet your mind, I will send you a short analysis

of what the treatise might be. My pen and age cannot attempt more.

'You may remember a book by Mr. Overton on *The True Churchman.* It satisfactorily proved that those who hold evangelical views are the true Churchmen.

'They who believe and follow all things taught by our Lord are the *true Christians.* (Perhaps this may also prove that evangelical faith is the Christian faith !)—Your ever affectionate W. MARSH.'

TO HIS YOUNGEST DAUGHTER.

'BECKENHAM RECTORY, *April* 7.

'I DAILY pray that all who come under our roof at Beddington (as well as visitors at Beckenham) may find it good and profitable, and pleasant to be there. There is a "house not made with hands," in which there is nothing but what is good, profitable, and pleasant.

'. . . I thank God for each new encouragement He grants to feeble efforts in His service. Mr. Simeon once said to a person who was praising him for having kindled a flame in the land: "To be sure, sir; quite right, always praise the poker, tongs, and shovel." That man will always remember in future that the praise is due only to the *Hand* that uses the instrument.

'It is one of the negative blessings of a future state that there shall be "no more pain." What must the positive blessings be! and what a crowning one in John xvii. 24!

'You and darling Lucy must not over-tire yourselves in furnishing for us, nor be burdened with "the cares of this life."—Ever your own loving father, W. M.'

To the Same.

'Beckenham, *May* 8, 1861.

'... I begged Mrs. W— to encourage the poor woman to continue in prayer, and to get a Christian friend or two to unite with her. I told her also the following anecdote, which I heard many years ago:—A lady was converted: her husband was opposed to religion;—but he said to a friend, "My wife obeys me cheerfully in everything, except where she thinks her duty to God is concerned." The friend said, "I will lay you a wager that she would not obey you in such a case as this:—You shall invite me and half a dozen more to sup with your wife at a very late hour, when you know she has retired to rest." "I take the bet," he said. The party arrived after midnight. He sent word to his wife that several friends had come to sup with him. She rose immediately, had the supper prepared, and received them kindly. The man who lost the wager said to her, "How could you keep your temper?" She answered, "Unless my husband's heart is changed, this is his only heaven, and therefore I wish to make it as happy to him as possible." When the husband heard it, he said, "This must be true religion;" and he began to read, and think, and pray for himself; and God put a new spirit within him. Sinners may be drawn, when they cannot be driven.

'Do ask the sun to shine, and the east wind to retire, that I may set off for Beddington.—My great love to my housekeepers. My love to everybody. Wm. Marsh.'

A few of his thoughts, noted down at the time, are inserted here :—

'St. Paul wrote against self-righteousness, St. James against un-righteousness.'

'Fire and wind are beautiful types of the agency of the Holy Spirit. Fire is penetrating, purifying, illuminating, comforting. So the Holy Spirit can penetrate the hardest, purify the most sinful, illuminate the darkest, and comfort the most distressed heart.

'Then, what can resist the wind? it can uproot the strongest trees, it revives, it invigorates, it refreshes. So, like the mighty rushing wind, the Holy Spirit can uproot the strongest prejudices, can revive dead souls, can strengthen and refresh believers.'

'The great object of the Church of Christ should be to humble the sinner, to exalt the Saviour, and to promote holiness.'

'The Jewish nation was compared to a fig-tree; and the words, "Let no fruit grow on thee henceforth for ever," have indeed been fulfilled, for that nation has borne no fruit since they rejected Messiah; but when we see the fig-tree again putting forth green leaves, we shall know that *summer is nigh.*'

'Whilst the righteousness of our Redeemer admits us into heaven, the fruits of faith will be rewarded there.'

'Love is the peculiar spirit, peace the peculiar blessing, of Christianity. "By this shall all men know that ye are my disciples, if ye have love one to another." "My peace I give unto you."'

'The imagery of Scripture is astonishing. It ransacks all nature to illustrate Divine Truth; from the sun in the firmament, to the worm that creepeth upon the earth.'

'What a difficulty, says one, when you believe in a free gift of salvation through Christ, where to put good works? Why, the answer is, "Put them in your life."'

'The memory of the beloved apostle, under the inspiration of the Holy Spirit, was the faithful depository of the deepest and highest thoughts revealed by His Lord to His disciples. The 14th chapter of St. John's Gospel was pointed out by an excellent old minister to a physician who held Unitarian sentiments, with the request that he would read it through first according to his own views, and then, divesting himself of prejudice, read it again as one would who believed in the divinity of the Saviour, and see with which view it best accorded. The physician rose up, as he concluded his second reading of the chapter, saying, with St. Thomas, "My Lord and my God!"'

'In these days we want *mines*, but the Lord accepts *mites*.'

After reading the 19th Psalm, he said, 'What a series of arguments it contains for the Bible Society. "The law of the Lord is perfect, converting the soul;" then let us give it to the unconverted of mankind. "The testimony of the Lord is sure, making wise the simple;" then let us give it to the uninstructed of mankind. "The statutes of the Lord are right, rejoicing the heart;" then let us give them to the miserable of mankind. "The commandment of the Lord is pure, enlightening the eyes;" then let us give it to the sinful of mankind. What a wonderful Psalm it is: and like the 1st of Romans it shows us that men are not converted by the works of God, but by the Revelation of His Word.'

The privilege which was eagerly sought by his married grandchildren, that the great-grandfather should himself publicly dedicate their babes to the service of Christ in baptism, occasioned another family gathering in the month of February 1861, for the christening, in Beckenham Church, of Margaret Louisa, the first-born child of one of his grand-daughters, who had married the eldest son of Hulbert Wathen, Esq. of Beckenham Lodge, a valued parishioner of Mr. Chalmers.

A few weeks later my father had the joy of welcoming back from India another married grand-daughter, who spent much of her time in England under his roof, and added not a little to his daily pleasure.

The first tea-party which my father gave in the grounds of Beddington Rectory was to the mill-workers and their wives. They had been assembled by one of his family, for Scripture readings, in a large tannery shed, belonging to Mr. M'Rae, who, from first to last, forwarded these plans for their religious benefit with hearty goodwill. It had been mentioned by a daughter-in-law of Mr. M'Rae, that many of these men would probably cease to attend after the week of the Epsom races. She said it had become an almost universal practice in that neighbourhood for the working-men to spend the 'Derby-day' on the race-course, and that this frequently resulted in betting and hard drinking, and, consequently, in making homes miserable for days afterwards. She earnestly urged, therefore, that an appeal should be made to the men to relinquish the holiday at Epsom.

After some consideration, and with a great dread of being hard upon working-men, by seeking to deprive them of one of their few pleasures before they had found higher and greater ones, it was at length suggested to them by their friend, at one of their Bible-readings, that if, on consideration, they found that they could not ask for the blessing of God to go with them to the race-course, and if they felt that the day's amusement would probably end in sin, would they seek the help of God to enable them to give it up? And it was added that, in this case, though a tea-party seemed a poor exchange for the excitement of attending the races, Dr. Marsh would most gladly welcome them to the rectory for the afternoon, and that he and his family would endeavour to make it as pleasant to them as they could. They were requested to take time for consideration, and at the end of two days, out of above a hundred 'hands,' all save three sent in their names to accept the invitation. To soften the sacrifice, and to extend the pleasure, their wives and widowed mothers were asked to accompany them, and the use of the park was obtained in order that they might have cricket in the earlier part of the day; and as Mr. M'Rae kindly provided refreshment there at noon, they were able to enjoy a whole holiday.

At three o'clock they walked in procession from the park, and were received at the rectory gate, where flowers and coloured favours had been previously prepared, to be distributed by ladies who came to assist at the tea-party. The tea was spread in a picturesque part of the rectory grounds; and, after a hearty meal, some sacred verses were sung by the women who worked at a paper-mill in the adjoining parish of Carshalton, where the rector had most kindly given his sanction, at the request of the mill-workers, for a weekly Bible-reading to be held by one of Dr. Marsh's family.

The singing ended, and prayer having been offered by Mr. Southey, they seated themselves on the grass around the aged rector; and whilst

> 'All
> Saw in his face contentment, in his life
> The path to glory and perpetual joy,'

he spoke to them on the happiness of 'being found in Christ' and of being employed in His service.

Six months afterwards, an unbeliever, referring to that address, said, 'Eighteen years before, I had a great shake away from Christianity by a clergyman treating me in a very hoity-toity way. I have been a free-thinker ever since. But I got a great shake back towards Christianity when I heard your father speak about faith in his Saviour making him happy; and yet not so much by what he said as by the sight of his face. It did your heart good to look at it.'

My father had invited some of his old clerical friends, and several laymen who also were devoted Christians, to make short addresses to the assembled party. Between each address a hymn was sung, and the whole was concluded with prayer by Mr. O'Rorke, after which all joined in singing the doxology before they parted.

A poor woman who had been bedridden for many years told us shortly afterwards that she had always dreaded the evening of the Derby-day, for that sounds of oaths and curses, mingled with snatches of profane songs, reached her ears, even through her closed window, when the men returned from the race-course; and that too often a drunken fight was the close of the day's revelry. 'But,' she continued, 'this year it *was* a different thing. I heard nothing but sweet hymns and cheerful "good-nights," as the neighbours parted at their garden gates.'

And from another parishioner, we heard that a young mill-worker, who lodged at her house, said, on his return from the rectory, 'No more races for me, landlady, I have found a happier way!'

On the 20th of July he gave a similar fête to the wives and widows of Beddington, inclusive also of the single women, so that not a few of the faces of the Derby-day tea-party reappeared. On this occasion, a table was also provided for a number of recruits from the Guards' barracks at Croydon, many of whom were in the habit of attending a Bible-reading, held for the poor of the parish, on Sunday evening, in the school-room; and some also came one evening in the week to receive Scriptural instruction from Mr. Baldwin, a young officer in the engineer service, who spent his last summer, before leaving for India, at Beddington Rectory. He had been one of the leaders of the band of young Christians at Addiscombe; and his high character and noble heart had endeared him in no slight degree to my father.

This year passed away calmly and happily, with health sufficient for the exercise of the duties in which he delighted, and in the enjoyment of the family circle and of his numerous friends.

TO HIS ELDEST DAUGHTER.

'DARLING MARY,— . . . The work here appears to be prospering, *Deo gratia!* We have encouragement enough to embolden us to ask for more.

'. . . Several pleasant Christian visitors have been with us,—last week, dear Lady Erroll and her young sister. Both are seeking to hear their Saviour's voice, to know His love, and to do His will.

'"To hear His voice;" then we have truth. "To know His love;" then we have peace. "To do His will;" then we have usefulness, and all leading to glory, honour, immortality, and eternal life.—Your ever loving father, W. M.'

CHAPTER XV.

'LIVE, WHILE YOU LIVE.'

'He liveth long who liveth well
  All other life is short and vain;
He liveth longest who can tell
  Of living most for heavenly gain.

. . . . .

Sow love, and taste its fruitage pure;
  Sow peace, and reap its harvest bright;
Sow sunbeams on the rock and moor,
  And find a harvest-home of light.'

H. Bonar.

'LIVE, WHILE YOU LIVE.'

England still remembers the days of anxious suspense, followed too quickly by the shock of grief which fell upon every heart and home throughout the land, when, in the prime of his noble manhood, the Prince Consort died.

Eyes that had scarcely ever been dimmed by tears, and those which had almost wept away the power of shedding them, alike overflowed then for their Queen in her desolating sorrow, and for their country in the loss of so wise a counsellor, so shining an example.

'We know him now, all narrow jealousies
Are silent; and we see him as he moved,
How modest, kindly, all-accomplished, wise,
With what sublime repression of himself;

. . . .

Wearing the white flower of a blameless life,
Before a thousand peering littlenesses,
In that fierce light which beats upon a throne,
And blackens every blot.'

The mournful tidings were known in Beckenham early on Sunday, but the knowledge of it was kept from my father, as he was to preach that morning, and his deafness prevented him from being conscious of the silent announcement that all hope was over, by the omission from the prayers for the Royal Family of that beloved and honoured name.

When he came home and heard that the blow had actually fallen, it seemed almost to overwhelm him; and a day or two later we were obliged to remove from his room a little picture of the Queen leaning on the Prince Consort's arm; for its aspect of happy confiding love, in contrast with the thought of the desolation of her widowhood, so pierced his heart that he wept until palpitation came on. During his subsequent severe illness, this incident was mentioned by one of the ladies-in-waiting to her Majesty, and it drew from her tender heart an expression of sympathy which was deeply gratifying to him.

About a year and a half after the Prince Consort's death, her Majesty, in going from Windsor to Blackheath to see Prince Leopold, had to pass through Beckenham station. A slight delay was necessary to change the carriages on to a different line, and during this time the train was standing at the corner of the rectory grounds, almost under the shadow of its tall old elms. The wish of the Queen, that she should have no greetings on her way, had been made known, and orders had therefore been given at the rectory that none of the family should go outside the gates. From the window of the boudoir, where my father was lying on his couch, he could see between the trees the white steam from the engine which had brought the royal carriage to Beckenham, and his loyal heart beat high with the consciousness of his Queen's presence in the place, whilst his fervent spirit poured itself out in prayer for her with such earnestness that, when he was told her Majesty had left, he sank back exhausted, and for some minutes was unable to return to his morning reading.

During the time of suspense, when a war with America was imminent, he was fervently engaged in prayer for the preservation of peace. He felt deeply for his eldest grand-daughter in parting with her husband in the expectation of active service; and this, together with his personal love for Colonel Anstruther, lent a private interest to the earnestness of his prayers for the public blessing. The announcement of the release of the prisoners, which sent a thrill of joy throughout the country, was received by him with profound thanksgiving, but scarcely with surprise. His faith had in a measure prepared him to expect it.

TO HIS YOUNGEST DAUGHTER.

'*January* 3, 1862.

'... I AM glad you like this new-year's tract.[1] A packet has been sent you, and you shall have as many more as you wish.

[1] At the close of every year he published an 'Invitation to United Prayer,' in a tract of four pages, in which a survey of present events was given, and future hopes were dwelt upon; but the main object was to entreat Christians to unite in prayer for the outpouring of the Holy Spirit. The plan was begun by Mr. Haldane Stewart; after his death it was taken up by my father, and the invitation is now made to the Church of God by Dr. M'Neile.

'How we thank God that our sweet Lucy is better, and that darling Louie bears her trial so well. May God in His providence watch over her Robert, and bring him and our army safe back from Canada. All well here; satisfied you should be at the seaside with your nurslings, yet longing to see you.

'We are very thankful for the mercy shown to our beloved Queen, in the power of resignation given her, and her intention to discharge her high and important duties.

'Though we are trembling as to America, yet of this we are certain, that all prayer on earth will terminate in endless praise in heaven. Infinite wisdom and infinite love direct all; and this we know,—"the Lord reigneth." "The government shall be upon His shoulder" who took our sins on His own person. Not a sparrow falls unseen, and wisdom directs love. "He doth not willingly afflict or grieve the children of men." In Him may we trust, in Him rejoice, and delight to make known His love.

'I had a very large party last Saturday evening at the rectory. I took Acts iv. 14.

'The power, when it comes, is omnipotent; so that I should have no objection to a congregation of infidels, profligates, self-righteous, or formalists. We must exercise faith in the power. "According to your faith be it unto you." We ask too little, look for too little, believe too little for blessing on the Word. "Lord, increase our faith!"—Ever your most loving father, W. M.'

To his daughter and grand-daughters, on the arrival of the news that the danger of war was averted :—

'BECKENHAM, *January* 9, 1862.

'MY DARLINGS,—"Glory to God in the highest! on *earth, Peace!*"

'It is a great answer to many prayers. And how pleasant that it should be sent before the "Week of Prayer" closes—to turn prayer into praise.

'May we, as *individuals,* seek for more grace to show forth His praises, not only with our lips but in our lives; and to lead us, as a *nation,* to show our gratitude, by honouring His word and His Sabbath more humbly and heartily.

'. . . I almost cried when I heard of the death of dear old Mrs. M'Rae. How well she carried her ninety years, and how much we shall miss her from our summer garden-tea-party. We feel for her son. The longer so good a mother was spared to him, the more he valued her. But it is only joy for herself. Safe for ever. Holy for ever. Happy for ever.—Your most loving father and grandfather, W. MARSH.'

In the spring of this year, he shared in the joy of the beloved grandchild who had recently returned from India, in welcoming back her husband, Captain Hay Forbes, son of the Honourable Robert Forbes, who, with his excellent Christian wife, had been for some time amongst my father's beloved and most attached friends. During his short leave, he and his young wife spent much of their time at Beddington Rectory; for he formed a devoted affection for my father, watching him with undisguised admiration, to anticipate his lightest wish. This love was returned with fatherly tenderness, and most fervent prayers for his spiritual welfare. Nor was the aged grandfather satisfied with prayer without effort. By earnest conversations on Scriptural subjects, by anecdotes related of souls brought to Christ, and of the happiness found in Him, no less than by the beauty of holiness in his daily life, was the young man drawn, almost insensibly, to determine, by the grace of God, to take no rest, and to give God no rest, until he too knew that his life was hid with Christ in God. But it was not until the day of their return to India, in the following November, when he and his wife were taking their last farewell of their beloved grandfather, that he knew how full an answer had been given to his prayers.

TO HIS ELDEST DAUGHTER.

'BECKENHAM RECTORY, *March* 26, 1862.

'DEAR DARLING MARY,— . . . Though our title to heaven is in Christ alone, yet, such is the Divine bounty, that right conduct is rewarded. You are now reaping the fruits of the good conduct you sowed when a child.

'You say you are "a worm." I am glad you think it, because it is "a worm that shall thresh the mountains."

'If you had said you were a Goliath, I should have been greatly afraid that your head would have been cut off!'

'*May* 29, 1862.

'MY SWEET LITTLE LUCY,—What a delightful account you give of the northern home. Your story of the children's "missiontery" box is very pleasant. But I fear we have *too many* on this side the Tweed to follow the example of the little one who thinks that "charity begins at home;" and alas, when that is the case, it generally *stays* there!

'When your time for returning comes, I have told them all that *I* mean to go for you, unless some thoroughly good escort is found. Kiss all the darlings for me, and tell them to love their Saviour, and to love one another, and to love all the world; which is all I ask at present.

'God bless you all. We enjoy your loving letters and pleasant stories of the little darlings.—Your most loving grandfather,
W. MARSH.'

The 'opposition'-Derby-day at Beddington Rectory had now become an institution, and was anticipated with scarcely less pleasure by many in the upper classes of society, than by those for whom its celebration was principally adopted. On this anniversary, there was a large attendance from London and other places, and amongst these friends my father had the pleasure of welcoming Sir Culling Eardley and the Rev. Edmund Hollond. With Sir Culling he had long been linked in many a Protestant and evangelical work of faith and love; and with Mr. Hollond he was associated in the Simeon Trust, and had found him also ever ready to help in every work of piety and benevolence.[1]

[1] The late Rev. Charles Simeon, Fellow of King's College, Cambridge, had spent an ample fortune in the purchase of livings in important stations, in order to present to them, on vacancies, the most

In June the College at Addiscombe was finally closed, as the cadets were to be transferred to the Academy at Woolwich, on the amalgamation of the Indian service with the Queen's army. Monday the 17th was chosen for a last meeting at Beddington Rectory with the members of the Addiscombe Bible-reading. A few friends, including Mr. Blackwood and Sydney Duchess of Manchester, who had for some time past invited several of the cadets to spend Sunday at their house alternately with Beckenham and Beddington, came to join in the meeting.

The afternoon was sultry, so the little band assembled in a shady part of the flower-garden; and there, after Mr. Blackwood had begun with prayer, we read together 2 Tim. ii., and spoke of the Christian's warfare, his hardships, his temptations, his sufferings, his assurance, his certain victory, and his glorious reward.

Before the conversation had quite ended, it was interrupted by a heavy thunder-storm, and all took shelter in the rectory. My father was reading in his library; for, as he had preached the day before, we feared to ask him

earnest and able evangelical clergymen whom he could find willing to undertake the charge. He first associated my father with himself in the Trust, and, shortly before his own death, vested it also in the hands of the late Archdeacon Hodson and Rev. William Carus Wilson, and of the Revs. William Carus and John Venn, men endowed with the 'spirit of power and of love, and of a sound mind.' When two of the number were removed by death, the vacancies were filled up by the appointment of the Rev. Edward Auriol and the Rev. Edmund Hollond, men of like spirit and principles.

The meetings of the trustees, which for several years took place under my father's roof, and the affectionate intercourse they ever maintained one with another, were always sources of refreshment to him and to them.

to give an address, lest the exertion should be too much for him. But no sooner did he know that the cadets were in the house, than he expressed his strong wish to meet them once more, to give them a parting blessing.

Like the high-priest in ancient days, when he came forth from the presence of the Lord to bless the people, he came from seeking the face of his God in the study of the Scriptures; and, taking his place in the midst of the bright young group, he first gave some heaven-taught counsel to guide them in the ordering of their daily life and conversation, if they desired not merely to be amongst the followers of Christ, but to have the honour and the happiness of being standard-bearers in the army of His chosen and faithful ones; and then concluded with the inspired benediction,—

'The Lord bless thee and keep thee:

'The Lord make His face shine upon thee, and be gracious unto thee:

'The Lord lift up His countenance upon thee, and give thee peace.'

Few could have seen unmoved the veteran warrior, whose courage was still as high, and whose devotion to his Master's cause was as unwearied as in the days of his prime, though age had obliged him to relinquish the more arduous part of the service, thus arming the recruits for the field on which, 'having fought a good fight,' his own warfare would shortly be accomplished. God grant that each of those young soldiers may be found at the right hand of the great Captain of our salvation, in the day of His appearing!

The Bishop of Winchester kindly preached for him on Sunday, June 29th, and my father much enjoyed his society.

He had a natural reverence for authority; and when he had, as in this case, perfect confidence in and sympathy with his diocesan, it was an especial pleasure to him to welcome him under his roof. There were many pleasant events in past years to recall together; and foremost in their memories seemed to be a visit which the bishop had paid to the Channel Islands, when my father was residing in Guernsey for part of the summer of 1829. It was the first time that a bishop had been there for years, and it produced quite an excitement of interest amongst the inhabitants. The bishop was accompanied, on that visit to Guernsey, by his chaplains, the Rev. Alexander Dallas, and the Rev. Philip (now Archdeacon) Jacob. They all united in promoting, in every way in their power, the work of the Lord. The bishop carried on his own special office of ordaining and confirming, and also united with his two excellent chaplains in preaching, visiting, and addressing schools. It was a time of great interest, and doubtless of much blessing. One remarkable instance of conversion may be recorded here. In the island of Jersey an unhappy young man was at the time in prison, and under sentence of death for murder, committed in a fit of passion. There had not been an execution in the island for twenty-four years, and the case excited painful interest among the inhabitants. Mr. Dallas and Mr. Jacob visited the poor criminal, and earnestly pointed him to the Saviour. He became truly penitent; and their conversations and prayers were made the means of leading him to cast himself as a guilty sinner on the Lamb of God, who taketh away the sin of the world: thus he was enabled to trust in that Saviour's pardoning love, and to meet without dread the awful fulfilment of his sentence.

In July, a family meeting took place at Beddington Rectory, for the christening of the third son of his eldest grandchild. Robert Hamilton Anstruther was the last infant for whom he was able to read the baptismal service. The little brothers and sister of the babe clustered round their great-grandfather as he stood by the font, looking up with reverent love into his heavenly face, as with tender solemnity he dedicated the unconscious child to be 'Christ's faithful soldier and servant unto his life's end.'

His birthday was celebrated, as usual, by a tea-party for the women of the parish, and the customary gathering from far and near, and by addresses given by several friends. Amongst many little tokens of love which were brought him on that occasion, was a text illuminated by a niece of my mother's, Mrs. Austen of West Wickham Rectory, which, from that time, was always placed opposite the foot of his bed,—'To me to live is Christ, to die is gain.'

Almost immediately afterwards, he had a severe attack of illness, accompanied by distressing palpitations of the heart; but his faith was strong that he would be restored to preach again 'the unsearchable riches of Christ.' He was much gratified by the interest and sympathy manifested, both by rich and poor; and shortly after he had begun to recover, he wrote the following note, and directed that a printed copy should be left at every house and cottage in the parish:—

'BEDDINGTON RECTORY, *August* 7, 1862.

'MY DEAR FRIENDS,—Your kind sympathy with me and my family during my late illness calls for my gratitude to God and to you.

'Mine hour, it appears, is not yet come to depart this life, as I am in a measure raised up again, and may, perhaps, be permitted to address you again from the pulpit. I am very thankful for the faithful and affectionate discharge of that, and other duties, by my beloved brethren, Mr. Southey and Mr. O'Rorke.

'If life be always uncertain, it must be emphatically so at my age. But my present motto is, "Work whilst it is day;" yet trust in *no* work except that which was wrought during thirty-three years, above 1800 years ago.

"Jesus, Thy blood and righteousness
My beauty are, my glorious dress."

'With reference to the hour of death, I have often thought I should like to have the humility of the publican,—"God be merciful to me, a sinner!" and to offer the prayer of Stephen,—"Lord Jesus, receive my spirit;" and to exercise the faith of David,—"Into Thy hands I commend my spirit, for Thou hast redeemed me, O Lord, Thou God of truth."

'May the Divine blessing rest on you and your families; and may we all, taking the Word of God as our guide, finally meet in the world of light and love.—Ever your faithful and affectionate friend, WILLIAM MARSH.'

TO HIS SECOND DAUGHTER.

'BEDDINGTON RECTORY, *August* 8.

'DEAR DARLING MATILDA,—Many thanks for your love-letter. There is no love lost. Never was a father more blessed in his daughters. Oh, what unspeakable happiness it will be to meet in that world, not only where all is light and all is love, but where there is no parting. "So shall we ever be with the Lord." Sweet word of the inspired apostle. That will be the sunshine on all. We do not take glory from the sun when we admire flowers and fruits. We know the sun to be the source of those beauties and benefits. So in heaven we shall see the glory of the Lord in all He does to make His people happy. The glory of Him will be seen in all. His wonderful prayer on earth will be fully answered (John xvii. 24).

'Love attends you. Dear Constance and Fred. are enjoying the quiet of Beddington Rectory and the fresh air from the downs. Their sweet little child is here also. My dear Mrs. Marsh takes great care of me. She unites in love. W. MARSH.'

To the Same.

'BEDDINGTON.

'DARLING MATILDA,—We had a pleasant visit yesterday from Lord Radstock. He is a faithful and devoted Christian.

'I am remarkably well to-day, but always hoping to be better; and shall never be satisfied till *quite* well, when

"Sin, my worst enemy before,
Shall vex my eye and ear no more.
My inward foes shall all be slain;
Nor Satan break my peace again.

Then shall I see, and hear, and know,
All I desired and wished below;
And every power find sweet employ
In that eternal world of joy."

And, next to the sight of the Saviour, to see you all there —Oh, what joy!

'Would you like to hear a dream I had last night? I saw before me—side by side—

'The Babe of Bethlehem—The Eternal King.

'The Man of sorrows—filled with unutterable joy.

'The outcast of men—the Judge of the world.

'He had not where to lay His head,—the universe as His property.'

On the 12th of August a telegram reached the rectory from the father of one who had been amongst the most devoted of the young Christians at Addiscombe. The telegram only said, 'Pray for the departing spirit of our beloved Arthur. He is quite conscious. All is peace.'

It was the first intelligence of his illness which had reached my father, and it deeply touched him. He had remarked the rapid ripening of the youth from the day when—trained from infancy in Scriptural knowledge, and blessed with the unceasing prayers of a tender mother—he had, at Beckenham Rectory, believed on the Lord Jesus Christ with the heart unto righteousness, and had gone forth 'to confess Him with the mouth unto salvation,' amidst his companions at a military college.

From that hour, sensitive as he was to an almost feminine degree, the brave and faithful spirit of that young soldier never flinched. To those who watched him closest, it seemed that he never even wavered, but that his light grew brighter and brighter until the sun of his earthly life went down at noon.

Delicacy of health obliged him to resign his commission as first engineer of the term, just as he had taken the highest honours of the college. After a time he turned his thoughts to studying for Orders, and matriculated at Trinity College, Cambridge, where, during his brief career, he was remarked as being 'pre-eminent amongst the number of those who deserve the name of consistent and happy Christians.' Wherever he went, during the vacations, his society was felt to be an influence for increased holiness and earnestness. At once he sought to be employed in visiting the sick, and constantly conversed with those of his own age on the subjects nearest his heart; and he has been known to give up travelling in the same carriage with his own friends, in order to carry on a conversation with a third-class passenger, begun on the platform of the railway station, that he might press upon his companion the blessedness of choosing the Way of Life.

When he was seized with fever at Interlachen, he said to his devoted mother, 'It is better to depart and be with Christ—*far* better.' So dear was the Bible to him, that he would fall asleep, at times, with it clasped in both hands. On one occasion he said to his French nurse, 'Je suis très-malade. Je suis pauvre, misérable pécheur, mais par l'amour de Jésus Christ qui est mort pour nos péchés, je serai sauvé.' The last three words she described him as saying most earnestly, with clasped hands. Then he ended by repeating the words, 'Le sang de Jésus Christ nous nettoye de tout péché.' And when the names of father, mother, and sisters fell on an unconscious ear, the name of Jesus lighted up his face with a radiant smile. So passed away the spirit of Arthur Elliott into the presence of that Saviour whom he had so early sought and so early found.

TO HIS ELDEST DAUGHTER.

'BEDDINGTON RECTORY, *Sept.* 1.

'DEAR DARLING MARY,—I prayed that you might have a safe, prosperous, and useful journey; and now I ought indeed to be thankful for your letter just received. Do tell Rose when she arrives that I am very fond of roses. I am so glad to hear that the rose-bud is prospering.

'We have had a glimpse of the dear Wildmans again —warm and bright as ever, and rejoicing in the hope of the appearing of our blessed Lord.

'Our dear Georgie has sailed for India. He has a brave spirit and a tender heart, and is, I believe, a true Christian. May grace be given him to be 'steadfast, unmovable, and always abounding in the work of the Lord.'

'Will Islip have a sermon for Lancashire? We are to have two next Sunday (*D.V.*) Some poor persons are sending in their pence beforehand. One young woman, apparently a servant, or a dressmaker, brought Katie a sovereign at the schoolroom last night, and slipped it into her hand wrapped up in paper.

'How many Christians seem to think that it is indeed the Last Time. Good news; though the enemy, knowing his time is short, may make a great effort to retain his power. Nature is, alas, *for* him, but grace is *against* him; and grace must reign: that also, is our individual hope (Rom. v. 20, 21). "Comfort ye, comfort ye." Love to the quartette. W. M.'

To the Same.

'BEDDINGTON RECTORY, *Sept.* 23.

'. . . A PENITENT and believing sailor said, "To save such a sinner as I am! *He shall never hear the last of it!*" This expression, so frequently made use of by unforgiving persons, never was, that I know, applied in a Christian sense, before this case. It was remarkably scriptural, for the hallelujahs of heaven will be eternal.

'I greatly enjoy the honest tar's expression, "He shall never hear the last of it." We are too apt to forget that praise is well-pleasing to God. "Whoso offereth Me praise, glorifieth Me;" and St. Paul states the same (Heb. xiii. 15). I am thankful also for the 16th verse: it is a wonderful thing that such sinners can please God. But, "accepted in the Beloved," we are "complete in Him."'

Since he had begun to rally from his attack of illness in the summer, the desire of his heart had become intense to preach again in his own church. Notwithstanding the doctor's fears, he determined that nothing less than the hand of God interposing should hinder him from making the effort; and all who heard him were astonished by the energy and power with which he delivered his Master's message.

His family watched him with rejoicing yet trembling hearts, as he entered his pulpit once more; but anxiety was soon absorbed in the deep and thankful interest with which they listened to the thrilling tones of that beloved voice, as he described the blessedness of Heaven like one familiar with the customs of that Country.

As we all left the church, Captain Forbes, who knew well the risk of life which had been incurred by the exertion, could not help exclaiming, 'Well, I never saw such pluck! Our old veteran would march up to the cannon's mouth before us all at the order of *his* commander-in-chief, and not waste so much as a thought upon danger!'

But the effort so soon after the exhaustion of illness had been too great; and the repetition of it on the following Sunday brought on a similar attack of the heart to that from which he had suffered in the summer, so that he was again laid by, to enter his pulpit no more; although he continued to give addresses on scriptural subjects from his wheel-chair in the rectory, or its grounds, where from two to five hundred persons from time to time were assembled to hear him.

In the preceding month of July, he had written to ask the Archbishop of Canterbury if he might claim his promise to plead the cause of the Church Missionary Society in Beddington Church. The Archbishop replied, 'My dear friend, I should have been delighted to preach for you; but my health is failing so much that I think the next place of worship I shall enter will be—

"Where congregations ne'er break up,
And Sabbaths never end."'

On the 6th of the following month of September, in simple trust in his Saviour, and in perfect peace, that blessed Archbishop passed into the eternal world; leaving behind him a name fragrant as 'precious ointment.'

TO HIS ELDEST DAUGHTER.

'BEDDINGTON RECTORY, *Sept.* 29, 1862.

'YESTERDAY I addressed a full and attentive congregation, and endeavoured to point them to something more beautiful than anything to be found on earth, from Rev. xxii. last part of 3d and whole of 4th verse. I gave them a dark view of our fall in the first Adam, but an exceedingly bright view of our recovery by the second Adam. The text shows, with reference to the blessed—

'1. Their perfect service. 2. Their intimate fellowship. 3. Their entire consecration.

'Application—

'1. Will any say, "We will not serve God?" Pause, and think of the consequence. Pause again, and think of the love that still invites you. "Let the wicked forsake his way, and the unrighteous man his thoughts; and let him return unto God, and He will have mercy upon him; to our God, for He will abundantly pardon" (Isa. lv.)

'2. Do any desire to serve God? Press forward

through difficulties; help will come. Let those who love His service think daily of the future state, where there will be knowledge without error, holiness without sin, and happiness without alloy.'

The following imaginary dialogue was sent in a letter to Captain Hay Forbes, shortly after his return to India, and will serve as a specimen of the pleasant way in which the grandsire gave his counsel while expressing his loving confidence:—

A Dialogue on Christianity between two Hindus, done into English by W. M.

'Dear friend, have you yet thought anything about this Christianity which is making such a stir in our country?'

'No! for I do not see that the Christian religion is any better than our own.'

'I thought so too, till one of them put their Shaster into my hands, which I found to be very beautiful, teaching men to love their Creator, and one another; and that, though they were sinners, there was a Saviour and a heaven for them. It is but fair to judge of their religion by their Book, and, next to that, by the conduct of those who love the Book and evidently desire to follow it. I do confess that, before I read the Book, I was much impressed in favour of it by the conduct of some Christians who were sincere. For instance, let me request you to look at Captain and Mrs. Hay Forbes; their just and upright conduct; their kindness to those who are in need or trouble. They tell me that there is a throne of grace for all who approach it, sensible of their need; and that such are sure to succeed, through their Redeemer; and that mercy and grace lead to everlasting happiness and glory. I confess that I begin to see that it is Christianity that can bless mankind, in life, in death, and in eternity. Dear friend, once more let me request you earnestly to look at Captain and Mrs. Forbes, and the Christian missionaries in our country, and to read their Book. Their Book calls true disciples "the light of the world," and "the salt of the earth;" the light, by their knowledge; the salt, by their practice. My dear friend, if I could work a miracle, I would turn you into light and salt immediately.'

'Ha-ha-ha! I believe you wish my happiness; I will read and think, and observe Captain and Mrs. Forbes all the time they are in India. Farewell!'

His annual tea-party for the men of the parish was given on the evening of the 7th of November. It happened to be most dreary weather—fog and rain,—so that it would have been a risk for his health, had he attended it. Still, so heartily had he enjoyed the anticipation of being present, that it was not until within the last half hour that he relinquished the opportunity of meeting so large a number of his parishioners, of witnessing their pleasure, and of pleading with them for their eternal profit. When he found that it would be really imprudent to go, he wrote the following letter, to be read to them by one of his curates:—

'*Nov. 7th*, 1862.

'DEAR FRIENDS,—If Providence had permitted, I should have had great pleasure in meeting you this evening. I shall be present with you in spirit, and shall hope that on all your hearts the impression will be made, that Christianity is a kind and a pleasant religion, and that it forbids no innocent pleasures, but only such as would be injurious to us as rational and accountable creatures.

'The book of Proverbs says of "wisdom," which is true religion, "that her ways are ways of pleasantness, and all her paths are peace." Alas! the children of men, in general, will not walk in her paths, and therefore is there so great a want of peace in our world. I could wish you, if you have not already done it, to read that book through, one chapter each day, till you come to the end; and if you have done it, I could wish you to repeat it. It does so clearly prove that "godliness is profitable unto all things, having the promise of the life that now is, and of that which is to come."

'But Christianity brings out this truth in all its fulness, by making known the Saviour, and making Him known as *willing* as well as *able* to save. A consciousness of sin may make us doubt, and that remaining in the mind might lead to despair. But "it is a faithful saying, and worthy of all acceptation, that Christ Jesus came into the world to save sinners," and He casts out *none* who come to Him. It was a wise reflection of a poor man called Joseph, who was but half-witted, "Jesus Christ came into the world to save sinners! Poor Joseph is a sinner; therefore Jesus Christ came into the world to save poor Joseph." Behold, therefore, we bring you "glad tidings of great joy;" for this Saviour is preached to you, His atoning blood takes away all sin, and His intercession in heaven keeps the way open for the honourable exercise of mercy; hence, "if we confess our sins, God is faithful and just to forgive us our sins, and to cleanse us from all unrighteousness."

'Oh, never get tired of a book that contains such good news; and remember that our heavenly Father will give the Holy Spirit to them that ask Him.[1] . . . .

'Dear friends, well may we exclaim, "*Who is a God like unto Thee, that pardoneth iniquity, and delighteth in mercy.*" And we should therefore never doubt of the success of our prayers for the mercy and grace that we need, till we arrive in that land where sin, sorrow, temptation, and death are known no more. I cannot close this short address without acknowledging with thankfulness your kind and generous feeling towards our suffering brethren in the north, shown in the liberal way you have contributed, and are continuing to contribute, for the supply of their wants.[2] I delight to subscribe myself, in conjunction with my beloved brothers and most useful helpers, Mr. Southey and Mr. O'Rorke—Your affectionate friend and pastor, WILLIAM MARSH.'

[1] Then followed the story of 'Praying Tom.'—See pp. 25, 26.

[2] The men and boys working at Mr. McRae's leather-mill and tannery voluntarily subscribed from 25s. to 27s. a week, as long as the distress continued in Lancashire and Cheshire; and scarcely less generous efforts were made by others in the parish who worked for their bread, and by the children of the schools.

It was in the month of November 1862 that he bade farewell to his beloved grandchild, Honoria Forbes and her husband, on their return to India—a parting he keenly felt. He took leave, about the same time, of Mr. Frederick Wathen, a young clergyman, known to him from childhood, who, after finishing his blameless and useful career at Oxford, gave himself up to the work upon which his heart had long been set—a missionary's life in India. His devoted service there was shortly brought to a close by a fatal fever, during which he was nursed with brotherly tenderness by Captain Forbes whilst his gentle wife soothed and supported the sorrowing heart of her who was soon to be left desolate.

When the young missionary had passed away, leaving this as his dying testimony, 'I am at perfect peace with God; Christ has washed away all my sins,'—the faithful wife, who had gone out with brave and cheerful heart to follow him through dangers, and nurse him in sickness, came on her lonely way back to England, a widow with her orphaned babes, within three years of her marriage.

The loving mother, who with Christian self-forgetfulness had fostered her son's noble purpose of life from his childhood, bore the sorrow of his death with a holy acquiescence in the will of her God. She did not long survive him. Within a year, her life of piety and usefulness on earth was exchanged for the rest that remaineth for the people of God.

TO HIS ELDEST DAUGHTER.

'Beckenham Rectory, *Dec.* 6.

'Darling Mary,—. . . . A bow shot at a venture does execution. We never shoot the right arrow altogether in vain.

'You will like to read the delightful letter enclosed, from Henry Clarke, one of the first of our young friends at Addiscombe. He is another of the frequent instances I have observed of the sons of Christian mothers, on whom a peculiar blessing has rested from their youth upward.

'Cumming's book on the *Great Tribulation*, like all his works, is very interesting. It may be that the time of that tribulation is at hand, and it may be very terrible. But it will usher in a great ecstasy of joy to those who trust alone in Jesus.

"E'en then shall this be all my plea:
Jesus has lived and died for me."

That name opens heaven's doors immediately.'

CHAPTER XVI.

THE THRESHOLD OF HEAVEN.

'He hath been near unto the golden gate;
Serene he waited for his Master's calling:
It came,—"A little longer thou must wait,
The sands of life have not yet ceased their falling."

Servant of God! thou hast not long to stay;
Soon the weak bonds that hold thee here shall sever;
Then shalt thou gaze upon the perfect day,
And Him thou lovest, for ever and for ever.'

THE THRESHOLD OF HEAVEN.

On the last night of the year 1862, my father was seized with a sudden attack of the heart. It was the commencement of a long and severe illness. The dangerous symptoms increased with such rapidity that, from the evening of the 5th of January until noon of the following day, his family, with his doctor, watched beside him, fearing that each hour must be his last. During that night—for us, full of anguish and suspense, for him, of serene calm and holy joy, there flowed from his lips a stream of heavenly teaching, to which those around him listened with wondering admiration.[1]

At first his thoughts were dwelling on the song of the aged Simeon, and, in a voice which rang through the silence of midnight, he exclaimed, '"Lord, now lettest Thou Thy servant depart in peace, for mine eyes have seen—*mine eyes have seen*—MINE EYES HAVE SEEN THY SALVATION!"' and, turning to us. he added, 'and this

[1] His eldest daughter was occupied during four hours of that night in writing down, unseen by him, the words that fell from his lips.

salvation is for you all.' A little while later he quoted the hymn—

> 'But timorous mortals start and shrink
> To cross that narrow sea.'

'Why should they?' he exclaimed. 'They may go over Jordan DRY-SHOD.'

Then lifting his eyes and hands to heaven, he said,—

> 'Blessed Saviour,—
> Washed in Thy Blood,
> Clothed in Thy Righteousness,
> Prepared by Thy Spirit,
> Employed in Thy Service,
> Received into Thy Kingdom,
> Praise, praise be to Thee!'

He quoted the words, 'LOOKING UNTO JESUS,' adding—

> 'Look and live;
> Look and love;
> Look and obey;
> Look and be happy;
> Look and follow Him;
> Look and go to Heaven.'

Children and grand-children had gathered around him for last blessings and last looks of love. But he was yet again to be raised up from the very gate of death, or rather it seemed to us that he awaited his Master's call at the gate of heaven, and when the order came, 'Tarry thou the Lord's leisure,' he turned back at that bidding to earth once more; as if to let us gain some idea by the shining of his face how those who are counted worthy to stand before the Son of Man 'are made like unto Him, when they see Him as He is.'[1]

But his recovery was subject to frequent relapses; and during the night of February the 4th, my sister and I were anxiously watching by his side during severe suffering in his chest and palpitation of the heart. Suddenly he mastered his faltering breath to say, 'Oh, *my* Saviour! who didst suffer for my sins, Thou wast *alone* in Thine agony. Thou hadst no words of loving comfort said to Thee. I *must* weep' (his tears were falling). 'I am standing with the Marys at the foot of Thy cross. O blessed, blessed Jesus, how Thy heart must have beat till Thou saidst, "IT IS FINISHED!" But it is quiet now. It has been at rest these eighteen hundred years; and it will be at rest for ever. Oh, I am so glad—I am so glad it was *all over* eighteen hundred years ago, when Thou saidst, "It is finished!" The claims of justice met—the law magnified—the door opened—the types fulfilled—the prophecies accomplished—the atonement completed—mankind redeemed—It is finished! Let all the angels of God worship Thee!'

[1] This was the week which had been set apart by many Christians, throughout the world, for special prayer. Amongst other places opened for a similar purpose in London, a daily prayer-meeting was held at Freemasons' Hall. To the chairman of this assembly a note was forwarded from Dr. Marsh's family to request him to ask those gathered together to plead with God that, *if* it would best promote His glory and the good of His Church, that beloved life might yet be spared for a season. This petition was read, and one who was present at the time wrote:—'Your request seemed to find a response from almost every soul there. If you had heard the "Amen" from countless voices, it would have strengthened your hearts.

From that hour he began to revive. 'Women received their dead raised to life again.'

After a time, ease was mercifully granted, and we heard him hushing himself to sleep with sweet fragments of joyful thoughts. The last we caught was, 'My Saviour, my righteousness, my happiness, my heaven, my Lord, my God, my Glory.'

On the morning of the 20th of January he called me to his side and said, 'Tell me which text in the Bible is a fountain of good to the guilty?'

'Is it this,' I asked,—' "The blood of Jesus Christ His Son cleanseth us from all sin"?'

'That is the meritorious cause—but not the Fountain. Shall I tell it to you? It is in the 16th verse of the 3d chapter of the Gospel of St. John,—" GOD SO LOVED THE WORLD, THAT HE GAVE HIS ONLY BEGOTTEN SON, THAT WHOSOEVER BELIEVETH IN HIM SHOULD NOT PERISH, BUT HAVE EVERLASTING LIFE."

'In that way justice and love are reconciled. It would have been inconsistent with the purity and integrity of the Divine Government to forgive the sinner without an atonement. By providing an atonement, and that through the sacrifice of the Son of God Himself, a further view was given of the wonders of Divine love. What an exhibition of love was the crucifixion of the Saviour—God sacrificing Himself in the Manhood for mankind. Creating, preserving, providing love, is not love in the highest sense—the essence of love is self-sacrifice.

'And this will be manifested to the universe. "Which things the angels desire to look into;" and they will be permitted to do so. "That unto principalities and powers in heavenly places might be known by the Church the manifold wisdom of God." Who shall put a limit to the effect of awe, adoration, and holiness, which shall be produced throughout creation by the knowledge of the whole of the Divine plan and of its success, when the final victory of this battle-field—the world, is won, and the proclamation of it is sounded to the utmost limit of creation.

'There is an answer, therefore, in two words, to all sceptical doubts,

"ETERNITY and the UNIVERSE."

'The first—because it may well take an Eternity for the Infinite God to reveal Himself to finite man; and the last—because the whole Universe will be benefited by God's dealings with our world.

'All mistakes touching the character of God arise from a want of trust in His own revelation of Himself in these words, "GOD IS LOVE."

'Here is the great battle between Faith and Unbelief.

'Some, to reconcile things in the Revealed Word, which seemed to them inconsistent with their human and therefore limited ideas of a God of Love, have chosen to believe but in part, or to reject revelation altogether; instead of humbly yet wisely waiting for the Infinite God to explain Himself in the fulness of time, and throughout the duration of Eternity.'

'I like that saying, "Sin, sin, what hast thou done!"
'But I like this saying better, "Saviour, Saviour, what hast THOU done!"'

'That is a beautiful description given by St. Paul, "The express image of His person." What THE SON OF GOD is, let the sons try to be—let them imitate the character of God. God is Love.

'One comes and says to Him, "But I have sinned against you." "And I have forgiven you! And I will bring you to a world where you shall sin no more." "I should *like* not to sin any more in thought, or word, or deed." "You are a pleasant child. Go in peace."

'"Be ye therefore perfect, even as your Father which is in heaven is perfect." I do not think it means sinless perfection, but imitation; you will see the context is that we are to do as our Father in heaven does, "who maketh His sun to shine on the evil and on the good." "I will not give up that text to John Wesley. If we had a walk together, I would say—"Now, Wesley, there's a wicked man, I am going to give him something; I would be a *perfect* man! That man has spoken ill of me, and treated me ill, notwithstanding I had shown kindness to him and to his family. I will give him a ten-pound note." Then the poor man says, "Oh, I'll never speak ill of him again; I'll tell every one to whom I abused him of this ten-pound note!"

'This is love. "If God so loved us, we ought also to love one another."'

In one of his last attacks of palpitation, as it was passing off he seemed much oppressed in spirit. My sister asked him, 'Does any particular thought trouble you?' —'Yes. I have two scenes before me,—sin, and my

Saviour; Calvary, and the glory to be revealed. And they are too much for me. I look at the one, and I feel as if my heart would break for sorrow. I turn to the other, and it is ready to burst with joy.'

In one of his wakeful nights, he was overheard saying, '*Beautiful!*' On being asked of what he was thinking, he replied, 'Of that prayer in the Litany, "By Thine agony and bloody sweat, by the cross and passion, by Thy precious death and burial, by Thy glorious resurrection and ascension, and by the coming of the Holy Ghost—good Lord deliver us!" And I have made a little commentary upon it,—"Deliver us from the guilt and power and love and practice, and finally from the existence of all sin!"'

Soon afterwards he added, 'I think, if I were a Dissenter, and read the Litany, I should become a Churchman, or at least adopt those prayers! For many years past I have prayed the prayer for "all conditions of men," just before going to sleep, every night. The chapter which I usually repeat then is the 14th of St. John. By it the Lord bids His people to 'rest in His love."'

One morning, when he was getting better, alluding to the comforts by which he was surrounded, he said, with clasped hands, 'Thanks for food and raiment, fitting and convenient; and thanks far more for robes of Righteousness and garments of Salvation! *Covered* with the justifying robes of a Saviour's righteousness, and adorned with the garments of Salvation wrought by the Holy Spirit; and both coming from and delighted in by God the Father!

'It has been one of the errors of the Church of Rome, to blend the two in one, until she lost sight of the completeness and perfection of the Title. The *one* is entirely the work of the blessed Redeemer; and our *only* ground of meritorious Title. The other is the work of the Holy Spirit, moulding us more and more unto the likeness of Christ, which becomes our meetness for the Heavenly Inheritance; "Who hath made us meet for the Inheritance of the Saints in Light."

'Let us remember, therefore, that there is the meetness of *merit*, ALL THROUGH CHRIST; and the meetness of *fitness*, through the work of the Holy SPIRIT.'

Another morning, whilst I was giving him his breakfast, he said to me, 'Would you like to hear my boasting? I can boast of thirty-three years without spot of sin, within or without!'

He looked at me earnestly, to see if I had caught his meaning; and so I replied to him in the words of an old hymn, in which the Saviour is supposed to be speaking to the sinner,—

'MINE all-sufficient merits
Shall appear
Before the Throne of Glory
In thy stead.
I'll put into thy story
What I did.'

'Right!' he rejoined, '*He is mine*, who so passed his years on earth: thus His spotless life on earth is mine: His righteousness is mine. "He of God is made unto us wisdom, and righteousness, and sanctification, and redemption."'

'I think our taste for the beautiful will be gratified to the uttermost in another world. How lovely is the description of the New Jerusalem! And when I think of those words of the blessed Saviour, "Father, I *will that they also whom Thou hast given me be with me where I am, that they may* BEHOLD MY GLORY," I can believe that the house that holds Him must be glorious too. And He is "preparing" it for *us!*

'"My thirsty spirit faints
To see the Land I love;
The bright inheritance of saints,
Jerusalem above."

'"Then shall I see, and hear, and know,
All I desired or sought below;
And every power find sweet employ
In that eternal world of joy."

'I have been thinking much of a volume in a word, "BRIGHTNESS of the Father's glory. Not merely Likeness, but Brightness."'

'Divine love differs from all human love in this, that human love sees something amiable in the creature, discerns a similarity, finds somewhat to sympathize with; but Divine love is "whilst we were yet sinners!"'

When speaking out of the abundance of his love to his children, touching 'the fellowship of heart there had been between himself and them,' he added, 'How tenderly and sacredly you have kept the Fifth Commandment. It is the link between heaven and earth, between the love to God and the love to the neighbour.'

'"Behold the Lamb of God, which taketh away the sin of the world." How vast is redemption! We shall never know *how* great its extent until we see the final result. Nor even then! for St. John tells us, that the redeemed will be "a great multitude which *no man can number.*" And they will be "out of EVERY kindred, and tongue, and people, and nation." That must include all heathen nations, as well as others. "The blood of sprinkling, which speaketh better things than that of Abel," which cries from the ground for pardon for the earth on which it was shed, may sprinkle and plead for unconscious numbers who are "feeling after God." They may go to sleep in dull twilight, and awake up in the brightness of the Sun of Righteousness.'

'HUMAN NATURE IS REDEEMED. Amongst those who have had the opportunity of knowing this, they only are benefited who *believe* it. "*God so loved the world*, that He gave His only begotten Son, that *whosoever believeth* in Him should not perish, but have everlasting life." That is distinct. But St. John made no exaggerated statement when he wrote by Divine inspiration Rev. v. 9.'

After quoting the text, 'The blood of Jesus Christ His Son cleanseth us from all sin,' he wrote down these words,—

'It is that blood which *justifies*' (Rom. v. 9).

'It is that blood which *sanctifies*' (Heb. ix. 13, 14).

'It is that blood which *glorifies*' (Rev. i. 5, 6).

'It is that blood which calls forth the hallelujahs of heaven' (Rev. v. 11, 12).

'There are two much greater objections to the Bible than any Bishop Colenso has brought forward: 1*st*, It is too humiliating for man's pride. 2*d*, It is too holy for man's practice.'

'I have had the presumption to make an answer to Pope's well-known lines,—

"For modes of faith let senseless bigots fight,
He can't be wrong whose life is in the right."

'It was this,—

'In Christian faith let Christian men be strong,
He can't be right whose faith is in the wrong.'

'I am going to set a task to all who reject the Bible; they are to write me four chapters that will be equal to the 14th, 15th, 16th, and 17th chapters of St. John. They will deserve a great prize if they write me four better!'

The delight which he always felt in little children was not lessened even in his extreme illness, and to them his sick-room seemed the happiest place in the house. Malcolm and Florence Forbes, two of his great-grand-children who were living at the rectory, could scarcely be persuaded to pass the door of his room, though one of them, who was too young to speak, could only hold out her hands in entreaty to be allowed to go to him. Their happiness was complete when allowed to sit on a pillow on either side of him. The earliest snowdrops, violets, and primroses were gathered for him by the little sons of Mr. Chalmers's coachman, and brought with hushed footsteps and reverent looks to his bedside. Ralph, Evelyn, and Harry Anstruther, by their own earnest request, were brought down by their parents (on one of their frequent visits) to see their great-grandfather when he was dangerously ill. It happened that he had fallen asleep just before they arrived, but the eldest was admitted into the room, and quietly climbed on a sofa at the foot of the bed, where he could stand and watch the placid face. On awaking, my father stretched out his arms to the child, who sprang forward to meet his embrace, and for some moments neither spoke. Then my father said, 'Mayest thou be satisfied with favour, and full with the blessing of the Lord!' adding, 'Love your Saviour all your days, dear little Ralph, remembering that He loves you.'

The other little ones were now summoned, and each received a tender blessing.

To one of his grandsons, who was going to a public school that winter, he gave a single word of advice, which was well remembered and followed,—'Do not, my dearest Ken, be afraid of saying, "No," but say it kindly.'

TO STEVENSON BLACKWOOD, ESQ.

'*Feb.* 10*th*.

'MY BELOVED BROTHER,—Indeed I have not forgotten those two verses! Frequently have I to resist the enemy with them by the help of the Holy Ghost.

'I want the power to sleep, and I remember that it is written, "So He giveth His beloved sleep." But I say, how is it possible that I can claim to be His beloved? Then I begin repeating to myself chaps. v., vi., and viii. of the Epistle to the Romans. And I find from chap. v. 8, that *sinners* may come under the title of beloved. "God commendeth His love towards us, in that, while we were yet sinners, Christ died for us." Hence I jump for joy at chap. viii. 29 to the end, and thus enter into the triumph of verses 38, 39. And what a triumph it is! An uninspired man could never have written those words. If you had an hour to spare, how glad I should be if you could cast your eyes over the manuscript of my little commentary on that epistle, with a pen and ink and sheet of paper by your side, making *addenda et corrigenda*. My love to you and to the dear Duchess. Blessings on you both, and on the children. I shall love to see you if my life be prolonged a little. And I shall love to see you with life prolonged for ever, in the presence of our Life, our Love, our Lord and Saviour, our all in all.—Yours ever affectionately, WM. MARSH.'

In conversing with one of his daughters, he said,—

'The longer I live, the more I see the value of an Episcopal Church government, with parochial divisions, but this is a preference, not an exclusion. It is not necessary to the Christianity of a nation. When we meet in heaven those from whom we have differed on such points, we shall say, "Brother, brother, we were all in the wrong; all too much warped in our views of the necessity of non-essentials!" Let the Gospel be preached and practised in a country, and blessed is that nation.'

The present Archbishop of Canterbury, shortly after

entering upon the duties of his diocese, had expressed a wish to see my father. When it was first proposed, he was too ill to be allowed to see a stranger, but as soon as he had rallied a little, the Archbishop came from Lambeth. My father welcomed him with warm thanks for his kindness, and soon afterwards said, 'I have a jewel for your Grace. I put it by when I first heard of your kind intention of coming to see me. Will you accept it? You will find it in the forty-first chapter of Isaiah. "Fear thou not; for I am with thee: be not dismayed; for I am thy God: I will strengthen thee; yea, I will help thee; yea, I will uphold thee with the right hand of My righteousness."'

'I shall keep it as your gift, thankfully indeed,' the Archbishop replied; 'and will you turn it into a prayer for me?'

Then my father spoke of the nearness of the Saviour, of His tender kindness to the sinner, and His far tenderer love to the believer; of His assurance to the sinner, "Him that cometh unto Me, I will in no wise cast out;" of His encouragement to the believer, "For whosoever shall give to drink unto one of these little ones a cup of cold water only in My name, verily, I say unto you, he shall in no wise lose his reward."'

In the course of conversation, the Archbishop told him that he well remembered having listened with delight to his address to the Jewish children some years before at Exeter Hall. At the close of the interview, my father asked him for his blessing. The Archbishop hesitated, saying, 'You should rather bless me;' but on its being requested a second time, he complied, pronouncing the blessing out of the service for the Visitation of the Sick; and then saying, 'Bless me now! let me have your blessing;' he knelt down by his side and guided my father's hands to his head, reverently kissing them at the close.

The visit produced a most gratifying impression on the heart of the beloved invalid, and made him even more earnest in prayer than before, for one holding so high and responsible an office.

In the summer of the previous year my father had offered a title to orders, with the third curacy of Beddington, to a son of his old and highly valued friend, Captain J. E. Gordon, R.N., well known, both in the House of Commons and in the country at large, for his able and fearless advocacy of Protestant principles, and for his earnest and faithful adherence to the truth of God, in doctrine and practice. Mr. George Gordon was ordained by the Bishop of Winchester at Christmas, and from that time devoted himself with almost filial reverence and affection to his rector, by whom he was beloved both for his father's sake and his own. After working earnestly for nearly two years in the parish of Beddington, he took a laborious cure in London, and then gave his services gratuitously to the work of the Church Missionary Society in India. Soon after Mr. Gordon's ordination, Mr. Southey was offered a more permanent sphere of duty, which he saw it right for the sake of his family to accept, though feeling deeply at parting from my father. When alluding to this prospect, he said, 'We must pray earnestly as well as seek diligently for a like-minded successor. How well and how happily dear Southey and O'Rorke have worked together. However closely I may keep the secret as to what my children have been to me, I must tell the world that it never knew two better or pleasanter curates! I pray for them daily, that as they have been taught of God to say,

> 'Happy day, happy day,
> When Jesus washed my sins away;"

They may also be ever able to add,

> " He taught my heart *to watch and pray*,
> And *live rejoicing* every day;"

and I pray for them that they may be kept from being in any way or degree "corrupted from the simplicity which is in Christ."'

When Mr. Gordon came to see him, just after his ordination, he said, 'You have in your possession the only lever which can raise our fallen world near to heaven—the Bible.' And a little while afterwards, 'In my mind I have been making a plan for correcting all the mistakes made by good Christians. It is to tell them not to read the first three chapters of Ephesians *only*, but to read the whole six; then they will make no mistakes, or at least *need* not. It is a partial comprehension of Christianity which is the cause of all erroneous views concerning it.'

He welcomed a visit from his friends Mr. and Mrs. Samuel Gurney towards the end of January; and as Mr. Gurney held his hand, he said to him, 'I have greatly enjoyed your friendship and that of dear Mrs. Gurney. Shall I give you my short view of Christianity? "*Henceforth* I call you not servants, but friends," said our Lord and Saviour. Believe in Him as your friend—*that* is faith; act as His friend—*that* is practice.

'Years ago I heard one of the Society of Friends say,—"Let us seek for simplicity of intention and simplicity of dependence." I have never forgotten it, but have prayed for it constantly. Intend only, intend all for the glory of the Lord Jesus. Depend wholly and entirely on the help of God the Holy Ghost.'

Soon afterwards he dictated the following letter:—

TO SAMUEL GURNEY, ESQ., M.P.

'My dear Friend,—Many thanks for the valuable volume you have sent me.

'Joseph John was a scholar—Joseph John was a philosopher—Joseph John was a Christian—Joseph John was an honour to the community of which he was a member. And what made him such but the Word and the Spirit of God?

'When Bishop Bedell, an ardent Protestant, but a most loving and benevolent man, died, a zealous Roman Catholic exclaimed, "May my soul be with Bishop Bedell's!"

'Joseph John was a Friend, and I am a Churchman, but—May my soul be with Joseph John's!

'If the Friends who are readers of that book, and the younger members in particular, are guided by it, they will be wise, holy, and useful Christians.'

During the whole time of his illness he received many visits, not only from old friends and relatives, but also from his curates and some of his parishioners. All were welcomed with his unvarying sweetness and serenity, and received messages of encouragement and comfort from his lips. His most frequent and beloved visitor was Mrs. Laurence, of Beddington, whose tender sympathy and constant thoughtfulness for his comfort and pleasure had made almost a tie of relationship between them.

One day he received a visit from Captain Harris, R.N., so well known throughout the navy, not only for his own high standing as an officer but also for his admirable training of the cadets, that it had been said by several distinguished officers in the service, 'He has regenerated the navy.' He had long been known to my father by character, and by his encouragement of a voluntary Bible-class, held every evening, by about eighty of the cadets, on board the 'Britannia.' My father had heard, with deep interest, of the elevated moral tone resulting from these meetings, not only amongst those who joined them, but spreading in its measure over the whole ship's company, until gambling, drinking, and swearing became almost unknown.

My father congratulated Captain Harris warmly upon the honour of having nurtured, at all risks and costs to himself, this confession of Christ amongst the boys under his care, and added, 'Would you like to hear how I class the Church of Christ on earth?—Apostles, prophets, martyrs, *sufferers for Christ's cause*, missionaries, ministers, and penitent believers. "Blessed are ye when men shall revile you, and persecute you, and shall say all manner of evil against you *falsely*, for My sake." "Rejoice, and be exceeding glad, for *great* is your reward in heaven."'

Within two years of this interview, that noble Christian, after passing through a stormy time of trial, closing with a few days' painful illness, departed with triumphant joy into the presence of his Saviour.

My father found great comfort, during the whole of his prolonged illness, in the unwearied kindness and care of his old friend and doctor, Mr. Williams of Bromley. He was also frequently visited by Mr. Skey,[1] whose cheering presence always seemed to do scarcely less good than his skilful remedies. Never did either of these friends leave his side without receiving a word of heavenly counsel, and unfeigned was the admiration and respect with which they both regarded him.

On one occasion, when prevented from coming himself, Mr. Skey sent his eldest son, who was associated with him in professional practice. My father was extremely charmed with this gifted and attractive young man, and spoke to him earnestly about making choice of Christ without delay. He listened with deep respect and evident feeling, and knelt whilst my father prayed for a blessing upon him.[2]

[1] President of the Royal College of Surgeons.

[2] He was then in the flower of his manhood, with apparently a long and successful career opening before him, to add celebrity to a name already made. He could have thought as little that morning as we did that his life was numbered by days, and would end without a moment's warning.

It was not known or imagined, until after his death, that he had

At the early part of this lingering illness, my father had commenced dictating to the beloved grand-daughter who constantly resided with him, and whose mind and feelings so blended with his own that she could almost anticipate his thoughts, a brief exposition of St. Paul's Epistle to the Romans. His mind had for a long time dwelt much on this epistle; and as the attacks from which he suffered increased in severity and danger, his anxiety not to leave this little work unfinished increased also.

Most touching was it to see him, during the intervals of comparative ease, exerting himself to dictate a few sentences, for this his *last* opportunity of spreading through the press the knowledge of the gospel of the grace of God. Several times he pursued the labour, which to him seemed only a mental recreation, until an attack of palpitation obliged him to desist. So earnest was his interest in this work, that his doctor thought that the energy of his desire to complete it might even be the means of prolonging his life. When told that the immediate danger of his illness was past, it mingled with his reasons for thankful content in the prospect of lingering for a season on earth, as soon as he knew that such was the will of his Lord. 'It will be delightful,' he said, 'to serve my Master and Saviour for a little longer on earth,

begun to bear his testimony for Christ. A patient from St. Bartholomew's Hospital, who came to Beckenham Rectory, when lamenting over his early removal, said, 'How he will be missed! he was so kind and good. And when a patient lay dying, he would stand by his side and say, "There is a Saviour who died for us all. You had better put your trust in Him, and then you will be all right."'

and to make my beloved ones happy again;' adding, in his own bright and playful manner, 'and now I can finish my Romans!'

It was finished early in the summer of that year; but was kept beside him, during the brief remainder of his life, for occasional enriching with some fresh thought or quotation, and, above all, for prayer for blessing upon it.

He sent the manuscript to be overlooked by two friends on whose opinion he set a high value,—the Rev. Charles Goodhart, of Park Chapel, Chelsea, whom he loved with the heartiest sympathy and regard, and counted as one of the noblest of the witnesses for God and His Truth in our country; and the Rev. T. Lloyd Phillips, one of Mr. Chalmers' curates, and for some time editorial secretary of the Bible Society; from whose clear intellect and sound judgment he coveted criticisms for his work, as truly as he prized the regard and affection which made light of any trouble which could render him a service.

My father had lost nothing of the vividness of his interest in all public matters, especially as connected with the concerns of his Master's kingdom.

The marriage of the Prince and Princess of Wales occupied his heart with tender enthusiasm. He was the first to propose plans for keeping the day, with general rejoicings, at Beddington, and a subscription for a dinner for the poor of his parish. After a part of one of his wakeful nights had been spent in earnest supplication for a blessing on the royal bride and bridegroom, he composed the following prayer, to be distributed amongst his friends, and all the parishioners of Beddington and Beckenham, with an earnest request that the subject of it should be constantly remembered before God :—

A PRAYER FOR THE PRINCE AND PRINCESS OF WALES.

'ALMIGHTY and most merciful Father, we thank Thee, amongst innumerable blessings, for great national mercies, for the free use of Thy Holy Scriptures, and the faithful preaching of Thine everlasting Gospel.

'And at this time, whilst Thou wilt not forbid us to lament our great loss in the death of so wise, useful, and Christian a man as the late Prince Consort, yet we thank Thee for the manner in which his children have been trained.

'We pray that the heart of our beloved Queen may be supported, and comforted, and stayed upon Thee, her God, and that all her royal family may be a joy to her.

'We pray for the Princess who is now connected with Prussia, that Thy blessing may ever rest upon her, and on her royal husband and children.

'But, at this time, we especially pray for His Royal Highness the Prince of Wales. We believe that Thou hast guided him to make a right choice; and we pray Thee to bless the young Princess whom Thou hast committed to his care and love; and to grant that domestic peace, harmony, and love may be their portion.

'Endue them with Thy Holy Spirit; enrich them with Thy Heavenly Grace; and prosper them with all happiness. May they ever follow the directions of Thy Holy

Word, given to Husbands and to Wives;[1] and be filled with that wisdom which is profitable to direct under all circumstances. If Thou art pleased to bless them with a family, may their children be to them what they have been to their honoured parents, to *their* joy, and for a blessing to the country (Eph. vi. 1-3).

'We pray that Truth and Justice, Religion and Piety, may be ever established in our land; and that the Nation may be kept faithful to the glorious privileges of a Christian Sabbath and an open Bible; so as to prize Thy Sabbaths, and *profit* by Thy Word, and ever abide by the Truth as revealed in it. Be Thou a wall of fire round about us, and the Glory in the midst of us.

'Hear us, Father of Mercies; and provide for the needy, means of obtaining sustenance; and bless all ranks and orders amongst us, that all may fill their different stations to Thy Glory and the general good; and may finally meet in that Kingdom which cannot be moved, wherein dwelleth Righteousness, free from all sin and sorrow, and in possession of perfect light, and love, and joy for ever.

'O hear us, of Thine infinite Mercy and Grace, through our Lord Jesus Christ, to whom, with Thee and the Holy Ghost, be the praise for ever and ever.'

[1] See Ephesians v. 25: 'Husbands, love your wives, even as CHRIST also loved the Church, and gave Himself for it.' And 1 Peter iii. 7: 'Likewise, ye husbands, dwell with them according to knowledge, giving honour unto the wife, as unto the weaker vessel, and as being heirs together of the grace of life; that your prayers be not hindered.'

Also see Ephesians v. 22, 23: 'Wives, submit yourselves unto your own husbands, as unto the Lord. Let the wife see that she reverence her husband.'

On the 24th of April, after a lingering illness, little Rosamond, my brother's only child, fell asleep in her Saviour's arms. She had borne her sufferings with great patience; and a short time before her death she said, 'I wish I were grown up, that I might do something to please the Lord Jesus.'

She was told that she need not wait to please Him until she was grown up, for that she could do so at once by obeying Him, and that He had said, 'Suffer little children *to come unto Me*, and forbid them not.'

'Oh, I am so glad!' she replied, 'for I *have* come to Him, I know. I am so glad it pleased Him.'

My father was tenderly attached to the gentle and lovely child; and so deeply did he sympathize with her bereaved parents in their great sorrow, that it occasioned a temporary return of his illness.

But from the end of the month of April his recovery was steady, and he began to anticipate with great delight the renewal of opportunities of speaking for his Master to the people committed to his charge.

One evening, after reading Bushnell's sermon on 'The Power of an Endless Life,' he said to Mr. Chalmers, 'That is a great and noble sermon. Some of the others in this volume have left an unsatisfied feeling in my heart. They display great intellect, but they lack *the sprinkling of the blood.* There should be *no sermon without that.* Never should a sinner leave one of our churches without hearing of the Saviour. Even in preaching to real Christians who required being built up, and exhorted, and led on to higher attainments, St. Paul said, "To write the same things to you, to me indeed is not grievous, but for you it is safe." For wherever these are gathered together, there may be also some soul ready to perish,—and he *might* perish before I could have another opportunity of bidding him "Behold the Lamb of God, which taketh away the sin of the world." When I preach again, may I preach Jesus more clearly, more freely, more persuasively, than ever before.'

During his illness he had spent much thought and prayer upon one who was at that time very prominently before the public—the Bishop of Natal; and at length, 'while he was musing, the fire burned,' and he could not refrain from entering into correspondence with him. It need scarcely be said that his words of argument, warning, and entreaty were written in gentle and deferential though uncompromising language. The bishop answered him at some length, and with most respectful courtesy, appearing to be touched by the faith and fervour which had led an old man, amidst a suffering and dangerous illness, thus to lay to heart that which he believed to be the peril of such views for him who held them and for those who should be led by him.

A few days afterwards the bishop enclosed for his perusal a letter from a working-man in Glasgow. Its object was to express thanks, on his own behalf and that of others of his class, for the deliverance which Bishop Colenso had given to their minds from the thraldom of old prejudices into the unfettered liberty of free thought and speculation.

There was something about the whole letter deeply

saddening. The writer had evidently been taught in his childhood from

'The big ha' Bible, once his father's pride,'

but now, leaving the simple faith of those early days, was wandering in the mazes of scepticism, without a light to guide him.

My father was greatly distressed by the tone of the letter, and wrote, by that day's post, to a Christian friend in Glasgow, begging him to go at once and see the man, seeking power from the Holy Ghost to reach his heart with the message of the gospel of life and peace—'God so loved the world, that He gave his only begotten Son, that whosoever believeth in Him should not perish, but have everlasting life.' Three days later came the solemn answer, 'I lost no time; but my visit was *too late*. The night before, the man had died suddenly.'

My father's thoughts were not a little occupied now in seeking for a successor to his curate, Mr. Southey, and he wrote to one of his daughters as follows:—

'How much we shall miss dear Southey and his active and useful wife. It will be difficult to fill the vacancy. Let us take the surest way to find that for which we are seeking—by going to Heaven for the right man. "Ask and it shall be given you." But as we are also to use means, you shall write for me to the friends of whose names I send you a list, and inquire whether they know of a suitable curate.

'I wish for one who, besides the great points required, would be a pleasant fellow-worker with my dear O'Rorke, who has been invaluable both to the parish and to myself. And I cannot forget that he twice refused a good living from our late beloved Archbishop to remain with me; although, had I known it in time, I could not have allowed him to do so. . . .

'Last night I found out the essence of Christianity in three short sentences: "My Master;" "My Lord and my God;" "Thou knowest that I love Thee."

'"My Master," whom I delight to serve.

'"My Lord, and my God," in whom I trust for time and for eternity.

'"Thou knowest that I love Thee;" Thy character, Thy sayings, Thy government, Thy salvation, and Thy person.

'. . . . Bless thee, my darling, for going over to do my work amongst my dear poor people. Yet I miss my tender nurse, and long for thy return to-morrow.

'Thy dearly loving father, WILLIAM MARSH.

'They are all taking the greatest care of me, and "keeping me in cotton wool!"'

His prayers touching the additional assistant in the parish were answered to his heart's desire. Mr. O'Rorke mentioned to him that it was possible Mr. French of Agra, who had returned from India for his health, might like such a charge. My father eagerly responded to the suggestion; and shortly afterwards Mr. French began his work at Beddington. There followed a time of united, earnest, and prayerful work, and of true and happy communion of spirit between Mr. French, Mr. O'Rorke, and Mr. Gordon. To my father the pleasure of their society was only second to the comfort and joy of having all his plans for the good of the parish carried out by men of no common gifts and devoted piety.

His return to Beddington, after so severe and prolonged an illness, was hailed with more than usual expressions of joy.

The school children stood outside his library window, singing a welcome; and he found the rectory adorned with the choicest flowers, brought thither and arranged with thoughtful care by Mrs. Laurence, and the two Miss Ferrers, daughters of a former rector, who had remained as residents in the parish.

To save him the fatigue of going upstairs, his bed, with its white curtains and sky-blue quilt, was now placed in the old oak-pannelled library, just where he could see, through the oriel window, round which white roses hung in clusters, the gay flower-beds on the smooth green lawn, and the shady little fir wood which led into the field beyond.

The summer passed away calmly and happily. My father, as he acquired strength, resumed his habit of giving addresses to young and old at the rectory, although he was forbidden by his doctors to enter the pulpit. Mr. Goodhart, of Park Chapel, Chelsea, preached for him twice in Beddington Church; and Dr. Ewald, who had married one of a family who had greatly valued my father's ministry in Leamington, and for whom he had a sincere regard, came to plead the cause of the Jews' Society.

Many of his old friends visited him in the course of the summer, and were astonished at the continued power of his mind and buoyancy of his spirit. The Miss Leycesters, who were paying a long visit at Beckenham Rectory, came frequently to see him. They both entered vividly into his chief interests, and he delighted in their society. It charmed him to hear, amongst many other plans of kindness, of macaroni breakfasts for poor Italian boys in London, and how a way had been won to their hearts thereby for readings from the Bible in the Italian tongue. The younger sister frequently corresponded with him on the business of the society for sending Englishwomen as missionaries to the women of the East, in the service of which she constantly employed herself, especially in examining the candidates and selecting those who were most suitable for the work in India. Those who knew Emma Leycester, and the charm of her cultivated mind, bright sweetness, and childlike unworldliness of spirit, with single-hearted desire to promote her Saviour's glory, will readily understand that there was between her and her aged relative a tie scarcely less endearing than that of father and daughter. Only seven months after he was taken from us, she too was called to endure a brief but sharp season of suffering; and then, with unfailing faith and triumphant joy, to pass through the dark valley into the presence of the Saviour, whom (she said) my father had led her, in her early days, to trust and love.

TO HIS ELDEST DAUGHTER.

'BEDDINGTON RECTORY, *Oct.* 9, 1863.

'DEAR DARLING MARY,— . . . You and I think and feel alike. I get so tired of my own heart. I like your remedy, "Simply to cast one's-self on Jesus." I add, "IT IS FINISHED." Remember that; and yet let us work as hard as we can. That is the way to grow in grace, and to prove it.

'Dear Susie came to us from Watlington Park, and paid us a little visit, which was very pleasant. "Our Car" arrived next, and then good Mrs. Scott from Colchester. So you see our old friends find us out in our new home. Can you, and dear little Mary and Fanny come on Tuesday next, when we shall have plenty of room? I wish Francis could also come. By-and-bye we shall all meet in one mansion, and say, "Thou hast placed my feet in a large room."

'My love to you all. Sweet Lucy, who writes for me, says, "How will you end your letter?" I tell her, *by love without end* from your loving father, W. M.'

'*P.S.*—Since I have been here I have read Chalmers's *Daily Readings on the Psalms.* Very enlarged views; very spiritual; very full of common sense! What a man he was! and at last, translated, as it were!

'You did not take the little book on prophecy, so I send it after you. . . . I have always shrunk from *fixing dates.* But I have not been afraid of *believing* "Surely, I come quickly," and of *praying* "*Even so, come,* Lord Jesus!"'

When entering on the charge of Beddington, my father had felt so tenderly for the parishioners in their sorrow at the recent loss of their beloved pastor, whose earnest labours they had enjoyed for nineteen years, that he was anxious to avoid making any unnecessary changes in the existing arrangements for the church and parish. The only exception he made was the substitution of a regular weekly service and sermon, instead of the prayers on saints' days. But, besides the services he found there, a cottage lecture had been added; and when the duties were shared by three curates, extempore lectures were delivered every week at two school-rooms in different parts of the widely-scattered parish, and a third at a cottage in another direction.

A Bible-woman was also employed, whose salary was generously given by Mr. Laurence. She was a simple and hearty Christian, and soon made her way into the confidence of the poor. Before she began her work at Beddington, she had been known and approved by Mrs. Ranyard, the foundress of the noble institution of 'the missing link' between rich and poor, the marvellous progress and success of which my father had watched and furthered with the warmest interest and sympathy.

It could not be expected but that, amidst the respectful and cordial kindness which he experienced in his parish, on all sides, deepening into tender anxiety during his illness, there should yet arise some shades of differing opinion on questions touching Church matters. His manner of dealing with such divergencies of judgment amongst his flock was marked by his habitual courteous and gentle consideration for the feelings of others, combined with a steadfast firmness where he felt principle to be concerned.

It will be seen by the following extracts from one of the letters written on the occasion, that a desire had been expressed by some to introduce the practice of monotoning the Church service.

To one of his parishioners he wrote as follows :—

'YOUR visit of yesterday was a great pleasure to me. I truly value your hearty friendship.

'With regard to our Church matters, there are many things which may seem harmless in themselves, but become dangerous by their affinity.

'A strong effort is being made to unite the Latin, Greek, and English Churches. This would be the ruin of our constitution, and of the prosperity of our country; because it is contrary to the Divine will, as revealed in the Holy Scriptures, to unite truth with error.

'The main object of introducing intoning, and other practices which usually accompany it, into the churches of our country, is to undermine the principles of the Reformation, by accustoming the congregations to listen to a service *performed for them*, appealing more to the senses than the spirit; and in that, and other ways, assimilated to the mode of worship of the Church of Rome.

'As patriots, no less than as Protestant Christians, we should resist everything which would help to open the flood-gates to Romanism. It is said by some that the spirit of the Church of Rome is now more in accordance with the tolerant spirit of the Church of England. But alas! while she claims for her prerogatives infallibility and unchangeableness, she must act upon her original persecuting dogmas, wherever she has the power; as we see in the case of those noble Spaniards, who have just been saved with great difficulty, by the appeals of several Governments, from the horrors of galley-slavery; to which they were sentenced solely for the crime of reading the Word of God!

'The Church of England has not only declared in her rubric the doctrine of the Church of Rome touching the sacrifice of the mass, to be "*idolatry abhorred of all faithful Christians*,"[1] but she deems the system in general to be so dangerous, that out of her Thirty-nine Articles she has sixteen expressly against the same, besides the strong protests in many of her Homilies. The sixth article is the glory of our Church; by that may she always abide, and may you and I, as individuals, do so likewise. "Holy Scripture containeth all things necessary to salvation; so that whatsoever is not read therein, nor may be proved thereby, is not to be required of any man, that it should be believed as an article of the Faith, or be thought requisite or necessary to salvation."

'It is on these grounds that I cannot give my consent to any change in our simple and scriptural form of worship which would tend to assimilate it to, or symbolize with, that of the Church of Rome.'

His anxious concern on the whole of this momentous question seemed only to intensify, as he was himself

[1] Rubric at the close of the Communion Service.

drawing nearer his rest. Not alone in the direction of Ritualism was he alarmed at the development of the Romanizing movement, but whilst doing all the justice of which his high nature was capable to the devout and self-sacrificing purpose of individuals, he viewed with equal distrust and anxiety the increase of the number of Sisterhoods. He saw in them the germ of conventual life, in all its rigidity and unhappiness, its line of demarcation between secular and religious life in place of the hallowing of common life, its severance of home-ties, and its injurious concentration of interest in spiritual directors and confessors. 'The system cannot but culminate in the Church of Rome,' he said, 'as surely as a river flows to the ocean.'

The principle of monastic life he believed to be opposed to the Divine will. 'God made the family,' he would say; 'priests made the nunnery. Asceticism demands the bondage of life-vows. God gives "glorious liberty" to His children to "serve Him with gladness" and with "a free heart," while watching, day by day, the guiding of His eye.'

It need scarcely be repeated here, that, whilst he thus clearly expressed and firmly stood by his life-long convictions as to the doctrines and practices of the Church of Rome itself, or those which paved the way for their reception, he was very tender towards the individual members of her communion. To one of his daughters who was visiting a dying Roman Catholic, he said, 'You are right not to disturb the mind of one who is drawing near to another world by alluding to churches or dogmas.

Seek only to lead him to rest on the Lord Jesus Christ *alone* for salvation; to let none stand between him and "the ONE Mediator between God and man, the man Christ Jesus;" and to believe in His "ONE sacrifice ONCE offered for the sins of the whole world;" and he is SAVED in the Lord with an everlasting salvation; he is one of those of whom the Master spoke, in the words recorded in John v. 24, "He that heareth my word, and believeth on Him that sent me, HATH EVERLASTING LIFE, and shall not come into condemnation; but IS PASSED FROM DEATH UNTO LIFE."'

The following letter, written about the same time, will show that, whilst faithfully caring for the spiritual welfare of his parish, not only for its own sake, but also as an integral part of the church to which he was devotedly attached, the temporal condition of the poor throughout the country shared in his thoughts, his sympathies, and his efforts:—

'THERE is a subject on which *The Times* might give its powerful and generous advice much to the honour of our country, and to the alleviation of the misery of many poor people—I mean as to the appointment of the governors of workhouses.

'The electors, in a town, or district, should never choose "A," or "B," "because he needs such a situation," but only men who are qualified for the office.

'Workhouses are not prisons for criminals, but asylums for the aged, the poor, and those who have met with misfortunes and have no means of relief. The governor, therefore, as to rules, order, and proper discipline, may be inflexible as a judge, but should be also tender as a mother.

'There are many persons, in the present day, who have such a dread of a workhouse that they would rather submit to starvation than become inmates of one, not so much because the workhouse lowers them in the scale of human society, as because they hear of the rigour and cruelty too often exercised within those walls.

'The Holy Scriptures speak frequently and strongly on the duty of showing kindness to the aged, the fatherless, and the widow.

'He is not best qualified who is *over*-shrewd in examining into the truth of cases in order that the public money may never be misapplied.

'If persons come to the workhouse late in the evening, and apparently in very great distress, why not give them a decent night's lodging and food until the case can be inquired into the next day?

'If young outcasts apply for admission, they might be received, and be taught some trade which would pay for their own expenses while in the workhouse. Very few would give up their free lives out of doors unless desiring to reform, or actually starving, and such in either case have a claim for attention and relief.

'You may ask me why I enter upon the subject. I have just been reading of cases even in London, of persons who have actually died of starvation; and in our courts of justice, workhouse officials have been blamed for refusing to admit such cases of distress until (as they said in excuse) they had had time to investigate the circumstances.

'A passage of Scripture occurs to me, which is as applicable to a nation as to the individual to whom it was originally addressed, "Break off thy sins by righteousness, and thy iniquities by showing mercy to the poor, if it may be a lengthening of thy tranquillity."'

TO THE REV. JOHN MILLER, D.D., THEN RECTOR OF BIRMINGHAM, NOW OF GREENWICH.

'BEDDINGTON RECTORY, *October* 15.

'MY DEAR DR. MILLER,—I take it for granted your sermon on "Controversy a Scriptural Duty" will be printed? Would it not be well also to have it put in the form of a little book for general circulation?

'We have met with sincere and good High Churchmen, but such are not aware of the tendency of their views. Yet one of them said, the other day, he had rather be a Roman Catholic than a Dissenter. Is it possible that he could ever have read the sessions of the Council of Trent, or the creed of Pope Pius IV.? It is impossible for common-sense to prove that system and the New Testament Christianity to be otherwise than antagonistic. We must continue to pray "that it may please Thee to lead into the way of truth all such as have erred and are deceived."

'There is a deep-laid conspiracy against the Protestantism of our Church and country. If permitted to succeed, judgments will fall on the land; but if Popery prevail a for short time, it will terminate in infidelity as the *last* antichrist. Satanic influence is not sufficiently recognised, yet it will prevail till the enemy be bound. "From the crafts and assaults of the devil, good Lord, deliver us!"

'May your health and strength continue, and that of dear Stowell and others, to be champions in the war of truth against error.—Yours ever affectionately,

'WILLIAM MARSH.'

TO THE LATE REVERED AND LAMENTED CANON STOWELL.

'*October* 16, 1863.

'MY DEAR STOWELL,—I am thankful for your faithfulness, and by grace you will be faithful unto death.

'That was a sterling saying of Dr. Hook, on the third day at the Manchester Conference: "The first thing a clergyman should do, should be to ascertain clearly, as an honest man, what are the real principles of the Church of England." The non-natural sense put upon the Articles by some, is a departure in heart from the Church of England; she requires them to be taken in their plain, literal, grammatical sense.

'The Archbishop of York's speech at the Church Missionary Anniversary, calling for devout thankfulness to Almighty God for what the Society has already accomplished, is a sufficient answer to the innuendoes lately uttered against it.

'My dear friend, the Jesuit is abroad, and if (as I fear) the Church of England is to be visited with chastisement for her want of faithfulness to her own principles, Romanism will prevail. After that, infidelity will succeed, and there may be a violent struggle. But after that, HE will come who will "put down all rule, authority, and power" opposed to the glorious gospel of the grace of God. "Amen: even so, come, Lord Jesus."

'I fear it is in vain for me to think that you would ever have a spare Sunday to occupy Beddington pulpit, otherwise you might plead here the cause of the Church Missionary Society before the end of the year.—Ever yours affectionately WILLIAM MARSH.'

TO THE REV. JOHN RYLE.[1]

'BEDDINGTON RECTORY, *October* 20.

'MY DEAR RYLE,—If I should ever visit you, I should like a "sitting" in your new schoolroom; so I pay for it in advance, £1—I only wish it were £100. I am so glad to hear of the movement at Ipswich. The great enemy is awake and astir; if we sleep, the land will be sown with tares. May truth conquer among our Suffolk brethren, and the wheat they sow produce an abundant harvest. Controversy, "with meekness and wisdom," in the present day is a bounden duty; silence would be too like neutrality, and *neutrality is treason.*—Yours most truly,

'WILLIAM MARSH.'

[1] Of Mr. Ryle's *Commentary on the Gospels*, he said, 'I know nothing of the kind likely to be more useful. It is clear as light. And Mr. Ryle's tracts were those which he gave away most widely, excepting only the series entitled 'CHRIST IS ALL,' by his beloved friend, Archdeacon Law, now Dean of Gloucester.

TO T. S. WRIGHT, ESQ.

'DEAR MR. WRIGHT,— . . . I fear the hope of gain has been a temptation to poor ——, inducing him to sell tracts of extreme views. How numerous and how subtle are the devices of the enemy! There is no safety but in adhering to the Word of God, and in prayer for the Spirit of God; and thus the will is strengthened to incur risks rather than to act contrary to truth, duty, and conscience. The laity must rise up, and see that error be put down, or the Church of England will fall, and all Protestantism in this country. Many Dissenters are little aware that the fall of our Church would remove the sea-wall, and they would then soon be overwhelmed in the flood. All lovers of Scriptural truth should unite (as they have done at Leamington), and should pray that the Government may act wisely and firmly.

'But our privilege is to look beyond it all, to a kingdom which can never be moved, and a Church which will be without spot, wrinkle, or any such thing. There cannot be such till "that which is perfect be come."

'Kindest remembrances to Mrs. Wright.—Yours affectionately, W. MARSH.'

During the summer my father's mind had been much occupied with thoughts concerning the Lord's return, which he was led to think, from many signs of the times, might not be very long delayed. He loved more than ever to dwell upon this hope when conversing with his own family, and with the friends who visited him.

Long ago he had given heed to the sure word of prophecy, but now his anxiety deepened that the subject should be kept prominently before the minds of the people of God as a powerful motive for increased activity in His service, and for seeking greater attainments in personal holiness. Whilst 'of that *day* and that *hour* knoweth no man,' he would quote; yet remember that it is also said, 'Ye, brethren, are not in darkness that that day should overtake you as a thief.' Then, alluding to passing events, and comparing them with the signs foretold by our Lord of His coming, he would add, in a triumphant tone, 'When these things *begin* to come to pass, then look up, and lift up your heads, for your redemption draweth nigh.'

In the hope of arousing the interest of many in the neighbourhood on this subject, he arranged that a conference should be held at Beddington in November. Having obtained the use of the large hall in the Park for two days, it was planned that the working-men's annual tea-party should be given on Monday the 2d, that the conference should meet in the morning and afternoon of the 3d; and that the day should be ended by an evening service in the church, with the celebration of the Lord's Supper, bearing in mind the words of St. Paul, 'As often as ye eat this bread, and drink this cup, ye do show the Lord's death till He come.'

When my father sent out the invitations,[1] he made a request in each that prayer might be offered that all who should meet on that occasion might receive 'an unction from the Holy One;' and that the presence of God the Holy Ghost, the Teacher, Sanctifier, and Comforter, might be felt and known amongst them.

These prayers received a full answer. Many wrote word afterwards that it had been a marked day in their heavenward journey;[2] and others said they had never before felt so conscious of the presence of the Lord Jesus as during those meetings, and in the intervals between them, which were chiefly spent in prayer and praise, and holy converse.

[1] The following letter was an answer received from one of those whose presence he had first invited :—

'LIVERPOOL, 28th *October* 1863.

'BELOVED FRIEND,—Impracticable! I am specially engaged here for Nov. 1, 2, 3, and 5.

'The vision is *yet* for an appointed time. Though it tarry, we will still be waiting for it. "It will surely come, it will not tarry."

'Then shall Isa. xxvi. be sung in the land of Judah, and the song of Moses raised in the same key with the song of the Lamb. The subject is the same,—the Lord's victory over the enemies of His Church. The enemy changes aspects,—Egypt, Assyria, Babylon, Rome; our Captain changeth not. Hallelujah! And what are we? "Weak and helpless;" yet "more than conquerors."

'Peace, His peace, perfect peace, be ever with you, my dear old friend. HUGH M'NEILE.'

[2] One of these was shortly called to enter her heavenly home. The account of the blessing which she found at this conference is told in the simple but beautiful story of her brief life and peaceful death, entitled, *Clear Shining; a Memoir of Gertrude Acklom.* By her Mother.

The following extract is taken from a letter written a few days afterwards, by the Rev. Marcus Rainsford, now incumbent of Belgrave Chapel, London :—

'REVEREND AND DEAR SIR,— . . . I can truly say I had a fresh and full baptism of the Holy Spirit at your conference, and I heartily joined with others in asking a special blessing on the dear aged servant of the Lord who had brought us together. . . . Probably, when next we meet, His name will be written on our foreheads; and, in the meantime, our names are written in His heart, engraven on His hands, and on His shoulders.'

The 3d of November set in with such storms of wind and rain as made us fear that comparatively few would be able to attend the meetings. But by ten o'clock, between sixty and seventy of my father's personal friends had arrived at the rectory, and assembled in the library to hear from him a short but heart-stirring address, in which he dwelt chiefly on the words, 'The Lord is at hand.' 'Not only providentially, not only spiritually, but personally; not alone to faith, but also to sight.' Afterwards they proceeded to the hall, which was already nearly filled. From some miles around the people had gathered together; and a remarkable spirit of solemnity and devotion prevailed.

Copies of the hymn-book called *The Praise of Jesus* had been distributed; and the service commenced with singing a hymn, in which every heart and voice seemed to join. This was followed by prayer and a short address from the Rev. William Pennefather, after which the following letter from my father was read aloud by Mr. O'Rorke:—

'BELOVED FRIENDS,—You are assembled together for the greatest object that can occupy the human mind,—the glory of God in the salvation of man. You are also employing the best means to promote that object, for

"Prayer is appointed to convey
The blessings God designs to give;"

and there appears to be a special honour set upon *united* prayer. Our blessed Lord has not only promised to hear it, but to grant His presence to it, for "where two or three are gathered together in My name, there am I in the midst of them."

'You have also in view that which will be so bright a manifestation of the Divine glory both to this world and to the universe,—the Second Advent of our blessed Lord. Not till then will the enemy be bound and error be banished, and Jew and Gentile form one flock, under One Shepherd.

'It is the great and constant subject of the Christian Scriptures. The apostolic writings employ it to awaken salutary fears, to excite joyful hopes, and to quicken believers in the discharge of every duty. Nor should we forget that with this subject Revelation closes: "Behold, I come quickly;" and St. John, as if personating all believers, answers, "Amen: even so, come, Lord Jesus."

'You will allow me to add to these few thoughts, that

till that glorious period, in the righteous judgment of God, Satanic influence will obtain over our world. And, dear brethren, none of us is likely to escape it but by daily prayer and daily reading of the Holy Scriptures. Thus "Resist the devil, and he will flee from you," terrified by the discovery that One is with you who has him in a chain. Our Lord himself, in His personal conflict with the devil, overcame him by the Scriptures. But we must have the Holy Spirit to apply the Word; therefore "draw nigh to God, and He will draw nigh to you." It is only by the diligent use of the Scriptures, and by constant prayer, that individuals or nations can be preserved in the truth to the end. Therefore, "I commend you unto God, and to the Word of His grace, which is able to build you up, and to give you an inheritance among them that are sanctified." Thus you will be useful in life, safe in death, and blessed in eternity.

'And let me ask your prayers for myself, that I may die resting only on the simple faith that a full, perfect, and sufficient sacrifice was made for sin, when our Lord proclaimed on Calvary, "*It is finished!*" After all His unknown sufferings for us, it will be heaven to behold His glory; and to this happiness may we all be brought, and to the Father, Son, and Holy Ghost shall be the eternal praise.'

The meeting was continued for about two hours with undiminished interest. The speakers were the Revs. Marcus Rainsford, Charles Goodhart, Claremont Skrine, and Daniel Wilson of Islington. Prayer was offered or a hymn sung between each address; and the whole was closed by a short exposition of Canticles ii. 8-17, given by Mr. Pennefather.

Dinner had been prepared in the school-room for a hundred guests who had received special invitations, and refreshments were provided for others in the ante-room of the hall.

When the meeting was resumed in the afternoon, it was carried on with unabated interest and fervour. Mr. O'Rorke commenced it with prayer, and then Mr. French, Colonel Rowlandson, and Mr. Blackwood, each spoke, in turn, faithful words of warning, counsel, and encouragement, touching the dangers, the duties, and the hopes of the Church of Christ in these days.

The twilight of the winter's evening soon deepened into night, and the only light in the old hall—the flickering blaze of the log-fire burning on the open hearth, its flames lighting for a few moments the uplifted faces, or showing the speaker pleading earnestly for his Lord—seemed to be in keeping with the deep solemnity of the last address; which touched upon the probability of a time of great tribulation intervening before the Lord's return, and urged a constant state of preparedness.

Just as it was ended, a message was brought from my father to say that he would speak a few words to any who liked to come to the rectory. Many gladly responded to his invitation, and again the library was filled with listeners, eager to hear his ripened experience.

The brief remembrances written down afterwards can give but little idea of the power of the spoken words, as the aged saint, his face radiant with the joy of his Lord, spoke out of the fulness of his heart in varying tones, now solemn, now persuasive, and now exulting. He spoke first of the character of God, then of the mistaken views of men concerning Him.

'God is not loved because He is not known: "Acquaint now thyself with Him, and be at peace, thereby good shall come unto thee."

'He has revealed Himself in His word: "God is light;" "God is love."

'He has manifested Himself in His Son: "In this was manifested the love of God toward us, because that God sent His only begotten Son into the world, that we might live through Him."

'But the heart of the natural man is so hard, and his will so stubborn, that they must be renewed and subdued by the power of the Holy Spirit: "For the love of God is shed abroad in our hearts by the Holy Ghost, which He hath given unto us."

'Then, when the Three Persons of the Blessed Trinity are known and believed in, "The name of the Lord is a strong tower," and the soul that is sheltered there is safe for eternity.'

An hour after tea had been served in the schoolroom, all who could remain joined in the evening service in the church and partook of the sacrament of the Lord's Supper. The preacher was the Rev. Thomas Nolan, who gave an excellent sermon on the words, 'Till He come!'

Just before my father left his parish to pay his winter visit to Beckenham, one of his churchwardens thus wrote to him:—

'REVEREND AND DEAR SIR,—I am much obliged by your kind remembrance of me, shown by your handsome present of a standard Church work.

'I shall very much value the gift for the honoured donor's sake, and also for its intrinsic merit.

'As I suppose we shall soon hear of your returning to your warm and comfortable winter quarters, permit me to express my hopes of your continued preservation in health during your absence, and of your return to your flock next spring in a good state of health. We all value you, and are proud of so bright an example of what the declining years of a clergyman ought to be.'

The close of the old year and the opening of the new, my father had always regarded as a very solemn season, and it had been his custom to hold a meeting in his parish for prayer and exposition of the Scripture on the last night of the old year, and to administer the Sacrament, in addition to the service and sermon on New-Year's Day. Even in the feeble health of his later years, he had been in the habit of waiting until the midnight hour had struck, ushering in the New Year, that he might meet it with prayer and with praise before retiring to rest. Quoting the words, 'We spend our years as a tale that is told,'—'humiliation for the past year,' he said, 'with its long catalogue of sins and shortcomings, and its tale of listless love and service to Him who so loved us as to give His life for us, should mingle with thankfulness for abounding mercies, and most of all for "the blood which cleanseth us from all sin;"' and for the coming year, 'there should be happy confidence in the promised grace and strength of our Redeemer, and in the fatherly wisdom and kindness of the Almighty Providence which has foreseen all its unknown events, with intent and power to make them work together for good to them that love God.'

More than once the first sound we heard, after the chiming of the church bells had announced the New Year, was his beloved voice repeating the following verses :—

'This God is the God we adore,
Our faithful unchangeable Friend,
Whose love is as great as His power,
And neither knows measure nor end.

'Tis Jesus, the First and the Last,
Whose mercy shall guide us safe home;
We'll praise Him for all that is past,
And trust Him for all that's to come.'

It was the moment his daughters especially prized to have with him, to receive his blessing. On one year he gave it in these words, to be turned into a daily prayer:

'"Be strong in the grace which is in Christ Jesus;" "The Lord give thee understanding in all things;" "The Lord lift up His countenance upon thee, and give thee peace."'

On being reminded of those words the following year, and asked, 'Can you ever give us any blessing so full as that?' he promptly replied, 'Yes; and fuller still. "Mercy unto you, and peace, and love, be *multiplied*."'

On this, the last of these solemn seasons which he spent on earth, he seemed to see every blessing as concentrated in the promise, 'I will be a GOD unto thee.'

He commenced the year 1864 in such fairly good health, that no mournful impression fell upon our hearts that it was to be the last New-Year's Day on which we should receive the greeting and the blessing so dearly prized; and look upon

> 'The sweet attractive kind of grace,
> A full assurance given by looks,
> Continual comfort in a face
> The lineaments of gospel books.'

As he was not allowed to venture out of doors in the cold weather, he wished to partake of the sacrament of the Lord's Supper at the rectory with his family; and Mr. O'Rorke came over in the afternoon and administered it to us. Just before the service, my father gave a short address on the words, 'As often as ye eat this bread, and drink this cup, ye do show the Lord's death till He come.' And after the close, his voice broke the stillness with prayer and praise.

Early in this year he welcomed with delight the Rev. John Sandys, who came to spend a few days with him,—not to revive their friendship, for its warmth had never been lessened, but to enjoy an intercourse which had become less frequent since my father's state of health had obliged him to give up his annual visit to Mr. Sandys in London, and owing also to his removal into Norfolk.

Referring to this visit, Mr. Sandys, in concluding the letter quoted before,[1] wrote as follows:—

'The little visit I paid to Beckenham in the February before dear Dr. Marsh's removal to his heavenly home, I

[1] See pages 75-78.

shall never forget. His mind seemed as clear as ever, his conversation as animated, and there was a radiancy of countenance, and a manifest ripeness for heaven, which it was indeed good to contemplate.

'Notwithstanding his great age, his cheerfulness was not a whit abated. At the time of my visit the snow was lying thick on the ground. His bedroom adjoined the drawing-room; and as he was coming from one to the other in a wheel-chair, he called to me and said, with his pleasant humour, 'Sandys, if any one asks you how friend Marsh is, say, "Oh, he takes his drive every day!" "What! not in such weather as this?" "Yes; every day!"'

'My feeling at the time of that visit was (I remember) this,—I wish all I love were here with me to witness the loveliness and power of religion as they shine forth in this old servant of the Lord.

'"Wherein, it may be asked, were his faults? for none here are perfect." None in the sight of God. "Behold, I am vile," was the confession of the pre-eminently humble Job. Like lowliness of heart characterized your dear father. But Daniel's enemies could find against him no occasion or fault; and for a friend or enemy to find occasion or fault in your dear father would, methinks, be a hard matter. Of our adorable Redeemer it is written, "Yea, He is altogether lovely." And to no other of His followers that I ever saw might the same words be, with an equal degree of truth, applied.

'My love and veneration for your dear father were very great. *You* will not think, but *some* may, that these have blinded my eyes to any defects that may have existed.

The character of my mind is just the reverse. The more deeply I love a person, the more sensitive am I to any failing or defect there may be in them. I mention this because the amount of weight to be given to what any one says depends in no inconsiderable measure upon the character of his mind.'

During the spring his health continued to improve. He carried on a large correspondence on public and private interests, including letters to various religious periodicals, and was able to enjoy his usual studies, as well as to read the *Times* in the morning and the *Record*[1] in the evening.

He was delighted with a pamphlet, on the subject of the Second Advent, sent to him about this time by Dr. Stevenson.[2] A warm friendship, arising from remarkable sympathies of heart and character, had long existed between them, to which a new link had been added, in the previous year, when, at the Beddington Prophetical Conference, Dr. Stevenson's thoughts had been first led to dwell on the hope of the *near* approach of the Coming of the Lord.

Before my father's return to Beddington, his heart was cheered by tidings that reached him from his parish, of a blessing which God was bestowing there, through the visit of a devoted clergyman,[3] who has taken these words for

[1] The reading of the *Record* was a great enjoyment to him, as it seemed for the time to carry him again into public religious interests, and amongst many of his old and valued friends.

[2] Vicar of Patrixbourne.

[3] Rev. William Haslam, Rector of Buckenham, Norfolk.

the motto of his life, 'Time is short—Souls are precious—Jesus is worthy.'

The ground had been well prepared by the faithful and earnest preaching of the Gospel of Christ; so that in many hearts the good seed already sown now took root, sprang up, and flourished. There could be no doubt as to the reality of the change in them, for it was attested by new lives and happy faces.

The work thus begun was carefully fostered and carried on by the three clergymen, who had the joy of seeing it steadily increase, as month after month went by.

A desire was soon felt by many to join in prayer for the furtherance of this blessing; and it was expressed to Mr. O'Rorke, with the suggestion that those who wished should be invited to remain in the schoolroom, at Beddington Corner, for united prayer, after the conclusion of the Sunday evening service.

He gave the plan careful consideration before proposing it to my father, who heartily assented to it; and Mr. French and Mr. Gordon gladly joined in carrying it out.

An evident blessing rested on this meeting. Not only were the newly awakened watched over and nurtured in the heavenly life, but the Christians of longer standing were also greatly strengthened by this bond of fellowship.

In the adjoining parish of Mitcham there was a similar work of the grace of God, accounts of which my father heard with deep interest, from the rector—a grandson of his late beloved friend Bishop Wilson, and his curate, the Rev. Richard Graves; whose love to their Saviour and earnest life in His service made their frequent visits to

Beddington Rectory a source of much pleasure to my father.

TO THE REV. J. H. J. HANDCOCK.

'BECKENHAM RECTORY, *February* 20, 1864.

'MY DEAR MR. HANDCOCK,—You ask whether I believe that the full assurance of faith is attainable, and that it should be sought for by *every one?* To this I reply, Assuredly I do, because I am a *Churchman.*

'The service of our Church opens with the announcement, "He *pardoneth* and *absolveth* all them that truly repent, and unfeignedly believe His holy Gospel." In the Collect for the Second Sunday in Advent, we are taught by our Church to pray "that we may embrace and *ever hold fast* the blessed hope of everlasting life," etc. Also, in the 17th Article, it is declared, "that the godly consideration of our election in Christ . . . doth greatly establish and confirm our faith of eternal salvation, to be enjoyed through Christ."

'Again, most assuredly do I believe that this full assurance is attainable, and should be sought for by all, because I am a *Christian*, and believe that it is the design of Christianity to bring us into a state of *peace* with God," by declaring that Christ has "died for our sins, and has risen again for our justification." And our Saviour Himself hath said, "He that heareth my word, and believeth on Him that sent me, *hath* everlasting life, and shall not come into condemnation, but *is passed* from death unto life."

'Yea, moreover, the object of Christianity is to raise us to that highest of all privileges, even *joy in the Lord.* No sooner had the Philippian jailor believed on the Saviour than he rejoiced in God. No sooner had Candace's treasurer believed on Christ as having made an atonement for sin, than "he went on his way rejoicing."

'This joy in the Lord gives great strength to meet trial and to perform duty. Then why do not all believers partake of it?

'*First,* Because some are of a naturally morbid and dejected turn of mind, and they do not attain to joy because they do not ask *believing that they shall receive* (Matt. xxi. 22).

'*Secondly,* Because of inadequate views of the fulness and freeness of the grace that is in Christ, causing doubts and fears, and so preventing perfect peace.

'*Thirdly,* Because of some indulged sin, in heart or life, that grieves the Holy Spirit, and therefore this joy, which is one of His fruits, is withheld. But such should pray, "Show me wherefore Thou contendest with me? If I have done iniquity, I will do so no more." And *all* should pray, "Remember me with the favour which Thou bearest unto Thy people, and visit me with Thy salvation, that I may *see* the felicity of Thy chosen, and *rejoice* in the gladness of Thy people, and *glory* with Thine inheritance."

'Thus I believe that assurance is attainable, and is to be *sought* by all; because I have read, and I believe, my Bible.

'See the following passages:—2 Cor. xiii. 5, and 1 John v. 13, which latter text is especially interesting when compared with John xx. 31. Paul would have the Philippians "rejoice in the Lord alway;" for Christianity is a happy as well as a holy religion.

'Little faith is safe, but it is not so happy or so useful as great faith; and no one should be content with *little*, when he might have *much*.—Yours affectionately,

'WILLIAM MARSH.'

TO JAMES GRANT, ESQ.

'DEAR MR. GRANT,—I am glad that your inkstand is not dry. I want you to write on the following subjects:—Grieving the Holy Spirit; quenching the Holy Spirit; resisting the Holy Spirit; doing despite to the Holy Spirit.

'I fear these important subjects are too much overlooked.

'I should like you to write also on the following subjects:—The evil spirit is represented as a *destroyer* (roaring lion); as a *deceiver* (the serpent); as an *adversary* (Satan); as an *accuser* (the devil).

'If the plans of the evil spirit were more considered, and the power of the Holy Spirit more invoked, what prayer there might be; and how would the influence of the Holy Spirit be cherished; and the injury of grieving or quenching Him be manifest; and the extreme danger of resisting Him, or doing despite to Him, be evident.—Yours faithfully,

WM. MARSH.'

A quarterly clerical meeting was held at the house of the Rev. Robert Tritton, rural dean at Morden, in the neighbourhood of Beddington, and although my father could not be present, yet Mr. Tritton's thoughtful kindness in letting him know beforehand what would be the passage of Scripture under discussion, enabled him each time to take his regular part in it, by writing down a few thoughts which were read aloud at the ensuing meeting. A copy of one of these letters had been taken, from which the following extracts are given :—

On 2 *Timothy* i.

'DEAR MR. TRITTON,—In accordance with your request, I willingly send a few thoughts on the passage of Scripture to be considered at your next meeting.

'Ver. 5.—I have often been much delighted in observing (for I have seen it in many families) the children of believing parents following in their steps, and the promise being fulfilled, "The children of Thy servants shall continue, and their seed shall be established before Thee" (Ps. cii. 28).

'With regard to the 7th verse, I have thought that it contains all that we principally need. In discussing this verse some time ago with a brother clergyman, I differed from him in thinking that the word "power" related to the authority of the minister over the people, believing it in that place to mean *courage*. When a doubt arises as to the correct rendering of a word, the context will often decide its true meaning.

'Here, in the 8th verse, it is opposed to fear, or cowardice, to which temptations the ministers of Christ in those days were especially subject, in consequence of the persecution they might have to endure.'

A well-known Greek scholar, who was present at the time, said, that undoubtedly the word *δύναμις* was used sometimes in the sense of 'courage.'

'But courage must be softened by love, and courage and love must be under the direction of a "sound mind" to make the completeness of the Christian character. "Wisdom is profitable to direct," and reading, meditation, and prayer will further the growth of this heavenly wisdom, and keep the fire burning—*ἀναζωπυρεῖν*, ver. 6.

'It would be a useful petition to offer up every morning,—"Give me the spirit of power, and of love, and of a sound mind."

'Ver. 9.—How careful the Apostle is to exclude human merit from any part in our salvation; yet there never was a more *special pleader* for good works than St. Paul.

'In this verse we may also notice that he ever maintains the sovereignty of God, which is always exercised in showing mercy.

'In the 6th verse he equally maintains the responsibility of man.

'Ver. 10.—How thankful we should be who live under the light and liberty of the Christian dispensation!

'Ver. 12.—What courage confidence in Christ will give!

'Ver. 14.—May we always remember how dependent we are on the Holy Ghost for the reception, maintenance, and preservation of Divine truth.

'Vers. 16-18.—The servant, like his Master, notices and remembers every act of kindness shown to him.

'Oh, *how much* is contained in that expression, "Find mercy of the Lord in that day!"

'My prayers often ascend for a blessing on your clerical meeting.

'The following Collects have occurred to me as suitable to this subject:—The Collect for St. Stephen's Day, for Quinquagesima Sunday, and for the Ninth Sunday after Trinity.—I am, dear Mr. Tritton, yours most sincerely,

'WILLIAM MARSH.'

TO HIS GRAND-DAUGHTER.

'*May* 11, 1864.

'DEAR DARLING LITTLE LUCY,— . . . "Faith cometh by hearing, and hearing by the Word of God," and the Word of God leads to the Saviour, and the Saviour leads us to heaven. That Word also leads us to seek to be useful to others by the way.

'A poor boy subscribed for a Bible. When it was brought to him, he said, "I only want the first part. I will not read your Christian Scriptures, I am a Jew." Those who carried the Bible, however, persuaded him to keep it. After more than a year the same collectors re-visited this district. They inquired for the boy; a poor woman said, "Ah! he is dead; we all remember him. He used to visit the sick in our court, read the Bible to them, and often out of his little earnings give them a few pence."

'We ask for "power from on high" to be given to Captain Trotter and Mr. Blackwood, for their addresses at Willis's Rooms. My love to dear Lord and Lady Kintore;

and tell them I pray for a deep and lasting blessing to rest on all their endeavours to hasten the coming and the kingdom of our Lord Jesus Christ. The sowing-time will soon be over, and then the sowers and reapers will shout together at the Harvest Home. You will like to read the enclosed. It gives a pleasant glimpse into the happy and useful lives which our dear little Mya and Mr. Bolland are leading in the midst of their crowded parish. What changes I have seen wrought in various places, during my long lifetime, by the untiring efforts of many a devoted evangelical clergyman of our Church. They have been workers, indeed! But still the labourers are few *compared* to the need of the vast fields of corn standing "white unto the harvest," so that we may bless God for sending us again, in these latter days, the help of laymen full of faith and power," "sanctified and meet for the Master's use." . . . Give my love to dear Car Maitland, and bid her come and see her old friend on her way back to Park Place.—Ever your loving grandfather.'

TO THE REV. DAWSON MASSEY.

'*June* 24, 1864.

'DEAR MR. MASSEY,—I shall receive with thankfulness such a gift. Sure I am that when I have read it I shall have to thank you again, and most readily to recommend it. You have taken the history of an interesting period. So many centuries under Pagan Rome and under Papal Rome, twin sisters.

'That the professed *teachers* of mankind should have

been the *deceivers* of mankind will form a melancholy chapter in the history of our world. Yet so it has been—to wit,—Brahmins among the Indians, Moulvies among the Mahometans, Rabbis among the Jews, and Priests among the Christians.

'Where the Scriptures are unknown or neglected, error must prevail. The Bible is the only infallible book of faith and practice. The opposition of the Church of Rome to the study of it, in itself proves that she is no longer a Church of Christ; and yet we hope that numbers of Romanists, after all, trust only in the Saviour,—and so will help to fill His kingdom.

'We are praying that Ireland may obtain increase of light. God bless you in all your labours to win sinners to the Saviour, and to lead believers to adorn His doctrine. Many thanks for the sweet text which you have sent to old eighty-nine.—Yours ever affectionately,

'WM. MARSH.'

He has more than once described the difference between a true and false religion, by standing before us, first as a teacher of a false religion with a closed Bible behind him, saying, 'You are to believe what I tell you, and be satisfied with the voice of the church.' Then coming forward as a teacher of the true religion, with the Bible wide open, he would say, 'Believe nothing that I teach you which you cannot prove for yourselves by most certain warrant from Holy Scripture.'

TO MISS MANN.

'. . . "The accuser of the brethren," in order to harass and hinder them, brings past sins before them again and again, after they have been repented of, and washed away in the blood of the Lamb, and forsaken. But they were all foreknown and pardoned when the Saviour said, "It is finished."

'"Only believe." The plan for us is,—Believe and be at peace; believe and love; believe and work; believe and suffer; believe and die; believe and go to heaven. "Lord, increase our faith!"

'One of the old divines said, when on a dying-bed, "A list of all my sins was presented to me. I knew it was done by the enemy; so I said, Write at the bottom, 'The blood of Jesus Christ cleanseth from *all sin;*' and the temptation to despair fled away."—Yours truly,

'WM. MARSH.'

The two following letters, although they have found a place here considerably beyond their date, could scarcely be omitted without loss:—

TO THE LATE COLONEL JACOB, BOMBAY ARTILLERY, ON THE DEATH OF HIS WIFE, WHICH TOOK PLACE ONLY A YEAR BEFORE HIS OWN.

'RECTORY, BECKENHAM, *March* 18.

'DEAR COLONEL JACOB,—I have known what it is to be turned out of Paradise, and can indeed sympathize with you. All I could say for some time was, "Thou art righteous, O Lord!" but when I could reflect upon the happiness of the departed, the grief was a little assuaged.

'How difficult it is not to look down into the grave when it is actually open—yea, and oftentimes after that; but she is not there. Wherever Paradise is, there are the blessed dead. We are therefore taught to look upward.

'I have just been preaching on Psalm xciv. 19: "In the multitude of my thoughts within me, Thy comforts delight my soul." *1st*, The state of mind here described. *2d*, The consolation afforded.

'I will only send you some of the latter.

'Sorrow may not be speedily removed, but it shall be alleviated by covenant truths and promises: By positive assurances of good from all events; and by the prospect of our future rest.

'God has loved His people with an everlasting love. Therefore all His arrangements for time have a reference to their good in eternity.

'But the Comforter alone can truly comfort (Prov. xxv. 20).

'May that Eternal Spirit bring every alleviating and consolatory thought to your mind.

'Tears, indeed, are not forbidden. It was at a grave that—"Jesus wept." HE can sympathize with you.

'God help us all to look forward to His kingdom, in which tears are for ever wiped away.—Yours very truly,

'WM. MARSH.'

TO THE LATE HONOURABLE MRS. MACKENZIE, ON THE DEATH OF HER LAST SURVIVING SON, AGED TWENTY-ONE.

'DEAR MRS. MACKENZIE,—What can I say to comfort you? Dear Frank came of age, and was immediately put in possession of his estate in Paradise. Follow him there in thought, as you will at the appointed time in person. Then also you will see what he has escaped in this world of trial, sin, and suffering.

'Some live a long life in a short time. It was so with him. Though not in age, yet in grace; he was "like a shock of corn that cometh in, in his season:"—

> "To such we'll follow on,
> Leaning on Jesus all the way,
> Who on our hearts lets down a ray
> Of comfort from His Throne."

'Perhaps faith could never be fully exercised, if circumstances we suppose improbable under the government of love, did not arise. "If thou hadst been here, my brother had not died." A natural thought. But we know the reason why Lazarus died, and though indeed the veil was very soon removed in that case, yet, it is but a little while and the veil will be removed in other cases.

'I was glad darling Katie was well enough to go at once to Cambridge. She found in your dear daughter a remarkable example of faith and resignation. The good Lord comfort you all, and give you bright views of the coming re-union—the coming glory of the Lord and all His people.—With hearty sympathy, yours very affectionately, WM. MARSH.'

CHAPTER XVII.

'WITHIN SIGHT OF THE CITY.'

'The Celestial City is full in my view. Its glories have shone upon me, its breezes fan me, its odours are wafted to me, its sounds strike upon my ears, and its spirit is breathed into my heart. Nothing separates me from it but the River of Death, which now appears but as a rill, that may be crossed at a step.'

Payson.

'WITHIN SIGHT OF THE CITY.'

At midsummer of 1864, Mr. French, whose services my father had highly appreciated for his parish, was appointed to a church in Cheltenham. The following extract from his farewell letter will show how deeply he, on his part, had valued the association with my father:—

'My dear Dr. Marsh,—I do thank you most sincerely for all the fatherly kindness and consideration you have shown me since I became your curate. And I trust my ministry, whether long or short, may ever bear the impression of Beddington and Beckenham,—the Bethany and Bethphage, I would fain believe, the blessed Lord would have chosen had He preached to London instead of to Jerusalem.'

The glowing beauty of the cloudless summer of that year seemed to be reflected about him. Never had we seen his face so brilliant in colouring and expression—never had the charm of his conversation been more rich and sparkling—never had his heart of love so poured forth its heavenly warmth and tenderness.

All the lingering symptoms of his long illness had been mercifully removed, and we only knew how fragile was the life just verging on its ninetieth year, by the increasing transparency and beauty of his face, just as our hearts faintly foretold his nearness to heaven by looks and tones and ways too lovely for earth.

More than ever he was the centre of delight to his family. Every hour seemed to have suffered loss which was passed away from him. Yet his presence, with his own close and evident communing with his Saviour, his earnest charges to all to work while it is day, and his warm sympathy and fervent prayers for blessing in every attempt to serve that Master, stimulated those about him to fresh efforts in such service.

The home circle was frequently enlarged by the visits of those whom we knew would especially value the privilege of seeing him, and hearing him converse. Amongst these, the youngest daughter of his valued friend the late Mr. Hardy, M.P. for Bradford, well known for his noble Christian character, clear scriptural views, and steadfast Protestantism, was staying at the rectory for part of that summer. The youngest sister of Hedley Vicars came to pay a farewell visit before leaving England with her husband, the Rev. Frederick Tayler, who had been appointed Head of the College of Perth in Australia. The young clergyman, whose frank and manly character at once attracted my father, beheld with admiration and delight the aged saint who had entered the land of Beulah, 'where the sun shineth night and day;' and just before they sailed he wrote, that the memory of that face would ever be a call to them to 'serve the Lord with gladness' in their distant home. The daughter of Lord Wriothesley Russell had asked to bring a friend who had been educated at a school in her father's parish, and was one of the members of his Bible class. After preparing her for confirmation, he had watched with hopefulness her growing interest in the things of God; but now, when she was returning to her home, with her heart still wavering between the world and Christ, it occurred to his devoted Christian wife and daughter that it might be the turning-point of her life if she could see how bright and beautiful was the sunset light of a day—the morning, noon, and evening of which had alike been spent in the Lord's vineyard. The answer to their prayers was granted; for, during the visit, that young heart surrendered itself to the Saviour's call.

The evenings were chiefly passed around my father's arm-chair in the drawing-room; and often he would lay down his book, and hold his listeners entranced by anecdotes of his early friends and early days, and of wonders wrought by the grace of God, all told with an animation and charm which carried his hearers into the very centre of the scenes he described.

Then he would pause for a time and resume his reading, and again his rejoicing spirit would break forth in singing some of the hymns of praise he loved so well.

It was his wish, with reference to his birthday gathering, that this year there should be connected with it a call to his clerical brethren, to meet specially for prayer and addresses on the subject of the Coming of the Lord. Several laymen were also invited, and the day fixed for it was Tuesday the 19th of July, the eve of his birthday. When we recall the thought and prayer with which he arranged the plans for both these meetings, it seems to us now that there must have mingled with the gladness with which he looked forward to the festival, a solemn yet joyful presentiment that it was to be his last anniversary on earth.

The following was the form of invitation which he sent for the 19th:—

'"THE NIGHT IS FAR SPENT, THE DAY IS AT HAND."

'We intend, therefore, in obedience to the apostolic command, to "assemble ourselves together, and to exhort one another, so much the more as we see the day approaching."

'Will you join our gathering here at half-past three o'clock in the afternoon of Tuesday, the 19th instant? And, in the meanwhile, unite with us in fervent prayer, that the power of the Lord may be present with us, that we may be "filled with joy and with the Holy Ghost," "looking for and hasting unto the coming of the day of God."—Your faithful servant and brother in the Lord,

'WILLIAM MARSH.'

Hearty and numerous were the responses to this invitation, and those who were present will not soon forget the power with which he spoke that day; the clear testimony to the blessedness of resting alone on the finished work of Christ, of walking in conscious, unbroken communion with Him, and of looking for His coming glory; nor the pouring out of his soul in prayer, and the sudden burst of sacred song—the overflow of the joy with which he 'drew water from the wells of salvation.'

After alluding to the more widely diffused expectation of the near Coming of the Lord, and to the numerous calculations of dates in the prophecies which converge in the present decade, he went on to say—'But be that as it may, we are expressly told by an apostle, that the First and Second Advents of the Messiah are the great subjects of Holy Writ, for the Spirit of Christ was in all the prophets, testifying beforehand of the sufferings of Christ and of the glory that should follow. For what end did the Redeemer come into this world? He came to glorify God, to magnify the law, to make "a full, perfect, and sufficient sacrifice" for the sins of the whole world, to offer a free pardon to guilty man, and so to take out of the way every obstacle which hindered his coming to God for pardon, peace, and grace here, and for glory hereafter.

'At the First Advent of our Lord and Saviour Jesus Christ, it appears to me that He came especially to exercise the office of a prophet, as the great Prophet that should come into the world.

'Since His ascension into heaven, His work as a prophet being ended, He has assumed the office of a priest; the forerunner is for us entered within the veil, "even Jesus, made an High Priest for ever." By His intercession, He keeps the way open to the throne of grace, and therefore mercy and grace can flow freely to us.

'Some, alas, have a very imperfect view of the way in

which God deals with man. They have not got a proper understanding of either His justice or His mercy. They look upon the work of Christ as accomplished in the perfect example which He left to us by His life, and overlook the purpose of His death as the sacrifice for the sins of the world, that He might be at the same time "a just God and a Saviour."

'Doubtless the blessed Redeemer left us an example that we should follow His steps; and the more watchfully, prayerfully, and faithfully we follow in that blessed pathway, the fuller will be our peace, the brighter will be our light, the wider will be our usefulness. But equally without doubt His death took place that we might be pardoned and accepted through it alone, and have life and peace in time, and glory in eternity.

'A poor man who had sought and found salvation through Jesus Christ, and was rejoicing in Him, was asked by a friend whether he did not fear that his soul would be in danger if he should lose his joy. He replied, "Never! for I am on the Rock, and though I may tremble on the Rock, the Rock never trembles under me."

'What a beautiful view is given to us of the perfection of the work of our blessed Redeemer, in that He could say with His dying breath, "IT IS FINISHED."

'Dear friends, on that short saying *I rest all my hopes of eternal life*, and I beseech you all to do the same.

'But now let me speak to you of the Second Advent, which is the Christian's great hope (as the First Advent is the foundation of his faith); for then Christ will assume His office of King; and not till then will the great enemy of souls, the "accuser of the brethren," be bound, error be banished, sin be subdued, and creation cease to groan; because at His coming He will establish the kingdom of truth, righteousness, and peace. What Christian is there who, believing this, when he hears the Saviour's voice saying, "Surely I come quickly," will not reply, "Amen, even so, come, Lord Jesus!"

'The First Advent is the source of all our hopes of eternal life; but when we have been admitted freely into the kingdom of glory through the Saviour's obedience unto death, we shall find, at the Second Advent, that there is nothing that we have either done or suffered for Him that will not be graciously remembered, and even rewarded by Him.

'"Therefore, my beloved brethren, be ye steadfast, unmoveable, always abounding in the work of the Lord, forasmuch as ye know that your labour is not in vain in the Lord."

'Be steadfast in this faith, that Christ died for our sins.

'Be unmoveable from this hope, that through His resurrection all who believe on Him shall have a joyful resurrection, when all sins and all infirmities shall be gone for ever. For "So also is the resurrection of the dead. It is sown in corruption; it is raised in incorruption. It is sown in dishonour; it is raised in glory. It is sown in weakness; it is raised in power. It is sown a natural body; it is raised a spiritual body."

'Lastly, be always abounding in the work of the Lord. The fruit of such work may be, and often is, seen even here, and most certainly shall be seen hereafter; for "the day shall declare it," and the reward shall be reaped, for "ye know that your labour is not in vain in the Lord."

'I remember a good minister, who said, when leaving a country parish for a charge in London, "I do not know that I have been a blessing to one soul in this place." But not long after this he received a letter, signed by a hundred and twenty persons, thanking him for the good they had derived from his ministry.

'A faithful and prayerful discharge of religious, moral, and social duties and services can never be "in vain in the Lord." This is illustrated in His parable of the talents (Luke xix. 12-28).

'Oh what a Saviour is ours, who forgets our sins! "I, even I, am He that blotteth out thy transgressions for mine own sake, and will not remember thy sins." "The blood of Jesus Christ cleanseth us from all sin."

'Oh what a Saviour is ours, who never forgets our services, however poor and imperfect! "Verily I say unto you, Inasmuch as ye have done it unto one of the least of these my brethren, ye have done it unto Me."

'Let us then diligently "search the Scriptures," which make known to us such a Saviour and such a Master.

'Trust in the finished work of salvation accomplished by Christ at His First Advent, and look for the glory to be revealed at His Second Advent; that, when He says, "Surely I come quickly!" you may be ready to reply, "Amen: even so, come, Lord Jesus."'

The 20th of July was celebrated as usual by a large gathering of poor and rich, all invited to an early tea on the rectory lawn. It was one of the sunniest days of that brilliant summer; friends gathered around him, from far and near, to wish him joy on entering his ninetieth year; and nothing seemed to be wanting to add to the interest and grace of the scene.

The first visitors who arrived were two who held places very near his heart, the Duchess of Sutherland and Lord Shaftesbury. Two years earlier the Duchess had made his acquaintance, and from that time had ever been regarded by him with tender and prayerful interest. On his preceding birthday, she had brought him a beautiful copy of the "Bible, with Commentary wholly biblical," which was treasured by him with special value. The charm of her bright and gentle presence from time to time, with her open communication and warm sympathy on the subjects nearest his heart, combined with her unvarying thoughtfulness about him in absence, were amongst the pleasures which a loving Father had provided so richly for his aged servant to enjoy in his last years out of Paradise.

The next who arrived was his valued old friend, the Rev. Henry Venn, of the Church Missionary Society, with the first black bishop, just then on the eve of his departure for his diocese of Abbeokuta and the Niger. To him my father said, 'If a man desire the office of a bishop, what saith the Word of God that he desireth?—a large income?—a palace?—to be called "my lord?" No! "he desireth a *good work*." Work for Christ is the true honour of the bishop!' And turning to Mr. Venn he said, 'You, dear brother, have large opportunities of working for Christ; continue to work zealously, faithfully, prayerfully. Work while it is day.'[1]

Between three and four hundred women and girls were assembled round the tea-tables on the lawn; and on the terrace which overlooked it, their aged rector, in his wheel-chair, was surrounded by others of his parishioners, and new friends, and old friends,—some of whom had not seen him for many a year; amongst these were Lord and Lady Mayo[2] and their daughter; a beloved sister of Hedley Vicars, with her husband, the Rev. Leonard Burrows of Rugby; Mr. Goodhart; Mr. Auriol, and several other of my father's clerical brethren, besides many of the laity, gathered around him. Behind his chair, in their scarlet turbans and dark-blue flowing robes, stood two Afghans;[3] and on his right hand stood the Archbishop of Canterbury, now benevolently enjoying the scene, again looking with reverence on the holy and radiant face of the patriarch by his side, and then, at his request, commencing the service of the day with prayer.

[1] From a letter from Mr. Venn, who also wrote of this interview as follows:—'Upon my rejoining Bishop Crowther, after seeing your beloved and revered grandfather, he said to me that the venerable man appeared so ready for his entrance into glory, that he almost expected it might take place that moment.'

[2] Since that time Lady Mayo has also entered into rest, saying on her dying bed, 'Lord Jesus, take me quickly to Thyself! I long to be with Thee.'

[3] Ghoolam, one of these Afghans, had formed such a reverent attachment to my father, that when the tidings reached him that he had passed into the presence of his Saviour, he exclaimed, 'His religion shall now be my religion, his God shall be my God; for I must go where he is, and see his face again!'

After this, many voices joined in the hymn which thus begins,—

'Lord, I hear of showers of blessing
Thou art scattering full and free,
Showers the thirsty land refreshing,
Let some droppings fall on me,
Even me.'

The singing was accompanied by a harmonium, which had been placed on the terrace, and was played by Mr. Hawkins (afterwards ordained to the curacy of Beckenham), who had won my father's affectionate regard from the days when he was one of the first to propose the Bible-reading amongst the cadets at Addiscombe, and, as a sub-officer, he opened his room for it.

Every sound was hushed, when the first words were heard from my father's lips, as he began:

'Beloved friends,—including all my dear parishioners here,—One of the first martyrs, at his trial, said, "*Eighty and six* years have I served Christ, and He has never forsaken me, and I will not forsake Him in my old age." And, faithful to his word, he died a martyr.

'Although I cannot number so many years in the service of that blessed Master, this I can say, *seventy-one* years ago a faithful and revered minister of Christ taught me to love my Bible, showed me that it was the Word of God, and the only book in our world which could teach us the way of salvation.

'That man was Mr. Cadogan. The Lord Chancellor of that day—Thurlow—passing through Reading, heard from the landlord of the Crown Hotel that the vicar of St. Giles's Church was just dead. The living was in his gift;

and Lord Thurlow made up his mind at once as to the disposal of it. Early the next morning he went to Caversham Park, then the residence of Lord Cadogan, for whom he inquired. The servant replied, "You can't see his lordship yet; but you may sit down in the hall, if you like."

'So the Lord Chancellor sat down; and, after some time had passed, Lord Cadogan came through the hall, and started with surprise as he recognised his unexpected guest.

'"Why, my Lord Chancellor! how came you here?"

'"Your servant gave me leave to sit down in your hall."

'So, after a good laugh together, they went into the breakfast-room. The Lord Chancellor then said, "I heard that the vicar of St. Giles's was dead, and I thought it might be pleasant to your family and to your son if I offered him the living."

'It was accepted. And that was the manner in which Mr. Cadogan's ministry was brought to Reading. I have thought very often of him lately, because he taught me to love my Bible, and to believe that it made known salvation to fallen man; and from that time a friendship was formed between us which lasted till his death. At his first entrance on the ministry he did not so clearly know the way of salvation as he afterwards learned and preached it; but he had great earnestness and zeal on the subject of religion, and that is a good beginning.

'A former acquaintance wished to lend him the works of Paine and Voltaire; he wrote him word in reply, that he had not yet done with Moses and the prophets. An admirable determination, that! And we shall never have done with Moses and the prophets, because they are "the servants of the Most High God, and show unto us the way of salvation;" afterwards more fully developed in the New Testament.

'On the death of Mr. Cadogan, a tablet was erected to his memory in St. Giles's Church. Bacon, who was chosen as the sculptor, begged permission to write the epitaph. Having given the name and date, he carved a pillar with these words upon it, "I will make him a pillar in the temple of my God." And on the tablet he thus described Mr. Cadogan as a minister: "Christ was his theme, his refuge, and his joy."

'It was this that gave energy to his ministry, and success to his labours. His last words were, "I die in the faith of Jesus Christ, and in love to all mankind, and in special love"—here his voice failed; it was supposed he was going to add, "to all Christian brethren."

'I have paraphrased that epitaph thus, "Christ was his theme as a minister, his refuge as a sinner, his joy as a believer."

'I need not dwell on "Christ his theme as a minister," before you, my beloved friends in the ministry, who are here to-day, because I believe Christ *is* your theme. But let me say a few words to all present on "Christ his refuge as a sinner." Dear friends, what other refuge have we? The law of God condemns us. Under that condemnation we must be banished from the Divine presence. But Jesus Christ is the refuge, "the shadow of a great rock in a weary land." By faith I come to my Saviour, and I find He has fulfilled the law for me; He has died for me; He has done all for me; and as it was with John Bunyan's pilgrim when he came to the foot of the cross, the burden of sin falls off and rolls into the Saviour's grave.

'Never enter any other refuge, whatever it may be, for all others are false. JESUS ALONE must be your refuge. In Him you will find the propitiation for the broken law of God, and all the righteousness which its precepts demand. I have no other hope, in the prospect of death, but in the Saviour's words, "IT IS FINISHED." When He uttered them, He ratified the promises, embodied the types, fulfilled the prophecies, and yielded a perfect obedience unto death, which glorified God and brought pardon and peace to man.

'Are we not in the habit of thinking of our Saviour as a great way off? It is not so. He is near, He is present —a refuge in temptation, under trial, and in the hour of death.

'But it was not only said of Mr. Cadogan that Christ was his refuge as a sinner, but also that "Christ was his joy, as a believer."

'And now I can blame my own ministry, doubting whether I have dwelt enough on this truth, that Christ brings *present* happiness. Christianity is for the present happiness of believers, as well as for their future joy in eternity.

'St. Paul writes to the Romans: "Being justified by faith, we *have* peace with God through our Lord Jesus

Christ;" and prays for them that they may "be *filled* with all joy and peace in believing, and *abound* in hope by the power of the Holy Ghost." And he thus exhorts the Philippian Christians: "*Rejoice* in the Lord *alway;* and again I say, Rejoice."

'I do not say that the assurance of hope is *essential* to salvation; but it is a very blessed privilege, and one that should be diligently sought after.

'There are two remarkable passages on this subject in the inspired writings of St. John; one in his Gospel, the other in his first Epistle.

'In the 31st verse of the 20th chapter, he assigns the reason for writing his Gospel:—

'"These are written, that ye might believe that Jesus is the Christ, the Son of God; and that believing ye might have life through His name."

'And in the 13th verse of the 5th chapter of his first Epistle, St. John addresses those who have believed, and tells them it is on their account that he has written the Epistle, as supplemental to the Gospel.

'"These things have I written unto you that believe on the name of the Son of God; that ye may *know* that ye *have* eternal life." Know it for your support amidst trials and persecutions, in the time of sorrow and in the hour of death; and that you may persevere in that blessed faith, knowing that "believing on the name" of our Lord Jesus Christ you *have* eternal life."[1]

[1] During the last few years of his life he always kept beside him a supply of the Bible Society's small edition of St. John's Gospel, and to each of his visitors he gave a copy, with this note written on the margin, by the 31st verse of chap. xx.: 'See 1 John v. 13.'

'Dear friends, the three cardinal graces of Christianity —Faith, Hope, and Love—have a direct tendency to promote our happiness.

'As sinners, *faith* leads us to the Saviour, and will divest us of all slavish fear.

'Whilst passing through a world of sorrow and trial, *hope* points us to Heaven as the world of uninterrupted joy and eternal rest.

'And sure I am (for in selfishness there can be no true happiness), that in the exercise of *love* to God and man there is real and lasting pleasure.

'Thus it can be clearly proved that faith in an atoning, pardoning Saviour, working by love, which is Scriptural Christianity, brings present happiness, as well as insures future bliss. Let me exhort you, therefore, diligently to "search the Scriptures," and earnestly to pray for the Holy Spirit, that, through His grace and power, you may live and die in the exercise of Faith, and Hope, and Love.

'Thus our Church would lead us to pray, in the words of one of her beautiful collects—

'"Almighty and everlasting God, give unto us the increase of faith, hope, and charity; and that we may obtain that which Thou dost promise, make us to love that which Thou dost command; through Jesus Christ our Lord. Amen."'

A few of the guests were obliged to leave early; and amongst them Lord Shaftesbury: not wishing to be called upon to make a speech, he was keeping out of sight. 'But I cannot let him go without his saying a few words to my people; and he is such an old friend, I must hear his voice again,' urged my father; and when, unable to resist the plea, Lord Shaftesbury came forward, and heard the entreaty, 'Do speak to them; tell them to read and love their Bibles;' he hesitated no longer, and gave them a brief and impressive address on the priceless value of the Scriptures.

After some hymns had been sung, Mr. Auriol and Mr. Goodhart, followed by Colonel Travers and Mr. Blackwood, spoke words of counsel and comfort to those assembled; and the meeting was concluded with prayer by Mr. O'Rorke and Mr. Gordon.

No shadow fell on our hearts amidst the gathering shades of that lovely summer's evening, foretelling that that day five weeks the 'hoary head,' which was our 'crown of glory,' would be laid upon the bed of death; and that his next birthday would be when 'an entrance was ministered unto him abundantly into the everlasting kingdom of our Lord and Saviour Jesus Christ.'

The following letter, though not received until some time later, may be inserted here:—

FROM H. PHILLRICK, ESQ.

'To me his memory is hallowed with such an elevation of Christian excellence as to be unrivalled. I never knew any one so altogether rooted in Christ—so altogether growing up and flourishing in Christ—as he was from first to last. I thank God for his holy teachings in my boyhood, and for his lovely life, which (as it seems to me) would need but little transformation to become that of the risen saint, with the exchange only of his earthly crown of joy, for the crown of glory that fadeth not away.'

An anecdote in the following letter, illustrative of his benevolence to animals, recalled to us his kindness to a white cat, the gift of one of his friends at Beddington. The little creature had attached itself so faithfully to him that it would watch from sunrise at the door of his room, ready to seize the first opportunity of springing in there to establish itself as his companion for the day. When he was dangerously ill, and scarcely able to bear any weight, it still maintained its accustomed place on his coverlet, because he refused to allow its comfort to be interrupted for his own:—

'BRETHERTON PARSONAGE, 10*th Oct.* 1864.

'ACCEPT my grateful thanks, for the remembrance of your dear father, whose loveliness by nature and grace is afresh brought before me. I have known not a few of God's best servants in our day, but—during forty years, since I first saw him—I have never yet come across any man to be measured with your now sainted and happy father for winning sweetness, heavenly-mindedness, and entire annihilation of self. . . . One day, when I called upon him, I found him in his study, but not in his accustomed place; for his favourite cat was asleep in his own easy-chair. He said to me, with that gentleness so peculiar to him, "Mr. Wilde, please not to disturb him."

It was so like him,—a tender word for dumb animals even, as well as for all his fellow-creatures, old and young, who happened to fall in his way.

'I had learned to esteem and admire his pure and exalted character long before I personally knew him. Mutual friends (amongst them the late Miss Hancock of Norwich, useful in her day and generation) prepared me for those rare excellences and attractions I met with in dear Mr. Marsh, while I was his curate in Birmingham. If all Christian ministers were of like mind and mould with that charming man, *how* the Gospel would win its way in the world, and its power, its wisdom, and its grace, so developed, would draw others to the Saviour.—Believe me, very faithfully yours, RALPH WILDE.'

It was during a wakeful night that the following little paraphrase of the Lord's Prayer was composed by him, and written down from his dictation the next morning:—

'*Our Father,*—
By right of creation,
By gracious adoption.

'*Which art in heaven,*—
The home of Thy angels,
The seat of Thy glory.

'*Hallowed be Thy Name,*—
By the thoughts of our hearts;
By the words of our lips;
By the actions of our lives.

'*Thy kingdom come,*—
Of Providence, to protect us;
Of Grace, to refine us;
Of Glory, to crown us.

'*Thy will be done on earth, as it is in heaven,*—
Submissively, cheerfully,
And, finally, perfectly.

'*Give us this day our daily bread,*—
Of temporal things for our bodies,
Of spiritual things for our souls.

'*And forgive us our trespasses,*—
Against the precepts of Thy law,
And the grace of Thy Gospel.

'*As we forgive them who trespass against us,*
In imitation of Thy love,
And to the glory of true religion.

'*And lead us not into temptation,*—
Of such honours, riches, or pleasures
As might war against the soul.

'*But deliver us from evil,*—
Of Satan to deceive us;
Of sin to defile us,

'*For Thine is the kingdom,*—
Of Providence and Grace.

'*The power,*—
To establish it.

'*And the glory,*—
Of all good.

'*For ever, and for ever: Amen,*—
So let it be;
So it is;
So it shall be.'

'By this Prayer of our Lord—
The Father bless,
The Son adore,
The Spirit praise,
For evermore.
Amen, and Amen.'

Towards the end of July, his eldest daughter, with her husband and children, was going abroad for a time, and she was able to leave with comparatively little anxiety, as he appeared remarkably well. On her birthday, which she usually spent with him, as it occurred within four days of his own, he gave her a travelling desk, and said, as he placed it in her hand, 'I was going to make you a speech, but Moses shall speak for me;' and then quoted Numbers vi. 24-26. It was his farewell blessing, for they were never to meet again in this life.

The days of that summer glided by, each one brighter and happier than that which had gone before. On Sunday the 14th of August, he seemed if possible to be even in fuller enjoyment than ever of the day so dear to his heart. His awaking was always bright and instantaneous, and generally announced by some morning song of praise. This time it was—

'To-day He rose and left the dead,
And Satan's empire fell;
To-day the saints His triumphs spread,
And all His wonders tell.'

It was the Sunday when the early communion was administered in the church; and, before we left the house to join in it, he gave us his blessing. On our return, he said, 'I was with you in spirit. I read the service here; it is a beautiful expression of depths of humiliation and heights of adoration. Our worship can take no higher flight than this ascription—rising above all thanksgiving connected with ourselves—"We give Thee thanks for THY GREAT GLORY." You find the same note struck by the Psalmist, "Give thanks at the remembrance of HIS HOLINESS!"'

He read, as had always been his custom whenever prevented from joining in public worship, the morning service inclusive of the psalms and lessons, with the utmost devotion of countenance and manner. Afterwards, he returned to the reading of the Bible, with which he had begun the day. Since he had been deprived of 'going to the house of God in company,' he had made Sunday a day for feasting on the Holy Scriptures, spending at least four hours in reading them; intent as a schoolboy on a new story, scarcely able to lay down the book. Yet, if any one came in, desirous of conversing with him on sacred subjects, he would put it away for the time, not only with his wonted gentle courtesy, but with thankful readiness to take up any work which the Lord had appointed for him.

On that Sunday evening, he was in gay spirits; and

when the family party had assembled round the tea-table, he said to a beloved young grand-daughter who had been spending the summer with him, 'Now, dear little Agnes, you shall hear a celebrated vocalist!' And then he sang a Hebrew chant:

> 'Ail bene, Ail bene,
> Bene, bene, beth cara.'

'Lord build, Lord build Thy house speedily! even in our day.' Then he resumed his reading; but shortly afterwards, with clasped hands and upraised eyes, he sang again, with wonderful power of voice, part of the Hallelujah chorus, commencing with the words, 'King of Kings, and Lord of Lords,' and 'He shall reign for ever.' Then passing, with the rapid transition of thought, from the coronation of the King of kings to the fulfilment of His promise, that His redeemed shall sit down with Him on His Throne, he sang the hymn beginning—

> 'There is a land of pure delight,
> Where saints immortal reign.'

Monday morning was spent as usual in reading and writing, but in the afternoon he suffered from faintness and oppression of breath; still the night brought refreshing sleep, and on Tuesday the 16th he was able to go out in his wheel-chair, to take what he called his 'grand tour' round the garden and field; and in the evening he remained in the drawing-room later than usual. Well do those who were around him remember how beautiful a picture he looked, as he sat in his own arm-chair, dressed in his sky-blue wrapper, reading a large New Testament beneath the shaded lamp which cast a glow of light upon the noble head, with its crown of silver hair, resting against a crimson cushion; while, for a background, on the white wall, hung coloured sketches of Jerusalem, and of scenery in the Holy Land; and beside him, through the bay window, surrounded by roses and jessamine, the rising moon could just be seen above the trees. Presently he put down his book, and began to sing—

'Israel, thy Creator bless,
And with joyful tongue express,
That His mercies far extend,
And His bounty knows no end.'

Then, as if his heart was too full of praise to restrain itself, again his voice rose with

'Salvation, oh! the joyful sound,
'Tis pleasure to our ears,
A sovereign balm for every wound,
A cordial for our fears.'

And he sang the whole hymn, ending with the chorus—

'Glory, honour, praise, and power,
Be unto the Lamb for ever,
Jesus Christ is our Redeemer,
Hallelujah, Amen.'

And yet once more he sang aloud his favourite Hebrew melody, 'Lord, build Thy house speedily.'

There was no undertone, in the glad music of that summer night, foreboding that it was the last of long years of happy family evenings, and that none other like it remained for us on earth. Little we thought, as the beloved voice sank into silence, that his next song of praise would be sung with 'angels and archangels, and all the company of heaven.'

'The twilight of a Sabbath eve
Was deep'ning in the west,
As one by one a household met
To share its sacred rest.

Around the window where they sat,
Beneath the moon's fair light,
Hung the bright stars of jessamine,
And trailing blossoms white.

But evermore each eye was turn'd
Where one, in honour'd age,
Mused in his tranquil solitude
Upon an open page.

For he who long his Master served,
In combat undismay'd,
Borne from the heat of battle now
Upon his shield was laid!

And in this patient waiting kept,
So long he tarries still!
"Till his Lord come," we almost said,
"What if it be His will!"

A light upon his brow serene,
Its fullest radiance beam'd,
And on the crown of silver hair,
Which like a glory seem'd.

But brighter far than all, the glance
Of calm, yet deep content,
And the sweet smile whose sparkling play
Like sunshine came and went:

'While now he sang of Canaan's land,
And of its bowers of light,
And of the perfect day which fears
No darkening shades of night.

And yet in louder, fuller strains
He raised his joyful song;—
Then waved his hands with parting grace,
As if he blessed the throng.'[1]

BECKENHAM RECTORY,
August 1864.

[1] By the author of *Grace and Remembrance*.

CHAPTER XVIII.

'THROUGH THE FLOOD ON FOOT.'

. . . . . .

' So we went slowly down
To the river side,
Till we stood in the heavy shadows
By the wild black tide.

We could hear that the Lord was speaking
Deep words of grace ;
We could see their blessed reflection
Upon our father's face.

" Farewell !—I cannot fear.
Do *you* not see His grace ?"
And even as he spoke he turn'd
Again to the Master's face.

So they two went closer down
To the river side,
And stood in the heavy shadows
By the wild black tide.

But when the feet of the Lord
Were come to the waters dim,
They rose to stand on either hand,
And left a path for Him.

So they two passed over quickly
Towards the goal,
But the wistful longing gaze
Of the parting soul

Grew only more rapt and joyful
As he held the Master's hand ;
We think, or ever he was aware,
They were come to the Holy Land.'

. . . .

B. M.

'THROUGH THE FLOOD ON FOOT.'

On the morning of the 17th of August, my father awoke weak and weary; and as the day wore on, he became more ill, so that in the afternoon his daughter Matilda, whom he was accustomed playfully to call his 'chief doctor,' was sent for. Although there was no alarming symptom, he evidently felt that his end was drawing near, for he said to Mrs. Marsh, as she sat anxiously and tenderly watching by him, 'It is right you should be prepared, dearest, —this is dying.'

Thursday morning brought no improvement, and Mr. Skey was sent for from London. He came at once, and pronounced the illness to be very serious, but at the same time he gave us some hope that the wonderful power of rallying in his constitution might yet enable him to recover; and we, who had so often seen him given back from the very gates of death, in answer to our prayers, took comfort from this hope.

Notwithstanding great suffering and weakness, his spirit of loving consideration for all around him, and the bright playfulness of his disposition, shone out continually. He had a kind word for every one who came into his room.

To Mr. Skey he said, 'Dear friend, what a shadow that vanisheth away is the longest human life! But there *is* a heaven, and there *is* a Saviour. Seek that Saviour, and heaven is yours, and all is well.'

In the afternoon he received a letter from his eldest daughter from Germany, which he read with great interest, and then said to us, 'Do not let darling Mary be made anxious, and her holiday be spoilt.'

Yet we longed to telegraph to her, knowing how earnestly she would desire to be beside him in his illness; but no address had been given where letters could reach the travellers until Saturday, and we still leant upon the hope that by that time there might be a change for the better.

In the afternoon he was moaning frequently, as if in much pain; but whenever any one spoke to him, or even stood by his side, he answered in a cheerful voice, and with his own bright smile. From his deafness he did not know that his expressions of pain were audible, and evidently thought that by speaking cheerfully he could spare us the knowledge of his suffering.

During the night he slept very little, but though worn and weary, his heart was overflowing with love. When his youngest daughter was standing by him, he said, 'Stay where you are a minute, my darling, that I may see your face well. If I were only a second Sir Joshua Reynolds, I would paint it at once, that I might wear it always next my heart.'

On Friday, Lady Emma Dalzell, who had been almost as a daughter to him, came from Beckenham; and he asked tenderly after her brothers, especially one who was an invalid; for no suffering of his own caused him to forget the anxieties of others. Never did we hear him utter a complaint or murmur. His lips were ever full of thanksgiving, and praise was the constant occupation of his dying days as it had been of his long lifetime.

It is impossible to describe the change that came over the whole household as day by day his illness increased. All longed to be with him constantly, but while there was any hope that the precious life might be preserved, it was right that his room should be kept as quiet as possible. The door was left open; and those who sat in the drawing-room, listening sadly to the heavy breathing, felt the shadow of the gathering cloud darken their hearts. Yet even then we scarcely thought that in less than a week the whole heaven of our happy home would be 'black with clouds,' and its sun have set for ever.

He had frequently of late expressed his conviction that we were entering upon troublous times; and in one of his latest letters had dictated the following sentence:—'I am a Jeremiah about my Church and my country. The Church is on an inclined plane towards the precipice of Romish error, and there are some who seem to be patting her upon the back who are in reality pushing her downwards.' At another time, he said, 'Avoid all that symbolizes with Rome.' And then, with an expression of deep distress in his countenance, 'I pray for those who are within convent walls—those prisoners without crimes. The whole system is opposed to the revealed will of God.'

To Dr. Carpenter he said, 'Train up your children in

Bible knowledge, for a time of great trouble is at hand, and no other knowledge will enable them to stand in the day of trial and temptation.'

In the course of the afternoon he sent to his grand-daughter, who had kept out of his room a good deal that day, as the doctors had requested that only three should be there at one time, saying, 'Surely I have not seen you since 1764!' Adding, 'My darling, how I have loved you!—and how I have prayed for you!'

On Saturday night he scarcely slept at all, but seemed enjoying a rapt communion with his Saviour, often saying, half aloud, as if answering one who had spoken to him, 'My Saviour—my dear Saviour. Yes, my Lord, my blessed Saviour.'

The days and nights had passed so strangely with him from the want of sleep and of his usual occupations, that on Sunday morning he awoke, for the first time probably for more than seventy years, without knowing that it was the Lord's Day. It was not till the afternoon that he said to a faithful and devoted nurse, who had come over from Beckenham, 'Is this really Sunday? What a thoughtless man I am! I never spent such a Sunday as this before!' adding, with a smile, 'You had better send me out of the world, that I may learn how to keep a Sabbath!' But seeing her eyes fill with tears, he said, 'There is the eternal Sabbath, you know, which we shall all spend together;' and continued, as if speaking to himself, 'The dear Archbishop wrote to me from his dying bed that we should meet soon "where Sabbaths never end."' In the morning he had dictated a beautiful and animated letter to Mrs. Joseph Sturge, whose husband's life he was reading, concluding with the words: 'Oh! blessed brother and sister, how happy they must be in a world where they can neither see, nor feel, nor hear anything contrary to true happiness. And not only so, but where they realize the certainty that the blessed system is becoming universal. "For He must reign until He shall have put down all rule, and all authority and power" opposed to truth, righteousness, and peace.'

By Sunday night his deafness had increased so much that he could not even hear a word. He continued patiently and gratefully to take the food and medicine offered him; and though it was evidently with great effort that he swallowed it, he always had some playful and tender saying for those who brought it.

His grandson, Mackenzie Chalmers, walked from Beckenham in the afternoon, and received his fervent blessing; and in the evening one of his grand-daughters, Katherine Wathen, arrived, with her husband, to take leave of him. He welcomed them with one of his bright, loving smiles, and blessed them.

He had a few hours' sleep on Sunday night, and we felt that it was given in answer to the prayers offered up for him, from far and near, that day; for by this quiet sleep his sufferings were lessened. He awoke on Monday morning repeating the verse—

'Poor, guilty, weak, and helpless worm,
Into thine arms I fall;
Thou art my strength, my righteousness,
My Jesus, and my all.'

When the doctor arrived he told us that he feared a few days only remained of that blessed life. Again was his absent daughter telegraphed for, and we began to count the hours till the time when we thought it possible she might arrive.

During the day he spoke but seldom, as his voice was very hoarse. But now and then he repeated a text or a verse of a hymn; and once remarked, 'I like that pretty saying,—

> "Give me a place at Thy saints' feet,
> Or some fall'n angel's vacant seat."'

To his second daughter, who was standing by him, he said, 'My Matilda—my sister' (and then smiling at his child, he added, 'and *you* are *my Matilda* too) said, when she was dying, and her throat was closing,

> "My days of praise shall ne'er be past,
> While life, and thought, and being last,
> Or immortality endures."

'*My* throat is closing now, and I say also,

> "My days of praise shall ne'er be past."'

Several times in that day we believe that he was allowed to see one or more of the redeemed spirits, who would, we felt, be crowding down to the brink of the river to watch for and to welcome him; for he spoke more than once to our mother—the beloved of his early days—saying, 'Maria, darling;' and two or three times smiled, and waved his hand towards the foot of the bed, when none whom *our* eyes could see were standing there.

As he tenderly bade his son good-night, he gave him

the texts, 'I will bless thee, and thou shalt be a blessing,' and 'Ye are my witnesses, saith the Lord of hosts.'

Dr. Carpenter came about ten o'clock, and after he had seen him, told us that this night would be a crisis in his illness, and a most anxious one. As he was unable to remain, we asked him to send Dr. Lanchester, one of his partners, who came at once, and whose attentions were a great comfort to the beloved one.

At twenty minutes to twelve he suddenly spoke, but in a voice so strange, *so distant*, that had we not known the words he was saying we could scarcely have understood them, and repeated the following hymn:—

'When all thy mercies, O my God!
My rising soul surveys,
Transported with the view, I'm lost
In wonder, love, and praise.

Ten thousand, thousand precious gifts
My daily thanks employ;
Nor is the least a thankful heart,
That tastes these gifts with joy.

Through every period of my life
Thy goodness I'll proclaim;
And after death, in distant worlds,
Resume the glorious theme.

Through all eternity to Thee
A joyful song I'll raise;
But, oh! eternity's too short
To utter all thy praise.'

Closing with the sentence, 'When I consider the works of God, in providence and in grace, they seem marvellous.'

His grand-daughter was waiting to write down any words that might fall from his lips, to be our treasures when we should hear that voice no more—but no words came—the silence of death had begun already; he was gradually being withdrawn from all intercourse with earth, for he could no longer hear our voices, or speak to us.

About six o'clock on Tuesday morning he signed for a slate, and when Mr. O'Rorke handed it to him, he wrote the following words with trembling hand:—'Tell the clergy to preach Christ, to live Christ, to serve Christ, and they shall joy and praise in eternity.' He could not speak, but we could tell by the movement of his lips that he several times repeated the words 'MY SAVIOUR.' He also wrote two or three short sentences on the slate: 'Do not sorrow, you are kept, etc.,' for he had not strength to finish the text. From having had little or no sleep, he thought it was the middle of the day, while it was still early morning, and, with his usual thoughtfulness for others, wrote on the slate, 'Dr. Lanchester, luncheon.'

The evening drew on, and with every sound of wheels our hopes pictured his eldest daughter's arrival, while we continued to pray (but it was *all* that we dared to ask *now*) that the Lord would leave him just long enough to see her, for we felt that for ourselves we could let him go that hour, rather than see him suffer, or detain him for our selfish pleasure from the sight of Him for whom his soul thirsted.

'A pilgrim for his new abode
  Is making preparation,
Who long hath closely walk'd with God
  In joy and tribulation.
Now faint and weary with his load,
He pants to reach the blest abode
  For which he long hath striven:

His soul is thirsting, God, for Thee;
O grant him, grant him soon to see
Thy glorious face in heaven.

Lord Jesus, through death's gloomy night
This pilgrim soon must wander;
Light of the world, be Thou his light,
Uphold, and guide him yonder.
In life he walk'd with Thee; in death
Do Thou receive his parting breath,
Sweet rest of weary mortals;
Thou wast his help in life; be Thou
His help and comforter e'en now,
Through heaven's eternal portals.'

At midnight the final change commenced; and for only one more night the privilege was ours of watching beside and ministering to him who was our joy, our crown, our glory. His daughter printed in large letters to catch his failing sight, the words, 'A pillow for my heart's beloved.' 'GOD IS LOVE.' (He says), 'I have loved thee with an *everlasting* love.'

It had been for some time his custom, the last thing every night, to ask for a text from one of his daughters for special meditation, and this he used to call his 'pillow.' Those were the last words on which his eyes rested, and as they rested there, a heavenly light shone in them.

We watched in silence through the night in the dimly lighted room, listening to the laboured breathing, and scarcely daring to think of what lay before us on the coming day.

Early in the morning he made a sign for his spectacles and put them on, himself, with a little help from Mrs. Marsh, and then looked round on us all with inexpressible tenderness; he tried to write again, but his hand could scarcely guide the pencil. Suddenly the voice which we thought we should hear no more till the Resurrection morning, broke the silence, and in a tone of wonderful love he said the one word, 'Mary!' whilst his eyes, which were already growing dim in death, were for a moment bright with life and power.

One by one we all drew near and knelt to kiss his hand, and to receive its gentle pressure, as he raised his eyes in prayer, and thus we took our silent farewell. His wife, son, son-in-law, daughters, grand-daughters, his curates, and several dear friends, besides the devotedly attached servants of the household, and from Beckenham Rectory, each in turn, received that unspoken blessing. Then most of them withdrew to the end of the room, leaving his family around his bed. He looked tenderly towards Mrs. Marsh, and pointed upwards, when he saw her tears.

He signed for the window to be thrown wide open, and the sunshine came streaming in on his heavenly face. After the heavy rain in the night, everything was looking refreshed and lovely, and the clematis, then in blossom, which hung around the library window, was glittering in the sun, as it formed the frame through which he took his last look into the garden.

He lay tranquilly, surrounded by those who loved him best. Presently Dr. Lanchester felt his pulse for the last time, and afterwards he himself signed to his daughter Matilda to come near, and placed the thin wrist in her hand, with a smile of tenderest confidence, knowing that she would like to be the last to feel its faint and now fast-failing beating. Then, with serene dignity, and almost a leisurely calm, he raised his hand, and closed his own eyes,—to spare us one pang, and to draw the curtain that would hide earth from his sight and leave him alone with his Saviour.

No sound of sorrow broke the stillness of that holy place. We had gone with him to the bank of the river, and there waited in silence for the arrival of the Shining Ones who were to carry him to the Celestial City.

The heart that had so overflowed with love still beat with tremulous motion; and the hand which clasped a hand of the daughter whose life's blessedness it had been never to be parted from him, closed firmly, as if he would have drawn her into the promised land at the same moment with himself, by the power of that 'love which is strong as death.'

Then as the church bells began to chime for the service, with a few gentle breathings his spirit passed away.

By the look of radiant joy, adoration, holy awe, and almost surprise, upon his face at the last, we felt that it was no angel guard alone that had come for him, but that his eyes had seen 'the King in His beauty;' that he had not only been made 'most blessed for ever,' but also 'exceeding glad with his Saviour's countenance.'

'Soft through the open casement
Stole in the summer air,
And faintly came the chiming
Of bells that called to prayer:

While on his couch reclining,
That loved one rested now;
The gracious lips were silent,
And chill the stately brow.

But on the face there deepen'd
A look of tender awe;
As when the loved disciple
His risen Master saw:[1]

As when the untold glory—
The unapproached light,—
Veil'd from our mortal vision,
Burst on the martyr's sight:

And in that hush of wonder,
And love, and awe, and praise,
Gently his spirit enter'd
Upon eternal days.

Still was that vision's rapture
Upon the face exprest,—
Only the silence told us
He was indeed at rest.

They say that Death has enter'd,
And here his vigil keeps!
But still we know the Master
Has said his servant "*sleeps.*"

He comes Himself to wake him;—
Perchance the morn is near—
So, though our home be darken'd,
Say not that Death is here.'[2]

BEDDINGTON RECTORY,
August 1864.

[1] John xxi. 7.
[2] By the author of *Grace and Remembrance.*

CHAPTER XIX.

'THE QUIET RESTING-PLACE.'

'And needest thou our prayers no more, safe folded 'mid the bless'd?
How changed art thou since last we met to keep the day of rest!
Young with the youth of angels, wise with the growth of years;
For we have pass'd, since thou hast gone, a week of many tears.'

. . . .

How wise, and great, and glorious, thy gentle soul has grown,
Loving as thou art loved by God, knowing as thou art known!
Yet in that world thou carest still for those thou lov'dst in this;
The rich man did in torments, and wilt not thou in bliss?

For sitting at the Saviour's feet, and gazing in His face,
Surely thou 'lt not unlearn one gentle human grace.
Human, and not angelic, the form He deigns to wear;
Of Jesus, not of angels, the likeness thou shalt bear.'

By the Author of 'The Three Wakings.'

'THE QUIET RESTING-PLACE.'

In accordance with his own wish, he was buried in the churchyard at Beddington: where his grave was made, beside the porch, by the little path leading to the vestry.

The 2d of September was the burial day; and from far and near friends gathered to follow him, mourners in heart for the father in Christ who was that day to come to his grave 'in a full age, like as a shock of corn cometh in in his season.' The precious body was laid in a plain coffin of polished oak, its only ornament a silver star, bearing the following inscription:—

'Rev. William Marsh, D.D., Rector of Beddington.

'Born July 20th, 1775; died August 24th, 1864.

'"All the days of my appointed time will I wait till my change come: Thou shalt call, and I will answer; Thou wilt have a desire to the work of Thy hands:" "For the Lord Himself shall descend from heaven with a shout, with the voice of the Archangel, with the trump of God: and the dead in Christ shall rise first."

'"Wherefore comfort one another with these words."'

The coffin was placed in the library until the hour came for its removal to the grave. In the interval of waiting, the executors opened a small packet of papers addressed to themselves, and thus found the following parting blessing, which came like a voice from heaven to comfort his heart-stricken children and grandchildren:—

'Darling Katie and all my Children,—Let not my departure over-grieve you. You will consider how long my life has been spared. But, above all, look forward to the happy meeting which the mercy of our Lord Jesus Christ will grant; and I know you will like to serve Him by the way.

'I thank you all for your most dutiful and affectionate, yea, most loving conduct. Never was a man so blessed with such children.

'I have often thanked God for my children, and those to whom four of them have been married; and since, those to whom my grandchildren have been married. They have all been most dutiful and affectionate. May the Lord "who has fed me all my life long"—the angel (or messenger of the covenant of grace, our blessed Redeemer) "who has redeemed me from all evil," bless them all, and my great-grandchildren. May they live in faith, and hope, and love. It is the happiest life in this world, and prepares for perfect happiness in the world to come.

'I pray God to bless my kind executors, and all my friends, especially the dear people among whom I have ministered.

'I have been spared to see my children's children. Oh that they might see "peace upon Israel," and all finally meet in the land of light, and love, and joy, to the praise of God and the Lamb for ever!

'I wish my executors to place all my papers, and manuscripts, and letters, etc., in the hands of my daughter Catherine, for any use she may wish to make of them. (Signed) W. Marsh.'

At length the hour came; to no stranger hands was the privilege granted of rendering the last act of respect, but 'devout men' from amongst the recent converts at Beddington, and some from an earlier work of the grace of God at Beckenham, were waiting with reverent tenderness to 'carry him to his burial.'

After a brief prayer by Mr. Chalmers in the library, the mournful procession was ready to depart. Many of the number, but a few weeks before, on his birthday, had rejoiced with them that did rejoice, as they saw him come forth from that very room, radiant with life and beauty; and now they stood as mourners in the hall, weeping with them that wept, as from the same door was carried forth the silent form of the dead.

Followed by his wife, his son, his daughters, and his grandchildren; by relations and friends, near and distant; by grey-haired brethren in the ministry, veterans in Christ's service; by laymen whose hands he had upheld with his counsel, his sympathy, and his prayers; by young officers whose faith he had strengthened to withstand the snares which surrounded them; by his old churchwarden from Colchester, and sons of friends who had died in the Lord there; by members of his old congregations in Leamington and Birmingham; by some of the Society of Friends; by a large company who loved him from Beckenham and Bromley; by many of the clergy from the neighbourhood; by numbers of his parishioners; by faithful and sorrowing servants from both rectories; by mourners old and young, rich and poor, the friends of years and the friends of weeks—the body was borne to the grave.

The road from the rectory was lined with people, who filled the churchyard when the procession had passed into the church; and by their solemn stillness showed their deep sympathy.

Mr. O'Rorke and Mr. Gordon, who sorrowed as sons for a father, met the funeral at the gate. In the pause, whilst the long train quietly took their places in the church,—to soft, low music, his favourite hymn was sung,—

'There is a land of pure delight.'

Profound silence reigned in the church during the reading of the service. The last declaration of faith had been made, the threefold blessing pronounced; and whilst the mourners were still standing around the open grave, and hundreds lingering sorrowfully, unwilling to leave the place where he was laid, words of comfort were spoken[1] on the Voices which bear their testimony at the beginning of the burial service.

The voice from heaven—

'I am the Resurrection and the Life; he that believeth in Me, though he were dead, yet shall he live; and whosoever liveth and believeth in Me shall never die.'

The voice from the dead—

'I know that my Redeemer liveth, and that He shall stand at the latter day upon the earth; and though after my skin worms destroy this body, yet in my flesh shall I see God; whom I shall see for myself, and mine eyes shall behold, and not another.'

The voice of the bereaved—

'The Lord gave, and the Lord hath taken away; blessed be the name of the Lord.'

[1] By the Rev. Edward Hoare, of Tunbridge Wells.

All day the rain had fallen heavily until just before the funeral left the rectory. But now, as the preacher's voice ceased, the setting sun broke forth from behind a bank of gloomy clouds, and poured such a flood of golden light over all the scene, that it seemed as if heaven's gate had been thrown open to let its glory stream a while upon earth. At the same moment a white dove was seen slowly descending towards the grave, over which it poised with outspread wings, and after resting there awhile, soared out of sight towards heaven:—meet emblem for him whose peaceful and loving spirit had passed into the skies.

As many had come from a distance, and wished to remain until late in the evening, refreshment was provided for them in the school-room; and afterwards a meeting was held there, by the curates, for prayer for the parish which had suffered so great a loss, for the bereaved family, and especially for the daughter whose absence from her father's death-bed added such poignancy to her share of the sorrow so deep for all.

It was whilst these prayers were being made for her, that she entered the desolated home. No tidings of his illness had reached her until five days after his death. Although hopeless then of looking upon the beloved face once more, she had travelled day and night to be in time to follow him to the grave. On her account the funeral had not taken place until after the arrival of the express train from Folkestone; but then all expectation of her return that day was at an end.

Watch was kept by the grave that night, for it was left open that she might see his quiet resting-place.

'Another chamber yet,
Its curtain is of grass, and closely drawn;
But the pale pilgrim, in its portal set,
Looketh toward the dawn.

Ofttimes red roses lie
On the green curtain of that chamber low,
And blossoms like the deep-blue summer sky,
Or like the winter snow.

Now lay the pilgrim down—
Set thou his feet, and face, and closed eyes,
Where they may meet the golden-raying crown
Of Christ's own great sunrise.

So let him rest.
Unheard all sound of mourning—let thy weeping cease:
Translate the grave into a gentler word—
Call it the chamber Peace!'[1]

On Sunday, the 4th of September, funeral sermons[2] were preached in Beddington Church by the Rev. John Venn (who, with great kindness, came from Hereford, at considerable inconvenience), and the Revs. Henry Elliott[3] and Charles Goodhart, who had each for many years known, loved, and honoured the aged saint, to whose holy living and dying they now bore their testimony.

To these was added another public tribute, when, on the following Sunday evening, the school-room was filled with sorrowing parishioners to hear an address given by his dear friend, Colonel Rowlandson, on the farewell words of St. Paul (2 Tim. iv. 1-8), as illustrated in the life and death of their aged pastor; by his following Christ, renouncing all righteousness of his own; his personal and heart-felt reliance upon the atoning blood and righteousness of the Lord Jesus; his liberty of access to the throne of grace; his abiding joy in God, which was the source

[1] 'The pilgrim they laid in a chamber whose window opened toward the sun rising; the name of the chamber was Peace, where he slept till break of day.'—*Pilgrim's Progress*.

[2] Published in a small volume, entitled, *Memorial Sermons on the occasion of the Death of the Rev. William Marsh, D.D.*

[3] The Rev. Henry Venn Elliott, incumbent of St. Mary's, Brighton, where he faithfully exercised his varied and eminent gifts in the work of the Lord for thirty-eight years. Though he had laboured for so long a period, with unceasing devotedness, in that glorious service, he was full of life and energy, as was shown by his coming from Brighton to attend the funeral on Friday, returning in the evening to prepare his sermon, and coming again on Saturday night to be ready for his Sunday's work. A twofold act of kindness, which can never be forgotten by those whose hearts experienced the comfort of his considerate and self-forgetting sympathy, and the help of his holy conversation and prayers, together with those of the two other valued and mutual friends.

Mr. Elliott preached in his own church on New Year's Day, 1865, from the text, '*Occupy till I come;*' but before the first month of that year had closed, he had heard the blissful words, 'The Master *is come*, and calleth for *thee*.'

and secret of his abiding victory over the world and sin; his reflection of the Saviour's image before his fellow-men, caused by the indwelling of the Holy Ghost; his constant recourse to the Wonderful Counsellor; hence his calmness, making the language of complaint a thing unknown to his lips; his love to all who belonged to the Lord Jesus, and his zeal for God; his chief delight and study in four books, within the reach of all: the book of God's creation; the book of God's providence; the book of the human heart; the Word of the Living God; his love for and earnest expectation of the appearing of the Lord Jesus Christ.

And lastly, his creed and motto through life were, 'Jesus only,' and 'My fresh springs are in Thee.'

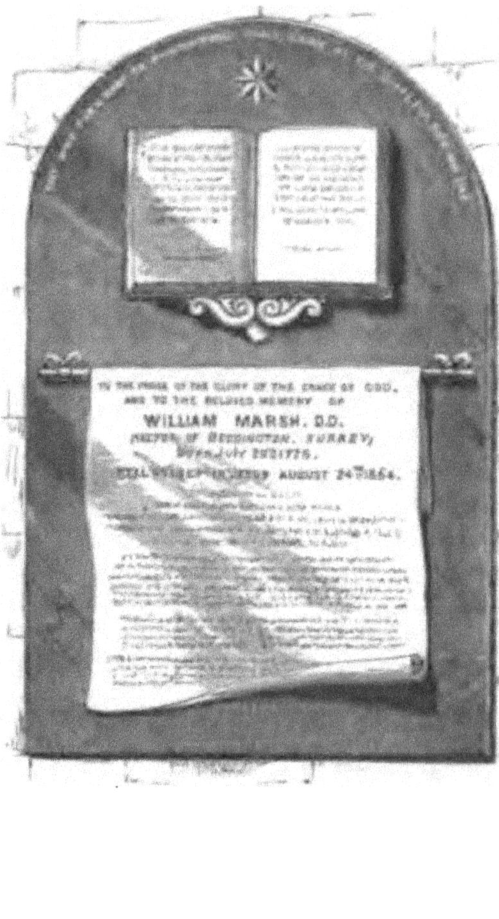

Milton Keynes UK
Ingram Content Group UK Ltd.
UKHW010027181123
432780UK00003B/72

9 783752 534498